Frank Podmore

Apparitions and Thought-Transference

An examination of the evidence for telepathy

Frank Podmore

Apparitions and Thought-Transference
An examination of the evidence for telepathy

ISBN/EAN: 9783337188252

Printed in Europe, USA, Canada, Australia, Japan

Cover: Foto ©Andreas Hilbeck / pixelio.de

More available books at **www.hansebooks.com**

THE CONTEMPORARY SCIENCE SERIES.

EDITED BY HAVELOCK ELLIS.

APPARITIONS
AND THOUGHT-TRANSFERENCE.

APPARITIONS

AND

THOUGHT-TRANSFERENCE:

AN EXAMINATION OF THE EVIDENCE FOR TELEPATHY.

BY

FRANK PODMORE, M.A.

WITH NUMEROUS ILLUSTRATIONS.

LONDON:
WALTER SCOTT, LTD.,
24 WARWICK LANE, PATERNOSTER ROW.
1894.

CONTENTS.

—◆◆—

CHAPTER I.

CHAPTER II.

CHAPTER III.

CHAPTER IV.

CHAPTER V.

CHAPTER VI.

CHAPTER VII.

CHAPTER VIII.

CONTENTS.

CHAPTER IX.

CHAPTER X.

CHAPTER XI.

CHAPTER XII.

CHAPTER XIII.

CHAPTER XIV.

CHAPTER XV.

CHAPTER XVI.

PREFACE.

———◦◦———

THE following pages aim at presenting in brief
compass a selection of the evidence upon which
the hypothesis of thought-transference, or telepathy,
is based. It is now more than twelve years since
the Society for Psychical Research was founded, and
nearly eight since the publication of *Phantasms of the
Living*. Both in the periodical *Proceedings* of the
Society and in the pages of Edmund Gurney's book,[1] a
large mass of evidence has been laid before the public.
But the papers included in the *Proceedings* are interspersed with other matter, some of it too technical for
the taste of the general reader; whilst the two volumes
of *Phantasms of the Living*, which have for some time

---

[1] The book actually bore on the title-page the names of Edmund
Gurney, F. W. H. Myers, and the present writer. But the division of
authorship, as explained in the Preface, was as follows :—" As regards
the writing and the views expressed, Mr. Myers is solely responsible
for the Introduction, and for the ' Note on a Suggested Mode of
Psychical Interaction; ' and Mr. Gurney is solely responsible for the
remainder of the book. . . . But the collection, examination, and
appraisal of evidence has been a joint labour."

been out of print, were too costly for the purse of some, and too bulky for the patience of others. The attention which, notwithstanding these drawbacks, that work excited on its first appearance, the friendly reception which it met with in many quarters, and the fact that a considerable edition has been disposed of, encouraged the hope that a book on somewhat similar lines, but on a smaller scale, might be of service to those—and their number has probably increased within the last few years—who take a genuine interest in this inquiry. Accordingly in the autumn of 1892 I obtained permission from the Council of the Society for Psychical Research to make full use, in the compilation of the present work, not merely of the evidence already published by us, but of the not inconsiderable mass of unpublished records in the possession of the Society.

It will be seen that the present book has little claim to novelty of design; but it is not merely an abridged edition of the larger work referred to. On the one hand it has a somewhat wider scope, and includes accounts of telepathic clairvoyance and other phenomena which did not enter into the scheme of Mr. Gurney's book. On the other hand, the bulk of the illustrative cases here quoted have been taken from more recent records; and, in particular, certain branches of the experimental work have assumed a quite new importance within the last few years. Thus the experiments conducted by Mrs. Henry Sidgwick at Brighton have strengthened the demonstration of

thought-transference, and have gone far to solve one
or two of the problems connected with the subject;
and the evidence for the experimental production of
telepathic effects at a distance has been greatly
enlarged by the work of MM. Janet and Gibert,[1]
Richet, Gibotteau, Schrenck-Notzing, and in this
country by Mr. Kirk and others.[2] It may be added
that some of the criticisms called forth by *Phantasms
of the Living*, and our own further researches, have led
us to modify our estimate of the evidence in some
directions, and to strengthen generally the precautions taken against the unconscious warping of
testimony.

To say, however, that the following pages owe
much to Edmund Gurney is but to acknowledge
the obligation which all students of the subject
must recognise to his keen and vigorous intellect and
his colossal industry. My own debt is a more personal
one. To have worked under his guidance, and to
have been stimulated by his example, was an invalu-
able schooling in the qualities demanded by an
inquiry of this nature. Of the living, I owe grateful
thanks, in the first instance, to Professor and Mrs.
Henry Sidgwick, who have read through the whole
of the book in typescript, and have given help and
counsel throughout. Miss Alice Johnson, Mr. F.
W. H. Myers, the late Dr. A. T. Myers, Miss Porter,

[1] Some account of the earlier experiments by MM. Janet and Gibert
was included in the supplementary chapter at the end of the second
volume of *Phantasms*.

[2] See Chapters V. and X. of the present book.

and others have also given me welcome help in various directions. In acknowledging this assistance, however, it is right to add that, though I trust in my estimate of the evidence presented, and in the general tenour of the conclusions suggested, to find myself, with few exceptions, in substantial agreement with my colleagues, yet I have no claim to represent the Society for Psychical Research, nor right to cloak my own shortcomings with the authority of others.

One word more needs to be said. The evidence, of which samples are presented in the following pages, is as yet hardly adequate for the establishment of telepathy as a fact in nature, and leaves much to be desired for the elucidation of the laws under which it operates. Any contributions to the problem, in the shape either of accounts of experiments, or of recent records of telepathic visions and similar experiences, will be gladly received by me on behalf of the Society for Psychical Research, at 19 Buckingham Street, Adelphi, W.C.

FRANK PODMORE.

August 1894.

APPARITIONS
AND THOUGHT-TRANSFERENCE.

APPARITIONS AND THOUGHT-TRANSFERENCE.

CHAPTER I.

INTRODUCTORY—SPECIAL GROUNDS OF CAUTION.

IT is salutary sometimes to reflect how recent is the growth of our scientific cosmos, and how brief an interval separates it from the chaos which went before. This may be seen even in Sciences which deal with matters of common observation. Amongst material phenomena the facts of Geology are assuredly not least calculated to excite the curiosity or impress the imagination of men. Yet until the middle of the last century no serious attempt was made to solve the physical problems they presented. The origin of the organic remains embedded in the rocks had indeed formed the subject of speculation ever since the days of Aristotle. Theophrastus had suggested that they were formed by the plastic forces of Nature. Mediæval astrologers ascribed their formation to planetary influences. And these hypotheses, with the alternative view of the Church, that fossil bones and shells were relics of the Mosaic Deluge, appear to have satisfied the learned of Europe until the time of Voltaire, who reinforced the rationalistic position, as he conceived it, by the suggestion that the shells, at

I

any rate, had been dropped from the hats of pilgrims
returning from the Holy Land. Yet Werner and
Hutton were even then preparing to elucidate the
causes of stratification and the genesis of the igneous
rocks. Cuvier in the next generation was to demonstrate the essential analogies of the fossils found in
the Paris basin with living species; Agassiz was to
investigate the relation of fossil fishes and to show
the true nature of their embedded remains. Nay,
even in the middle of the present century, so slow is
the growth and spread of organised knowledge, it was
possible for a pious Scotchman to ascribe the origin
of mountain chains to a cataclysm which, after the
fall of Man, had broken up and distorted the once
symmetrical surface of the earth;[1] for a Dean of
York to essay to bring the Mediæval theory up to
date and prove that the whole series of geological
strata, with their varied organic remains, were formed
by volcanic eruptions acting in concert with the
Mosaic Deluge;[2] and for another English divine to
warn his readers against any sacrilegious meddling
with the arcana of the rocks, because they represented
the tentative essays of the Creator at organic forms—
a concealed storehouse of celestial misfits![3]

The subject-matter of the present inquiry has
passed, or is now passing, through stages closely
similar to those above described. "Ghosts" and
warning dreams have been matters of popular belief
and interest since the earliest ages known to history,
and are prevalent amongst even the least advanced
races at the present time. The Specularii and Dr.
Dee have familiarised us with clairvoyance and
crystal vision. Many of the alleged marvels of

[1] *Primary and Present State of the Solar System*, by P. McFarlane.
Edinburgh, Thomas Grant, *circa* 1845.
[2] At the meeting of the British Association in 1844; quoted by
Hugh Miller, *Testimony of the Rocks*, pp. 358, 359.
[3] *A Brief and Complete Refutation of the Antiscriptural Theory of
the Geologists*, by a Clergyman of the Church of England. London,
1853; quoted by Hugh Miller, *loc. cit.*

witchcraft were probably due to the agency of hypnotism, which in later times, under the various names of mesmerism, electrobiology, animal magnetism, has attracted the curiosity of the unlettered, and from time to time the serious interest of the learned. These phenomena indeed were made the subject of scientific inquiry, first in France and later in England, during the first half of the present century; have now again, after a brief period of eclipse, been investigated for the last two decades by competent observers on the Continent, and are at length winning a recognised footing in scientific circles in this country. Yet within the last two or three years we have witnessed the spectacle of more than one medical man, of some repute in this island, laughing to scorn all the researches of Charcot and Bernheim, just as their prototypes a generation or two ago ignored the results of Cuvier and Agassiz, and held it an insult to the Creator to accept the scientific explanation of coprolites.

And as regards the other subjects, to which must be added the alleged marvels of the Spiritualists, there have indeed been one or two isolated series of observations by competent inquirers, but for the most part the learned have held themselves free to ascribe the phenomena without investigation to fraud and hysteria, and the unlearned to "magnetism," "psychic force," or the Devil. For whilst men of science, preoccupied for the most part with other lines of inquiry, have kept themselves aloof, the vacant ground was naturally occupied by the ignorant and credulous, and by those who looked to win a harvest from ignorance and credulity. It is not of course implied that all persons who interested themselves in such matters came under one or other of these categories. There were many sensible men and women amongst them, but they lacked for the most part the special training necessary for such inquiries, or they failed through want of co-operation and support. No serious and organised attempt at investigation was made until, in 1882, the Society for Psychical Research was founded in London, under the presidency of Professor Henry Sidgwick. He and his colleagues were the pioneers in the research, and their example has been widely followed. Two years later an American society under the same title (now a flourishing branch of the English society) was founded in Boston; and there are at the present time societies with similar objects at Berlin, Munich, Stockholm, and elsewhere. Moreover, the Société de Psychologie Physiologique, which was founded in Paris, under the presidency of M. Charcot, in 1885, has devoted much attention to some forms of telepathy.

But the forces of superstition and charlatanry, to which this vast territory has been ceded for so long, have bequeathed an unfortunate legacy to those who would now colonise it in the name of Science; and the preliminary difficulties of the undertaking can perhaps most effectually be met by a frank recognition of that fact. On the one hand, a large number of thinking men have been repelled, and still feel repulsion, from a subject whose record is so unsavoury. On the other hand, the appetite for the marvellous which has been so long unchecked is not easily restrained. The old habits of inaccuracy, of magnifying the proportions of things, of confusing surmises with facts, cannot be eradicated without long and careful discipline. To one writer, indeed, those dangers seemed so serious that he solemnly warned the Society for Psychical Research, at the outset of its career, against the risk of stimulating into disastrous activity inborn tendencies to superstition, by even the semblance of an inquiry into these matters. Without going to such lengths, it may be conceded to the critic that even with those who endeavour to apply scientific methods to the investigation the mental attitude is liable to be warped by the environment, and that here, as elsewhere, evil communications may corrupt.

As regards the actual investigators this difficulty is growing less serious, as more men who have received their training in other branches of science are attracted to the inquiry, and as the affinities of the subject to long-recognised departments of knowledge become daily more apparent. In another direction, however, this mental attitude presents still a more or less formidable obstacle. Many of the observations on which students of the subject are compelled to rely are derived from persons who have had no training in such habits of accuracy as are required in scientific research. When accounts of the ornithorhynchus first reached this country naturalists laughed at the traveller's tale of a beast with the tail of a beaver and the bill and webbed feet of a duck. In the same way scientific men for long refused to admit the existence of aerolites, as they now decline to credit the reports of a Sea Serpent of colossal proportions. In all these cases, so long as the alleged facts rest solely on the testimony of men untrained in habits of close observation and accurate reporting, a suspension of judgment seems to be justified. And if these considerations are valid in ordinary cases, a much higher degree of caution may be reasonably demanded of investigators who leave the neutral ground of the physical sciences to enter upon a field in which the emotions and sympathies are most keenly engaged, and in which the incidents narrated may have served to afford support to the dearest hopes and sanction to the deepest convictions of the narrator. So insidious, in such a case, is the work of the imagination, so untrustworthy is the memory, so various are the sources of error in human testimony, that it may be doubted whether we should be justified in attaching weight to the phenomena of telepathic hallucination and clairvoyance, to which a large part of this book is devoted, if the alleged observations were incapable of experimental verification. Certainly in such a case, though the recipient of an experience of this kind might cherish a private conviction of its significance, it would hardly be possible for such a view to win general assent.

In fact, however, the clue to the interpretation of the more striking phenomena, in the case of which, since they occur for the most part spontaneously, direct experiment or even methodical and continuous observation are rarely possible, is furnished by actual experiment on a smaller scale and with mental affections of a less unusual kind. The thesis which these pages are designed to illustrate and support is briefly: *that communication is possible between mind and mind otherwise than through the known channels of the senses.* Proof of the existence of such communication, provisionally called *Thought Transference* or *Telepathy* (from *tele* = at a distance, and *pathos* = feeling), will be found in a considerable mass of experiments conducted during the last twelve years by various observers in different European countries and in America. Before proceeding, in the course of the next four chapters, to examine this part of the evidence in detail, it will be well to consider its various defects and sources of error—defects common in some degree to all experiments of which living beings are the subject, and sources of error for the most part peculiar to this and kindred inquiries. The word *experiment* in this connection usually, and rightly, suggests the most perfect form of experiment, that in which all the conditions are known, and in which the results can be predicted both quantitatively and qualitatively. If, for instance, we add a certain quantity of nitric acid under given conditions to a certain quantity of benzine, we know that there will result a certain quantity of a third substance which is unlike either of its constituents in taste, smell, and physical properties. Or if we burn a given quantity of coal in a particular engine, we can predict, within narrow limits of error, the total amount of energy which will be evolved. That we cannot in the second instance predict with absolute accuracy the amount of energy produced is simply due to the difficulty of measuring with precision all the factors in the case. But when we leave the problems of chemistry and physics and approach the problems of biology, the difficulties increase a hundredfold. Here not only are we unable to measure the various factors, we cannot even name them. No skill or forethought would have enabled an observer, from however patient a study of parentage and environment, to have predicted the appearance, say, of Emanuel Swedenborg or Michael Faraday. Of the seven children of John Lamb and his wife it might have seemed easier to conjecture that the majority would not survive childhood, and that one would become insane, than that another should take his place amongst those whose writings the world would not willingly let die. And even where, as in most biological researches, the results drawn from observation can be to some extent checked and controlled by direct experiment, generations may elapse before the balance of probabilities on one side or the other becomes so great as to lead to unanimity amongst the inquirers. One of the most interesting, and certainly not the least important, of the questions now occupying biologists, is that of the transmission to the offspring of characters acquired in the lifetime of the individual. Observations have been accumulated on the subject since before the days of Lamarck; and these observations, interpreted and confirmed by experiment, have been adduced and are still held by many as evidence that such transmission occurs. On the other hand, Weismann and his followers contend that no such inference can legitimately be drawn from the observations and experiments quoted, and that the occurrence of such transmission is irreconcilable with what is known of the growth and development of the germ. And for all that has been said and written the opinion of competent biologists is still divided upon the question.

But in many biological problems the conditions are much simpler, and the questions at issue can more readily be brought to the test of experiment. Yet even so various unknown factors are included, and the results obtained are correspondingly difficult of interpretation. No question affects us more nearly than the part played by the several kinds of food in repairing the daily waste of the human body. Statistics and analyses have been collected of workhouse, prison, and military dietaries; innumerable experiments have been conducted on fasting men and hypertrophied dogs and rabbits; and yet the precise function of nitrogenous substances in nutrition is still undetermined. Again, the import of the experiments made during the last few decades by Goltz, Hitzig, Ferrier, Horsley, and others on the functions of various areas of the brain substance, and the exact nature and degree of localisation which those experiments imply, are still matter of debate amongst the physiologists concerned.

To take yet another instance, and one which has a more intimate bearing upon the experiments to be discussed. Some years ago Dr. Charlton Bastian claimed to have proved experimentally the fact of abiogenesis, or the generation of living organisms from non-living matter. He had placed various organic infusions in glass tubes, which were heated to the boiling point and then hermetically sealed. When the tubes were, after a certain interval, unsealed, the contained liquid was found in some cases to be swarming with bacteria. Believing that these micro-organisms and their germs were invariably destroyed by the heat of boiling water, Dr. Bastian saw no other conclusion than that the bacteria were formed directly from the infusion. His conclusions were not accepted by the scientific world. But they were rejected, not because the fact of abiogenesis was regarded as in itself improbable, nor yet because Dr. Bastian was unable to indicate by what steps or processes the transformation of an infusion of hay into living organisms of definite and relatively complex structure could be conceived to take place, but because Pasteur, Tyndall, and others showed that the germs of some of these micro-organisms are capable of sustaining for some minutes the heat of boiling water; and further, that when elaborate precautions were taken, by filtering and otherwise purifying the air, tubes containing similar infusions would remain sterile for an indefinite period.

The conclusion that under certain conditions thought-transference may occur rests upon reasoning similar to that by which Dr. Bastian sought to establish a theory of abiogenesis. Neither the organs by which nor the medium through which the communication is made can be indicated; nor can we even, with a few trifling exceptions, point to the conditions which favour such communication. But ignorance on these points, though a defect, is not a defect which in the present state of experimental psychology can be held seriously to weaken the evidence, much less to invalidate the conclusion. That conclusion rests on the elimination of all other possible causes for the effect produced. But at this point the analogy between the two researches fails. Dr. Bastian's conjecture was based on a short series of experiments conducted by a single experimenter under one uniform set of conditions. At the first breath of criticism the whole fabric collapsed. The experiments here recorded represent the work of many observers in many countries, carried on with different subjects under a great variety of conditions. The results have been before the world for about twelve years, and during that period have been subjected to much adverse and some instructive criticism. But no alternative explanation which has yet been suggested has attained even a momentary plausibility.

Whether the elimination of all other possible causes

is indeed complete, or whether, as in Dr. Bastian's case, there may yet lurk in these experiments some hitherto unsuspected source of error, the reader will have the opportunity of judging for himself. To assist him in forming a judgment some of the main disturbing causes will be briefly indicated.

(1) *Fraud.*—In nearly all the experiments referred to in this book the agent was himself concerned in the inquiry as a matter of scientific interest. But it necessarily happens on occasion that neither agent nor percipient are by education and position absolutely removed from suspicion of trickery in a matter where trickery might to imperfectly educated persons appear almost venial. If any such cases have been admitted, it is because the precautions taken appear to us to have been adequate. At the same time, the investigators of the Society for Psychical Research have come across some instances of fraud in cases where they had grounds for assuming good faith, and it may be useful, therefore, to illustrate some of the less obvious methods of acquiring intelligence fraudulently. The conditions of the experiment should of course, as far as possible, preclude, even where there is no ground for suspecting fraud, communication between the percipient and the agent, or any one else knowing the idea which it is sought to transfer.

In the autumn of 1888 some experiments were conducted with a person named D., whose antecedents afforded, it was thought, justification for the belief that the claims which he put forward were genuine. D. acted as agent, the percipient being a subject of his own, a young woman called Miss N., who was apparently in a light hypnotic sleep during the experiment. It was soon discovered that the results were obtained by means of a code formed from a combination of Miss N.'s breathing with slight noises—a cough or the creak of a boot—made by D. himself. I have seen a somewhat similar code employed in Prince's Hall, Piccadilly, where the conjurer stood in the middle of the hall with a coin or other object in his hand, a description of which he communicated to his confederate on the platform by means of a series of breathings, deep enough visibly to move his dress-coat up and down on the surface of his white collar, punctuated by slight movements of head or hand. The novel feature in the first case, however, was that the percipient herself furnished the groundwork of the code, the punctuation alone being given by the conjurer. A still more elaborate form of collusion is described at length by Bonjean.[1] In this case the subject, a young woman named Lully, appears to have read the words to be conveyed after the fashion of a deaf mute, by the motion of the lips of the showman. Lully was apparently in a hypnotic trance, with the eyes fast closed. Another form of fraud, since it does not require the aid of a confederate, is perhaps worthy of note. Some years ago a young Australian came to this country with a reputation for "genuine thought-reading," based on the successful mystification of some members of a certain Colonial Legislature. The writer had a few experiments with this person, in which several small objects—a knife, a glass bottle, etc.—placed in the full light of a shaded lamp, were correctly named. The object was in each case placed behind the back of the "Thought-reader," who looked intently at the writer's eyes, which were in turn fixed upon the brightly illuminated object. Experiments made under more usual conditions, not dictated by the "Thought-reader," completely failed ; and there can be little doubt that the initial successes were due to the "Thought-reader" seeing the image of the object reflected in the agent's cornea.

(2) *Hyperæsthesia.*—But, after all, it is rarely necessary to take special precautions against fraud, for there are dangers to be guarded against of a more subtle kind. There are various, and as yet imperfectly

---

[1] *L'Hypnotisme et la suggestion mentale.* Germer Baillière et Cie. Paris, pp. 261-316.

known methods of communication by which indications may be unconsciously given and as unconsciously received. Thus, to take the last instance, it is pretty certain that cornea-reading does not always imply fraud, and that hints may be gained in all good faith from any reflecting surface in the neighbourhood of the experimenter; or the movements of lips, larynx, and even hands and limbs may betray the secret to eye or ear. We know little of the limits of our sensory powers even in normal life; and we do know that in certain subconscious states—automatic, hypnotic, somnambulic—these limits may be greatly exceeded, and that indications so subtle as frequently to escape the vigilance of trained observers may be seized and interpreted by the hypnotic or automatic subject. It is clear, therefore, that results which it is possible to attribute to deliberate fraud stand almost necessarily self-condemned. For if the precautions taken by the investigators left such an explanation open, much more were those precautions insufficient to guard against the subtler modes of communication referred to. It is not the friend whom we know whose eyes must be closed and his ears muffled, but the "Mr. Hyde," whose lurking presence in each of us we are only now beginning to suspect.

There is a case recorded by M. Bergson,[1] in which a hypnotised boy is said to have been able to state correctly the number of the page in a book held by the observer, by reading the corneal image of the figures. The actual figures were three millimetres high, and their corneal image is calculated by M. Bergson to have been 0.1 mm., or about $\frac{1}{250}$ of an inch in height! In some other experiments conducted by M. Bergson with the same subject the acuteness of vision is said to have exceeded even this limit. In another case, recorded by Dr. Sauvaire,[2] a hypnotised

[1] *Revue Philosophique*, Nov. 1887, quoted in *Proceedings of the Soc. Psych. Research*, vol. iv. p. 532.
[2] *Revue Philosophique*, March 1887.

subject was able to recognise the King of Clubs, face downwards, in two different packs of cards. In the first of these cases the results, which could not have been attained by the senses under normal conditions, must apparently be attributed to hyperæsthesia. Instances, especially of auditory hyperæsthesia, are of course quite familiar to those who have studied the phenomena of hypnotism. In Dr. Sauvaire's case, however, the power of distinguishing the cards by touch may have been the result of practice. Mrs. Verrall records (*Proceedings Soc. Psych. Research*, vol. viii. p. 480) that she acquired such a power by means of "a longish series of experiments"; and Mr. Hudson, in *Idle Days in Patagonia*, tells of a gambler who by careful training had developed the same faculty in a very high degree.

It seems probable in the cases described by M. Bergson and Dr. Sauvaire, and possible also in the case of Mr. D.'s subject, that there was no intentional deception, and that the hypnotised person was not himself aware of the means by which his knowledge was attained.[1] The same remark probably applies to the following case, in which, though the conditions of vision were certainly unusual, it seems not clear whether the degree of success attained should be attributed to abnormal sensibility of the eyes, or to the facility acquired by long practice. In a series of experiments at which the writer assisted, in 1884, an illiterate youth named Dick was hypnotised, a penny was placed over each eye, and the eyes and surrounding features were elaborately bandaged with strips of sticking-plaster; a handkerchief being bound over all. Under these conditions Dick named correctly objects held in front of him, even at a considerable distance, a little above the level of his eyes. Normal vision appeared to be impossible. Mr. R. Hodgson, how-

---

[1] Mrs. Verrall states that after long practice she " lost all consciousness of the means which enabled her to guess, and *saw* pictures of the cards."

ever, repeated the experiment upon himself, and found after several trials that he also could see objects, though fitfully and imperfectly, under the same conditions, the channel of vision being a small chink in the sticking-plaster on the line where it was fastened to the brow.

(3) *Muscle-reading.*—From this last case we may pass to the illustrations of "thought-reading" given by professional conjurers and others, where it seems clear that the skill exhibited in the interpretation of unconscious movements and gestures is due rather to long practice and careful observation than to any abnormal extension of faculty. It hardly needs saying that experiments in which contact is permitted between the agent and percipient can rarely be regarded as having evidential value. It has been demonstrated again and again that with the fullest intention of keeping the secret to themselves, most "agents" in such circumstances are practically certain to betray it to the professional thought-reader by unconscious movements of some kind. Indeed, it is difficult to place any limit to the degree of susceptibility to slight muscular impressions which may be attained. A careful experimenter has assured the writer that when acting as percipient in some experiments with diagrams the slight movements of the agent's hand resting upon her head gave her in one case a clue to the figure thought of. And Mr. Stuart Cumberland has exhibited feats still more marvellous before kings and commoners. Nor is it necessary, as already said, for successful muscle-reading that there should be actual contact in all cases. The eye or the ear can sometimes follow movements of the lips or other parts of the body. But though we can look for little evidence from experiments conducted with contact, or under conditions which allow of interpretation by gesture, etc., and their repetition in this connection can rarely be expected to serve any useful purpose, it seems worth pointing out that, if

telepathy is a fact, we should expect to find it operating not merely where, from the conditions of the
experiment, it must be presumed to be the sole source
of communication, but also as an auxiliary to other
more familiar modes of expression. It seems not
improbable, therefore, that some of the more startling
successes of the professional "thought-reader" and
some of the results obtained in the "willing game"
may be due to this cause.

(4) *Thought-forms.*—There remains one other
source of error to be guarded against. An image—
whether of an object, diagram, or name—which is
chosen by the agent may be correctly described by
the percipient simply because their minds are set
to move in the same direction. It must be remembered that, however unexpected and spontaneous
they may appear, ideas do not come by chance, but
have their origin mostly in the previous experience of
the thinker. Persons living constantly in the same
physical and intellectual environment are apt to
present a close similarity in their ideas. It would not
even be *prima facie* evidence of thought-transference,
for instance, if husband and wife, asked to think of a
town or of an acquaintance, should select the same
name. And investigation has shown that our
thoughts move in grooves which are determined
for us by causes more deep-seated and more general
than the accident of particular circumstances. Thus
it is found that individuals will show a preference for
certain figures or certain numbers over others ; and
that the preference for some geometrical figures tends
to be tolerably constant. The American Society for
Psychical Research [1] made some interesting observations on this point in 1888. Blank cards were
issued to a large number of persons, with the request
that the recipients would draw on the card "ten
diagrams." 501 cards were returned, and the diagrams
inscribed on them were carefully tabulated. It was

---

[1] *Proceedings of the American Soc. Psych. Research*, pp. 302 *et seq.*

found that of the 501 persons no less than 209 drew
circles, 174 squares, 160 equilateral triangles and
crosses, while three only drew wheels, two candlesticks, and one each a corkscrew, a ball, and a knife.
It was found that the simpler geometrical figures[1]
occurred not only most frequently but as a general
rule early in each series of ten. It follows, therefore,
that in an experiment the success of the percipient
in reproducing a circle, a square, or a triangle raises
a much fainter presumption of thought-transference
than if the object reproduced had been a corkscrew
or a pine-apple. But so much was perhaps obvious
even without a detailed investigation. From a
similar analysis of the guesses made, it can be
shown that some percipients have decided preferences
amongst the simple numerals. And in the same way
it seems probable that others have a preference for
particular cards. An important illustration of the
working of the "number-habit" has been brought
forward by Professor E. C. Pickering of the Harvard
College Observatory, U.S.A.[2] A revision of part of
the Argelander Star-Chart had been undertaken
by several observatories, of which the Harvard Observatory was one. For the purposes of the revision the
assistant had the Argelander chart before him, whilst
the observer, who was in ignorance of the magnitude
assigned in the chart, made an independent estimate
of the magnitude of each star. If no thought-transference or other disturbing cause affected the result,
the amount of deviation of the later observations
from the earlier in each tenth of a degree of magnitude would be represented by a smooth curve. As a
matter of fact, it was found that the number of cases

[1] No doubt the great preponderance of geometrical figures is in some
measure due to the use of the word "diagram," which in English
would probably suggest to most persons a geometrical diagram. But
possibly the word has a different shade of meaning in American. It is
certain too that a considerable proportion of the persons who filled in
the cards were acquainted with the object of the inquiry.

[2] *Proc. American Soc. Psych. Research*, pp. 35-43.

of complete agreement were much greater, with some observers more than 50 per cent. greater, than they should have been on an estimate of the probabilities. At first sight this excess of the actual over the theoretical numbers suggested the action of thought-transference between the assistant and the observer. But Professor Pickering shows, on a further analysis of the figures, that almost the whole of the excess was due to the preference of both the earlier and the later observers for 5 and 10 over all other fractions of a degree.

The practical deduction from this investigation is that in any experiment care should be taken to exclude, as regards the agent at any rate, the operation of any diagram or number-habit.[1] If an object is thought of, it should if possible be chosen by lot, and should not be an object actually present in the room. If a card, it should be drawn from the pack at random ; if a number, from a receptacle containing a definite series of numbers ; if a diagram, it is preferable that it should be taken at random from a set of previously-prepared drawings. It will be seen that in the majority of the cases quoted in the four succeeding chapters these precautions have been observed.

[1] It is not possible to eliminate the operation of such preferences in the percipient. But if care be taken that the series of things to be guessed is chosen arbitrarily, the only effect of even a decided preference for particular cards, numbers, etc., on the part of the percipient will be to lessen the number of coincidences due to thought-transference.

CHAPTER II.

EXPERIMENTAL TRANSFERENCE OF SIMPLE SEN-SATIONS IN THE NORMAL STATE.

IT is somewhat remarkable that the facts of thought-transference should only have attracted serious attention within the last two decades. With waking percipients, indeed, such phenomena do not seem to occur unsought with sufficient frequency, or—if we leave on one side for the moment telepathic hallucinations—on a sufficiently striking scale to afford evidence of any transmission of thought or sensation otherwise than through the familiar channels. But the hypnotic state appears to offer peculiar facilities for such transmission, and hypnotism, under the name of mesmerism, has now been closely studied by numerous observers for upwards of a century. The earlier French observers,[1] indeed, occasionally recorded instances of what appears to have been thought-transference between the mesmerist and his subject. But these facts were observed by the way, in the search for phenomena of another kind; and no attempt appears to have been made to follow up the clue by means of direct experiment. Even the English observers of 1840 and onwards, though familiar with what they termed "community of sensation" between the operator and his subject,

---

[1] See, for instance, Puységur, *Memoires pour servir à l'établisse-ment du magnétisme*, pp. 22, 29 *et seq.*, and Pététin, *Electricité Animale*, p. 127, etc. (quoted by Dr. Ochorowicz, *De la Suggestion mentale*).

appear never to have realised its possible significance. Dr. Elliotson, for instance, describes in the *Zoist* (vol. v. pp. 242-245) some experiments in which a lady, mesmerised by himself, was able to indicate correctly the taste of salt, cinnamon, sugar, ginger, water, and pepper, as Dr. Elliotson placed successively these various substances in his mouth. But he seems to have recorded the results chiefly from curiosity, and to have regarded them as of little scientific interest compared with the stiffening of a limb, or the painless performance of an operation under mesmeric anæsthesia. Dr. Esdaile (*Practical Mesmerism*, p. 125), Mr. C. H. Townshend (*Facts in Mesmerism*, pp. 68, 72, 76, etc., etc.), Professor Gregory (*Animal Magnetism*, p. 231), and other writers of that time, record similar observations. But the subject seems to have been crowded out, on the one hand, with the more cautious observers, by the growing importance of hypnotism as an anæsthetic and a curative agency, on the other by the greater marvels of "clairvoyance" and "spirit" communications.

It was Professor Barrett, of the Royal College of Science, Dublin, who, in a paper read before the British Association at Glasgow in 1876, first isolated the phenomenon from its somewhat dubious surroundings, and drew public attention to its importance. Up to that time "community of sensation" or thought-transference seems to have been known only as a rare and fitful accompaniment of the hypnotic trance. But in the course of the correspondence arising out of his paper Professor Barrett learnt of several instances where similar phenomena had been observed in the waking state. The Willing game was just then coming into fashion, and cases had been observed in which the thing willed had been performed without contact between the performer and the person willing, and apparently without the possibility of any normal means of communication between them. Later, in the years 1881-82, a long series of experiments, in which Professor Sidgwick, the late Professor Balfour Stewart, the late Edmund Gurney, Mr. F. W. H. Myers and others joined with Professor Barrett, seemed to establish the possibility of a new mode of communication. And these earlier results have been confirmed by further experiments continued down to the present time by many observers both in this country and abroad. In the present chapter some account will be given of experiments in the transference of simple ideas and sensations performed with percipients in the ordinary waking state. The next chapter will deal with similar results obtained with hypnotised persons. In Chapters IV. and V. results of a more complicated or unusual character will be described and discussed.

Transference of Tastes.

The particular form of telepathy which first attracted attention to the whole subject, the transmission to the percipient of impressions of taste and pain experienced by the agent, appears to have been observed in the normal state very rarely. One such case may be here quoted. In the years 1883-85 Mr. Malcolm Guthrie, J.P., of Liverpool, the then head of a large drapery business in that city, conducted a long series of experiments with two of his employees, Miss E. and Miss R. In September 1883 Mr. Guthrie, Mr. Edmund Gurney, and Mr. Myers, indicated respectively by the initials M. G., E. G., and M., had a series of trials with these percipients in the transference of tastes. The percipients, who were fully awake, were blindfolded; the packets or bottles containing the substances experimented upon were placed beyond the range of possible vision; and in the case of strongly smelling substances, either at a distance or outside the room; and other precautions were taken by the agents, by keeping the mouth closed and turning the head away, etc., in order that the percipients should not become aware by the sense of smell of the nature of the substance experimented with. Strict silence was of course observed. It may be conceded that when all possible precautions are taken, experiments with sapid substances must be inconclusive when the agent is in the same room with the percipient; since nearly all such substances have an odour, however faint. In view, however, of the extreme sensibility already demonstrated (see below, pp. 23, etc.) of these particular percipients to transferred impressions of other kinds, it seems probable that the results in this case also were actually due to telepathy. The alternative explanation is to attribute to persons in the normal waking state a degree of hyperæsthesia for which we have no exact parallel even in the records of hypnotism. For to persons of normal susceptibility the odour of a small quantity, *e.g.* of salt or alum, in the mouth of another person at a distance of two or three feet would certainly be quite inappreciable.

No. 1.—By Mr. Guthrie and others.

September 3, 1883.

EXPT.	TASTER.	PERCIPIENT.	SUBSTANCE.	ANSWERS GIVEN.
1	M.	E.	Vinegar.	"A sharp and nasty taste."
2	M.	E.	Mustard.	"Mustard."
3	M.	R.	Do.	"Ammonia."
4	M.	E.	Sugar	"I still taste the hot taste of the mustard."

September 4.

5	E. G. & M.	E.	Worcestershire sauce	"Worcestershire sauce."
6	M. G.	R.	Do.	"Vinegar."
7	E. G. & M.	E.	Port wine.	"Between eau de Cologne and beer."
8	M. G.	R.	Do.	"Raspberry vinegar."
9	E. G. & M.	E.	Bitter aloes	"Horrible and bitter."
10	M. G.	R.	Alum	"A taste of ink—of iron—of vinegar. I feel it on my lips—it is as if I had been eating alum."
11	M. G.	E.	Alum.	(E. perceived that M. G. was *not* tasting bitter aloes, as E. G. and M. supposed, but something different. No distinct perception on account of the persistence of the bitter taste.)

EXPT.	TASTER.	PERCIPIENT.	SUBSTANCE.	ANSWERS GIVEN.
12 ..	E. G. & M...	E.....	Nutmeg.............	"Peppermint—no—what you put in puddings—nutmeg."
13 ..	M. G.	R.....	Do.	"Nutmeg."
14 ..	E. G. & M...	E.....	Sugar...............	Nothing perceived.
15 ..	M. G.	R.....	Do.	Nothing perceived. (Sugar should be tried at an earlier stage in the series, as, after the aloes, we could scarcely taste it ourselves.)
16 ..	E. G. & M...	E.....	Cayenne pepper......	"Mustard."
17 ..	M. G.	R.....	Do.	"Cayenne pepper." (After the cayenne we were unable to taste anything further that evening.)

Throughout the next series of experiments the substances were kept outside the room in which the percipients were seated.

September 5.

18 ..	E. G. & M...	E.....	Carbonate of Soda...	Nothing perceived.
19 ..	M. G.	R.....	Caraway seeds.......	"It feels like meal—like a seed loaf—caraway seeds." (The *substance* of the seeds seems to be perceived before their *taste*.)
20 ..	E. G. & M...	E.....	Cloves..............	"Cloves."
21 ..	E. G. & M...	E.....	Citric acid..........	Nothing felt.
22 ..	M. G.	R.....	Do.	"Salt."
23 ..	E. G. & M...	E.....	Liquorice	"Cloves."
24 ..	M. G.	R.....	Cloves..............	"Cinnamon."
25 ..	E. G. & M...	E.....	Acid jujube..........	"Pear drop."
26 ..	M. G.	R.....	Do.	"Something hard, which is giving way—acid jujube."
27 ..	E. G. & M...	E.....	Candied ginger......	"Something sweet and hot."
28 ..	M. G.	R.....	Do.	"Almond toffy." (M. G. took this ginger in the dark, and was some time before he realised that it was ginger.)
29 ..	E. G. & M...	E.....	Home-made Noyau ..	"Salt."
30 ..	M. G.	R.....	Do. ..	"Port wine." (This was by far the most strongly smelling of the substances tried; the scent of kernels being hard to conceal. Yet it was named by E. as salt.)
31 ..	E. G. & M...	E.....	Bitter aloes..........	"Bitter."
32 ..	M. G.	R.....	Do.	Nothing felt.

(*Proceedings of the Society for Psychical Research*, vol. ii. pp. 3, 4.)

Further experiments in this direction are much to be desired. But apart from the difficulty above referred to, experiments of the kind are liable to be tedious and inconclusive because of the inability of most persons to discriminate accurately between one taste and another, when the guidance of all other senses is lacking. To conduct such experiments to a successful issue, it would probably be necessary that the percipients should have some preliminary training to enable them to distinguish by taste alone between various salts and pharmaceutical preparations.

Transference of Pains.

Experiments in the transference of pains are not attended with the same difficulties, nor open to the same evidential objections; and some interesting trials of this kind with one of the same percipients, Miss R., met with a fair amount of success. The experiments were carried on at intervals, interspersed with experiments of other kinds, by Mr. Guthrie at Liverpool during nine months in 1884 and 1885. The percipient on each occasion was blindfolded and seated with her back towards the rest of the party, who each pinched or otherwise injured themselves in the same part of the body at the same time. The agents in these experiments—the whole series of which is here recorded—were three or more of the following :—Mr. Guthrie, Professor Herdman, Dr. Hicks, Dr. Hyla Greves, Mr. R. C. Johnson, F.R.A.S., Mr. Birchall, Miss Redmond, and on one occasion another lady. The results are given in the following table :—

No. 2.—By Mr. Guthrie and others.

1.—Back of left hand pricked. Rightly localised.
2.—Lobe of left ear pricked. Rightly localised.
3.—Left wrist pricked. "Is it in the left hand?" pointing to the back near the little finger.
4.—Third finger of left hand tightly bound round with wire. A lower joint of that finger was guessed.
5.—Left wrist scratched with pins. "Is it in the left wrist, like being scratched?"
6.—Left ankle pricked. Rightly localised.

7.—Spot behind left ear pricked.   No result.

8.—Right knee pricked.   Rightly localised.

9.—Right shoulder pricked.   Rightly localised.

10.—Hands burned over gas.   "Like a pulling pain . . . then tingling, like cold and hot alternately," localised by gesture only.

11.—End of tongue bitten.   "Is it the lip or the tongue?"

12.—Palm of left hand pricked.   "Is it a tingling pain in the left hand here?" placing her finger on the palm of the left hand.

13.—Back of neck pricked.   "Is it a pricking of the neck?"

14.—Front of left arm above elbow pricked.   Rightly localised.

15.—Spot just above left ankle pricked.   Rightly localised.

16.—Spot just above right wrist pricked.   "I am not quite sure, but I feel a pain in the right arm, from the thumb upwards to above the wrist."

17.—Inside of left ankle pricked.   Outside of left ankle guessed.

18.—Spot beneath right collar-bone pricked.   The exactly corresponding spot on the left side guessed.

19.—Back hair pulled.   No result.

20.—Inside of right wrist pricked.   Right foot guessed.

(Proc. S.P.R., vol. iii. pp. 424-452.)

Transference of Sounds.

It is noteworthy that there is little experimental evidence for the transmission of an auditory impression.   Occasionally, in trials with names and cards the nature of the mistakes made has seemed to indicate audition, as when, *e.g.*, *three* is given for *Queen* or *ace* for *eight*.   But obviously a long series of experiments and a long series of mistakes would be necessary to afford material for any conclusion.   Sometimes a percipient has stated that he heard the name of the thing thought of; as, for instance, in a case recorded in Chapter V., where the percipient "heard" the word *gloves* before "seeing" a vision of them.   But such cases appear to be rare.   Experiments with a view to test the transmission of *actual* sounds could of course only be carried out under special conditions, of which one would be the separation of the agent from the percipient by a considerable intervening space—and this condition is, of itself, found to interfere with success. Some evidence, indeed, of a quasi-experimental character for the transference of musical sounds at a distance will be given in a later chapter (Chapter V., No. 33). Experiments with imagined sounds appear to have been rarely tried, or at least, successful results have rarely been recorded.[1] Occasionally indeed experimenters have put on record that in thinking of an object they have mentally repeated the name of the object as well as pictured the object itself, and there are a few cases where the general idea of the object thought of appears to have reached the percipient before the outlines of the form, which may possibly be explained as due to the reception of an auditory before a visual impression.[2]

This lack of evidence for auditory transmission is no doubt largely due to a desire on the part of experimenters in the first instance to make the proof of actual thought-transference as complete as possible. Experiments with sounds would impose a greater strain upon the agents, since in most cases they must be imagined sounds. Moreover, in such experiments it would be at once more difficult to estimate with precision degrees of success, and to preserve a permanent record of the result ; and finally, the subject thought of would be more easily communicated either fraudulently, by a code, or by unconscious indications on the part of the agent. In this connection it is possibly significant that whilst in morbid conditions auditory hallucinations are much commoner than visual, the proportion appears to be reversed with

---

[1] Some trials were made by Mr. Guthrie with imagined tunes. But they were in no instance successful without contact ; and as obviously the chances of unconscious indications being given, in any case considerable where tunes are in question, are much increased by contact, we should not be justified in regarding successful results, under such conditions, as even *prima facie* due to Thought-transference. (See *Proc. S.P.R.*, vol. iii. pp. 426, 447, 448.)

[2] See below, Chapter III.—Mrs. Sidgwick's experiments.

telepathic hallucinations. It seems probable that the apparent infrequency of auditory transmission may be in part due to the fact that in the modern world the sense of vision is for educated persons the habitual channel for precise or important information. To the Greek in the time of Socrates no doubt the ear was the main avenue for all knowledge; it was the ear that received not merely the current talk of the market-place and the gymnasium, but the oratory of the law-court, the literature of the stage, and the philosophy of the Schools. But for modern civilised societies the newspaper and the libraries have placed the eye in a position of unquestioned pre-eminence. It seems likely therefore, apart from all defects in such evidence, that the agent would find a greater difficulty, as a rule, in calling up a vivid representation of a sound than of a vision; and that the percipient would experience a corresponding difference in the reception and discrimination of the two classes of impressions.

Transference of Ideas not definitely classed.

Experiments by PROFESSOR RICHET and others.

In the following cases, where the exact nature of the impression received was not apparently consciously classified by the percipient, it may be presumed to have been either of a visual or an auditory nature. M. Charles Richet (*Revue Philosophique*, Dec. 1884, " La suggestion mentale et le calcul des probabilités ") conducted a series of experiments in guessing the suits of cards drawn at random from a pack. 2927 trials were made : ten persons besides M. Richet himself—who acted sometimes as agent and sometimes as percipient—taking part in the experiments. In the 2927 trials the suit was correctly named 789 times, the most probable number of correct guesses being 732. A similar series of trials was conducted, on Edmund Gurney's initiative, by some members of the S.P.R. and others. There were 17 series, containing 17,653 trials, and 4760 successes; the theoretically probable number, on the assumption that the results were due to chance, being 4413. The probability for some cause other than chance deduced from this result is .999,999,98, which represents perhaps a higher degree of probability than the inhabitants of this hemisphere are justified in attaching to the belief that the ensuing night will be followed by another day.[1] In a similar series of experiments carried out under the direction of the American S.P.R. the proportion of successes was little higher than the theoretically probable number.[2] But in the absence of details as to the conditions under which the experiments were made, no unfavourable inference can fairly be drawn from these results. At any rate some very remarkable results were obtained later, in a series of trials made on the lines laid down by the committee of the American Society. The agent in this case was Mrs. J F. Brown, the percipient Nellie Gallagher, "a domestic lately come from the county of Northumberland, in New Brunswick." The experiments appear to have been carried out with great care, and the results are recorded and analysed at length (*Proc. Am. S.P.R.*, pp. 322-349). 3000 trials were made in guessing the numbers from 0 to 9 or from 1 to 10 inclusive. The order of the digits in each set of 100 trials was determined by drawing lots. The agent sat at one side of a table, the percipient at the other side. At first the percipient sat facing the

---

[1] The calculation is by Professor F. Y. Edgeworth. (See *Proc. S.P.R.*, vol. iii. p. 190.) Of course the statement in the text must not be taken as indicating the belief of Mr. Edgeworth or the writer or any one else that the above figures demonstrate Thought-transference as the cause of the results attained. The results may conceivably have been due to some error of observation or of reporting. But the figures are sufficient to prove, what is here claimed for them, that *some* cause must be sought for the results other than chance.

[2] *Proc. American S.P.R.*, pp. 17 *et seq.*

agent, but after about 1000 trials had been made her back was turned to the table—and this position was continued to the end. The paper containing the numbers to be guessed was placed in the agent's lap, out of sight of the percipient. There was no mirror in the room. In the result the digits were correctly named 584 times, or nearly twice the probable number, 300. The proportion of the successes steadily increased, from 175 in the first batch of 1000 trials, to 190 in the second, and 219 in the third batch.

No. 3.—By Dr. Ochorowicz.

In the following set of experiments, made by Dr. Ochorowicz, ex-Professor of Psychology and Natural Philosophy at the University of Lemberg, described in his book *La Suggestion mentale* (pp. 69, 75, 76), there are not sufficient indications in most cases to enable a judgment to be formed as to the special form of sense-impression made on the percipient's mind. The percipient was a Madame D., 70 years of age. She had been shown to be amenable to hypnotism, but during these experiments she was in a normal condition. She is described as being of strong constitution and in good health ; intelligent above the average, well read, and accustomed to literary work. The first experiments with Madame D. are not quoted here, not having been conducted, as Dr. Ochorowicz explains, under strict conditions. The objects thought of had been selected by the agent, instead of being taken haphazard, and the choice had frequently been directly suggested by his surroundings. It seemed possible, therefore, to explain the results as due to an unconscious association of ideas common to agent and percipient. Dr. Ochorowicz, however, has shown by his careful analysis of the experiments recorded in the earlier chapters of his book that he is fully aware of the risk of error from this and other causes, and in the series of the 2nd May and the following days he tells us that adequate precautions were taken.

An Object.

36. A bust of M. N.	Portrait . . . of a man . . . a bust.
37. A fan.	Something round.
38. A key.	Something made of lead . . . of bronze . . . it is iron.
39. A hand holding a ring.	Something shining, a diamond . . . a ring.

A Taste.

40. Acid.	Sweet.

A Diagram.

41. A square.	Something irregular.
42. A circle.	A triangle . . . a circle.

A Letter.

43. M.	M.
44. D.	D.
45. J.	J.
46. B.	A, X, R, B.
47. O.	W, A ; no, it is an O.
48. Jan.	J . . . (go on !) Jan.

Third Series, May 6th, 1885.—Twenty-five experiments were made, of which, unfortunately, I have kept no record, except of the three following, which impressed me most. (The subject had her back to us, held the pencil and *wrote* whatever came into her head. We touched her back lightly, keeping our eyes fixed on the letters we had written.)

49. Brabant.	Bra . . . (I made a mental effort to help the subject, without speaking.) Brabant.
50. Paris.	P . . . aris.
51. Telephone.	T . . . elephone.

Fourth Series, May 8th.—Same conditions.

52. Z.	L, P, K, J.
53. B.	B.
54. T.	S, T, F.
55. N.	M, N.
56. P.	R, Z, A.
57. Y.	V, Y.

Fourth Series—continued.

58. E.	E.
59. Gustave.	F, J, Gabriel.
60. Duch.	E, O.
61. Ba.	B, A.
62. No.	F, K, O.

A Number.

63. 44.	6, 8, 12.
64. 2.	7, 5, 9.

(I told my assistant to imagine the look of the number when written, and not its sound.)

65. 3.	8, 3.
66. 7.	7.
67. 8.	8 ; no, o, 6, 9.

Then followed thirteen trials with fantastic figures, details of which Dr. Ochorowicz does not record. He tells us, however, that only five of the representations presented even a general resemblance to the originals.

It is to be observed that in this series of experiments contact was not completely excluded in all the trials. But if Dr. Ochorowicz's memory may be relied upon for the statement that the agent looked at the original letters and diagrams, and not at the percipient's attempts at reproducing them, the hypothesis of involuntary muscular guidance must be severely strained to account for the results. At any rate, in the three remaining trials in this series it seems clear that muscle-reading is inadequate as an explanation.

A person thought of.

Subject.	*Answer.*
68. The percipient.	M. O——— ; no, it's myself.
69. M. D——.	M. D——.

An Image.

70. We pictured to ourselves a crescent moon. M. P—— on a background of clouds, I in a clear dark blue sky.	I see passing clouds . . . a light . . . (in a satisfied tone)—it is the moon.

Transference of Visual Images.

No. 4.—By DR. BLAIR THAW.

The experiments which follow were made by Dr. Blair Thaw, M.D., of New York. The series quoted, which took place on the 28th of April 1892, comprises all the trials in which Dr. Thaw was himself the percipient. Dr. Thaw had his eyes blindfolded and his ears muffled, and the agent, Mrs. Thaw, and Mr. M. H. Wyatt, who was present but took no part in the agency, kept silent, except when it was necessary to state whether an object, card, number, or colour was to be guessed. The objects were in all cases actually looked at by the agent, the "colour" being a coloured disc, and the numbers being printed on separate cards.[1]

1st Object. SILK PINCUSHION, in form of Orange-Red Apple, quite round.—Percipient : *A Disc.* When asked what colour, said, *Red or Orange.* When asked what object, named *Pincushion.*

2nd Object. A SHORT LEAD PENCIL, nearly covered by the nickel cover. Never seen by percipient. Percipient : *Something white or light. A card. I thought of Mr. Wyatt's silver pencil.*

3rd Object. A DARK VIOLET in Mr. Wyatt's button-hole, but not known to be in the house by percipient. Percipient : *Something dark. Not very big. Longish. Narrow. Soft. It can't be a cigarette because it is dark brown. A dirty colour.* Asked about smell, said : *Not strong, but what you might call pungent; a clean smell.*

Percipient had not noticed smell before, though sitting by Mr. Wyatt some time, but when afterwards told of the violet knew that this was the odour noticed in experiment.

Asked to spell name, percipient said : *Phrygian, Phrigid, or first letter V if not Ph.*

4th Object. WATCH, dull silver with filigree. Percipient : *Yellow or dirty ivory. Not very big. Like carving on it.* Watch is opened by agent, and percipient is asked what was done. Percipient says : *You opened it. It is shaped like a*

---

[1] See Dr. Thaw's paper, *Proc. Soc. Psych. Research*, vol. viii. pp. 422 *et seq.*

butterfly. Percipient held finger and thumb of each hand making figure much like that of opened watch. Percipient asked to spell it, said: *I get r-i-n-g with a W at first.*

PLAYING CARDS.

KING SPADES.—*Spades. Spot in middle and spots outside.*
7 *Spades.* 9 *Spades.*
4 CLUBS.—*4 Clubs.*
5 SPADES.—*5 Diamonds.*

NUMBERS OUT OF NINE DIGITS.

4.—Percipient said: *It stands up straight. 4.*
6.—Percipient said: *Those two are too much alike, only a little gap in one of them. It is either 5 or 6.*
3.—*3.*
1.—Percipient said: *Cover up that upper part if it is the 1. It is either 7 or 1.*
2.—*9, 8.*
[From acting so much as agent in previous trials, I knew the shapes of these numbers printed on cardboard, and as agent found the 5 and 6 too much alike. After looking hard at one of them I can hardly tell the difference, and always cover the upper projection of the 1 because it is so much like a 7.
The numbers were printed on separate pieces of cardboard, and there were about a hundred in the box, being made for some game.]

COLOURS, CHOSEN AT RANDOM.

Chosen.		1st Guess.		2nd Guess.
BRIGHT RED	...	*Bright Red.*		
LIGHT GREEN	...	*Light Green.*		
YELLOW ...	...	*Dark Blue* ...	...	*Yellow.*
BRIGHT YELLOW ...		*Bright Yellow.*		
DARK RED	...	*Blue*	...	*Dark Red.*
DARK BLUE	...	*Orange*	...	*Dark Blue.*
ORANGE ...	...	*Green*	...	*Heliotrope.*

The percipient himself told the agents to change character of object after each actual failure, thus getting new sensations.
Percipient was told to go into next room and get something.
1st Object. SILVER INKSTAND chosen.—Percipient says *I think of something, but it is too bright and easy. It is the silver inkstand.*
Percipient told to get something in next room.
2nd Object. A GLASS CANDLESTICK.—Percipient went to right corner of the room and to the cabinet with the object on it, but could not distinguish which object.

Percipient had handkerchief off to be able to walk, but was not followed by agents, and did not see them. Agents found percipient standing with hands over candlestick undecided.

From the percipient's descriptions it would seem that the impression here was of a visual nature, though Dr. Thaw himself says, " I cannot describe my sensation as a visualisation of any kind. It seemed rather to be by some wholly subjective process that I knew what the agents were looking at." It is not always, however, an easy task to analyse one's own sensations ; and, on the whole, it seems more probable that there was visualisation, but of a very faint and ideal kind.

No. 5.—By MR. MALCOLM GUTHRIE.

Reference has already been made to the long series of experiments carried on during the years 1883-85 by Mr. Malcolm Guthrie of Liverpool. During a great part of the series he was assisted by Mr. James Birchall, Hon. Sec. of the Liverpool Literary and Philosophical Society. Professor Oliver Lodge, Edmund Gurney, Professor Herdman, and others co-operated from time to time. Throughout there were two percipients only, Miss R. and Miss E. The experiments were conducted and the results recorded with great care and thoroughness ; and the whole series, in its length, its variety, and its completeness, forms perhaps the most important single contribution to the records of experimental thought-transference in the normal state.[1] Summing up, in July 1885, the results attained, Mr. Guthrie writes :—

"We have now a record of 713 experiments, and I recently set myself the task of classifying them into the 4 classes of successful, partially successful, misdescriptions, and failures. I en-

---

[1] Records of these experiments will be found in the *Proc. of the Soc. Psych. Research*, vol. i. pp. 263-283 ; vol. ii. pp. 1-5, 24-42, 189-200 ; vol. iii. pp. 424-452.

deavoured to work it out in what I thought a reasonable way, but I experienced much difficulty in assigning to its proper column each experiment we made. This, however, is a task which each student of the subject will be able to undertake for himself according to his own judgment. I do not submit my summary as a basis for calculation of probability. A few successful experiments of a certain kind carry greater weight with them than a large number of another kind; for some experiments are practically beyond the region of guesses. . . .

"The following is a summary of the work done, classified to the best of my judgment :—

FIRST SERIES.

Experiments and Conditions.	Total.	Nothing perceived.	Complete.	Partial.	Misdescriptions.
Visual—Letters, figures, and cards— Contact - - - - -	26	2	17	4	3
Visual—Letters, figures, and cards— Non-contact - - - -	16	0	9	2	5
Visual—Objects, colours, etc.—Contact-	19	6	7	4	2
Do. do. Non-contact-	38	4	28	6	0
Imagined visual—Non-contact - -	18	5	8	2	3
Imagined numbers and names—Contact and Non-contact - - - -	39	11	12	6	10
Pains—Contact - - - - -	52	10	30	9	3
Tastes and smells—Contact - - -	94	19	42	20	13
	302	57	153	53	39
Diagrams—Contact - - - -	37	7	18	6	6
Do. Non-contact - -	118	6	66	23	23
	457	70	237	82	68

"There were also 40 diagrams for experimental evenings with strangers, in series of sixes and sevens, all misdrawn, and not fairly to be reckoned in the above.

457 experiments under proper conditions.
70 nothing perceived.
———
387

319 wholly or partially correct ; 68 misdescriptions = 18 per cent."

In the second series there were 123 trials; in 15 cases no impression was received, and in 35 cases, or 32 per cent. of the remainder, an incorrect description was given. In the third series, of 133 trials there were 24 in which no impression was received and 40 failures: proportion of failures = 37 per cent. Mr. Guthrie attributes this gradual decline in the proportion of successes to the difficulty experienced by both agents and percipients in maintaining the original lively interest in the proceedings.

No. 6.—By PROFESSOR LODGE, F.R.S.

Subjoined is a detailed description of experiments made on two evenings in 1884, recorded by Professor Lodge,[1] which leaves no room for doubt that the impressions received in this instance by the percipient were of a visual nature. The agent on the first evening was Mr. James Birchall, who held the hand of the percipient, Miss R. The only other person present was Professor Lodge. The object was placed sometimes on a wooden screen between the percipient and the agent, at other times behind the percipient, whose eyes were bandaged. The bandage, it should be observed, was a sufficient precaution against cornea-reading; but for other purposes no reliance was placed upon it. It is believed that the precautions taken were in all cases adequate to conceal the object from the percipient if her eyes had been uncovered. In the account quoted any remarks made by the agent or Professor Lodge are entered between brackets.

Object—a blue square of silk.—(Now, it's going to be a colour; ready.) " Is it green?" (No.) "It's something between green and blue. . . . Peacock." (What shape?) She drew a rhombus.

[N.B.—It is not intended to imply that this was a success by

---

any means, and it is to be understood that it was only to make a start on the first experiment that so much help was given as is involved in saying "it's a colour." When they are simply told "it's an object," or, what is much the same, when nothing is said at all, the field for guessing is practically infinite. When no remark at starting is recorded none was made, except such an one as "Now we are ready," by myself.]

Next object—a key on a black ground.—(It's an object.) In a few seconds she said, "It's bright. . . . It looks like a key." Told to draw it, she drew it just inverted.

Next object—three gold studs in morocco case.—"Is it yellow? . . . Something gold. . . . Something round. . . . A locket or a watch perhaps." (Do you see more than one round?) "Yes, there seem to be more than one. . . . Are there three rounds? . . . Three rings?" (What do they seem to be set in?) "Something bright like beads." [Evidently not understanding or attending to the question.] Told to unblindfold herself and draw, she drew the three rounds in a row quite correctly, and then sketched round them absently the outline of the case, which seemed therefore to have been apparent to her though she had not consciously attended to it. It was an interesting and striking experiment.

Next object—a pair of scissors standing partly open with their points down.—"Is it a bright object? . . . Something longways [indicating verticality]. . . . A pair of scissors standing up. . . . A little bit open." Time, about a minute altogether. She then drew her impression, and it was correct in every particular. The object in this experiment was on a settee behind her, but its position had to be pointed out to her when, after the experiment, she wanted to see it.

Next object—a drawing of a right-angled triangle on its side. —(It's a drawing.) She drew an isosceles triangle on its side.

Next—a circle with a cord across it.—She drew two detached ovals, one with a cutting line across it.

Next—a drawing of a Union Jack pattern.—As usual in drawing experiments, Miss R. remained silent for perhaps a minute; then she said, "Now I am ready." I hid the object; she took off the handkerchief, and proceeded to draw on paper placed ready in front of her. She this time drew all the lines of the figure except the horizontal middle one. She was obviously much tempted to draw this, and, indeed, began it two or three times faintly, but ultimately said, "No, I'm not sure," and stopped.

ORIGINAL.

REPRODUCTION. [N.B.—The actual drawings made in all the experiments are preserved intact by Mr. Guthrie.]

[END OF SITTING.]

Experiments with MISS R.—*Continued.*

I will now describe an experiment indicating that one agent may be better than another.

Object—the Three of Hearts.—Miss E. and Mr. Birchall both present as agents, but Mr. Birchall holding percipient's hands at first. "Is it a black cross . . . a white ground with a black cross on it?" Mr. Birchall now let Miss E. hold hands instead of himself, and Miss R. very soon said, "Is it a card?" (Right.) "Are there three spots on it? . . . Don't know what they are. . . . I don't think I can get the colour. . . . They are one above the other, but they seem three round spots. . . . I think they're red, but am not clear."

Next object—a playing card with a blue anchor painted on it slantwise instead of pips.—No contact at all this time, but another lady, Miss R——d, who had entered the room, assisted Mr. B. and Miss E. as agents. "Is it an anchor? . . . a little on the slant." (Do you see any colour?) "Colour is black. . . . It's a nicely drawn anchor." When asked to draw she sketched part of it, but had evidently half forgotten it, and not knowing the use of the cross arm, she could only indicate that there was something more there but she couldn't remember what. Her drawing had the right slant exactly.

Another object—two pairs of coarse lines crossing; drawn in red chalk, and set up at some distance from agents. No contact. "I only see lines crossing." She saw no colour. She afterwards drew them quite correctly, but very small.

Double object.—It was now that I arranged the double object between Miss R——d and Miss E., who happened to be sitting nearly facing one another. [See *Nature*, June 12th, 1884.] The drawing was a square on one side of the paper, a cross on the other. Miss R——d looked at the side with the square on it. Miss E. looked at the side with the cross. Neither knew what the other was looking at—nor did the percipient know that anything unusual was being tried. Mr. Birchall was silently asked to take off his attention and he got up and looked out of window before the drawings were brought in, and during the experiment. There was no contact. Very soon Miss R. said, "I see things moving about . . . I seem to see two things . . . I see first one up there, and then one down there . . . I don't know which to draw. . . . I can't see either distinctly." (Well, anyhow, draw what you have seen.) She took off the bandage and drew first a square, and then said, "Then there was the other thing as well . . . afterwards they seemed to go into one," and she

ORIGINALS.

REPRODUCTION.

drew a cross inside the square from corner to corner, adding afterwards, "I don't know what made me put it inside."

No. 7.—By Herr Max Dessoir.

In June 1885 some successful experiments in thought-transference were made by Herr Dessoir, of Berlin, author of *A Bibliography of Modern Hypnotism*, and other works, with the co-operation of some friends, Herren Weiss, Biltz, and Sachse. There were in all eighteen trials with diagrams in which Herr Dessoir was the percipient. The diagrams which follow— reproduced from the original drawings—were the result of six consecutive trials. They are, as will be seen, not completely successful; but they convey a fair idea of the amount of success attained in the whole series. It should be noted that the impression received by the percipient appears to have been persistent; and that the second attempt at reproduction, in five out of the six cases, was more successful than the first. Herr Dessoir states that he was generally out of the room whilst the figure was being drawn; he returned at the given signal, with eyes closely bandaged; "I set myself at the table, and in many instances placed my hands on the table, and the agent placed his hands on mine; the hands lay quite still on one another. When an image presented itself to my mind, the hands were removed . . . and I took off the bandage and drew my figure."

A full account of these experiments, and of others conducted by Herr Dessoir, will be found in *Proc. S.P.R.*, vol. iv. pp. 111-126; vol. v. pp. 355-357.

I.

ORIG.

REP. 1.

REP. 2.

While the second reproduction was pro-ceeding, an interruption occurred which prevented its completion.

Agent: W. S.

II.

ORIG.

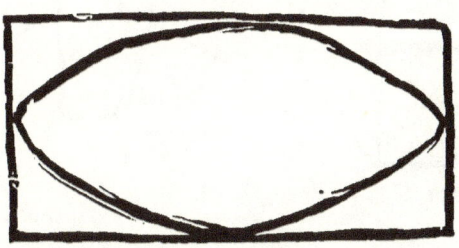

Agent: II. B.

REP. 1.   REP. 2.   REP. 3.   REP. 4.

III.

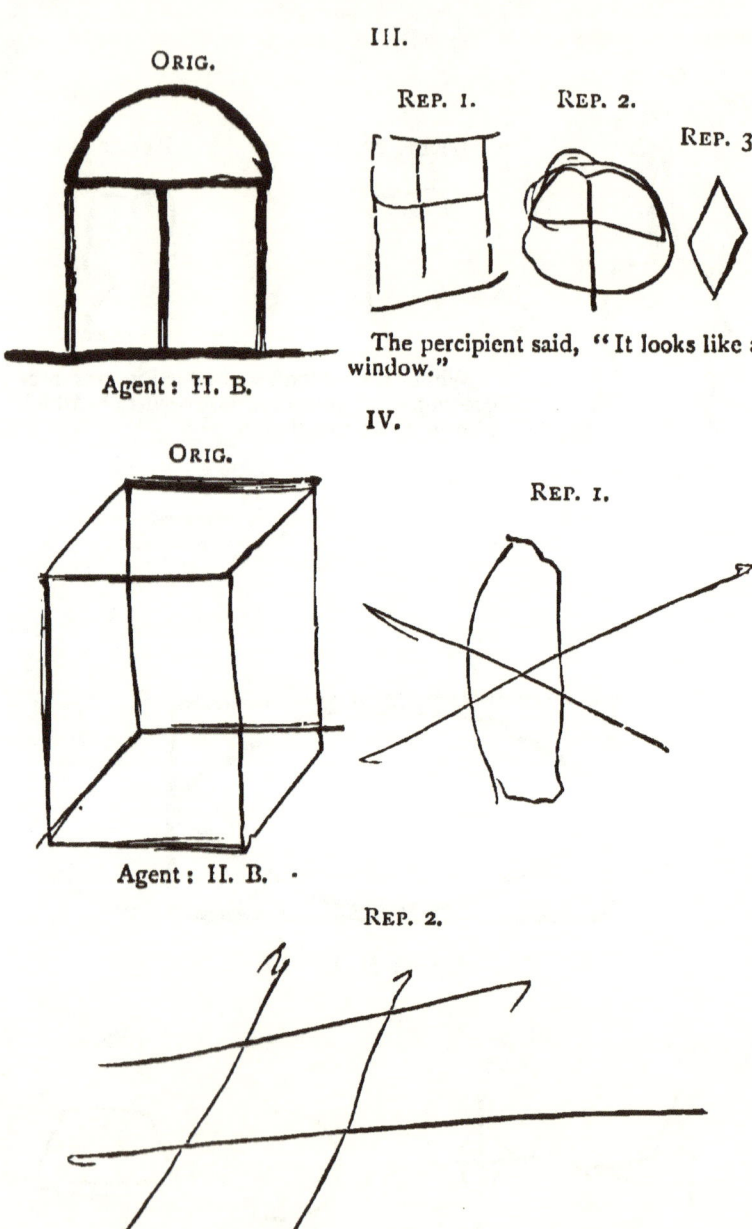

Orig.

Rep. 1.   Rep. 2.

Rep. 3.

The percipient said, "It looks like a window."

Agent: H. B.

IV.

Orig.

Rep. 1.

Agent: II. B.

Rep. 2.

REP. 3.

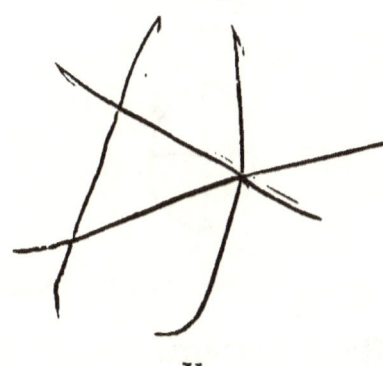

V.

ORIG.

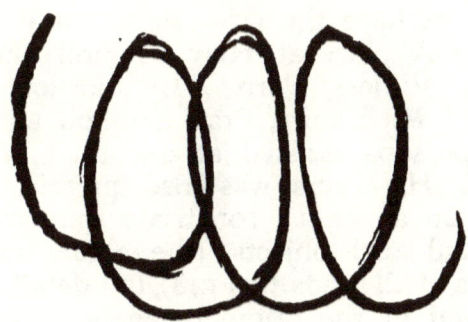

Agent : H. B.

REP. 1.   REP. 2.

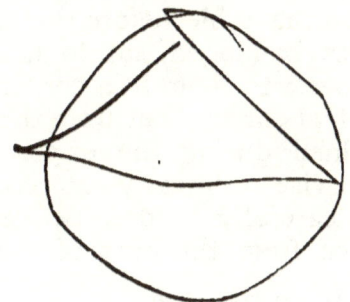   

VI.

ORIG.   REP. 1.   REP. 2.

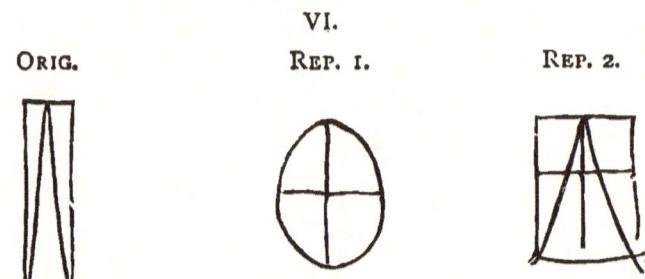

Agent: E. W.   The percipient said, "It looks like a window."

No. 8.—By HERR SCHMOLL and M. MABIRE.

Of more recent experiments with diagrams, those recorded by Herr Anton Schmoll and M. Etienne Mabire are perhaps the most important.[1] The experiments took place at Herr Schmoll's house, 111 Avenue de Villiers, Paris. In addition to Herr Schmoll and M. Mabire, Frau Schmoll and four or five other persons assisted at one time or another. Mr. F. W. H. Myers was also present on three occasions. In all about 100 trials were made with diagrams and real objects (the actual number of experiments of all kinds was 148), full details of which will be found in the original papers. The experiments were made in the evenings, in a room lighted by a hanging lamp. The agents, usually three or four in number, sat at a round table immediately under the lamp, and fixed their eyes on the diagram or object, which was placed on the table before them. The percipient, with his eyes bandaged, sat in full view of the agents with his back to them in a corner of the room at a distance of about ten feet from the object. Silence was maintained during the experiments, except where otherwise expressly stated. The object or diagram was carefully hidden before the handkerchief was removed from the eyes of the

[1] *Proc. Soc. Psych. Research*, vol. iv. pp. 324 *et seq.*; vol. v. pp. 169 *et seq.*

percipient to enable him to draw his impression.   In
the first nineteen experiments the figure was drawn
with the end of a match dipped in ink, whilst the percipient was in the room.   It was not likely, under
the circumstances, as the match moved almost noiselessly over the paper, that any indication of the
figure drawn could by this means have been given to
the percipient.   Nevertheless, in the later experiments
quoted the precaution was taken to draw the figure
whilst the percipient was in another room, and a soft
brush was substituted for the match.   The following
is a record, by Herr Schmoll, of the last two evenings
of the first series :—

18.—*August 24th*, 1886.

Agents—Mdlle. Louise, Frau Schmoll, Schmoll.
Percipient—M. Mabire.
Object (drawn)—

Result—M. Mabire saw "a sort of semicircle like the tail of a
  comet, but of spiral construction, like some of the nebulæ."
  What he saw he reproduced in the following manner :—

19.—*The same evening.*

Agents—Mdlle. Louise, M. Mabire, Frau Schmoll.
Percipient—Schmoll.
Object (drawn)—

Result—" I see two double lines, that cross each other at about
  right angles." (Pause.)   " The two double lines now appear

single, but like rays of light, and in the form of an X."
(Another pause.) "Now I see the upper part of the X
separated from the lower by a vertical line." I draw :—

 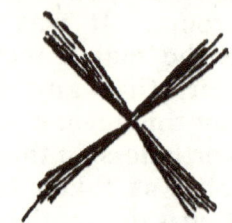 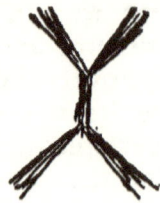

20.—*The same evening.*

Agents—Mdlle. Louise, M. Mabire, Schmoll.
Percipient—Frau Schmoll.
Object—A brass weight of 500 grms. was placed on the table.

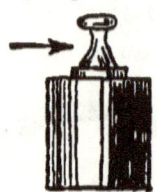

Result—"What I see looks like a short piece of candle, without
a candlestick. It must be burning, for at the upper end I
see it glitter."
Remark—At the upper part of the object, indicated by the
arrow, bright reflections, caused by the oblique lighting,
were seen by all the agents (the weight was rubbed bright).
The form seen decidedly resembles the original, especially
the outline.

21.—*The same evening.*

Agents—M. Mabire, Frau Schmoll, Schmoll.
Percipient—Mdlle. Louise.
Object—My gold watch (without the chain) was noiselessly
placed before us, the back turned towards us ; on the face
are Roman numbers.
Result—After five minutes : " I see a round object, but I cannot
describe it more particularly." (During the pause that
followed, without causing the slightest noise, I turned the
watch round, so that we saw the face.) Soon Mdlle. Louise
called out : "You are certainly looking at the clock over
the piano, for now I quite clearly see a clock face with
Roman numbers."
[The watch, as was ascertained after the experiment, was not
going at the time.]

22.—*September 10th*, 1886.

Agents—Mdlle. Louise, M. Mabire, Frau Schmoll.
Percipient—Schmoll.
Object—A pamphlet (in 8vo) was slantingly placed on the table.
Result—Completely failed. I saw nothing whatever.
Remark—At the beginning of our trials to-day we had neg-
lected to clear the table. The book was surrounded by
other objects, and also badly lighted.

23.—*The same evening.*

Agents—Mdlle. Louise, M. Mabire, Schmoll.
Percipient—Frau Schmoll.
Object—A piece of candle, 20 centimetres long, was placed on
the table.
Result—After eight minutes: " I see it well, but not clearly
enough to say what it is. It is a thin, long object."
" How long ? " asked M. Mabire.
Frau Schmoll tried by separating her hands to give a measure-
ment, but could not do it with certainty, and said, " A full
hand's length, about 20 centimetres." Begged for a further
description, she said, " I see something like a walking-stick,
but at one end there must be gold, for something shines
there." (The candle was *not* burning.)

24.—*The same evening.*

Agents—M. Mabire, Frau Schmoll, Schmoll.
Percipient—Mdlle. Louise.
Object—A Faience tea-pot was placed on the table :—

Result—After five minutes : " It is not a drawing, but a real
object. I see very clearly a little vase, a little pot or pan."

25.—*The same evening.*

Agents—Mdlle. Louise, Frau Schmoll, Schmoll.
Percipient—M. Mabire.
Object—The stamp of the firm was placed on the table :—

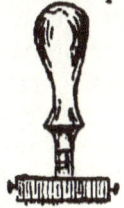

Result—After twenty minutes: "The picture appears to be rather confused. But I believe that I see the lower part of a drinking glass." (Pause.) "Now it has gone again." (A pause of five minutes.) "Now I see another form, like two symmetrical S-shaped double curves, placed side by side." Then M. Mabire drew :—

Remark—Apparently the lower part was seen first, and then the upper.

26.—*The same evening.*

Agents—M. Mabire, Frau Schmoll, Schmoll.
Percipient—Mdlle. Louise.
Object—The double eye-glasses (pince-nez) belonging to M. Mabire were laid on the table.

Result—After five minutes: "I see two curves, open above, that do not touch each other." Then Mdlle. Louise drew :—

Unfortunately, the original drawings and reproductions in this series were not preserved. The figures given are facsimile reproductions of those in Herr Schmoll's MS. record, which were copied at the time on a reduced scale from the actual drawings made by the agent and the percipient respectively. In the second series the actual drawings have been preserved. In the experiments quoted below, as already stated, the figure was drawn whilst the percipient was out of the room, and (with the exception of No. 58)

several copies were made of the drawing, "in order that each agent might be able to see the drawing in an upright position, and that he might be able to place it at the most favourable point of view." The percipient when ready withdrew the bandage from his eyes and, still seated in the chair with his back to the agents, executed the reproduction.

April 5th, 1887.

No. of Trial.	Percipient.	Agents.	Original Drawing.	Result.
51	Mdlle. Louise M.	4. Mme. D. Mdlle. Jane. Mme. Schmoll M. Schmoll.	Each agent had a copy of the original.	Before drawing the above figure, Mdlle. Louise said, "a terrestrial globe on a support." 10 minutes.
52	Mdlle. Jane.	4. Mdlle. Louise in place of Mdlle. Jane.	Four copies of the original were used by the agents.	10 minutes.
53	Mme. Schmoll	3.	Three copies used.	During the experiment Mme. Schmoll said that she saw "a little roof." 10 minutes.
54	Mdlle. Jane.	3. Mme. Schmoll in place of Mdlle. Jane.	Three copies used.	15 minutes.

Mdlle. Jane, *after having seen the original*, said that her first idea had been that of a glass.

April 5th, 1887 *(continued)*.

No. of Trial.	Percipient.	Agents.	Original Drawing.	Result.
55	Mme. D.	4.	Four copies used.	10 minutes.
56	M. Schmoll.	4. Mme. D. in place of M. Schmoll.	Four copies used.	10 minutes.
57	A Failure.			
58	Mdlle. Jane.	6.	This was the first time that an animal had been drawn.	After five minutes Mdlle. Jane said, "I see a cat's head." On being asked to draw what she saw, she produced the following figure :—
59	Mdlle. Jane.	6.	This was the first time that a head had been drawn.	At the end of five minutes, Mdlle. Jane having said, "*it is a head in profile*," a cry of joy unfortunately escaped one of those present. This cry having betrayed to Mdlle. Jane that she had guessed rightly, no drawing was made. In order to repair the wrong as much as possible, Mdlle. Jane was asked which way the head was turned. "To the left," she replied.

Experiments 60, 61, 62, 63, 64 were failures. No. 65 was not an experiment with a diagram.

April 8th, 1887.

No. of Trial.	Percipient.	Agents.	Original Drawing.	Result.
66	Mdlle. Louise.	5. (plus Mr. Myers)	This figure was drawn by Mr. Myers.	At the end of a few minutes, Mdlle. Louise said, "I see three fish on a skewer." Not being well understood, she explained, "Three fish held by a skewer, that is as they are sold in the fish markets; but everybody knows that!" Then she took off her bandage and drew—
67	Failure.			
68	Failure.			
69	Mdlle. Louise.	5. (plus Mr. Myers)		

Appended is a statement from Mdlle. Jane D., a young lady of 20, who appears to have been one of the most successful percipients in this series :—

" Whenever I have taken part in the experiments as percipient, I have endeavoured to expel from my mind all thoughts and images, and have remained inactive, with my hands over my eyes, waiting for the production of an impression ; sometimes I have tied up my eyes, but this plan has not always been

4

successful. At other times the *idea* of an object has presented itself to me before I have seized its form, but most frequently I seemed to see the picture either black on a white ground, or white on a black ground. In general, the objects present themselves in an undecided manner, and pass away very rapidly ; usually I only grasp a portion of them.

"Whenever I have been most successful, I have remarked that the picture has presented itself to my imagination almost instantaneously. Sometimes also I have been led to draw an object of which the name was forced on me, as if by some external influence.

"JANE D.

"Paris, *February 17th*, 1888."

Appended are a few facsimiles of the most successful of the above results, reproduced in the original size.

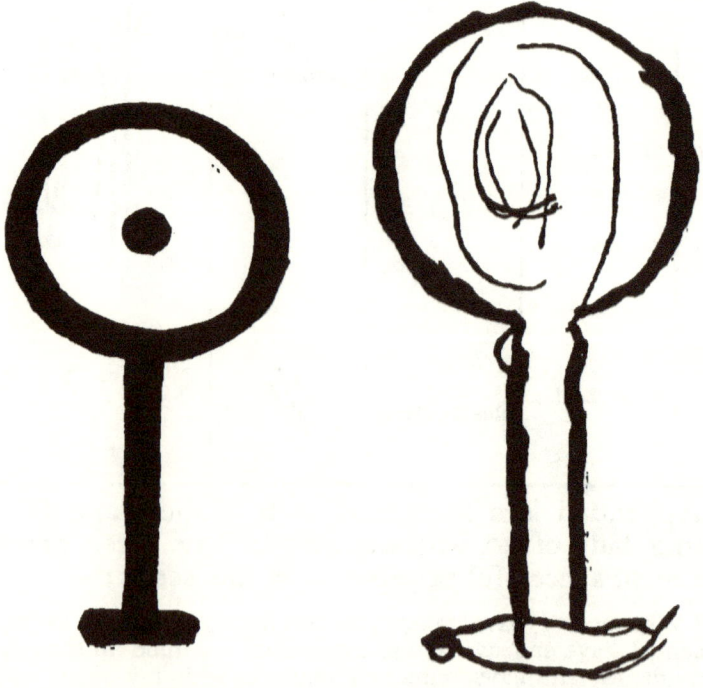

<table>
<tr><td>No. 51.—Original.</td><td>No. 51.— Reproduction.</td></tr>
</table>

No. 53.—ORIGINAL.

No. 53.—REPRODUCTION.

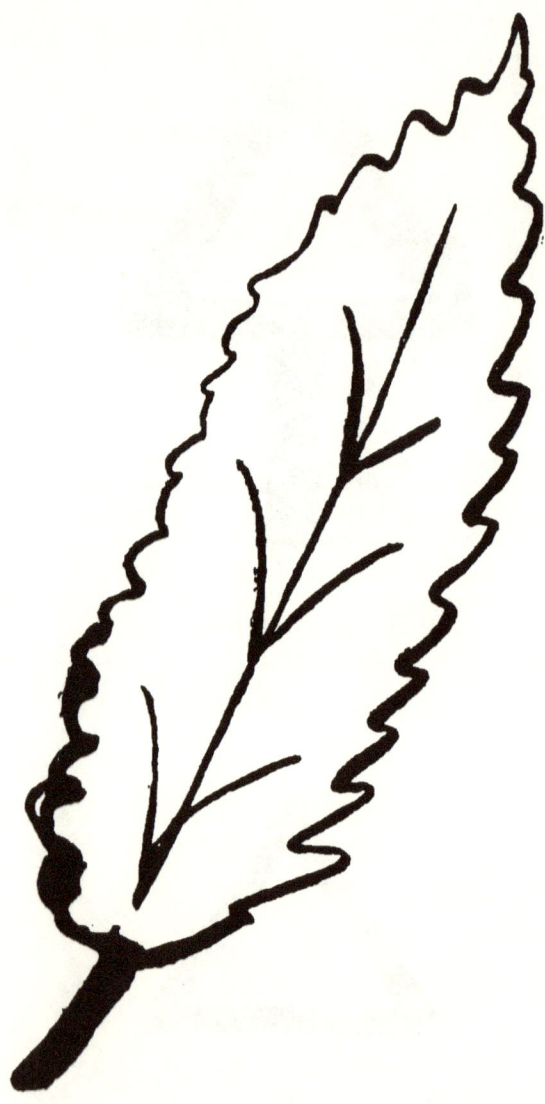

No. 56.—ORIGINAL.

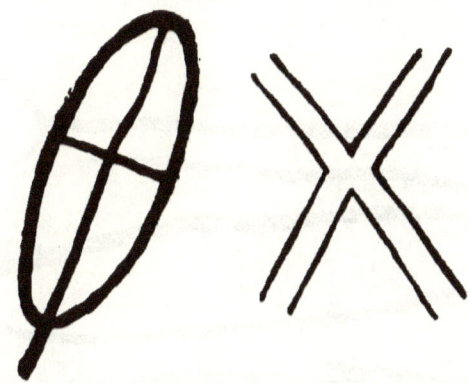

No. 56.—Reproduction.

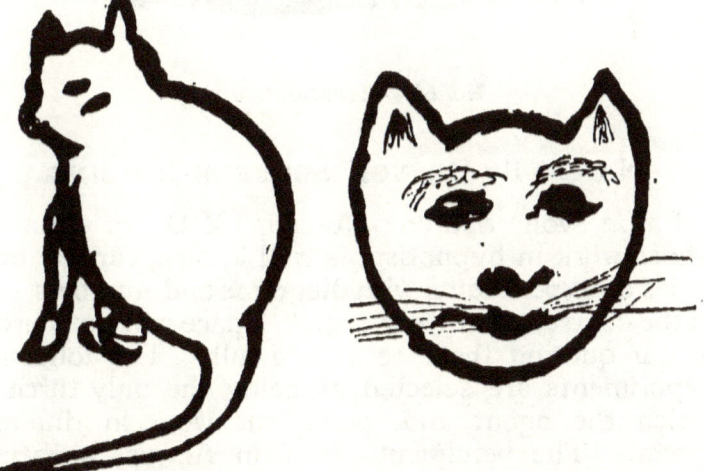

No. 58.—Original.   No. 58.—Reproduction.

No. 66.—Original.

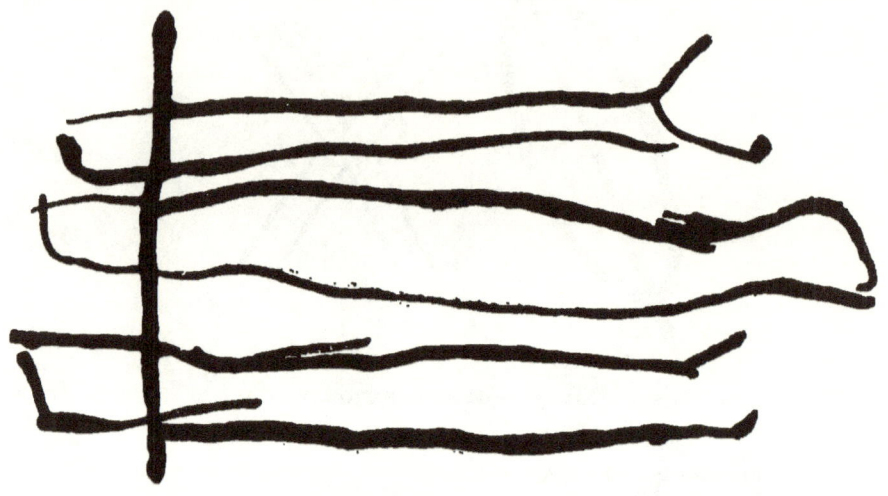

No. 66.—REPRODUCTION.

No. 9.—By DR. VON SCHRENK-NOTZING.

Baron von Schrenk-Notzing, M.D., of Munich, whose work in hypnotism is well known, carried on a series of experiments with diagrams and numbers, etc., in the course of the year 1890.[1] Space will not permit of our quoting these results in full. The following experiments are selected as being the only three in which the agent and percipient were in different rooms. The percipient, Fräulein A., was a patient of Dr. von Schrenk-Notzing's, of rather hysterical temperament; throughout the experiments she was in a normal condition and fully awake. In these three trials, which took place between 10.12 P.M. and 10.23 P.M. on the 15th October 1890, Fräulein A. sat on a chair in the agent's study about a yard from the door leading into the adjoining room, and with her back towards it; paper and pencil were on the table before her. In the adjoining room, about 12

[1] *Proc. S.P.R.*, vol. vii. pp. 3-22.

feet in a direct line from the percipient, with the door
of communication closed, Dr. von Schrenk-Notzing
stood, beside a small table, and drew a rough diagram
representing the staff of Æsculapius and the Serpent.
When the drawing was complete, to quote Dr.
Schrenk-Notzing,

"I call 'Ready?' The percipient says, 'Yes.' We have
been drawing at the same time in different rooms. On returning to the study I compare the drawings and see with astonishment that Fräulein A. has drawn a serpent. Even the open
mouth and the thickened end of the tail in the reproduction
agree with the original. The experiment has succeeded in its
essential part, and as regards strictness of conditions I think it
quite unassailable. Unconscious suggestion is absolutely excluded, when agent and percipient are in different rooms.
Any corresponding association of ideas seems to me also impossible, for the idea of the staff of Æsculapius first occurred to me
in the other room. In the study there is no object which could
have led up to the idea—no indication which could have pointed
out the way."

The percipient had, in fact, drawn a spiral figure
apparently intended to represent a serpent.

The two other experiments here referred to were
performed in immediate succession, and under precisely similar conditions, the time allowed in each
case being about two minutes.

In the second experiment the agent drew an arrow;
the percipient drew another spiral, with intersecting
loops. In this case, as the agent points out, the
original idea of the serpent appears to have persisted in the percipient's mind.

In the third experiment the agent drew a triangle
inscribed in a circle; also two diameters to the circle,
crossing each other at right angles, the vertical
diameter bisecting the upper angle of the triangle.
The agent writes :—

"The drawing was done in the following way. I began
with the triangle, and then drew the perpendicular on the
base. The idea that thereupon occurred to me, that the
figure was too simple, induced me to add a circle and
to prolong the perpendicular to the circumference; finally I

added the horizontal diameter. The percipient was drawing at the same time at table *b*, sitting on chair 5, with her back to the closed door of communication. Question from the next room, 'Are you ready?' Answer, 'Stop,' as I am about to open the door. Then, 'Now.' I open the door and enter the room. The two drawings agree except that the circle and the horizontal diameter are wanting. Even the perpendicular of the triangle, which has become obtuse angled, is prolonged beyond the base, just as in the original. This prolongation and addition of the perpendicular cannot be explained by any tendency of ideas to recur (diagram-habit). Only the fact that a triangle was drawn might, taken alone, be explained in some such way."

Figures of the original diagrams in this case are given in the *Proceedings of the S.P.R.*

Some experiments with diagrams, conducted in July 1890 by Drs. Grimaldi and Fronda, have been published by Lombroso.[1] The subject was a young man of twenty, subject to hysterical attacks and spontaneous somnambulism. The first experiments were made in the hypnotic state, with numbers, and met with only moderate success. Later, however, the trials were made in the normal state. At the first sitting diagrams were tried. The subject had his eyes firmly bandaged and his ears plugged with cotton wool. The diagrams were drawn at a certain distance (*ad una certa distanza*) from the subject, and behind him. Under these conditions the first five experiments were completely successful; the subject reproduced in turn a rhomb, a circle, a triangle, an irregular pentagon, shaped something like the profile of a barn, and a cone. The next experiment failed, only a formless scribble being obtained. The subject was much exhausted, and fell into a semi-cataleptic state as soon as the bandage was removed.

Some success was obtained in later sittings, in the guessing of names and in the execution of mental commands. But the experiments had soon to be abandoned, on account of the health of the percipient.

Other experiments with diagrams, in addition to

[1] *Trasmissione del Pensiero*, etc., Naples, 1891.

those above referred to, will be found in the *Proceedings of the S.P.R.*, vol. i. pp. 161-215, by Mr. Gurney, the writer, and others; vol. ii. pp. 207-216, by Mr. W. J. Smith. The paper on Thought-transference, etc., by Professor C. Richet, *Proceedings*, vol. v. pp. 18-168, should also be consulted in this connection.

CHAPTER III.

EXPERIMENTAL TRANSFERENCE OF SIMPLE SENSA-TIONS WITH HYPNOTISED PERCIPIENTS.

As already stated, the hypnotic state offers peculiar facilities for observing the transmission of thought and sensation. It is possible that the superior suscept-ibility of the hypnotised percipient is in some measure due simply to the quiescence and freedom from spontaneous mental activity very generally induced by the state of sleep-waking. There are indications, moreover, that the hypnotic state itself may present in many cases a specialised manifestation of that rapport which would appear to exist generally be-tween Agent and Percipient in thought-transference. But the close association of the telepathic activities with the consciousness which emerges in hypnotism and allied states suggests an explanation of a more general kind, and may possibly throw light on the evolution of the faculty itself.[1] However this may be, there can be no question that the most remarkable results in experimental telepathy so far recorded are those given in this and the following chapters with hypnotised percipients.

Transference of Tastes.

The fact that notwithstanding this recognised facility comparatively few observers have experimented with hypnotised subjects, except in one or two direc-

[1] See the discussion on this question in Chapter XVI.

tions, calls for some explanation.   There are, indeed, innumerable records of the transmission of sensations of taste and pain in the hypnotic state.   The uncertainty attending any experiment in the first direction with subjects in whom special exaltation of any particular sense is not merely possible, but even under the conditions of the experiments probable, has been already pointed out.   Such trials, conducted with a variety of substances nearly all of which are in some degree odorous, must necessarily lie under suspicion. To the references quoted in the preceding chapter (p. 21) and to the experiments of this nature recorded in the *Proceedings of the S.P.R.*[1] it will suffice here to add one further instance, in which the hypothesis of hyperæsthesia seems hardly an adequate explanation of the result. In a communication to the *Revue Philosophique* in February 1889, Dr. Dufay quotes the following passage from a letter received by him from Dr. Azam, the veteran historian of Félida X.:—

No. 10.—By Dr. Azam.

"I myself, and I believe many other medical men, have observed cases of this or of a similar nature.   I will quote two, in which I think I took all necessary precautions before being convinced of their truth.

"1st. About 1853 or 1854, I had under my care a young woman with confirmed hysteria : nothing was easier than to put her to sleep by various means. I consider myself entitled to state that, while holding her hand, my unspoken thoughts were transferred to her, but upon this I do not insist, error and fraud being possible.

" But the transmission of a definite sensation seemed to me to be absolutely certain.   This is how I proceeded : Having put the patient to sleep, and seated myself by her side, I leaned towards her and dropped my handkerchief behind her chair ; then, while stooping to lift it up, I quickly put into my mouth a pinch of common salt, which, unknown to her, I had beforehand put into the right-hand pocket of my waistcoat.   The salt being absolutely without smell, it was impossible that the patient should have known that I had some in my mouth ; but as soon

---

[1] Vol. i. pp. 226, 241 ; vol. ii. pp. 17-19.

as I raised myself again I saw her face express disgust, and she moved her lips about. 'That is very nasty,' she said ; 'why did you put salt into my mouth ?'

" I have repeated this experiment several times with other inodorous substances, and it has always succeeded. I report this fact alone because it seems to me to be certain."

Transference of Pain.

Experiments with sensations of pain, as has been pointed out, stand on a different footing. There is no special source of error to be guarded against. The following trials, conducted by Mr. Edmund Gurney, with the assistance of the present writer and others, on two evenings in the early part of 1883, will perhaps suffice to indicate the possibility of such transmission. The percipient was a youth named Wells, at the time of the experiments a baker's apprentice. He was hypnotised by Mr. G. A. Smith. During the trials Wells was blindfolded, and Mr. Smith stood behind his chair. On the first evening Mr. Smith held one of the percipient's hands ; and throughout the series it was necessary for Mr. Smith to hold communication with Wells ; the only words used, however, being the simple uniform question, "Do you feel anything ?"[1]

No. 11.—By EDMUND GURNEY.

First Series. January 4th, 1883.

1. The upper part of Mr. Smith's right arm was pinched continuously. Wells, after an interval of about two minutes, began to rub the corresponding part on his own body.
2. Back of the neck pinched. Same result.
3. Calf of left leg slapped. Same result.

---

[1] It is a frequent experience that hypnotised subjects are incapable of responding to any voice other than that of the person who has hypnotised them. The difficulty can, indeed, generally be removed by asking the hypnotiser to place some other person in rapport with the subject—*i.e.*, to give the subject the suggestion that he should also be able to hear the person indicated. At this early stage of our experiments it would appear, however, that this device had for some reason not been adopted.

4. Lobe of left ear pinched. Same result.
5. Outside of left wrist pinched. Same result.
6. Upper part of back slapped. Same result.
7. Hair pulled. Wells localised the pain on his left arm.
8. Right shoulder slapped. The corresponding part was correctly indicated.
9. Outside of left wrist pricked. Same result.
10. Back of neck pricked. Same result.
11. Left toe trodden on. No indication given.
12. Left ear pricked. The corresponding part was correctly indicated.
13. Back of left shoulder slapped. Same result.
14. Calf of right leg pinched. Wells touched his arm.
15. Inside of left wrist pricked. The corresponding part was correctly indicated.
16. Neck below right ear pricked. Same result.

In the next series of these experiments Wells was blindfolded, as before ; but in this case a screen was interposed between Mr. Smith and Wells ; and there was no contact between them. During two or three of the trials Mr. Smith was in an adjoining room, separated from Wells by thick curtains.

Second Series. April 10th, 1883.

17. Upper part of Mr. Smith's left ear pinched. After a lapse of about two minutes, Wells cried out, "Who's pinching me?" and began to rub the corresponding part.
18. Upper part of Mr. Smith's left arm pinched. Wells indicated the corresponding part almost at once.
19. Mr. Smith's right ear pinched. Wells struck his own right ear, after the lapse of about a minute, as if catching a troublesome fly, crying out, "Settled him that time."
20. Mr. Smith's chin was pinched. Wells indicated the right part almost immediately.
21. The hair at the back of Mr. Smith's head was pulled. No indication.
22. Back of Mr. Smith's neck pinched. Wells pointed, after a short interval, to the corresponding part.
23. Mr. Smith's left ear pinched. Same result.

After this, Mr. Smith being now in an adjoining room, Wells began, as he 'said, "to go to sleep ;" and said that he "didn't want to be bothered." He was partially waked up, and the experiments were resumed.

[Four experiments with tastes are here omitted.]

28. Mr. Smith's right calf pinched. Wells was very sulky, and for a long time refused to speak. At last he violently drew up his right leg, and began rubbing the calf.

After this Wells became still more sulky, and refused in the next experiment to give any indication whatever. With considerable acuteness he explained the reasons for his contumacy. "I ain't going to tell you, for if I don't tell you, you won't go on pinching me. You only do it to make me tell." Then he added, in reply to a remonstrance from Mr. Smith, "What do *you* want me to tell for? they ain't hurting *you*, and *I* can stand their pinching." All this time Mr. Smith's left calf was being very severely pinched.

To the onlooker the situation was rendered additionally piquant by the fact that the boy, at the very time when he was apparently acutely sensitive to pain inflicted upon Mr. Smith, showed no sign of susceptibility when any part of his own person was pretty severely maltreated. The only point in the trials which seems to call for special notice is the failure on two occasions to indicate the seat of pain when the agent's hair was pulled (7 and 21). Numerous trials with the same and other percipients have shown that this particular experiment rarely succeeds, possibly because the pain so caused is with many people not of an acute kind.[1]

Transference of Visual Images.

But when we leave these experiments in the transfer of the less specialised forms of sensation we find that but few observers have paid attention to the phenomena of telepathy in the hypnotic state. Probably this is in some measure due to one or two initial difficulties in conducting experiments on such subjects. Opening the eyes to permit the subject to reproduce a diagram will in many cases have the effect of wakening him. Again, with some persons it is a matter of difficulty to maintain the exact stage of the hypnotic trance when they are quiescent enough for the alien impression to meet with little risk of disturbance from the subject's own mental activities, and yet

[1] Cf. No. 19 in the series of similar trials conducted with Miss Relph, p. 24.

sufficiently alert to prevent them from relapsing, as was frequently the case with Wells, the percipient just referred to, into a torpid sleep from which no further response could be elicited.   But, after all, these difficulties when they occur can readily be overcome by the exercise of a little patience.   If the study of thought-transference in the hypnotic state has been comparatively neglected, it is mainly because, as already suggested, with most persons the more salient phenomena of the trance—hallucination, anæsthesia, rigidity, etc.—have distracted attention from what may ultimately prove to be a more fruitful line of inquiry.

For the following record we are indebted to Dr. Liébeault, of Nancy, who sent us the account in 1886.

No. 12.—By Dr. LIÉBEAULT.

[The first series of experiments were made on the afternoon of the 10th December 1885, in Dr. Liébeault's house at Nancy. There were present, in addition, Madame S., Dr. Brullard, and Professor Liégeois, who acted as agent, and Mademoiselle M., the subject.   The subject was hypnotised by Professor Liégeois, and experiments were made with diagrams, and in two cases the design—a water-bottle (*carafe*) and a table with a drawer and drawer-knob—was reproduced with exactness.   Precautions had, of course, been taken to conceal the original design from the percipient.   The account of the seventh and last experiment is quoted in full.]

"7. M. Liégeois wrote the word *mariage*, Mdlle. M. then wrote 'Monsieur.'   Then she said 'Decanter,—no—picture—no.'   [What is the letter?]   'It is an *l*—no, it is an *m*.'   Then after thinking for some minutes, 'There is an *i* in the word, an *a* after the *m*—a *g*—another *a*—an *e*—there are six letters—no —seven.'   When she had found all the letters and their places, *ma iage*, she could not find the letter *r*.   After a few minutes it was suggested to her that she should try combinations with the different consonants, and finally she wrote *mariage*."

[Further experiments were made by Dr. Liébeault, in conjunction with M. Stanislas de Guaita, on the 9th January 1886. The subject in this case was Mademoiselle Louise L., who was hypnotised by Dr. Liébeault.   The first two experiments, which are not quoted here, suggest lip-reading or unconscious audition as a possible explanation ; but the third experiment of this series and the two subsequent trials with Mdlle. Camille

Simon present interesting illustrations of a telepathic hallucination superimposed upon a basis of reality.]

"3. Dr. Liébeault, in order that no hint should be given even in a whisper, wrote on a piece of paper, 'Mademoiselle, on waking, will see her black hat transformed into a red one.' The paper was first passed round to all the witnesses, then MM. Liébeault and De Guaita placed their hands silently on the subject's forehead, mentally formulating the sentence agreed upon. After being told she would see something unusual in the room, the young woman was awakened. Without a moment's hesitation she fixed her eyes upon the hat, and with a burst of laughter exclaimed that it was not her hat, she would have none of it. It was the same shape certainly, but this farce had lasted long enough—we must really give her back her own. ['Come now, what difference do you see?'] 'You know quite well. You have eyes like me.' ['Well what?'] We had to press her for some time before she would say what change had come over her hat; surely we were making fun of her. At last she said, 'You can see for yourselves that it is red.' As she refused to take it we were forced to put an end to her hallucination by telling her that her hat would presently resume its usual colour. The doctor breathed on it, and when it became, in her eyes, her own again, she consented to take it back. Directly afterwards she remembered nothing of her hallucination. . . .

"Nancy, 9th January 1886.
          "Signed,   A. A. LIÉBEAULT.
                  STANISLAS DE GUAITA."[1]

.   .   .   .

"We had one very successful experiment with a young girl of about fifteen, Mdlle. Camille Simon, in the presence of M. Brullard and several other persons. I gave her a mental suggestion that on waking she should see her hat, which was brown, changed to yellow. I then put her *en rapport* with all the others, and I passed round a slip of paper indicating my suggestion, and asking them to think of the same thing. But, by a lapse of memory not unusual to me, I did not think after all of the colour which I had written down; I had a distinct impression that she would see her hat *red*. On awaking her I told her she would see something representing our common thought. When she was wakened she wondered at the colour of her hat. 'It was brown,' she said. After having thought for a long time, she assured us that really it did not look at all the same, that she could not quite define the colour, but that it seemed to her a sort of yellow-red. Then I remembered my

[1] Quoted in *Le Sommeil Provoqué, etc.*, by Dr. Liébeault, Paris, 1889, pp. 295, 296.

aberration. In the present case the others thought of yellow, I of red: thus the object appeared yellow and red to the awakened somnambule; which proves that the mental suggestion may be the echo of the thought of many minds."

[The following experiment, made with the same "subject," and sent to us by Dr. Liébeault on June 3, 1886, is an interesting example of temporary latency of the telepathic impression :—]

"In another experiment with the same young girl it was suggested to her, mentally, by several persons that on awaking she would see a black cock walking about the room. For a considerable time after waking, nearly half-an-hour, she said nothing, although I told her she would see something. It was about half-an-hour afterwards that, having gone into the garden and looked by chance into my little courtyard, she came running back to us to say, 'Ah, I know what I was to see : it was a black cock. This came into my head when I was looking at your cock.' My cock is greenish-black on the wings, tail and breast; everywhere else he is yellowish-white. Here we have an idea caused by the sight of a real object associated with a fictitious idea mentally transmitted by the persons present."

Between the beginning of July and the end of October 1889 a series of trials in the transference of numbers was conducted by Mrs. H. Sidgwick, with the assistance of Professor Sidgwick and Mr. G. A. Smith. The conditions were as follows:—Some small wooden counters, belonging to a game called Loto, and having the numbers from 10 to 90 stamped on them in raised figures, were placed in a bag. From this bag, which it will be seen contained 81 numbers in all, Mr. G. A. Smith drew a counter, placing it in a little wooden box, the edges of which effectually concealed it from the view of the percipient. The percipient, who had been previously placed in the hypnotic state by Mr. Smith, sat with his eyes closed and guessed the number drawn. The remarks, if any, made during the experiments, and the results, were recorded by Mrs. Sidgwick. After the first few days it was arranged, in order to avoid all possibility of bias in recording the numbers, that Professor Sidgwick should draw the counter from the bag and hand it to Mr. Smith, and that Mrs. Sidgwick should be herself ignorant of the number drawn. Through-out the experiments, although eight or more other persons tried to act as agent, Mr. Smith alone was successful. Mr. Smith himself failed to produce any result when the percipients were not hypnotised. The following detailed account of part of the experiments on one day, July 6th, 1889, will give a fair idea of the whole; but it should be added that in later experiments Mr. Smith kept complete silence, and that on several occasions a newspaper was placed over P.'s head. These precautions do not appear to have affected the success of the experiment.

The percipient was Mr. P., a clerk in a wholesale business, aged about nineteen, who had been frequently hypnotised by Mr. Smith, and now passes into the hypnotic state very quickly, his eyes turning upwards as he goes off, before the eyelids close. He is a lively young man, with a good deal of humour, and preserves the same character in the sleep-waking state.

No. 13.—By PROFESSOR and MRS. SIDGWICK.

NUMBER DRAWN.	NUMBER GUESSED, AND REMARKS.
87 ...	S.: "Now, P., you're going to see numbers. I shall look at them, and you will see them." P. (almost immediately): "87. You asked me if I saw a number. I see an 8 and a 7." (Number put away.) P.: "I see nothing now."
19 ...	P.: "18. What are those numbers on? I see only the letters like brass numbers on a door; nothing behind them."
24 ...	P. (after a pause): "I keep on looking. . . . I see it! an 8 and a 4—84."
35 ...	P.: "A 3 and a 5—35." S.: "How did that look?" P.: "I saw a 3 and a 5, then 35."
28 ...	P.: "88. One behind the other, then one popped forward, and I could see two eights." (Illustrated it with his fingers.)
20 ...	P.: "I can't see anything yet." S.: "You will directly." P.: "23." S.: "Saw that clearly?" P.: "Not so plain as the other." S.: "Which did you see best?" P.: "The 2."

NUMBER DRAWN.	NUMBER GUESSED, AND REMARKS.
27 ...	P.: "I can see 7, and I think a 3 in front of it. I can see the 7." S.: "Make sure of the first figure." P.: "The 7's gone now."
48 ...	S.: "Here's another one, P." (This remark, though not always recorded, almost always began each experiment, until July 27th, when, to avoid the possibility of unconscious indications, Mr. Smith adopted the plan of not speaking at all.) P.: "Another two, you mean. You say another one, but there are always two." S.: "Yes, two." P.: "Here it is. You said there were two! There's only one, an 8." Some remarks here not recorded. We think that Mr. Smith said there were two, and told him to look again. P. said he saw a 4. Mrs. Sidgwick: "Which came first?" P.: "The 8 first, then the 4 to the left, so that it would have been 48. I should like to know how you do that trick."
20 ...	P.: "A 2 and an 0; went away very quickly that time."
71 ...	P.: "71."
36 ...	P.: "3 . . . 36."
75 ...	P.: "I might turn round. Should I see them just the same over there?" (Changed his position so as to sit sideways in the chair, and looking away from Mr. Smith.) S.: "Well, you might try." P.: "I don't think I see so well this way." (He did not move, however.) "I see a 7 and a 5—75. Why don't you let them both come at once? I believe I should see them better if you let me open my eyes." (No notice was taken of this.)
17 ...	S.: "Now then, P., here's another." P.: "Put it there at once." (Then, after some time:) "You've only put a 4 up. I see 7." S.: "What's the other figure?" P.: "4 . . . the 4's gone." S.: "Have a look again." P.: "I see 1 now." S.: "Which way are they arranged?" P.: "The 1 first and the 7 second."
52 ...	S.: "Here's another." P.: "52. I saw that at once. I'm sure there's some game about it." (He had said something about this before, when the number was slow in coming. He said Mr. Smith was making game of him, and pretending to look when he was not looking.)
76 ...	P.: "76."

It will be observed that P. always speaks of "seeing" the figures, but as a matter of fact his eyes were closed, or appeared to be closed, throughout the experiments, and the pupils, as already stated, were introverted, at least at the commencement of the trance. That the impression was of a visual nature there can be no reasonable doubt. This may have been due to Mrs. Sidgwick's suggestion to the percipient that he would *see* the figures: though it seems equally probable that it was owing to the fact that Mr. Smith's impression was a visual one. That the vision in most cases was perfectly distinct seems equally clear. It is difficult to decide whether impressions received under such circumstances, with the eyes closed, are properly to be classed as hallucinations.[1] That under appropriate conditions the percept was capable of rising to the level of an externalised sensory hallucination, the following experiments, which took place later on the same day, July 6th, seem to show :—A blank sheet of paper was spread out on the table. P. was told that he would see numbers on it, and was then partially awakened and his eyes opened. He was at once told to look at the paper and see what came, but saw nothing for some time. Different stages of the hypnotic trance frequently exhibit different and mutually exclusive memories, and P. now had evidently forgotten all about the previous state in which he had been guessing numbers, and appeared so wide awake that it was hard to believe that he was not in a completely normal condition. Mr. Smith stood behind him.

NUMBER DRAWN.	NUMBER SEEN ON THE PAPER, AND REMARKS.
18 ...	P. : "23." S. : "Is that what you can see?" P. : "Yes" (but he added later that he did not see it properly).
87 ...	P. : "A 7, o. Oh, no, 8, 78. Funny! I saw a 7 and a little o, and then another came on the top of it, and made an 8."
37 ...	P. : "There's a 4, 7." Asked where, he offered to trace it,[2] and drew 47 in figures 1½ inches long.

---

[1] For such impressions seen with closed eyes Kandinsky has proposed the name *pseudo-hallucinations*.

[2] He had been, on previous occasions, asked to trace hallucinations.

NUMBER
DRAWN.   NUMBER SEEN ON THE PAPER, AND REMARKS.

44   ...   P.: "No. I see 5, 4; it's gone again." S. : "All
           right, look at it." P. : "45." S. : "Sure?"
           P. : " There's a 4 ;—the other's not so clear."
           (Then quickly:) " Two fours ; 44."

As he looked one of them disappeared, and he turned the
paper over to look for it on the other side ; then looked back at
the place where he saw it before and said, "That's funny!
while I was looking for that the other one's gone." When looking
under the paper he noticed some scribbling on the sheet below
and said, "Has that writing anything to do with it?" He
seemed puzzled by the figures, which were apparently genuine
externalised hallucinations. He could not make out why they
came, nor why they disappeared.

37   ...   P. (after long gazing): "37." S. : "Is that what you
           see?" P. : "It's gone. I'm pretty sure I saw
           37."

Mr. Smith then looked at the 37 again, and we told P. to
watch whether it came back, but after a little while he said he
thought he saw 29.

Similar trials were made with three other subjects,
Miss B., T., and W. In all 644 trials were made with the
agent in the same room with the percipient, of which
131 were successful, that is, both digits were given
correctly, though in 14 out of the 131 cases in reverse
order. The chance of success was of course 1 in 81,
and the most probable number of complete successes
was therefore 8. 218 trials were also made with Mr.
Smith in a different room from the percipient, but of
these only 9 succeeded, one having its digits reversed;
8 of these successes, however, occurred in the course
of 139 trials with P., whilst 79 trials with T. yielded
only one success. (*Proc. S.P.R.*, vol. vi. pp. 123-170.)
As regards the possibility of unconscious indications of the number thought of being given by the
agent, it seems certain that no such clue could have
been perceived through the sense of sight or touch,
contact between agent and percipient having been
absolutely excluded throughout the experiments.
It remains to consider whether any indication could
have been given by means of sounds. In the pres-

ence of two or more attentive and vigilant witnesses any indications by sounds—*e.g.*, an unconscious whispering of the number by Mr. Smith—could only have been perceived by persons of abnormal suscepti- bility. We know, indeed, of no precise limit which can be set to the hyperæsthesia of hypnotised subjects. But, on the other hand, hyperæsthesia of any sense in such subjects is generally the result of suggestion, direct or indirect, on the part of the operator; and in these experiments the only sugges- tion given—a suggestion apparently acted on through- out—was that they should *see* the result. Since, indeed, hypnotised persons are apparently not neces- sarily aware of the channel by which information reaches them, this circumstance is not in itself con- clusive; but taken with the fact that no direct sug- gestion to hear was given, it tends to make auditory hyperæsthesia less probable. It is perhaps more important to note that the experimenters, including Mr. Smith himself, were fully aware of this source of error, and on their guard against it; that no move- ments of Mr. Smith's lips, such as must have occurred if he had whispered the number, were observed; and that a careful analysis of the failures shows no tendency to mistake one number for another similar in sound—*e.g., four* for *five, six* for *seven,* or *five* for *nine.*

Experiments with Agent and Percipient in different Rooms.

However, the later experiments by the same ob- servers, recorded below, in which a marked degree of success was obtained with agent and percipient in different rooms, will no doubt be considered to render untenable any explanation of the kind above indicated. This further series was carried on through the years 1890-1-2. Mrs. Sidgwick, aided by Miss Johnson, conducted the experiments throughout, with the

occasional assistance of Professor Sidgwick, Dr. A. T.
Myers, and others.   The percipients were P., T., Miss
B., and three others, and Mr. G. A. Smith was in
nearly all cases the agent.   Some of these experiments, as in the last series, were with numbers of
two digits ; but the percipient was now in a different
room from the agent.   At first the trials were
carried on in an arch, fitted up with two floors, under
the Parade at Brighton.   On the ground-floor was
a little lobby, kitchen, etc. ; on the upper floor a sitting-
room about 15 feet square.   The staircase, which, as
shown in the plan subjoined, led directly out of the
upper room, was not enclosed above, but had a door

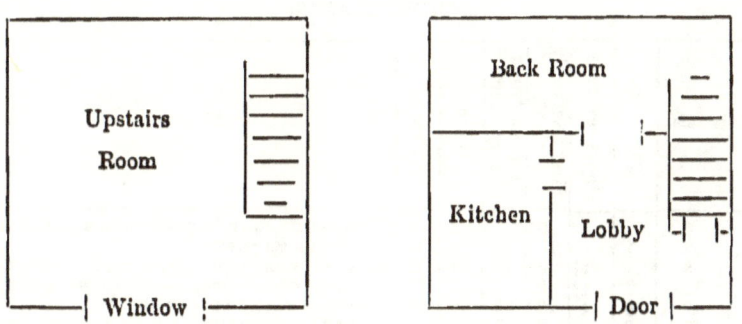

below, which was kept shut during the experiments.
The floor of the room above was covered with a thick
Axminster carpet.   Even so the sound-insulation was
not perfect; but it was found that words spoken in
ordinary conversation on one floor were indistinguishable on the other unless the ear was pressed against
the door or wall of the staircase.   In the experiments
carried on at Mrs. Sidgwick's lodgings in Brighton
the percipient sat in the room at a distance from the
door, which was closed, varying from 9 to 13 feet, and
Mr. Smith was in the passage outside, Miss Johnson
sitting between him and the door.   Of course strict
silence was observed by the agent.   One of the ex-

perimenters, in most cases Miss Johnson, accompanied the agent, drew the number from the bag, and noted each as it was drawn. Mrs. Sidgwick, of course in ignorance of the number drawn, sat by the percipient and took notes of his remarks. As in the previous series, the impressions received by the percipient, who in the first experiments was Miss B., appear generally to have been of a visual nature. Details of all the trials with Miss B. as percipient and Mr. Smith as sole agent are given in the following table :—

No. 14.—By Mrs. Sidgwick and others.

(1) Place, the Arch. Percipient upstairs; Agent downstairs.

Date 1890.	Quite right.	Digits reversed.	First Digit only right.	Second Digit only right.	Wrong.	Totals.	Notes.
Jan. 6 ..	..	..	6*	..	2	8	{ Professor Barrett present in addition to the usual party.
„ 7 ..	1	1	10	1	4	17	
„ 8 ..	..	1†	2	..	3	6	This set was done under very unfavour-
„ 11 ..	1	1†	8	..	10	20	able conditions, as there were three
„ 12 ..	9	1	13	2	8	33	other percipients in the room guessing
Mar. 17 ..	3	..	2	1	6	12	at the same time, which was very con-
„ 18 ..	1	1	1	1	4	8	fusing.
„ 22 ..	1	..	5	1	4	11	Drs. Myers, Penrose, and Lancaster present in addition to the usual party.
„ 23 ..	2	..	6	..	10	18	Drs. Myers and Rolleston present in addition to the usual party.
July 8 ..	..	..	..	1	2	3	
„ 9 ..	..	..	1	3	2	6	
Nov. 6 ..	1	..	1	1	..	3	Dr. Myers present.
„ 10 ..	1	..	..	..	2	3	
Totals	20	5	55	11	57	148	

(2) Place, the Arch. Percipient downstairs; Agent upstairs.

Date	Quite right.	Digits reversed.	First Digit only right.	Second Digit only right.	Wrong.	Totals.	Notes.
Mar. 17 ..	..	..	4	1	13	18	
„ 23 ..	..	..	2	3	7	12	
June 16 ..	..	..	1	..	2	3	Miss McKerlie present.
Totals	..	..	7	4	22	33	

* Two of these were given completely right first and then changed.
† The first digit of the number drawn was guessed first.

(3) PLACE, MRS. SIDGWICK'S LODGINGS. PERCIPIENT IN ROOM, AND AGENT IN PASSAGE.

Date 1890.	Quite right.	Digits reversed.	First Digit only right.	Second Digit only right.	Wrong.	Totals.	Notes.
Mar. 19 ..	..	..	1	..	2	3	
Dec. 17 ..	2	..	11	2	12	27	These guesses were made by table-tilting, Miss B. normal, having her hands on the table. Miss Robertson present on December 17, 19, and 20.§
,, 19 ..	2	1	3	1	..	7	Agent in room across passage, but only one of the two intervening doors closed.
,, 19 ..	..	..	..	1	4	5	
,, 20	1	1	2	..	..	4	Guesses made verbally by Miss B. hypnotised, having her hands on the table.
	..	..	1	1	2	4	Guesses tilted by the table, at the same time as the above.§
,, 20 ..	1	..	1	1	4	7	Miss B. hypnotised, guessing in the usual way.
	1	1‡	4	2	6	14	Guesses made by table-tilting, Miss B. normal, having her hands on the table.§
Totals	7	3	23	8	30	71	
Totals of (1)(2) & (3) together	27	8	85	23	109	252	

‡ This was given completely right first and then changed.
§ See Chapter iv., pp. 96-100.

It will be seen that in 252 trials the number was guessed quite correctly 27 times, and with digits in reverse order 8 times—the most probable number of complete successes by chance being 3. Further, in the unsuccessful trials the first digit was correctly guessed no fewer than 85 times. The proportion of successes in a series of trials carried on during the same period with Mr. Smith in the same room with Miss B. was, however, much higher—viz., 29 (three with digits reversed) out of 146 trials. It is noticeable that in the short series of trials with Miss B. in the lobby downstairs a very much smaller degree of success was obtained, a result attributed by Mrs. Sidgwick to the percipient's feeling ill at ease in her surroundings.

Another noteworthy point is the large proportion

of cases in which the first digit was correctly named.[1] This disproportion is not found in the trials made with the agent and the percipient in the same room, and is possibly due, as suggested by Mrs. Sidgwick, to Mr. Smith in all cases concentrating his attention originally on the first digit. When in the same room with the percipient he would hear when the first digit had been named, and would then turn his attention to the other; but when out of the room he could not, of course, follow the process of guessing.

A further series of trials was conducted with the percipient under the same conditions, except that either P. or T. acted as agents jointly with Mr. Smith. In all 53 trials were made, resulting in 9 complete successes and two with the digits reversed. The proportion of successes, it will be seen, is much higher than in the experiments first described; but the series is too short to allow of a safe conclusion being drawn as to the superior efficacy of collective agency.

Experiments conducted under similar conditions with four other percipients yielded a slight but appreciable measure of success. A large number of trials—nearly 400 in all—were made with Miss B. as percipient, the agent or agents being at a still greater distance—viz., being either in a separate building, or with two closed doors and a passage intervening; but practically no success was obtained. Miss B. complained of the numbers being so far off. "They are all muddled up," she said on one occasion; "they seem miles off." It is not easy to account satisfactorily for this failure, but it may probably be attributed partly to a prejudicial effect exercised by the novel conditions on the agent's or percipient's anticipation of success, and partly to the tedious

[1] As all numbers above 90 were excluded, and as 0 cannot come first, the first digit should, by pure chance, have been correctly named more often than the second; but the disproportion, it will be seen, is far greater than could be thus accounted for.

waiting inseparable from experiments of this kind, where there is no ready means of communication at the end of each trial. (*Proc. S.P.R.*, vol. viii. pp. 536-552.)

Transference of Mental Pictures.

By Mrs. Sidgwick and Miss Johnson.

Later on, after various trials had been made with little success with letters, playing cards, and diagrams, a series of experiments was made in the transference of mental pictures. There were in all 108 trials, with 5 percipients—Miss B., P., and T., and two men, Whybrew and Major, who had been subjects of an itinerant lecturer on Hypnotism. The method of experiment was as follows :—A subject for a picture was written down by Mrs. Sidgwick or Miss Johnson and handed to Mr. Smith, who then summoned up a mental representation of the subject suggested, which he tried to transfer to the percipient. Occasionally, to aid his imagination, he drew on paper a rough sketch of the subject. During the experiment Mr. Smith was sometimes close to the percipient, sometimes behind a screen, sometimes in another room.

When in the same room it was occasionally necessary for Mr. Smith, in order to keep alive the percipient's interest and attention, to say a few words to him from time to time. These remarks were always recorded. In the earlier experiments the percipient's eyes were open, and he was given a white card or a crystal to look at ; and he appears to have seen the pictures as if projected on these objects. In the later trials the percipient's eyes were closed, but this change in the conditions does not appear in any way to have affected the vividness of the impressions.

Successful experiments were made with all five percipients, full details of which will be found in the paper referred to.[1] It will suffice here to quote

[1] *Proc. S.P.R.*, vol. viii. pp. 554-577.

a few illustrative cases of success, complete or partial.

The first experiments were made on July 9th, 1890. Miss B. was the percipient. I quote the account of the first two trials :—

No. 15.

The percipient, being in a hypnotic trance, had her eyes opened and was given a card and told to look out for a picture which would come on it.

The subject, chosen by Mrs. Sidgwick, was *a little boy with a ball*. Mr. Smith sat close to Miss B., but neither spoke to her nor touched her. Miss B. presently said: "A figure is coming—a little boy." Mrs. Sidgwick asked what he had in his hand, and Miss B. replied: "A round thing; a ball, I suppose."

For the next experiment Mr. Smith got behind a screen. The subject, *a kitten in a jar*, was again set by Mrs. Sidgwick. Miss B. said: "Something like an old cat—a cat—I think it's a cat." Mrs. Sidgwick: "What is the cat doing?" Miss B. (doubtfully): "Sitting down." Mrs. Sidgwick: "Is there anything else but a cat?" Miss B.: "No; only scratches about."

In all 21 experiments of the kind were tried with Miss B., of which 8, including the two above recorded, may be classed as more or less successful.

The following experiments were made with P. on November 5th, 1890. The notes of these cases were taken by Miss Johnson, who was herself ignorant of the subject, which was chosen by Mrs. Sidgwick.

The first experiment on this day was a failure.

No. 16.

Subject: *A black kitten playing with a cork.* P.: "Something like a cat; it's a cat." Mrs. Sidgwick: "What is it doing?" P.: "Something it's been feeding out of—some milk, is it a saucer? Can't see where its other paw is—only see three paws."

Subject: *A sandwich man with advertisement of a play.* P. said: "Something like letter A—stroke there, then there." Mrs. Sidgwick: "Well, perhaps it will become clearer." P.: "Something like a head on the top of it; a V upside down—two legs and then a head.—A man with two boards—looks like a man that goes about the streets with two boards. I can see a head at the top and the body and legs between the boards. I couldn't see what was written on the boards, because the edges were turned towards me." Mr. Smith told us afterwards that he had pictured to himself the man and one board facing him, thus not corresponding to the impression which P. had.

Subject : *A choir-boy.*[1] P. said : " Edge of card's going a dark colour. Somebody dressed up in white, eh ? Can see something all white ; edge all black, and like a figure in the middle. There's his hands up " (making a gesture to show the attitude) " like a ghost or something—you couldn't mistake it for anything but a ghost. It's not getting any better, it's fading—no, it's still there. It might frighten any one." He also made remarks about the difficulty of seeing a white figure on a white card (the blank card he was looking at was white), which Mr. Smith afterwards said corresponded with his own ideas.

Subject : *A vase with flowers.* (Mr. Smith, still behind P., was looking at a blue flower-pot in the window containing an indiarubber plant.) P. said : " I see something round, like a round ring. I can see some straight things from the round thing. I think it's a glass—it goes up. I'll tell you what it is ; it must be a pot—a flower-pot, you know, with things growing in it. I only guessed that, because you don't see things growing out of a glass.—It's not clear at the top yet. You see something going up and you can't see the top, because of the edge of the paper—it's cut off. I don't wonder, because it's no good wondering what Mr. Smith does, he does such funny things. I should fancy it might be a geranium, but there's only sticks, so you can't tell." Mrs. Sidgwick : " What colour is the pot ?" P. : " Dark colour, between terra-cotta and red—dark red you'd call it." Here the somewhat confused impression, apparently corresponding to the struggle of ideas in Mr. Smith's mind between what he was seeing and what he was trying to think of, is an interesting point.[2]

In all 50 trials were made with P., 26 with agent and percipient in the same room, 24 with agent and percipient in different rooms. Of the former 14 were successful, of the latter only one. In the 35 unsuccessful experiments no impression at all was received in 14 cases, 7 of which occurred while agent and percipient were in the same room.

Two trials with Whybrew are worth quoting as illustrating the gradual development of the impression.

---

[1] This was an idea extremely familiar to P., who had been a chorister and was still connected with the choir of his church.
[2] *Proceedings Soc. Psych. Research*, vol. viii. pp. 565, 566.

The percipient's eyes were closed during these experiments. The first was made on July 11th.

No. 17.

Subject: *A man riding.* Mr. Smith downstairs with Miss Johnson; Whybrew, upstairs with Mrs. Sidgwick, said, after some remarks on the former pictures: "There's another one —I think it's like the other two—a puzzle [to see]—if I can find the picture. I hope I'll be able to see it properly. A kind of a square—square shadow—blowed if I can understand what it's meant for—I don't know what to make out of that. I don't know if that's meant to be the lower part of a pair of legs. Do you see a picture?" Mrs. Sidgwick: "I see something." Whybrew: "I see them two spots, but I don't know what to make of them. If they're legs, the body ought to come.—Don't seem to come any brighter, but there's those two things there, that look like a pair of legs." Here Mr. Smith was asked to come upstairs and talk to him. He told him the picture was coming up closer and that he had turned the gas on to make it brighter. Whybrew: "There's them pair of legs there." Mr. Smith: "Yes" (doubtfully). Whybrew: "Why, there's another. I never see that other pair before. Why, it's a horse. I expect it's like them penny pictures that you fold over. That horse— that's plain enough; but what's that other thing?" Mr. Smith: "Yes, I told you there was something else." Whybrew: "Why, I see what it is now—it's supposed to be a man there, I expect." Mr. Smith: "Yes." Whybrew: "Riding him. But that ain't so good as the boy and the ball." Mrs. Sidgwick: "How is the man dressed?" Whybrew: "Ordinary."

The second took place on July 16th, 1891.

Mr. Smith having hypnotised Whybrew, sat by him, but did not speak to him at all after he knew the subject—*a man with a barrow of fish*—given him by Mrs. Sidgwick. Miss Johnson, not knowing what the subject was, carried on the conversation with Whybrew. He said: "It's the shape of a man. Yes, there's a man there. Don't know him. He looks like a bloke that sells strawberries." Miss Johnson asked: "Are there strawberries there?" Whybrew: "That looks like his barrow there. What's he selling of? I believe he's sold out. I can't see anything on his barrow—perhaps he's sold out. There ain't many—a few round things. I expect they're fruit. Are they cherries? They look a bit red. Aren't they fish? It don't look very much like fish. If they're fish, some of them hasn't got any heads on. Barrow is a bit fishified—it has a tray on. What colour are those things on the barrow? They looked red, but now they look silvery." He was rather pleased with this picture and asked afterwards if it was for sale.

Of 18 experiments with Whybrew 6 were successful. Of the 12 failures, 8 occurred when agent and percipient were in separate rooms. There were only two cases in which no impression was received—one with the agent in the same room.

Seven trials were made with Major, of which 1 was completely and 2 partially successful. Subjoined is the record of the only complete success, which occurred on July 8th, 1891. The percipient was hypnotised and his eyes were closed ; Mr. Smith sat by him, talking to him and telling him that he was to see a picture.

No. 18.

The subject given was *a mouse in a mouse-trap*. Regarding himself as a man of culture and being generally anxious to exhibit this, Major asked if it was to be an old master or a modern "pot-boiler." He was told the latter, and he then discoursed on "pot-boilers" and how he knew all the subjects of them—mentioning two or three—in a very contemptuous manner. He did not seem to see anything, however, and appeared to be expecting to see an artist producing a rapid sketch. Then, when told that the picture was actually there, he suddenly exclaimed : "Do you mean that deuced old trap with a mouse? He must have been drawing for the rat vermin people."

Thirty-two trials were made with T., of which only four were successful—two completely, one partially, one completely, but deferred—*i.e.*, the subject of the preceding experiment, a black dog, came before his vision after the agent had already passed to another subject, the Eiffel Tower. T. had, of course, not been told the subject of the previous experiment. Instances of deferred impressions of this kind occurred also with Miss B. A few experiments were tried with another percipient, a man named Adams, but without success ; his own imagination appeared to be so fertile that any telepathic impression must have been crowded out.

An analysis of the impressions showed that most of

them were reproductions of objects familiar to the percipient, in certain cases of hallucinations previously imposed upon them in the course of these or other experiments. With some of the successful percipients these spontaneous impressions showed a marked tendency to recur. Thus P. had a wrong impression— of an elephant—no less than four times in the course of the experiments; and T. of a woman and a perambulator three times. One of these coincided with the subject actually set, and the coincidence may perhaps therefore be attributed to chance. Speaking generally, however, this tendency to repetition amongst the percipient's native impressions constitutes an additional argument, if any such is needed, for attributing the frequent coincidences of the impression with the subject set to some other cause than the automatic association of ideas.

An instance of a quasi-experimental character, which closely resembles the cases above described, is recorded by Dr. A. Gibotteau :—[1]

No. 19.—By Dr. Gibotteau.

"Madame P. complained of headache. I placed my hand upon her forehead, and in a few minutes she was in a light hypnotic sleep. Without deepening the trance I endeavoured to give her a sensation of calm and well-being, and to procure this sensation for myself in the first place, I called up a picture of the sea, in which air and water were full of sunlight. 'I feel a little better,' she said; 'how fresh the air is!' I then proceeded to imagine myself walking along the *Boulevard Saint Michel*, in a slight rain. I saw the hurrying people and the umbrellas. 'How strange it is!' said Madame P.; 'I seem to be at the corner of the *Boulevard Saint Michel* and the *Rue des Écoles*, in front of the *Café Vachette*' (the exact spot I pictured); 'it is raining, there are a great many people, a hurrying crowd. They are all going up the street, and I with them. The air is very fresh. It gives me a pleasant, restful feeling.' With these words she opened her eyes and gave me further confirmation of her impressions.

"I should add that this scene took place in the provinces; I had not been in Paris for some months, nor Madame P. for several years.

"There had been no mention of the subject in the course of our conversation that day."

It will be seen that Dr. Gibotteau attempted to transfer to the percipient only the general sensation of calm and rest induced in himself by the imagined scene, and that the success obtained was therefore of a kind by no means anticipated.

Another experiment of the same nature is recorded by Dr. Blair Thaw in the article already referred to (p. 31). The percipient was Mrs. Thaw, Dr. Thaw and Mr. Wyatt were the agents. We are not told whether in this instance, as on some other occasions, the percipient was actually hypnotised, but judging from previous experiments it may perhaps be inferred that she was at least in a condition called by Dr. Thaw "a passive state," not easy to distinguish from the lighter stages of sleep-waking. The experiment took place on the 28th April 1892.

No. 20.—By DR. BLAIR THAW.

1st *Scene.* Locomotive running away without engineer tears up station.—Missed.

2nd *Scene.* The first real FLYING MACHINE going over Madison Square Tower, and the people watching.—Percipient: *I see lots of people. Crowds are going to war. They are so excited. Are they throwing water?* (Percipient said afterwards she thought it was a fire and that was the reason of the crowd.) *Or sailors pulling at ropes.* Agent said, "What are they doing?" Percipient: *They are all looking up. It is a balloon or some one in trouble up there.* Agent said, "Why balloon?" Percipient: *They are all looking up.* Agent said, "I thought of a possible scene in the future." Percipient: *Oh, it's the first man flying. That's what he's doing up there.* Agent: "Where is it?" Percipient: *In the city.*

An account of a similar instance of the transfer to a hypnotised percipient of an imagined scene has been recorded by Mr. E. M. Clissold and Mr. Auberon Herbert.[1]

---

[1] See *Phantasms of the Living,* vol. ii. pp. 677, 678.

CHAPTER IV.

EXPERIMENTAL PRODUCTION OF MOVEMENTS AND OTHER EFFECTS.

IN the two preceding chapters we have discussed experiments where the impression received by the percipient may be interpreted as having been a more or less accurate reproduction of the sensation experienced by the agent, or at most a translation of it into some other simple sensation. There have now to be considered various cases in which the transmission of thought is productive of other results in the percipient than the simple duplication or translation of a sensation. The most usual case is where the telepathic impulse leads to some action on the part of the percipient. It was frequently stated by the older mesmerists[1] that the operator, by a silent act of will, could induce a good subject to do or refrain from doing some prescribed or customary action. Isolated observations on such a point are little likely to compel belief; the vanity or the credulity of the recorder may be supposed to have led to his overlooking the negative instances, and attributing to his own peculiar gifts a result in reality due to chance. But, following on the clue thus

---

[1] Cases are recorded in the *Zoist* and other publications of the period. See the instances, quoted in *Phantasms of the Living*, vol. i. pp. 89-91, of the Rev. J. Lawson Sisson, Mr. Barth, Mr. N. Dunscombe, and Mr. H. S. Thompson. Traditions of the marvels wrought by the last-named gentleman still linger in Yorkshire society, and will no doubt demand the serious attention of future students of folk-lore.

obtained, the Committee on Mesmerism appointed by the S.P.R. in 1882, to some of whose work reference has already been made (Chapter III., p. 60), succeeded in obtaining results less open to question.

Inhibition of Action by Silent Willing.

The first experiments of the kind were conducted on our friend Mr. Sidney Beard, who was for some time an Associate of the Society and took an active interest in its work. Mr. Beard, who was easily hypnotised, would be entranced by Mr. Smith, and sit in a chair with closed eyes. Then, to quote the account of a single experiment, a list of twelve *Yeses* and *Noes* in arbitrary order was written by one of ourselves and put into Mr. Smith's hand, with directions that he should successively will the subject to respond or not to respond, in accordance with the list. A tuning-fork was then struck and held at Mr. Beard's ear, and the question, "Do you hear?" was asked by one of ourselves. This was done twelve times in succession, Mr. Beard answering or failing to answer on each occasion in accordance with the "yes" or "no" of the written list—that is to say, with the silent will of the agent. Similar trials on other occasions with Mr. Beard were equally successful. The percipient's own account of the matter is as follows: "During the experiments of January 1st [1883], when Mr. Smith mesmerised me, I did not lose consciousness at any time, but only experienced a sensation of total numbness in my limbs. When the trial as to whether I could hear sounds was made I heard the sounds distinctly each time, but in a large number of instances I felt totally unable to acknowledge that I heard them. I seemed to know each time whether Mr. Smith wished me to say that I heard them; and as I had surrendered my will to his at the commencement of the experiment, I was unable to reassert my power of volition whilst under his influence." (*Proceedings of the Soc. Psych. Research,* vol. i. p. 256.)

No. 21.—By PROFESSOR BARRETT.

Further trials of the same kind were carried on in November 1883 by Professor Barrett, at his own house in Dublin. The hypnotist and agent was again Mr. G. A. Smith, the percipient a youth named Fearnley, a stranger to Mr. Smith. In the first series of trials Professor Barrett asked Fearnley, " Now will you open your hand ? " at the same time pointing to " Yes " or " No," written on a card, and held in sight of Mr. Smith, but out of view from the percipient. Mr. Smith, who was not in contact with the subject, directed his silent will in accordance with the written indication. In twenty experiments conducted under these conditions there were only three failures   Later, to quote Professor Barrett,

"The experiment was varied as follows :—The word 'Yes' was written on one,. and the word 'No' on the other, of two precisely similar pieces of card. One or other of these cards was handed to Mr. Smith at my arbitrary pleasure, care of course being taken that the 'subject' had no opportunity of seeing the card, even had he been awake. When 'Yes' was handed Mr. Smith was silently to will the 'subject' to answer aloud in response to the question asked by me, 'Do you hear me?' When 'No' was handed Mr. Smith was to will that no response should be made in reply to the same question. The object of this series of experiments was to note the effect of increasing the distance between the willer and the willed,—the agent and the percipient. In the first instance Mr. Smith was placed *three feet* from the ' subject,' who remained throughout apparently asleep in an arm-chair in one corner of my study.

"At three feet apart, 25 trials were successively made, and *in every case* the 'subject' responded or did not respond in exact accordance with the silent will of Mr. Smith, as directed by me.

"At 6 feet apart six similar trials were made without a single failure.

"At 12 feet apart six more trials were made without a single failure.

"At 17 feet apart six more trials were made without a single failure.

" In this last case Mr. Smith had to be placed outside the study door, which was then closed with the exception of a narrow chink just wide enough to admit of passing a card in or out, whilst I remained in the study observing the 'subject.' To avoid any possible indication from the tone in which I asked the question, in all cases except the first dozen experiments, I shuffled the cards face downwards, and then handed the unknown 'Yes' or 'No' to Mr. Smith, who looked at the card and willed accordingly. I noted down the result, and then, and not till then, looked at the card.

"A final experiment was made when Mr. Smith was taken across the hall and placed in the dining-room, at a distance of about 30 feet from the 'subject,' two doors, both quite closed, intervening. Under these conditions, three trials were made with success, the 'Yes' response being, however, very faint and hardly audible to me, who returned to the study to ask the usual question after handing the card to the distant operator. At this point, the 'subject' fell into a deep sleep, and made no further replies to the questions addressed to him."

Further trials were made under different conditions, the results being almost uniformly successful.

In interpreting these results there is no justification for assuming direct control by the agent over the organism of the percipient. Nor does the current phrase, endorsed as it is in the first case by the percipient himself, that the operator's will dominated the will of the subject, give an adequate account of the matter. When, as in the case of experiments previously described, the percipient's impression reproduces the sensation of the agent, there is nothing to indicate that the impulse transferred directly affects the external organs, or even the intermediate sensory centres. In the absence of any direct evidence it is at least equally probable that the higher brain centres only are concerned in the transmission in the first instance, and that the transmitted idea is reflected downwards, until it actually assumes, as in some of the experiments recorded with P. and Miss B., the form of a sensory hallucination. Upon this view no fundamental distinction need be drawn between the results before described and those now under discussion. In the latter case the question is not one of transference of will or of a motor or inhibitory impulse. What is actually transferred from the agent is probably only a simple idea. Its subsequent translation into action, or the inhibition of action, is as much the work of the percipient's mind as, in the other case, the transformation of the idea of a number into a visual hallucination. As regards the particular effect produced, it must be remembered that the prime characteristic of the hypnotic state is its openness to suggestion, and especially to suggestion coming through a particular channel. It is the establishment of this suggestible state, which consists essentially in the suppression of the controlling faculties which normally pass judgment on the suggestions received from without, and select those which are to find response in action, that Mr. Beard describes as the surrender of his will. So that when Mr. Beard answered our questions he did what his natural courtesy led him to do ; when he maintained silence his tendency to respond to the stimulus of our questions was momentarily overcome by the stronger stimulus of the idea received from the agent. But the superior efficacy of the idea so transferred resulted not from any impulsive quality in the idea itself, but from the previously established relations between agent and percipient. The fact that experiments of this kind have rarely succeeded in the waking state is no doubt due to the inferior suggestibility of that state.

Actions originated by Silent Willing.

In the paper already referred to (*supra*, p. 31) Dr. Blair Thaw records some experiments which present us with a modification of the Willing Game, but without contact. In most of the experiments the person who was willed to perform a certain action—the nature of which had been previously communicated **to the other experimenters in writing**—was in the same room as the agents. But the agents did not follow the percipient about the room, nor did the percipient look at the agents for guidance. The percipient appears to have been awake throughout the experiments, but it seems probable that her condition was not that of complete normal wakefulness.

Of 26 experiments conducted under such conditions, 10 were completely and 12 partially successful. When, however, as in this case, there are several agents, all of whom are actually watching the movements of the percipient, it is impossible to feel convinced that no indication by the movements of the eyes or by breathing was given to the percipient to show her whether or not she was moving in the right direction. In the last four trials of the series, however, the percipient was willed to fetch an object from another room which was out of sight from the agents, and it is difficult to conceive that any indication could have been given to her of the object selected.

No. 22.—By Dr. Blair Thaw.

April 7th, 1892.

Mrs. Thaw, Percipient. Mr. M. H. Wyatt and Dr. Thaw, Agents. In the next four experiments an object was selected in another room, and then the percipient sent in for it. No clue was given as to what part of the room.

1st *Object Selected.* A Wooden Cupid, from a corner-piece in room with eight other objects on it.—Percipient first brought a photo from the lower shelf of corner-piece, then said: "It's the wooden Cupid."

2nd *Object.* Match-box on mantel.—Percipient seemed confused at first and brought two photos, then said: "It's the brass match-box on mantel."

3rd *Object.* A Vellum Book on table, among twenty other books, chosen; but a bag under one window was thought of first.—Percipient went to table, put her hand on the book, then went to the bag and took it up, then back to the table and took the vellum book and then the bag, and appeared with both. Percipient was in sight of agents during this time, but did not see them.

4th Object. BOOK on small table, among ten others.—Missed.

In commenting on these experiments, Dr. Thaw is himself inclined to attribute some of the results to "an indistinct motor impulse of some kind, leading the percipient near the object." But in the experiments above recorded, at any rate, it is sufficient, probably, to suppose the transference of the idea of the object.

Experiments of a somewhat similar nature are recorded by Dr. Ochorowicz (*La Suggestion mentale,* pp. 84-117). The subject in this case, Madame M., was sunk in the deep hypnotic state (*l'état aidétique*), a condition in which she would usually remain motionless until aroused by the doctor. Under these circumstances Dr. Ochorowicz conducted upwards of forty experiments in conveying mental commands, a large proportion of which were executed by the subject with more or less exactness. These trials have the drawback above indicated, common to all experiments of the kind with the agent in the same room; moreover, each experiment appears to have extended over a considerable period, and the command—*e.g.,* to rise from the chair and hand a cake from the table to Dr. Ochorowicz—was frequently executed in stages. In judging of the results, however, it should be remembered that Dr. Ochorowicz has elsewhere shown himself to be acute in criticism and accurate in observation.

Some experiments made by Dr. Gibert on Madame B., and recorded by Professor Pierre Janet,[1] seem open to a similar objection. Dr. Gibert communicated the mental command by touching Madame B.'s forehead with his own whilst concentrating his thoughts on the ideas to be conveyed. It is difficult to feel sure that the success of the experiment under such conditions was not due to the command having been

[1] *Bulletin de la Soc. de Psychologie Physiologique,* 1885.

unconsciously muttered by Dr. Gibert within the hearing of the percipient. In the following account, however, thought-transference would seem to be the simplest explanation of the results. The narrator, unfortunately, remains anonymous; he is, however, personally known to Dr. Dariex, the editor of the periodical from which the account is extracted, and the experiments were obviously conducted with care.[1] In this case it seems clear, since the command, though understood, was on more than one occasion disobeyed, that the idea telepathically intruded into the percipient's mind was not necessarily associated with an impulse to action.

No. 23.—By J. H. P.

[On the 6th December 1887], having placed M. in a deep trance, I turned my back upon her, and, without any gesture or sound whatever, gave her the following mental order:—

"When you wake up you are to go and fetch a glass, put a few drops of Eau de Cologne into it, and bring it to me."

On waking up, M. was visibly preoccupied; she could not keep still, and at last came and placed herself in front of me, exclaiming—

"What an idea to put in my head!"

"Why do you speak so to me?"

"Because the idea that I have got can only come from you, and I don't wish to obey."

"Don't obey unless you like; but I wish you to tell me at once what you are thinking of."

"Well, then, I was to go and look for a glass, put some water in it, with some drops of Eau de Cologne, and take it to you; it is really ridiculous."

My order had then been perfectly understood for the first time. From that moment, December 6th, 1887, till to-day, with only two or three exceptions, the mental transmission, whether in the waking or sleeping state, has been most vivid. It is only disturbed at certain times, or when M. is feeling very anxious.

On the 10th of December 1887, unknown to M., I hid a watch, that was not going, behind some books in my bookcase. When she arrived I put her to sleep, and gave her the following mental command:—

"Go and fetch me the watch that is hidden behind some books in the bookcase."

I sat in my armchair with M. behind me, and was careful not to look in the direction where the object was hidden.

M. suddenly got up from her armchair and went straight to the bookcase, but could not open it; making energetic movements the while, whenever she touched the door, and especially the glass.

"It is there! it is there! I am certain; but this glass burns me!"

I decided to open it myself; she rushed at my books, took them out, and seized the watch, delighted to have found it.

Similar trials have been made with commands that one of my friends passed to me, written beforehand, and not in the presence of the subject, and the success has been complete; but if the person who passes me the order is unknown to her, she refuses to obey, saying that the command is not mine.

.   .   .   .

M. N., who was convinced that mental transmission is a fraud, assured me that I should never be able to transmit an order from him to M.

I invited him to come to my house, at five o'clock in the evening, with a command written, which he was to give me only when M. was asleep, and outside my study.

At 5.10 N. arrived and we went out, leaving M. in a trance; when we were separated from my study by the two intervening rooms, with all the doors shut, N. pulled out a small paper and said—

"You will read this command, we will both come back to M., and without any gestures, you will communicate it to her."

"Certainly."

In the note was written, "Give the mental command to M. to count out loud from 5 to 1; 5, 4, 3, 2, 1."

We came back to my study; I sat at my desk as usual—I am in the habit of making notes during the progress of the experiments, so as to report them with scrupulous accuracy—and I sent N.'s mental command, while pretending to write. M. suddenly exclaimed—

"Doubtless, you imagine that I cannot count! I can count from 1 to 50,000, if I wish."

Mental command—"Count from 5 to 1."

"No, I will not obey a strange command; it is not a command of yours."

All my efforts were useless; we had to abandon the experiment. The command was certainly understood; but M. N. retired, convinced that it had not been understood, and that even the trance was a sham!

Automatic Writing.

Sometimes the working of the telepathic impulse is of a more apparently mysterious kind. We have seen that Mr. Beard was fully conscious of the action of a restraining force; and Mrs. Thaw, who was in a condition little if at all removed from the normal, appears also to have been aware of what she was doing, if perhaps without explicit recognition of her motives at the time of performing the prescribed actions. But in the various cases now to be described the telepathic impulse seems never to have affected the normal consciousness of the percipient at all ; and the results produced through the agency of his organism were due to no recognised volition on his part. The intelligence directing his hand was an intelligence working below and apart from his ordinary life.

Now this subterranean intelligence presents many points of analogy with the secondary consciousness of the hypnotic subject ; in both states we find indications of thought and will distinct from those of waking life, and of a memory not shared with that life. Moreover, it has been shown experimentally, by Mr. Edmund Gurney,[1] Professor Pierre Janet,[2] and others, that the consciousness which makes itself known through planchette is, in certain persons at any rate, identical with the consciousness found in the hypnotic trance, so far as the test of a common memory can be relied upon to prove identity. The superior susceptibility to telepathic influences, already referred to, of the hypnotic subject, may perhaps, therefore, in the light of these later experiments, be found to indicate a superior susceptibility of those parts of the brain whose workings lie below the ordinary consciousness, and reveal themselves only in the activities of trance and automatism.

[1] See the account of his experiments on " Peculiarities of certain Post-hypnotic States," *Proc. S.P.R.*, vol. iv. pp. 268-323.
[2] " L'Automatisme Psychologique."

The following is an illustrative case. The account is derived from contemporary notes, made by the late Mr. P. H. Newnham, Vicar of Maker, Devonport, of a series of experiments conducted by himself and his wife during eight months in 1871.[1] Mr. Newnham would write, in a book kept for the purpose, a question of the purport of which Mrs. Newnham was in ignorance; and Mrs. Newnham, holding her hand on a planchette, would write an answer to the question. The conditions of the experiments are described by Mr. Newnham, in an account written in 1884, as follows :—

No. 24.

"My wife always sat at a small low table, in a low chair, leaning backwards. I sat about eight feet distant, at a rather higher table, and with my back towards her while writing down the questions. It was absolutely impossible that any gesture, or play of features, on my part, could have been visible or intelligible to her. As a rule she kept her eyes shut; but never became in the slightest degree hypnotic, or even naturally drowsy."

In all 309 questions with their answers were recorded under these conditions, before the experiments were finally abandoned on account of their prejudicial effect on Mrs. Newnham's health. The extracts from Mr. Newnham's note-book given below show that Mrs. Newnham throughout had some kind of knowledge, not always apparently complete, of the terms of the question.[2] But she was not herself consciously aware of the purport either of the question or of the answer written through her hand.

January 29th.

13. Is it the operator's brain, or some external force, that moves the Planchette? Answer "brain" or "force."
A. Will.

---

[1] *Proc. Soc. Psych. Research*, vol. iii. pp. 6-23.
[2] Mr. Newnham explains that "five or six questions were often asked consecutively without her being told of the subject that was being pursued."

14. Is it the will of a living person, or of an immaterial spirit, distinct from that person? Answer "person" or "spirit."
    A. Wife.
15. Give first the wife's Christian name; then, my favourite name for her. (This was accurately done.)
27. What is your own name?
    A. Only you.
28. We are not quite sure of the meaning of the answer. Explain.
    A. Wife.

Failing to get more than this at the outset, we returned to the same thought after question 114; when, having been closely pressed on another subject, we received the curt reply—"Told all I know."

February 18th.

117. Who are you that writes, and has told all you know?
     A. Wife.
118. But does no one tell wife what to write? If so, who?
     A. Spirit.
119. Whose spirit?
     A. Wife's brain.
120. But how does wife's brain know (certain) secrets?
     A. Wife's spirit unconsciously guides.
121. But how does wife's spirit know things it has never been told?
     A. No external influence.
122. But by what *internal* influence does it know (these) secrets?
     A. You cannot know.

Mr. Newnham, who was a Mason, took the opportunity on several occasions of questioning the planchette on details of the Masonic ritual and archæology—of which Mrs. Newnham was of course ignorant—with very surprising results. It will be seen from the extracts which follow that Mrs. Newnham's answers showed not only an acquaintance with the terms of the question, but even a fragmentary knowledge of the correct answer—knowledge which under the circumstances could hardly have been derived elsewhere than from the questioner's brain.

March 26th.

166. Of what language is the first syllable of the Great Triple
R.A. Word?[1]
A. Don't know.

167. Yes, you do. What are the three languages of which
the word is composed?
A. Greek, Egyptian, Syriac first syllable (*correctly given*),
rest unknown.

168. Write the syllable which is Syriac.
A. (First syllable correctly written.)

169. Write the syllable which is Egyptian.
A. Second.

170. Can you not write the syllable itself?
A. Third Greek.

174. Write down the word itself.
A. First three and last two letters were written correctly,
but four incorrect letters, *partly borrowed from another
word of the same degree*, came in the middle.

176. Why do you write a word of which I know nothing?
A. Wife tried hard to tell the word, but could not quite
catch it.

177. Catch it from whom?
A. Not quite sure.

178. Not quite sure of what?
A. I know nothing. Wife doesn't quite know.

182. Write out the prayer used at the advancement of a
Mark Master Mason.
A. Almighty Ruler of the Universe and Architect of all
worlds, we beseech Thee to accept this, our brother,
whom we have this day received into our most honour-
able Company of Mark Master Masons. Grant him to
be a worthy member of our brotherhood; and may he
be in his own person a perfect mirror of all Masonic
virtues. Grant that all our doings may be to Thy
honour and glory, and to the welfare of all mankind.

This prayer was written off instantaneously and very rapidly.
It is a very remarkable production indeed. For the benefit of
those who are not members of the craft, I may say that no
prayer in the slightest degree resembling it is made use of in the
Ritual of any Masonic degree; and yet it contains more than
one strictly accurate technicality connected with the degree of
Mark Mason. My wife has never seen any Masonic prayers,

---

[1] Previous questions had been asked on the same subject, and the
first syllable had already been correctly written. On a subsequent
occasion the same question was repeated and a wholly incorrect answer
was given.

whether in "Carlile," or any other real or spurious Ritual of the Masonic Order.

183. I do not know this prayer. Where is it to be found?
    A. Old American Ritual.
184. Where can I get one?
    A. Most likely none in England.
185. Can you not write the prayer that I make use of in my own Lodge?
    A. No, I don't know it.

We have to remark here not merely the exhibition of a will and an intelligence differing from the writer's normal self, but the display of a yet more alien disingenuousness. Similar evasions and inventions occur more than once in the course of these experiments. Indeed, a certain degree of moral perversity is a frequent and notorious characteristic of automatic expression.

Some interesting experiments of the same kind were conducted, in the winter of 1892-93, by Mr. R. H. Buttemer, of Emanuel College, Cambridge, and Mr. H. T. Green. Throughout the series the questions were, as in the preceding case, written down, so that the percipient was completely ignorant of their purport. The following is the record of the last experiments of the series.

No. 25.—By MR. R. H. BUTTEMER.

February 18th, 1893, 8 P.M. Mrs. H., Miss B., Mr. and Miss M. present, in addition to Mr. Green, and Messrs. S., W., and Buttemer.

Mr. Green, as usual, operated Planchette, and on this occasion sat with his back to all the other persons present.

Q. (from Mr. M.): What was I doing this afternoon?
A. i. —— the sun —— (all else illegible). ii. Enjoying the fresh air of heaven.
Q. What was Mr. Rogers doing in Cambridge?
A. i. (Irrelevant, or possibly connected vaguely with the question.) ii. Ask another, but Mr. Rogers came up on important business connected with the Lodge. (Correct.)

Q. Where has Mrs. M. gone ?

A. i. (Irrelevant.) ii. Far, far away, but more next time. iii. Her mother has gone to—oh, what a happy place is London! iv. All change here for Bletchley. (Mrs. M. had possibly passed this station on her journey.)

Q. Who has won the Association Match to-day?

A. i. (Illegible.) ii. O ye simple ones, how long will ye love simplicity? Why, Oxford, of course. [This fact was known to some persons in the room, but not to Mr. Green.]

One of the company then suggested the attempt to get the name on a visiting card transmitted, and the question was written, "Write name on card." Mr. Green did not know that this experiment was about to be tried, and the card was picked from a pile at random. The name was John B. Bourne. A sentence was written by Mr. Green, which proved to be, "Think of one letter at a time and then see what will happen." We did so.

A. i. J for Jerusalem, O for Omri, H for Honey, and N for Nothing. ii. B for Benjamin, O for Olive, U for Unicorn. (The remaining letters were given incorrectly.)

Q. How many of the Society's books are here? (There were two volumes of *Proceedings* on the table.)

A. i. (Irrelevant.) ii. The answer is 100-98.

Q. What is 2 × 3?

Two irrelevant answers were given, possibly owing to a slight disturbance in the room. The third answer was— "When that noise has ceased and S. has finished knocking the lamp over, I say 6."

A trial shortly after this, February 19th, gave no results, and the power of automatic writing appears to have entirely left Mr. Green for the present. (*Proc. Soc. Psych. Research*, vol. ix. pp. 61-64.)

In this, as in Mr. Newnham's case, the mode of expression is again characteristic of the automatic consciousness. It is explained by Mr. Buttemer that when two or more answers are given, the operator had been simply told to write again, after the first irrelevant answer, without being shown the question.

Table Tilting.

No. 26.—By the AUTHOR.

We pass on to experiments in which the ideas transmitted from the agent find other subterranean channels in the percipient's organism for their expression. Of all forms of intelligent automatism writing, next to speaking, is probably in an educated percipient the easiest, because in normal life the commonest. In the cases, therefore, recorded below the actual movements involved, though of a relatively simple kind, as being unaccustomed called possibly for the exercise of a degree of mental activity as high as would have been the case had writing been the vehicle of expression. In the preceding chapter it was recorded, in the experiments with numbers, that some of the answers were given through the movements of a table on which the percipient's hands rested (p. 73). A series of experiments of this nature was made by the writer in November and December 1873, with the assistance of a few friends, amongst whom were Mr. F. H. Colson, now Head Master of Plymouth College, and the Rev. W. E. Smith, of Corton, near Lowestoft. The following is a description of the methods adopted. Three or four of us would sit round a small centre-legged table, cane-bottomed chair, waste-paper basket, or metal tripod, with our hands resting on it. We found that in a few minutes the table (or other instrument) would tilt on one side, or move round and round, with considerable freedom. When these motions had once been fairly established, one or two of those present in the room would retire to a distance, keeping their backs to the table, and think of a letter of the alphabet. The table would move freely up and down, under the varying pressure of the hands laid on it, in a succession of small tilts. Those sitting at the table would count the tilts—one tilt standing for A, two for B, three for C, and so on. Excluding second trials, there were 70 experiments conducted under these conditions. The right letter was tilted in 27 cases, and in two others the next succeeding letter was given. On some occasions the proportion of successes was much higher; thus, on the 28th November, out of a total of 16 trials, 10 were correct. On the 1st December, on the other hand, 10 trials were made without any success. It was the rule throughout that the agents should stand with their backs to the table at some distance from it, and after the first few experiments we found, or thought we found, that the thought-transference succeeded best with a single agent. In order that the letter might not be guessed from the context, we generally took the initial or initial and final letters only of a word ; in four cases only did the agent select as many as three consecutive letters of a word. If the letters had been arbitrarily chosen, the chances against the right letters being indicated would be 25 to 1. But as the letters actually selected were in most cases constituent parts of a word, generally the initial letter, and as in some cases two or three consecutive letters were selected, the adverse chances would be reduced, roughly speaking, to something like 15 to 1. But even so the results attained are sufficiently striking.[1]

In these experiments the percipient or percipients themselves counted the tilts ; and it is probable that occasionally one or other of those seated at the table half-consciously guided its movements in conformity with his own ideas of what the letter would be. But in a modified form of the experiment, introduced by Professor Richet, the percipients, two or three in number, were seated at one table and a printed alphabet was placed on another table behind the percipients and out of their range of vision. When

---

[1] There were nine sittings in all, but the records of one were imperfectly kept, and have not been preserved. In two cases the details given are insufficient ; in the notes of the first evening it is stated that the person seated at the table "failed three or four times, succeeded once in giving word of (*i.e.*, selected from) newspaper (which agent) held in his hand." These trials have been omitted altogether from the results given in the text. On the third evening there is a record, "gave S H but got wrong afterwards." The word thought of was *Sherry*. I have counted this trial as two successes and two failures, judging from the other experiments recorded that not more than four consecutive letters at most would have been attempted.

the first table tilted,[1] under the automatic movements of the hands resting on it, it caused a bell to ring. M. Richet or some other experimenter sat at the second table and drew a pen slowly backwards and forwards over the printed alphabet. The letters to which the pen was pointing when the bell rang were noted, and it was found that they made up intelligible words and sentences, provided that in some cases the next letter or the next but one were substituted for that actually given.[2] All necessary precautions were taken that the alphabet should be out of sight of the "mediums," who were in most cases personal friends of M. Richet, and whose good faith was, he believes, in all cases unimpeachable. Subjoined is an account of the results obtained on one evening. M. Richet appears from the account to have been one of those seated at the tilting table.

No. 27.—By PROFESSOR RICHET.

"On the 9th of November we took the same precautions, but used an ordinary alphabet, not the circular one.[3] The name of the 'spirit' who came to the table was given as V I L L O N.

---

[1] In this case it will be observed the table tilted only once for each letter. The method adopted (after trial of the alternative) in my own experiments, though slower and more cumbrous, was apparently productive of more accurate results. It will be readily understood that it might be easier for the transmitted impulse to check a movement, at once uncertain and spasmodic, which had been already initiated, than to overcome, in a short space of time, the resistance of inertia and generate a new movement. The distinction may perhaps be illustrated by the difference between the amount of force required to start a railway truck at rest on the level, and that which would suffice to arrest one actually in gentle motion.

[2] Of course substitutions of this kind considerably reduce the value of the results obtained, but it will be found that when full deduction has been made on this score, the coincidences remain overwhelmingly in excess of anything which could have been produced by chance.

[3] In some previous experiments a circular alphabet had been used, with a view of preventing any of those seated at the first table from learning by the movements of the operator's hand what point of the alphabet he had reached. The other precautions described seemed, however, as M. Richet points out, sufficient to exclude all considerations of this kind.

Then we made a great noise, we repeated poetry, sang, and counted to such good purpose that P., who was at the alphabet, could hardly follow the ringing of the bell. We asked for some French poetry. The reply was—

QUSNNTKFSNEIGDRDAMSAM
OU,SONT,LES,NEIGES,DANTAN

That is, "Ou sont les neiges d'Antan?"—a verse of Villon's, obviously known to us all.

We then asked, what were the relations of Villon with the kings of France?

KOUHTLECRUEL
LOUIS,LE,CRUEL

Louis le cruel.
What book ought we to read?

ESSAYSURDADMONINMANHP
ESSAY,SUR,DAEMONIOMANIE

The reader will understand that if I mention these experiments, it is not because the answers are interesting in themselves, but because the precautions taken seemed sufficient to prevent the medium from gaining any knowledge of the movements of the operator at the alphabet. . . . I add a few more replies; but the number and intrinsic significance of these replies is a matter of but little importance.

FESTINALENTE
LOFAMDTMREIINAJUBR
INFANDUM,REJINA,JUBES
RENOVAREDOLOREM
RENOVARE,DOLOREM

The old spelling of the word "Rejina" should be noticed. (*Proc. Soc. Psych. Research*, vol. v. pp. 142, 143.)

In this case it will be observed that P. alone was in possession of the knowledge, without which all the efforts of those at the table could have produced only a meaningless sequence of letters. In some other experiments of the series the procedure was more complicated. M. Richet, standing apart from both tables, asked a question, the answer to which was given by the percipients with a certain approximation to correctness. The results, though less striking than those already quoted, are yet such as to suggest that they were not due to chance.[1]

Production of Local Anæsthesia.

We now pass to experiments of another kind, resembling those last quoted, inasmuch as the effects were produced without the consciousness of the percipient, but differing in the important particular that no deliberate and conscious effort on his part could have enabled him to produce them. In experiments carried on with various subjects at intervals through the years 1883-87, at some of which the present writer assisted, Mr. Edmund Gurney had shown that it was possible by means of the unexpressed will of the agent to produce local anæsthesia in certain persons. (*S.P.R.*, vol. i. pp. 257-260; ii. 201-205; iii. 453-459; v. 14-17.) In these experiments the subject was placed at a table, and his hands were passed through holes in a large brown paper screen, so that they were completely concealed from his view. Mr. G. A. Smith then held his hand at a distance of two or three inches from the finger indicated by Mr. Gurney, at the same time willing that it should become rigid and insensible. On subsequently applying appropriate tests it was found, as a rule, that the finger selected had actually become rigid and was insensible to pain. In the last series of 160 experiments Mr. Gurney, as well as Mr. Smith, held his hand over a particular finger. In 124 cases the finger over which Mr. Smith's hand had been held was alone affected; in 16 cases Mr. Gurney and Mr. Smith were both successful; in 13 cases Mr. Gurney was successful and Mr. Smith failed. In the remaining 7 cases no effect at all was produced. It is noteworthy that in a series of 41 similar trials, in which Mr. Smith, while holding his hand in the same position, willed that no effect

---

[1] *Rev. Phil.*, Dec. 1884; see also *S.P.R.*, vol. ii. pp. 247 *et seq.*

should be produced, there was actually no effect in 36 cases; in 4 cases the finger over which his hand was held, and in the remaining case another finger, were affected. The rigidity was tested by asking the subject, at the end of the experiment, to close his hands. When he complied with the request the finger operated on—if the experiment had succeeded —would remain rigid. The insensibility was proved by pricking, burning, or by a current from an induction coil. In the majority of the successful trials the insensibility was shown to be proof against all assaults, however severe.

In these earlier experiments it seemed essential to success that Mr. Smith's hand should be in close proximity to that of the subject, without any intervening barrier. These conditions made it difficult to exclude the possibility of the subject learning by variations in temperature, or by air currents, which finger was actually being operated on; though it is hard to conceive that the percipient could by any such means have discriminated between Mr. Gurney's hand and Mr. Smith's. On the other hand, even if this source of error was held to be excluded, the interpretation of the results remained ambiguous. As a matter of fact, Mr. Gurney himself was inclined to attribute the effects produced, not to telepathy, as ordinarily understood, but to a specific vital effluence, or, as he phrased it, a kind of nervous induction, operating directly on the affected part of the percipient's organism. (*Proc. S.P.R.*, vol. v. pp. 254-259.)

With a view to test this hypothesis further experiments of the same kind were made by Mrs. Sidgwick during the years 1890 and 1892, the subjects being P. and Miss B. already mentioned. The percipient was throughout in a normal condition. As before, he sat at a table with his hands passed through holes in a large screen, which extended sufficiently far in all directions to prevent him from seeing either the operator or his own hands. Mr. Smith, as before, willed to produce the desired effect in the finger which had been intimated to him, either by signs or writing, by one of the experimenters. Passing over the trials, very generally successful, made under the same conditions as Mr. Gurney's experiments— *i.e.*, with the agent's hand held at a short distance without any intervening screen from the finger selected—we will quote Mrs. Sidgwick's account of the later series performed under varied conditions. (*Proc. S.P.R.*, vol. viii. pp. 577-596.)

No. 28.—By MRS. H. SIDGWICK.

In the second division, (*b*), of our experiments come those in which a glass screen was placed over the subject's hands. For the first four of these we used a framed window pane which happened to be handy. Then we obtained and used a sheet of 32 oz. glass, measuring 22 by 10 inches and ⅙ inch in thickness. This was supported on two large books placed beyond the subject's hands on each side, and in this position the upper surface of the glass was 2¼ inches above the surface of the table, so that there was ample room for the hands to rest underneath without touching the glass. Mr. Smith held his hand in the usual position over the selected finger, above the glass and not touching it. Under these conditions we tried 21 experiments with P., of which 18 were successful, and 6 with Miss B., all successful. In the case of the 3 failures with P., no effect was produced on any finger. In one successful case, the time taken was long, and we interrupted the experiment by premature testing in the way explained above.

Division (*c*) includes those experiments in which Mr. Smith did not approximate his hand to that of the subject at all, but merely looked at the selected finger from some place in the same room as the subject, but out of his sight. The distances between him and the subject varied from about 2½ to about 12 feet. Under these conditions we tried 37 experiments with P., 18 in 1890, of which 6 were failures, and 2 only partially successful, and 19 in 1892, of which 10 were failures. The proportion of success was, it thus appears, much less than under the previously described conditions, but still much beyond what chance would produce. Of the 6 failures in 1890, one was a case in which Mr. Smith made a mistake as to which finger we had selected, but succeeded with the one he thought of. In another case the left thumb instead of the right thumb became insensitive. In the other 4 cases no finger at all was affected.

Of the 10 failures in 1892, no effect was produced in 4 cases; in another the right (viz., the little) finger of the wrong hand became insensitive;[1] in 4 cases an adjoining finger was affected—once only slightly—instead of that selected, and in the remaining case a finger distant from the selected one was slightly affected.

Six experiments were made with Mr. Smith looking at the finger through the opera-glass at a distance of from 22 to 25 feet; in three cases the experiment succeeded, in three another finger was affected instead of that selected. Fourteen experiments were made with a closed door intervening between percipient and agent; 2 only succeeded, and in 8 a wrong finger was affected, no effect at all being produced in the remaining 4 cases. In a further series of 4 trials Mr. Smith held his hand near the percipient, and willed to produce no effect. The trials were successful. In all these experiments P. was the percipient.

The rigidity was tested, as before, by asking the subject to close his hands; the anæsthesia, as a rule, by touches or the induction coil. Tested by the latter means it was found, as the current was gradually increased to the maximum, that the insensibility was not always complete. Flexibility and sensation were usually restored, for economy of time, by means of upward passes; but a few trials made later in the series served to show that the finger could be restored to its normal condition by a mere effort of will on the part of the agent. In some cases when their attention was specially directed to their sensations the subjects were able to indicate beforehand the finger operated on, by reason of the feeling of cold in it. But as a rule they appeared to be unaware which finger was affected. It is perhaps needless to point out that no conscious effort on their part could have produced the results described.

[1] It happened on another occasion under these conditions that the right little finger was slightly affected when the left little finger, which had been selected, was so in a more decided manner.

CHAPTER V.

EXPERIMENTAL PRODUCTION OF TELEPATHIC EFFECTS AT A DISTANCE.

IN the cases so far described, where success has been attained, the agent and percipient, if not actually in the same room, have been separated by a distance not exceeding at the most 25 or 30 feet. The analogy of the physical forces would, of course, have prepared us to find that the effect of telepathy diminishes in proportion to the distance through which it has to act. And in fact we have but few records of successful experiments at a distance. Yet, on the other hand, we are confronted by a large body of evidence for the spontaneous affection of one mind by another, and that at a distance frequently of hundreds of miles. It is difficult to resist the conclusion, in view of the close similarity, in many cases, of the effects produced, that the force operating in these spontaneous phenomena is identical with, or at least closely allied to, that which causes the transfer of sensations or images from agent to percipient within the compass of a London drawing-room. It is probable, indeed, that the non-experimental evidence, for reasons already alluded to, and discussed at length in the succeeding chapter, should be generously discounted. But it is not easy for an impartial inquirer to reject it altogether. Nor indeed is any such summary solution required by the results of experimental telepathy. It is true that experiments at a distance have seldom succeeded, and that we have no record of any long-continued series of such experiments at all comparable to those conducted, *e.g.*, by Mr. Guthrie or Mrs. Henry Sidgwick at close quarters. But it is also probably true that such experiments have been comparatively seldom attempted. And if account be taken of the various drawbacks incident to experiments at a distance, the amount of success already achieved, though no doubt less in proportion to the number of serious and well-conceived attempts than is the case with experiments conducted under the more usual conditions, is yet far from discouraging. For trials at a distance are tedious; they consume much time, and call for long preparation and careful pre-arrangement. The difficulties of securing the necessary freedom from disturbance are probably increased when agent and percipient are separated. The interest in such experiments is difficult to maintain apart from the stimulus of a rapid succession of trials with an immediate record of the results. Lastly, such experiments would generally be undertaken only after a series of trials at close quarters; after, that is, some portion at least of the original stock of energy and enthusiasm has been exhausted. And even when such considerations have no effect upon the experimenter, it is likely, as has been already pointed out, that the novel conditions would of themselves affect unfavourably the imagination of the percipient, and thus prejudice the results. That, notwithstanding these various drawbacks, there have been several successful series of experiments at a distance is a matter of good augury for the future.

It is much to be desired that investigators should give attention to obtaining more results in this branch of the inquiry. For independently of the fact that results of the kind form an indispensable link between instances of thought-transference at close quarters and the more striking spontaneous cases at a distance, it is important to observe that in experiments of the kind described in the present chapter the gravest objection which is at present urged, and may fairly continue to be urged, against most experiments at close quarters—viz., the risk of unconscious apprehension through normal channels—is no longer applicable. Moreover, the results can only be attributed to fraud on the extreme assumption that both parties to the experiment are implicated in deliberate and systematic collusion.

Induction of Sleep at a distance.

Some of the most striking experimental cases, which are concerned with the production of hallucinations, are reserved for later discussion. (See Chapter X.)

But perhaps the most valuable body of testimony for the agency of thought-transference at a distance is to be found in the experiments recorded by French observers in the induction of sleep. It is not a little remarkable that this, one of its rarest and most striking manifestations, should have been among the first and, until recently, almost the only form of telepathy which attracted attention amongst French investigators. Moreover, of late years at any rate, this particular form of experiment has rarely succeeded except in France, and with hypnotic subjects. But as the number of physicians who practise hypnotism increases in other countries, we may no doubt hope to see the observations already made confirmed and enlarged. The analogy of the experiments in the induction of anæsthesia by thought-transference, recorded in the last chapter, would perhaps have prepared us to accept the induction of sleep as a not improbable effect of telepathy. But we are not without more direct testimony. The opening sentences of Professor Janet's account of the experiment with Madame B. show us that, in this case at all events, the conscious will of the operator was necessary to produce the hypnotic trance, even at close quarters. When, therefore, we find that the same cause, operating at a distance, is constantly followed by a like effect, there can be no reasonable ground for refusing to recognise the operator's will as in this case also the cause of the sleep; unless, indeed, we are prepared to attribute all the results to chance.

No. 29.—Experiments by MM. GIBERT and JANET.

In the autumn of 1885 Professor Pierre Janet of Havre witnessed some trials made by Dr. Gibert of the same town on Madame B., a patient of his own. Madame B., whose fame has now reached beyond her native land, is described by Professor Janet as an honest peasant woman, in good health, with no indications of hysteria. She has been hypnotised since childhood by various persons, and is occasionally liable to spontaneous attacks of somnambulism. One of the most remarkable features presented by Madame B.'s induced trances is that she can be awakened by the person who hypnotised her and by no one else; and that his hand alone can produce partial or general contractures, and subsequently restore her limbs to their normal condition.

"One day," to quote Professor Janet ("Note sur quelques Phénomènes de Somnambulisme," *Revue Philosophique*, Feb. 1886), "M. Gibert was holding Madame B.'s hand to hypnotise her (*pour l'endormir*), but he was visibly preoccupied and thinking of other matters, and the trance did not supervene. This experiment, repeated by me in various forms, proved to us that in order to entrance Madame B. it was necessary to concentrate one's thought intensely on the suggestion to sleep which was given to her, and the more the operator's thought wandered the more difficult it became to induce the trance.

This influence of the operator's thought, however extraordinary it may seem, predominates in this case to such an extent that it replaces all other causes. If one presses Madame B.'s hand without the thought of hypnotising her, the trance is not induced; but, on the other hand, one can succeed in sending her to sleep by thinking of it without pressing her hand."

Of course in experiments of this kind no precautions could exclude the chance that some suggestion of what was expected might reach the percipient's mind through the gestures, the attitude, or even the silence of the experimenter. But, acting on the clue thus given, MM. Gibert and Janet succeeded in impressing mentally on Madame B. commands which were punctually executed on the following day. During the same period Dr. Gibert made three attempts, all of which met with partial success, in inducing the hypnotic trance by mental suggestion given at a distance. Subsequently, during February and March 1886, and again during April and May of the same year, these trials were repeated with striking results. During one of the trials which took place in April Mr. F. W. H. Myers and Dr. A. T. Myers were present, and from their contemporary record the following account is taken. Throughout these trials, it should be stated, Madame B. was in the Pavillon, a house occupied by Dr. Gibert's sister, and distant about two-thirds of a mile from Dr. Gibert's own house. The distance intervening between agent and percipient in this series of experiments was in no case less than a quarter of a mile or more than one mile. In the first trial described by Mr. Myers (18 in the subjoined table) Madame B. actually went to sleep about twenty minutes after the effort at willing had been made; but as some of the party had in the interval entered the house where she was and found her awake, it seems possible that their coming had suggested the idea of sleep. In the second case (No. 19) an attempt to will Madame B. to leave her bed at 11.35 P.M.

and come to Dr. Gibert's house had failed—the only result, possibly due to other causes, being an unusually prolonged sleep and a headache on waking. Subsequently, to quote Mr. Myers' account,

"(20) On the morning of the 22nd we again selected by lot an hour (11 A.M.) at which M. Gibert should will, from his dispensary (which is close to his house), that Madame B. should go to sleep in the Pavillon. It was agreed that a rather longer time should be allowed for the process to take effect; as it had been observed (see M. Janet's previous communication) that she sometimes struggled against the influence, and averted the effect for a time by putting her hands in cold water, etc. At 11.25 we entered the Pavillon quietly, and almost at once she descended from her room to the *salon*, profoundly asleep. Here, however, suggestion might again have been at work. We did not, of course, mention M. Gibert's attempt of the previous night. But she told us in her sleep that she had been very ill in the night, and repeatedly exclaimed: 'Pourquoi M. Gibert m'a-t-il fait souffrir? Mais j'ai lavé les mains continuellement.' This is what she does when she wishes to avoid being influenced.

"(21) In the evening (22nd) we all dined at M. Gibert's, and in the evening M. Gibert made another attempt to put her to sleep at a distance from his house in the Rue Séry,—she being at the Pavillon, Rue de la Ferme,—and to bring her to his house by an effort of will. At 8.55 he retired to his study; and MM. Ochorowicz, Marillier, Janet, and A. T. Myers went to the Pavillon, and waited outside in the street, out of sight of the house. At 9.22 Dr. Myers observed Madame B. coming half-way out of the garden-gate, and again retreating. Those who saw her more closely observed that she was plainly in the somnambulic state, and was wandering about and muttering. At 9.25 she came out (with eyes persistently closed, so far as could be seen), walked quickly past MM. Janet and Marillier without noticing them, and made for M. Gibert's house, though not by the usual or shortest route. (It appeared afterwards that the *bonne* had seen her go into the *salon* at 8.45, and issue thence asleep at 9.15 : had not looked in between those times.) She avoided lamp-posts, vehicles, etc., but crossed and recrossed the street repeatedly. No one went in front of her or spoke to her. After eight or ten minutes she grew much more uncertain in gait, and paused as though she would fall. Dr. Myers noted the moment in the Rue Faure; it was 9.35. At about 9.40 she grew bolder, and at 9.45 reached the street

in front of M. Gibert's house. There she met him, but did not
notice him, and walked into his house, where she rushed
hurriedly from room to room on the ground-floor. M. Gibert
had to take her hand before she recognised him. She then
grew calm.

"M. Gibert said that from 8.55 to 9.20 he thought intently
about her; from 9.20 to 9.35 he thought more feebly; at 9.35
he gave the experiment up, and began to play billiards; but in
a few minutes began to will her again. It appeared that his
visit to the billiard-room had coincided with her hesitation and
stumbling in the street. But this coincidence may of course
have been accidental. . . .

"(22) On the 23rd, M. Janet, who had woke her up and left
her awake,[1] lunched in our company, and retired to his own
house at 4.30 (a time chosen by lot) to try to put her to sleep
from thence. At 5.5 we all entered the *salon* of the Pavillon, and
found her asleep with shut eyes, but sewing vigorously (being
in that stage in which movements once suggested are automati-
cally continued). Passing into the talkative state, she said to
M. Janet, 'C'est vous qui m'avez fait dormir à quatre heures
et demi.' The impression as to the hour may have been a
suggestion received from M. Janet's mind. We tried to make
her believe that it was M. Gibert who had sent her to sleep, but
she maintained that she had felt that it was M. Janet.

"(23) On April 24th the whole party chanced to meet at M.
Janet's house at 3 P.M., and he then, at my suggestion, entered
his study to will that Madame B. should sleep. We waited in
his garden, and at 3.20 proceeded together to the Pavillon,
which I entered first at 3.30, and found Madame B. profoundly
sleeping over her sewing, having ceased to sew. Becoming
talkative, she said to M. Janet, 'C'est vous qui m'avez com-
mandé.' She said that she fell asleep at 3.5 P.M." (*Proc. S.P.R.*,
vol. iv. pp. 133-136.)

The subjoined table, taken, with a few verbal
alterations, from Mr. Myers' article, gives a complete
list of the experiments in the induction of trance at
a distance (*sommeil à distance*) made by MM. Janet
and Gibert up to the end of May 1886:—

---

[1] An experiment of another kind, the description of which is here
omitted, had been made on the morning of this day.

No. of Experiments.	Date.	Operator.	Hour when given.	Remarks.	Success or failure.
	1885.				
1	October 3	Gibert	11.30 A.M.	She washes hands and wards off trance.	?
2	,, 9	do.	11.40 A.M.	Found entranced 11.45.	1
3	,, 14	do.	4.15 P.M.	Found entranced 4.30: had been asleep about 15 minutes.	1
	1886.				
4	Feb. 22	Janet	..	She washes hands and wards off trance.	?
5	,, 25	do.	5 P.M.	Asleep at once.	1
6	,, 26	do.	..	Mere discomfort observed.	0
7	March 1	do.	..	do. do.	0
8	,, 2	do.	3 P.M.	Found asleep at 4: has slept about an hour.	1
9	,, 4	do.	..	Will interrupted: trance coincident but incomplete.	1
10	,, 5	do.	5-5.10 P.M.	Found asleep a few minutes afterwards.	1
11	,, 6	Gibert	8 P.M.	Found asleep 8.2.	1
12	,, 10	do.	..	Success—no details.	1
13	,, 14	Janet	3 P.M.	Success—no details.	1
14	,, 16	Gibert	9 P.M.	Brings her to his house: she leaves her house a few minutes after 9.	1
15	April 18	Janet	..	Found asleep in 10 minutes.	1
16	,, 19	Gibert	4 P.M.	Found asleep 4.15.	1
17	,, 20	do.	8 P.M.	Made to come to his house.	1
18	,, 21	do.	5.50 P.M.	Asleep about 6.10: trance too tardy.	?
19	,, 21	do.	11.35 P.M.	Attempt at trance during sleep.	0
20	,, 22	do.	11 A.M.	Asleep 11.25: trance too tardy.	?
21	,, 22	do.	9 P.M.	Comes to his house: leaves her house 9.15.	1
22	,, 23	Janet	4.30 P.M.	Found asleep 5.5, says she has slept since 4.30.	1
23	,, 24	do.	3 P.M.	Found asleep 3.30, says she has slept since 3.5.	1
24	May 5	do.	..	Success—no details.	1
25	,, 6	do.	..	Success—no details.	1
					18

We have then in 25 trials 18 complete and 4 partial or doubtful successes. In two of the latter Madame B. was found washing her hands to ward off the trance, and in two others the trance supervened only after an interval of twenty minutes or more, and under circumstances which rendered it

doubtful whether telepathy were the cause. It is
important to note that during these earlier visits of
Madame B. to Havre, about two months in all, she .
only once fell into ordinary sleep during the daytime,
and twice became spontaneously entranced; and
that she never left the house in the evenings except
on the three occasions (14, 17, 21), on which she
did so in apparent response to a mental suggestion.
There is little ground, therefore, for attributing the
results above given to chance.

A further series of trials with the same percipient
was conducted by Professor Janet during the autumn
of 1886. The results, communicated by him to
Pro. sor Richet, were published by the latter in the
Proceeaings of the S.P.R., vol. v. pp. 43-45.[1] In
order to facilitate comparison I have thrown these
later results also into tabular form. In the later trials
it will be observed that there is a tolerably constant
retardation of the effect. The exact degree of the
retardation it was not always possible to ascertain, as
it was not practicable to keep Madame B. continually
under observation, and to have let those at the
Pavillon into the secret, and to have asked them to
exercise special vigilance at the time of the experiments would have entailed the risk of vitiating the
results. Moreover, in order to avoid giving any
suggestion by the hour of his arrival, M. Janet made
it a rule during a great part of this period to come to
the house at the same hour—4 P.M. in most cases—
for several days consecutively. When an early hour,
therefore, had been chosen for the experiments, the
exact degree of success could only be determined if
Madame B.'s movements had chanced at the right
time to come under the observation of those in the
house. During the period of the trials Madame B.
fell asleep in the daytime spontaneously only four
times.

---

[1] An account of these experiments is also contained in an article by
M. Richet in the *Revue de l'Hypnotisme* for February 1888.

No. of Experiments.	Date.	Hour when given.	Remarks.	Success or Failure.
	1886.			
1	8th Sept.	3 P.M.	Found asleep at 4 P.M. M. J. entered unseen and without knocking	?
2	9th Sept.	3 P.M.	Madame B. complained of headache	F.
3	11th Sept.	9 (? A.M.)	Found at 10, "troublée et étourdie"	F.
4	14th Sept.	4 P.M.	M. J. enters at 4.15. Madame B. says she was asleep, but wakened by ringing of door-bell	?
5[1]	18th Sept.	3.30 P.M.	Found asleep at 4 P.M.; states she was put to sleep at 3.30	S.
6[1]	19th Sept.	3 P.M.	Went to sleep at about 3.15	S.
7	23rd Sept.	2 P.M.	She was out walking ...	F.
8	24th Sept.	3.15 P.M.	Found asleep at 4. Had been seen awake at 3.15 ...	?
9	26th Sept.	3 P.M.	Walking in garden	F.
10	27th Sept.	8.30 P.M.	Commanded by M. Gibert to come to his house. Left the Pavillon, entranced, at 9.5 P.M. [in the account in the *Revue de l'Hypnotisme* the latter hour is given at *9.15*]	S.
11	29th Sept.	3.50 P.M.	Found asleep at 4.5 [given in *Revue* as *5.5*]	S.
12	30th Sept.	3.30 P.M.	... ...	F.
13	1st Oct.	2.40 P.M.	She was out walking ...	F.
14	5th Oct.	4 P.M.	Fell asleep suddenly at 4.5, whilst talking with nurse in garden	S.
15	6th Oct.	3 P.M.	... ...	F.
16	9th Oct.	3.15 P.M.	... ...	F.
17	10th Oct.	3.20 P.M.	Found asleep at 4.5 ...	?
18	12th Oct.	3 P.M.	... ...	F.
19	13th Oct.	5 P.M.	Found asleep. Executed a mental command given at a distance—viz., to rise at M. J.'s entrance	S.
20	14th Oct.	2.30 P.M.	Found asleep at 3.20 ...	?
21	16th Oct.	3 P.M.	Found asleep at 3.30 ...	S.

[1] M. Richet also took part in these two experiments.

No. of Experiments.	Date.	Hour when given.	Remarks.	Success or Failure.
22	24th Nov.	2.30 P.M.	... ...	F.
23	3rd Dec.	4.10 P.M.	... ...	F.
24	5th Dec.	4.10 P.M.	... ...	F.
25	6th Dec.	4.10 P.M.	Found awake, washing her hands	?
26	7th Dec.	2.30 P.M.	Found asleep at 3.5... ...	?
27	10th Dec.	4.20 P.M.	She was out walking ...	F.
28	11th Dec.	3.15 P.M.	... ...	?
29	13th Dec.	4.5 P.M.	Found asleep at 4.25. Had been seen awake a few minutes after 4 P.M. ...	S.
30	14th Dec.	11.30 A.M.	... ...	F.
31	18th Dec.	...	... ...	F.
32	21st Dec.	...	... ...	F.
33	22nd Dec.	...	... ...	F.
34	23rd Dec.	3 P.M.	Found asleep at 3.40 ...	?
35	25th Dec.	3.15 P.M.	She was out walking. Bad headache came on at 3.20. Returned hurriedly, and at once fell asleep in the *salon*.	S.

Throughout the series, except in case 10, M. Janet was the operator. It will be seen that in the 35 trials there were nine cases in which Madame B. was found asleep within half-an-hour of the attempt being made to entrance her. In six other cases she was found asleep after a longer interval, but there is nothing to indicate that the sleep did not actually supervene at the right time. In one case she was found awake within fifteen minutes of the trial, but stated that she had been awakened by the ringing of the bell which announced M. Janet's arrival. In one other case she was found washing her hands to ward off the trance. Of the 17 failures Madame B. was out walking in four cases at the time of the trial, a circumstance which no doubt diminished the chances of success. In two cases headache or disturbance were produced; of the remaining 11 trials no details are given, and it is presumed that no unusual effect was observed, and that there was no apparent cause for the failure. Of course, experiments carried on under these conditions, the trials being confined for the most part within a narrow range of hours, and the subject liable to spontaneous trance, offer some scope for chance coincidence. But as Madame B. actually fell asleep spontaneously on only four occasions during the period over which the trials extended, it will probably be considered that the number of coincidences, imperfect as they were, was considerably more than could plausibly be attributed to accident or self-suggestion.[1]

In January 1887 M. Richet made some experiments of the same kind on Madame B. Of 9 trials, however, two only could be described as completely successful, and three more as doubtful. A few further trials, in December 1887 and January 1888, were even less successful. M. Richet has attempted on several occasions to influence other subjects at a distance, but no series of successful results was attained ; and isolated coincidences of the kind have, of course, little evidential value (*loc. cit.*, pp. 47-51).[2]

No. 30.—Experiments by DR. DUFAY.

In a paper published in the *Revue Philosophique* of September 1888, M. Dufay, a physician formerly in practice at Blois, and now a Senator of France, records several instances in which he has himself succeeded in producing sleep at a distance. In one case he hypnotised from his box in the theatre, as he believes without her knowledge, a young actress who had been a patient of his, and caused her, whilst in the state of lucid somnambulism, to play a new and

---

[1] It is not stated whether the hour of the experiment was chosen by lot, but this precaution was taken in many of the earlier experiments.

[2] An account of these experiments was also contributed by M. Richet to the *Revue de l'Hypnotisme*, Feb. 1888.

difficult part with more success than she would have been likely to achieve in the normal state.   In this particular case, however, it seems possible that the subject may have received some intimation of Dr. Dufay's presence in the house, and that the hypnotic state may have been due to expectation.   Another case was that of Madame C., who had been for some time treated hypnotically by Dr. Dufay for periodical attacks of sickness and headache.   So sensitive did this patient become to his suggestions that she would fall into the hypnotic sleep as soon as the bell rang to announce his coming, and before he had actually entered the house.   The circumstances under which Dr. Dufay first made a deliberate attempt to influence Madame C. at a distance were as follows :—He was in attendance on a patient whom he was unable to leave, when he was unexpectedly summoned by Monsieur C. to hypnotise Madame C., who was in the height of an attack.   He assured Monsieur C. that on his return home he would find Madame C. asleep and cured, as proved actually to be the case.   However, here also, as Dr. Dufay points out, self-suggestion is a possible explanation.   The following case seems less open to suspicion on this ground :—

"On another occasion," Dr. Dufay writes, "Madame C. was in perfect health, but her name happening to be mentioned in my hearing, the idea struck me that I would mentally order her to sleep, without her wishing it this time, and also without her suspecting it.   Then, an hour later, I went to her house and asked the servant who opened the door whether an instrument, which I had mislaid out of my case, had been found in Madame C.'s room.

"'Is not that the doctor's voice that I hear?' asked Monsieur C. from the top of the staircase ; 'beg him to come up.   Just imagine,' he said to me, 'I was going to send for you.   Nearly an hour ago my wife lost consciousness, and her mother and I have not been able to bring her to her senses.   Her mother, who wished to take her into the country, is distracted.   . .'

"I did not dare to confess myself guilty of this catastrophe, but was betrayed by Madame C., who gave me her hand, saying, 'You did well to put me to sleep, Doctor, because I was going to allow myself to be taken away, and then I should not have been able to finish my embroidery.'

"'You have another piece of embroidery in hand?'

"'Yes ; a mantle-border . . . for your birthday. You must not look as though you knew about it, when I am awake, because I want to give you a surprise.'

.   .   .   .

"I repeated the experiment many times with Madame C., and always with success, which was a great help to me when unable to go to her at once when sent for. I even completed the experiment by also *waking* her from a distance, solely by an act of volition, which formerly I should not have believed possible. The agreement in time was so perfect that no doubt could be entertained.

"To conclude, I was about to take a holiday of six weeks, and should thus be absent when one of the attacks was due. So it was settled between Monsieur C. and myself that, as soon as the headache began, he should let me know by telegraph ; that I should then do from afar off what succeeded so well near at hand ; that after five or six hours I should endeavour to awaken the patient ; and that Monsieur C. should let me know by means of a second telegram whether the result had been satisfactory. He had no doubt about it ; I was less certain. Madame C. did not know that I was going away.

"The sound of moanings one morning announced to Monsieur C. that the moment had come ; without entering his wife's room he ran to the telegraph office, and I received his message at ten o'clock. He returned home again at that same hour, and found his wife asleep and not suffering any more. At four o'clock I willed that she should wake, and at eight o'clock in the evening I received a second telegram : 'Satisfactory result, woke at four o'clock. Thanks.'

"And I was then in the neighbourhood of Sully-sur-Loire, 28 leagues—112 kilometres—from Blois."

Similar experiments have been recorded by, amongst others, Dr. J. Héricourt,[1] a colleague of M. Richet in the editing of the *Revue Scientifique*, Dr. Dusart,[1] and Dr. Dariex.[2] In the last case there were only five trials, the experiments being then discontinued at the request of the patient. The first three trials were completely successful, the sleep supervening within,

---

[1] *Revue Philosophique*, February and April 1886. A translation of these accounts is given in the *Proc. S.P.R.*, vol. v. pp. 222, 223.

[2] *Annales des Sciences Psychiques*, vol. iii. pp. 257-267.

at most, a few minutes of the time chosen by the agent.

The following narrative resembles those cited above in its general features. But in view of the nature of the effect produced—a painful hysterical attack—it is perhaps hardly a matter for regret that the case is without any exact parallel.

No. 31.—By DR. TOLOSA-LATOUR.

In this account, taken from a letter written to M. Richet by Dr. Tolosa-Latour on the 5th March 1891 (*Annales des Sciences Psychiques*, Sept.-Oct. 1893), Dr. Latour explains that he had repeatedly hypnotised a lady who was seized in September 1886 with hysterical paralysis, and had ultimately succeeded in effecting by this means a complete cure. Prior to his treatment, in 1885, she had suffered for some time from daily hysterical attacks, and when she came under Dr. Latour she was still occasionally subject to them, and found relief in the hypnotic sleep. Both symptoms had at the time which he writes almost completely disappeared.

"I had made some very curious experiments, but I had never thought about either action at a distance or clairvoyance. It was while leaving Paris and reading your [M. Richet's] pamphlet in the carriage that the idea occurred to me of sending Mdlle. R. to sleep. It was Sunday, October the 26th, the very day of my departure. I remember the hour too ; it was just before reaching Poitiers, where some relations of my grandmother were expecting me. I told my wife that I was going to try the experiment, and begged her to say nothing about it to any one. I began to fix my thoughts about six o'clock, and during the journey from Poitiers to Mignie (where we stayed several days) I again and again thought of this question, especially during the intervals of silence which always occur during a journey.

"I wished to cause a violent hysteric attack, as I knew that she had not been dangerously ill for a long time. So on Sunday, October the 26th, from six till nine o'clock in the evening, I fixed my thoughts intently on the experiment.

"Then, on my return, I asked my brother if Mdlle. R. had called him in, as she always did when she was ill. Among the patients' names I did not find hers. It seemed almost certain that my experiment had failed. A week afterwards I called on her, and was agreeably surprised to learn that, on the contrary, it was a success, as you will judge by her letter. She does not fix the day, but her sister and the nurse have told me that it was the second Sunday after the festival of St. Theresa—that is to say, after Wednesday the 15th; the first Sunday being the 19th, the second is of course the 26th.

"This is the letter :—

"*From* MDLLE. R. TO M. TOLOSA-LATOUR.

"*March 23rd*, 1891.

"MY EXCELLENT FRIEND AND DEAR DOCTOR,—I wanted to write to you yesterday to give you the particulars of the attack I had about the middle of last October, but I was not able to do so till to-day.

"As I told you, it was about the middle of October; I do not remember the date, but I recollect very well that it was a festival day, and at half-past six in the evening.

"We had just been to see my sister and brother; we had had luncheon with them. I was perfectly well, without any excitement; it was five o'clock, and I reached home all right, but when I was sitting down, in the act of eating, I found myself unable to speak or open my eyes, and, at the same moment, I had a very severe, long, and violent attack, such as I do not remember to have had for a long time.

"I was so ill that I thought of sending for Raphael,[1] and my sister proposed it, but I thought that I ought not to disturb him, for, knowing that you were away, nobody could stop the convulsions and the excitement.

"I suffered horribly, for it was an attack in which I experienced, so to say, all my previous sufferings combined. I was completely broken down, but I have had no other attacks since, not even a spasm."

No. 32.—By J. H. P.[2]

The next case records the execution by the subject of a simple command to approach the operator, as in some of M. Gibert's experiments already described, and the partial execution of an order of a more

---

[1] Dr. Latour's brother, house-surgeon at the hospital.
[2] See No. 23, chap. iv.

complicated kind, given from a distance of more than twenty-five miles :—

It is possible to give M. a command in the waking state, but she must be quiet at the moment when she receives it.

We had never made experiments of this kind until R. one day proposed that we should try to make M. come to the room where we were. M. was in a neighbouring house, and could not know that we were actually in a kiosk at the end of the garden.

For three minutes I gave her the mental command to come. I began to think that I had failed, and continued energetically for three minutes more; she did not come, however.

We were just thinking that the experiment had failed when the door opened suddenly and M. appeared.

"Well, do you think I have nothing else to do ! Why do you call me ? I have had to leave everything."

"We wanted to say 'good morning' to you."

"Very well ! I am going away now."

She shook hands with us and went away quickly; whereupon it occurred to me to make her stop just at the gate.

(Mental command)—"I forbid you to go out. You cannot open the gate; come back." And back she came, furious, asking if we were laughing at her.

Now, to send this last command I had not moved at all from my place, and M. was completely invisible behind the garden wall; moreover, I was a long way from the window. I told her that this time she could open it, and let her go.

I will finish with another experiment of the same kind, which only partly succeeded, but which will serve to show the intensity of the mental transmission between M. and me. I went away, one morning, without thinking of M. I had to be away all day, 38 kilomètres from her. At 2.30 it occurred to me to send her a mental command, and I repeated it for ten minutes.

"Go at once to the dining-room ; you will take a book there that is on the mantelpiece ; you will take it up to my study, and you will sit in my armchair before my writing-table." I reached home at night. The next day, as soon as I saw M., and even before saying good morning to me, she cried: "I did a clever thing yesterday. I must be losing my wits, I suppose ! Just imagine ! I came down without knowing why, opened the dining-room door, then went up to your study, and sat in your armchair. I moved your papers about, then I went back to my work."

The command had then been understood; but she did not go into the dining-room, and she did not take the book from there.

J. H. P.

(*Annales des Sci. Psych.*, May-June 1893.)

Transference of Simple Sensations.

We may now pass to experiments in the transference of simple impressions of the same kind as those dealt with in Chapters II. and III. The following is a record of a series of trials in the transference of auditory impressions :—

No. 33.—From Miss X.

Miss X. is a lady resident in London, who is known personally to the present writer and other members of the S.P.R. She has experienced all her life frequent interchange of telepathic impressions with some of her friends. At the request of Mr. F. W. H. Myers, Miss X. and a friend D., also living in London, throughout the year 1888, with the exception of three months during which they were living in the same house, kept diaries in which any incident or feeling which might seem to be telepathically connected with the other was recorded. The ladies during a great part of the time saw each other constantly, and compared notes of their experience. In D.'s diary for the year there are thirty-five entries of the kind, of which twenty are believed to have been recorded before it was known whether or not there was any actual event to correspond with the impression. Of the twenty entries fourteen refer to hearing music played by Miss X., and two to reading books at, as D. believed, her telepathic instigation.

The entries in D.'s diary are given in italics. The degree of correspondence with the entries in Miss X.'s diary is indicated in the words included between brackets.[1]

(1) *Jan. 6th. Tried several books . . . finally took to "Villette."*

---

[1] Miss X.'s notes have been in some cases slightly abbreviated, in order to save space. Full details of the experiments will be found in *Proc. S.P.R.*, vol. vi. pp. 377-397.

(From Miss X.'s diary it appears that she willed D. to read *The Professor*, also by Charlotte Brontë.)

(2) *Jan. 23rd. Sonnets, E.B.B.* 10.30 P.M.
(In Miss X.'s diary, written at about 10 P.M., appears the entry, " Sonnets viii.-ix., E.B.B.")

(3) *March 6th. Hellers*, 7.30. (*i.e.*, D. had an impression of hearing Miss X. playing. Miss X. states that she was actually playing Hellers at the time, but there is no note in her diary of the fact.)

(4) *March 7th. Beethoven waltzes*, 10. (Correct—recorded in X.'s diary after seeing D.'s entry.)

(5) *March 8th. No practice.* (*i.e.*, X., contrary to her custom, was not playing at this hour: correct.)

(6) *March 9th. Music* 7.30-8. (Correct.)

(7) *March 10th. ?Music* 9.30-10 A.M. (Correct. Miss X. had told D. that she would be out at that hour, and had subsequently changed her plans, so that the music was unexpected to D., hence the note of interrogation.)

(8) *March 13th.* 7.40. *Music.* (Correct.)

(9) *March 14th.* 9.30 A.M. [Music.] *Evening of same day. Nothing but organs and bands, popular airs and Mikado. ?Flash of Henselt* 9 (P.M.)

(10) *March 15th.* 9-10. *?Faint Henselt.*
(Miss X. writes :—" I remember that when D. showed me these entries I was specially interested. I was practising at the time some music of Henselt's she had never heard, and was playing this on all five occasions. D. notes it on the first three vaguely as ' Music,' something which she did not recognise. On the 14th I played it over to her, and afterwards she recognised it imperfectly. I was practising it for her, knowing she would like it, so that she was much in my mind at the time.")

The following entries were made whilst D. and X. were in different and distant counties :—

(11) *August 15th. Hellers*, 9.10-25. (Correct.)

(12) *August 17th. Slumber Song*, 7.35-50. (Correct. D. wrote of her two experiences, and X. read the letter aloud to her hostess, who remembered that X. had actually played the music named above at the time referred to.)

(13) *September 14th. Hallé*, 9 A.M. (Incorrect. X. was not playing.)

(14) *November 18th. Chopin Dead March, War March Athalie*, 7.15-8 P.M.

(15) *November 25th. Lieder*, 7.30.

(16) *November 26th. Lied, never gets finished.* 5.15-20.
(Miss X. writes :—" On each of the above three occasions D.

asked me next day what I had played and found she was right. My playing of the Lied on November 26th was interrupted by the arrival of visitors, and the unfinished air naturally haunted me. D. writes:—On the day in question H. and I were together. I said to her that I could hear you [Miss X.] playing—a Lied we both associated with you—but that you never got beyond a certain part, which seemed to be repeated. H. replied, 'It is strange you should say that. I can't *hear* her, but I have been seeing her at the piano for some minutes.' H. corroborates this.")

It will thus be seen that in these 16 cases there were only two instances (1 and 13) in which D.'s impression failed to correspond with the facts. The remaining four entries (out of 20 recorded before-hand) relate to impressions which also appear to have corresponded with the event, but the degree of correspondence is more difficult to estimate.

In Miss X.'s own diary there are 55 entries during this period, of which 27 were made before the event was known. Of these 3 are failures, and in two other cases it is doubtful whether the impression was actually telepathic, or whether the coincidence should not be attributed to accident. In the other 22 cases of correspondence, presumably telepathic, Miss X. was sometimes the agent, sometimes the percipient. The impressions relate to events of various kinds, such as meeting particular persons, receiving letters, and playing music. Of the veridical impressions four were visual and one was a dream.[1]

No. 34.—From M. J. CH. ROUX.

The following record is taken from a paper by M. Jean Charles Roux, medical student, published in the *Annales des Sciences Psychiques* (vol. iii. pp. 202, 203). These experiments in thought-transference at a distance were preceded by a series of fairly successful trials with playing-cards at close quarters, and by some other experiments designed to test clairvoyance.

[1] Miss X. kindly submitted her diaries for inspection to Mrs. Sidgwick, who has carefully examined them.

Third Series: Experiments at a distance.

Lemaire is in his room, I in mine, with two rooms intervening. At an hour previously fixed on, I suggest a card to him.

Date.	Card thought of.	Card guessed.
(1) Mar. 15, 1892...	4 hearts...	red, hearts; low number, five
(2) ,, 18, ,, ...	10 hearts...	3 diamonds
(3) ,, 27, ,, ...	6 spades...	6 clubs
(4) ,, ,, ,, ...Kg. diamonds...		Knave diamonds
(5) ,, ,, ,, ...ace diamonds...		5 clubs
	(Agent had failed to concentrate his attention.)	
(6) ,, ,, ,, ...Queen spades...		King spades
(7) ,, ,, ,, ...	4 clubs...	6 clubs
(8) Apr. 6, ,, ...	3 clubs...	5 clubs
(9) ,, ,, ...	2 spades...	2 spades

Fourth Series.

The account of the following six trials at a distance in space and time, which are imperfectly recorded in the *Annales*, is taken from a letter received from M. Roux, dated the 19th December 1893 :—

(10) Paris, 2nd April.—Lemaire having gone out I drew a card from the pack, the 9 *Hearts*, and tried to transfer it to him. Then I wrote a note to the following effect : "Guess the card that I am thinking of as I write these words," and left it on the table. A few minutes after Lemaire entered and guessed the 7 *Hearts*.

(11) 3rd April.—Lemaire was out. I drew a card from the pack, the ace *Hearts*, and tried to transfer it to him. As on the previous day, I left a note on the table and went out immediately. When I came back at midnight I found a line from Lemaire saying he had guessed the ace *Hearts*.

The four other experiments took place in a country town, at Chateauroux. We lived about 500 or 600 yards apart.

(12) 13th April.—In the morning I saw Lemaire and said to him, "At 2 o'clock you must guess a card that I shall suggest to you." I went home, and at a quarter to twelve I drew from the pack the 5 *Hearts*. I saw Lemaire again in the evening. He had guessed the 6 *Hearts*. He was walking in the street with a friend. At about two minutes to 2 P.M. he looked at his watch, remembered the experiment, and immediately the idea of *Hearts* came to him. A few minutes later, when alone, he tried to guess the exact card, and decided on the 6 *Hearts*.

(13) 13th April.—I said to Lemaire that on the 14th April, at 9 A.M., he was to guess a card. After going home on the 13th April, at 10 P.M. I drew a card from the pack—4 *Clubs*. Next day, at 9 A.M., Lemaire guessed 2 *Clubs*.

(14) July 17th.—Lemaire was to guess a card at 9 o'clock. At 10 minutes to 9, from my house, I tried to transfer the 4 *Spades*. (I have forgotten to make a note of whether I merely thought of this card or whether I drew it from a pack.) At 9 o'clock Lemaire guessed 5 *Spades*.

(15) 30th July.—This experiment is more complicated but none the less interesting. On the 30th July, at 11 A.M., Lemaire was to guess a card which I had tried to suggest to him on the 26th July. This card was the *Knave Diamonds*. But he forgot to do it, and did not remember to guess the card till 7 P.M. on the 30th July. Now on this same day, the 30th July, from 6 to 6.30 P.M. I was myself engaged in guessing a card by clairvoyance, and after many attempts I decided on 7 *or* 8 *Clubs*, and Lemaire, guessing the card at 7 P.M., also decided upon 7 *Clubs*. So that I had suggested the card to him unconsciously.

Thus, omitting the last trial as of doubtful interpretation, we find that in 14 trials the card was guessed correctly twice, the number alone once, and the suit alone nine times, or three times the probable number.

Transference of Visual Impressions.

In the four cases which follow the impression was of a well-marked visual character; reaching, indeed, in the two last to the level of actual hallucination. It should be observed that in none of these four cases is the possibility of chance coincidence so entirely precluded as in many of the experiments at close quarters already cited. In the first of the cases recorded by Dr. Gibotteau (No. 40), and in some of Mr. Kirk's experiments (No. 37), the luminous patches seen by the percipients are not unlike rudimentary hallucinations of a sufficiently common type, and their resemblance in these instances to the objects actually looked at or thought of by the agents should not therefore be pressed very far. In the other cases, however, the percipient received a well-marked impression of a definite object. But here there is a flaw of another kind. The coincidences may have been due, as indeed Miss Campbell (No. 35) is careful to suggest, to a lucky shot on the part of the percipient at the object the agent would be likely to choose. The very distinct nature of the impression produced in each case upon the percipient, as contrasted with the vague images called up, *e.g.* in Miss Campbell's case, by more or less conscious conjecture, is, however, against this interpretation ; and the fact that in the first narrative the experiments quoted were the culmination of a successful series of experiments at close quarters tells in favour of a telepathic explanation for these also.

No. 35.—By MISS CAMPBELL and MISS DESPARD.

A series of experiments in thought-transference at close quarters had been carried on by the narrators at intervals from November 1891 to October 1892. In sending the account of these experiments at a distance, Miss Campbell explains that in the trial on October 25th, " there was first an auditory impression, as if some one had said the word 'gloves,' and then the gloves themselves were visualised."

(No. 1.)   "*June 22nd*, 1892.

"Arranged that R. C. Despard should, when at the School of Medicine in Handel Street, W.C., between 11.50 and 11.55, fix her attention upon some object which C. M. Campbell, at 77 Chesterton Road, W., is by thought-transference to discover."

PERCIPIENT'S ACCOUNT.

"Owing to an unexpected delay, instead of being quietly at home at 11.50 A.M., I was waiting for my train at Baker Street, and as just at that time trains were moving away from both platforms, and there was the usual bustle going on, I thought it hopeless to try on my part; but just while I was thinking this I felt a sort of mental pull-up, which made me feel sure that Miss Despard was fixing *her* attention, and directly after I felt 'my —compasses—no, scalpel,' seemed to see a flash of light as if on bright steel, and I thought of two scalpels, first with their points together, and then folding together into one; just then my train came up.

"I write this down before having seen Miss Despard, so am still in ignorance whether I am correct in my surmise, but as I know what Miss Despard would probably be doing at ten minutes to twelve, I feel that that knowledge may have suggested the thought to me—though this idea did not occur to me until just this minute, as I have written it down.

"C. M. CAMPBELL.

"77 Chesterton Road, W."

AGENT'S ACCOUNT.

"At ten minutes to twelve I concentrated my mind on an object that happened to be in front of me at the time—two scalpels, crossed with their points together—but in about five minutes, as it occurred to me that the knowledge that I was then at the School of Medicine might suggest a similar idea to Miss Campbell, I tried to bring up a country scene, of a brook running through a field, with a patch of yellow marsh marigolds in the foreground. This second idea made no impression on Miss Campbell—perhaps owing to the bustle around her at the time.

"R. C. DESPARD."

(No. 2.)   "*October 25th*, 1892.

"At 3.30 P.M. R. C. Despard is to fix her attention on some object, and C. M. Campbell, being in a different part of London, is by thought-transference to find out what that object is."

PERCIPIENT'S ACCOUNT.

"At 3.30 I was at home at 77 Chesterton Road, North Kensington, alone in the room.

"First my attention seemed to flit from one object to another while nothing definite stood out, but soon I saw a pair of gloves, which became more distinct till they appeared as a pair of baggy tan-coloured kid gloves, certainly a size larger than worn by either R. C. D. or myself, and not quite like any of ours in colour. After this I saw a train going out of a station (I had just returned from seeing some one off at Victoria), almost immediately obliterated by a picture of a bridge over a small river, but I felt that I was consciously thinking and left off the experiment, being unable to clear my mind sufficiently of outside things."

AGENT'S ACCOUNT.

"At 3.30 on October 25th I was at 30 Handel Street, Brunswick Square, W.C. C. M. C. and myself had arranged beforehand to make an experiment in thought-transference at that hour, I to try to transfer some object to her mind, the nature of which was entirely unspecified. I picked up a pair of rather old tan-coloured gloves—purposely not taking a pair of my own—and tried for about five minutes to concentrate my attention on them and the wish to transfer an impression of them to C. M. C.'s mind. After this I fixed my attention on a *window*, but felt my mind getting tired and therefore rather disturbed by the constant sound of omnibuses and waggons passing the open window.

"R. C. DESPARD.

"*October 25th*, 1892."

Miss Campbell writes later :—

"77 CHESTERTON ROAD, NORTH KENSINGTON, W.,
November 24th, 1892.

"With regard to the distant experiments, the notes sent to you were the only ones made. In the first experiment (scalpels) I wrote my account before Miss Despard's return, and when Miss Despard returned, before seeing what I had written [she] told me what she had thought of, and almost directly wrote it down.

"In the second experiment (gloves), I was just going to write my account when Miss Despard returned home, and she asked me at once, 'Well, what did I think of?' and I told her a pair of tan gloves—then sat down and wrote my account, and, when she read it through, she said, 'Yes, you have exactly described Miss M.'s gloves, which I was holding while I fixed my attention on them,' and then she wrote her account."

The next account is taken from the *Annales des Sciences Psychiques*, vol. iii. pp. 114-116. M. Hennique, the agent, had acted as agent in four experiments at a distance with another percipient in the previous year (*Annales*, vol. i. pp. 262-265). In the first the percipient saw vague lights, and finally a vase of flowers (very clear); the agent was looking at a lamp covered by a transparent shade, with a vase of flowers painted on it. In the second the percipient again saw vague lights, and then a luminous sphere; the agent was looking at the lamp globe placed on the table in full light. In the third, the percipient only saw brilliant lights, like stars or jewels; the agent was looking at the word *Dieu*, in big letters. In the fourth the percipient, to his astonishment, saw *nothing;*

the agent had willed him to see nothing. In each case the percipient's impression was recorded in writing before any communication was received from the agent. In the present case, it will be seen, the percipient received, not the impression which the agent wished to transfer, but the image of another object within the agent's field of vision, and which had entered his thoughts in connection with this very experiment.

No. 36.—From M. LEON HENNIQUE and M. D.

"On Friday, the 8th of July last, my friend Hennique and I made a further experiment in telepathy. Hennique was away from Paris, and separated from me by a distance of 171 kilomètres. At midnight I wrote to Hennique the following letter :—

"'PARIS, *July 8th*, 1892, *midnight*.

"'MY DEAR HENNIQUE,—A friend came unexpectedly to dinner. At 10.30, looking through the open window at the blue sky under the full moon, I thought all of a sudden of the experiment planned by us, of the telepathic meeting that we had fixed for eleven o'clock this evening, and my brain received at the same time the impression of a puppet. It seemed to me that you were trying to show me a little cardboard man fitted with strings to make his arms and legs move.

"'Reminded by this impression of my telepathic duty, I said good-night to my friend, and at eleven o'clock I waited, with my eyes closed, in the darkness of the dining-room. Nothing happened till twelve or fifteen minutes past eleven, when there appeared to me for an instant a small black silhouette, a Chinese shadow, as if you had cut out a little black figure and placed it in front of a light ; for the round part, which seemed to be its head, was surrounded by a bluish halo. It was mostly this little black sphere—which I thought was a head—that I saw ; the body I rather deduced than saw.   'D.'

"M. Hennique replied to me as follows :—

"'RIBEMONT (AISNÉ), *Sunday*, 10*th July* 1892.

"'MY DEAR FRIEND,—It was a bottle full of water, surmounted by its cut-glass stopper, a large stopper, very bright, that served for our experiment. But the most curious part of the affair is that about four inches from the bottle there was actually hanging on the wall a nigger-doll, of the kind which you describe, belonging to my daughter. Was it reflected on the crystal? A mystery ! For one second, but scarcely for a second, I had intended to telepathise the jumping-jack to you before choosing the water-bottle. It is certainly very odd !

"'LEON HENNIQUE.'

"M. Hennique added to this letter a water-colour drawing of the above-mentioned 'nigger-doll.' The head is a black circle, in which only the lips are red ; the arms and legs are black ; the chest is white, crossed with red ; arms, thighs, and legs are jointed, and can be worked by a string.

"I wrote to my friend to ask him if, at 10.30—that is to say, at the moment when I had conceived of a jumping-jack, he had not, on his part, thought at the same moment, of the same object. He answered me :—

"'RIBEMONT, 14th July 1892.

"'No; at 10.30 I was not thinking in the least of the jumping-jack; but, if I remember rightly, once or twice last year I wished to make use of it. It was only at the moment of choosing a simple object for the experiment that for an instant the idea of that little man came into my head; it was, you see, before beginning our experiment. This puppet was not four inches, but only two inches away from the water-bottle. There is something very curious in it, a physical or psychical effect, which I can't account for. The more so that this doll, *in cardboard mounted on strings*, is always fixed to the wall, above the table from which I am sending you my good wishes. It must have been about 9 o'clock, while tidying the before-mentioned table, that I had the idea of transmitting to you the image of the jumping-jack.

"'LEON HENNIQUE.'"

No. 37.—By MR. JOSEPH KIRK and MISS G.

During the year 1890 and onwards, Mr. Joseph Kirk, of 2 Ripon Villas, Plumstead, has carried on with a friend, Miss G., a series of experiments in thought-transference at a distance varying from 400 yards to about 200 miles. Some account of these experiments will be found in the *Journal of the S.P.R.* for February and July 1891 and January 1892. There are 22[1] trials in the transference of diagrams, etc., there recorded. The object looked at by Mr. Kirk was generally a square or oblong card, or a white disc with or without a picture, diagram, or letter on it. The object was always illuminated by a strong light.

[1] Excluding two in which the distance was only a few yards.

Notes of the experiments were in every case made independently in writing by agent and percipient. In each case, with the exception of two occasions (on which Mr. Kirk's notes record his anticipation of failure), the percipient saw luminous appearances, often taking the form of round or square patches of light, in correspondence with the shape of the surface looked at by the agent. When Miss G. was at Pembroke or Ilfracombe (Mr. Kirk remaining at Plumstead) the correspondence did not go beyond this; but in two or three cases, when Miss G. was also at Plumstead, at a distance of only 400 yards, the percipient appears to have seen some details of the diagram on the card, and in one instance a fairly accurate reproduction of the diagram was given. Mr. Kirk on this occasion, 5th June 1891, was trying to impress three percipients—of whom Miss G. was one —and used three diagrams, viz., a Maltese cross, a white oval plate with the figure 3 on it, and a full-sized drawing of a man's hand in black on white. Miss G.'s report is as follows :—

"5/6/91. Sat last night from 11.15 to 11.45. After a few minutes wavy clouds appeared [these are drawn as a group of roundish objects], followed by a pale bluish light very bright in centre. [This is drawn of an indefinite oval shape with roundish white spot in centre.] Near the end of experiment saw a larger luminous form, lasting only a moment but reappearing three or four times ; it had lines or spikes about half an inch wide darting from it in varied positions."

Appended are reproductions of Miss G.'s original drawings of her impression, which bear, it will be seen, a marked likeness to a man's hand.

 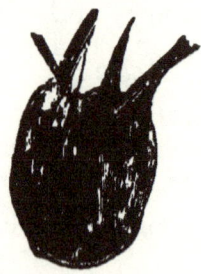

It should be added that Miss G. has not had any hallucinations of the kind except at times when Mr. Kirk was experimenting; and the amount of correspondence between her visions and the images which Mr. Kirk endeavoured to transfer would certainly seem beyond what chance could produce.

No. 38.—By MR. KIRK and MISS G.

A further series of seven trials with the same percipient in April-June 1892 produced some interesting results. Full notes of the experiments were, as in the previous cases, made by Mr. Kirk and Miss G. independently. Mr. Kirk wrote his notes immediately after the conclusion of the experiments, which were made late in the evening, at a time previously agreed upon. Miss G., who was in the dark, and as a rule in bed, wrote her notes on the following morning before hearing from Mr. Kirk. No diagrams were used in this series, "the object being," in Mr. Kirk's words, "to test the possibility of influencing the imagination, and inducing the percipient to visualise hallucinatory figures of persons or animals thought of by the agent." Miss G. knew only that diagrams would not be used. The distance between agent and percipient was about 400 yards.

In the first three trials (April 10th, 17th, and 24th, 1892) Mr. Kirk pictured to himself some ducks in a room, a witch, and other figures. On the 17th Miss G. saw at one time a small sunlike light, but with this exception she had no impression at all on any of the three occasions.

At the fourth trial (1st May) Miss G. records the same night that she saw "a broken circle ∪, then only patches of faint 'light, not cloudlike, but flat, which alternated with vertical streaks of pale light." Afterwards, however, she had another vision, which she thus records on the following morning before meeting Mr. Kirk:—

"Soon after lying down last night, I had a rapid but most realistic glimpse of Mr. Kirk leaning against his dining-room mantelpiece ; the room seemed brightly lighted, and he looked rather bothered, and just as I saw him he appeared to say, ' Doctor,[1] I haven't got my pipe.' This seems very absurd, the more so as I do not know whether Mr. Kirk ever smokes a pipe. I see him occasionally with a cigar or cigarette, but cannot remember ever seeing him with a pipe ; if I have, it must have been years ago. I do not know whether my eyes were open or closed, but the vividness of the impression quite startled me. This occurred just after the expiration of time appointed for experiment (10.45-11.15)."

Mr. Kirk reports in his account of the trial, written on the 1st May, that he tried to transfer an image of himself, sitting on a low chair, and also the part of the room facing him in the light of the lamp. But after seeing Miss G.'s report, he adds—

"The fact that I had another experiment to make [*i.e.*, after the trial with Miss G.] enables me to trace minutely my actions before beginning it. Immediately the time had expired with Miss G., I got up and rapidly lit the gas and three pieces of candle, which I had ready in the cardboard box-cover, to illuminate the diagram. The room was therefore brilliantly lighted. I now rested with my right shoulder against the mantelpiece, with my face towards Miss G., but with my eyes bent on the carpet. In this position I thought intensely of myself and the whole room, and feeling really anxious to make a success, for at least six minutes. By this time my shoulder was aching very much with the constrained attitude and the pressure on the mantelpiece, and I broke off, using words (talking to myself) very similar to those given by Miss G. What I muttered, as nearly as I can remember, was, '*Now*, Doctor, I'll get my pipe.' . . . Until within the last few weeks I have not smoked a pipe for many years, and I do not think it probable that Miss G. has ever seen me use one ; but it is an absolute certainty that she was not aware I had taken to smoke one recently."

In the fifth experiment of the series, made on the 9th May, the impression which appears to have been transferred was fortunately recorded beforehand. Mr. Kirk's report of that date, after describing an attempt to transfer an image of the room, and of an imaginary witch, runs as follows :—

[1] A familiar name given to Miss G. by Mr. and Mrs. Kirk.

"Continued to influence her some minutes after limit of time for experiment (11.30 P.M.). During this time I was much bothered by a subcurrent of thought, which I in vain strove to cast off. In the morning, just before time to get up, I had a vivid dream of my lost dog ('Laddie').[1] I dreamt he had returned, and that my wife, Miss G., and myself, made much of him. I thought of him all day, and tried to suppress the thought, fearing it would interfere with the success of experiment; feel worried and irritated at this, being really anxious to make an impression. Do not expect favourable result. Written same night.   "J. K."

Miss G.'s report is as follows :—

"Experiment last night (9-5-92) most unsatisfactory. Saw only a glow of light and once for a few seconds a figure [of a vase]. Some minutes after 11.30 (time for conclusion of experiment) it seemed as if the door of my room were open, and on the landing I saw a very large dog, moving as though it had just come upstairs. I cannot conceive what suggested this, nor can I understand why I thought of Laddie during time of experiment. I do not think we have mentioned him recently. My door was locked as usual.   "L. G."

The sixth experiment (15th May 1892) was, in the words of Mr. Kirk's contemporary report, "devoted to making hypnotic passes, done with great energy and concentration of mind. The passes were made, not only over Miss G.'s [imagined] face and arms, but specially over her hands," with the view of inducing hypnotic sleep.

Miss G. reports that she "fell asleep before the time arranged had expired. But it was only to awake again very soon, through dreaming I was in a basement room . . . making frantic efforts to strike a match, prevented doing so by some one behind clasping my wrists. The sensation was so unpleasantly real that it awoke me." The time fixed for the experiment had then passed. This was the only occasion in this series on which Miss G. went to sleep during an experiment.

[1] Mr. Kirk explains later that this dog had been lost six years before. They had all been much attached to him, and his loss was still an occasional topic of conversation and of dreams by Mr. Kirk.

In the seventh experiment (5th June 1892) Mr. Kirk again made passes to send Miss G. to sleep. Miss G., on her side, saw only something " like the varied but regular movements one sees in turning a kaleido-scope, only without the colouring; it was simply luminous, and lasted more or less distinctly from 15 to 20 minutes." This impression may conceivably have been due, as Mr. Kirk suggests, to the regular movements of his hands in making the hypnotic passes.

In estimating the value of the coincidences between Mr. Kirk's thought and Miss G.'s impressions in the fourth and fifth trials, it should not be overlooked that the percipient's impressions were not vague images, such as are wont to crowd through our minds on the near approach of sleep, but clear-cut visions, approximating to visual hallucinations.

No. 39.—By MR. KIRK and MISS PRICKETT.

Mr. Kirk conducted another short series of experi-ments in March 1892, with Miss L. M. Prickett, the distance between agent and percipient being about twelve miles. The results are given below. It is to be noted that the percipient's impressions in this series seem generally to have been deferred. But in weighing the amount of correspondence between the diagrams and the percipient's reproductions, it should be observed that of the four diagrams employed, three were reproduced with substantial accuracy, and in their chronological order ; and that even on the second and third evenings the per-cipient's impressions—rectilinear figures inscribed in a circle—bore a general resemblance to the diagram actually selected. It is perhaps unfortunate that three out of the four diagrams included circles or figures akin to circles, but as the percipient had not seen any of the diagrams beforehand, this circumstance does not in any way invalidate the results, though it weakens the argument against chance-coincidence.

No. of Experiment.	Date and Hour.	Diagram looked at by Agent.	Impression received by Percipient.	Percipient's Remarks.
1	Tuesday, 1st March, 1892. 10.30 to 11.0 P.M. White circle with blue border, about 7 in. diam.—cross in centre blue.			"No result whatever."
2	Friday, 4th March, 1892. 10.30 to 11.0 P.M.	Agent did not experiment. Percipient sat, in ignorance of agent's intentions.		Percipient wrote, "Saw particularly one clear circle, at first all light, but after a little a dark centre, with a V, or triangle on it; * * * one or two flakes in the shape of bright crescents." Drew rough diagrams accordingly.
3	Tuesday, 8th March, 1892. 10.30 to 11.0 P.M.			Drew a figure like a capital E inscribed in a circle; also one other form with circular lines, "all very indistinct."

No. of Experiment.	Date and Hour.	Diagram looked at by Agent.	Impression received by Percipient.	Percipient's Remarks.
4	Friday, 11th March, 1892. 10.30 to 11.0 P.M.	Spots painted in blue on raised disc of whitening on white cardboard about 14" x 12".		Drew first a, then b ; "then several times I saw your eyes, and that was all." Later on percipient sent diagram c. "These spots represent what I called in my letter your eyes ; not two, for there appeared more." [b, it will be observed, is a reproduction of the diagram looked at by the agent on the 1st and 8th March.]
5	Tuesday, 15th March, 1892. 10.30 to 11.0 P.M.	In blue on white, about 4½" in longer diam. In blue on white about 4" high.		Was unable to sit.
6	Friday, 18th March, 1892. 10.30 to 11.0 P.M.	Was unable to experiment.		"Knowing you were not sitting, I tried to reproduce what you intended on Tuesday [15th inst.] with the result shown here." [The first figure, it will be seen, is a partial reproduction of 8.]

Mr. Kirk has conducted several other series of experiments in the transfer of diagrams and ideas and in the induction of hypnotic sleep at a distance, with Miss G., Miss Porter, of 16 Russell Square, Mr. F. W. Hayes, and others. In one case the percipient was at Cambridge, a distance of more than fifty miles from Plumstead. The results in nearly all these cases raise a certain presumption of thought-transference, though the presumption is in most cases—owing partly to the conditions of the experiments—not so strong as in the two series last quoted. It is to be remarked that the series of experiments between Plumstead and Cambridge were perhaps the least successful of any, a result which may perhaps be attributed partly to the distance, partly to the fact that the agent and percipient were not personally acquainted.

It should be recorded that Mr. Kirk is strongly of opinion, as the result of a careful analysis of the experiments conducted by him, that telepathy, in these cases at any rate, operates as a rule subconsciously, and that we ought to be prepared to find the most striking proofs of its action in such undesigned coincidences as are quoted in Nos. 4 and 5 of the second series with Miss G.

No. 40.—From Dr. Gibotteau.

Dr. Gibotteau, in the year 1888, made the acquaintance, at a *crèche* in connection with a Paris hospital, of a peasant woman named Bertha J. Bertha was a good hypnotic, and Dr. Gibotteau succeeded on many occasions in inducing sleep at a distance. But Bertha claimed also to have the power of influencing others telepathically—a power which in her case seems to have been hereditary, as her mother had a reputation for sorcery. Bertha professed to be able, by the exercise of her will, to cause persons to stumble, or to lose their way, or to prevent them from proceeding in any given direction. She gave Dr. Gibotteau several illustrations of these powers, and he believes her pretensions to be well founded (*Annales des Sciences Psychiques*, vol. ii. pp. 253-267, and pp. 317-337). The following instances of hallucinatory effects of a more ordinary kind are taken from the same paper. In the last case, it will be observed, the experience was collective. In none of the three cases were the percipients aware of Bertha's intention to experiment. It will be seen that in the second case she succeeded in producing the emotional effect desired, though the imaginary object by which she intended to inspire terror was hardly of a kind calculated to frighten a hospital surgeon. Dr. Gibotteau writes :—

"I am a good sleeper, and I do not remember ever waking of my own accord in the middle of my sleep. One night, about 2 or 3 o'clock, I was abruptly awoke. With my eyes still shut I thought, 'This is one of B.'s tricks. What is she going to make me see?' I then looked at the opposite wall; I saw a circular luminous spot, and in the centre a brilliant object, about the size of a melon, that I stared at for several seconds, being wide awake, before it disappeared. I could not distinguish any form clearly, nor any detail, but the object was round, and parts of it appeared to be less luminous. I imagined that she had wished to show me a skull, but I could not recognise it ; the wall was lighted up in that place as if by a strong lamp; the room was not completely dark, because the window had outside blinds, and the curtains were drawn back ; but this brilliant object did not seem to give out any light beyond the area of which it occupied the centre on the wall. That was all. I waited a moment without seeing anything else, then I went fast asleep again. The next day I found Bertha, who had come to visit the hospital, and I questioned her cautiously. She had tried to show me first of all some dogs round my bed, then some men quarrelling, and finally a lantern. That was all. It will be seen that though the first two attempts failed, the third succeeded perfectly.

"After that, Bertha very often tried to hallucinate me; but I have never either seen or heard anything.

"I was more sensible to transmissions of a vague and general character. I have written elsewhere of illusions of the sense of space : I had a complete illusion of this kind, and P. a very curious commencement of an hallucination. I have also described the causeless terror that Bertha could inspire.

"Here is another account of a fright. One evening I was entering my house, at midnight. On the landing, as I was putting my hand on the door-handle, I said to myself, 'What a nuisance! here is another of B.'s tricks! She is going to make me see something terrifying in the passage; it is very disagreeable.' I was really a bit nervous. I opened the door suddenly, with my eyes shut, and seized a match; in a few minutes I was in bed, and, blowing out my candle, I put my head under the bed-clothes, like a child. The next day Bertha asked me if I had not seen a skeleton in the passage or in my room, and been very much frightened. It need hardly be said that a skeleton was the last thing in the world that could frighten me; and frankly, I think that I am not more of a coward than the common run of men."

On another occasion Dr. Gibotteau was in the company of a friend, M. P. They had just parted from Bertha.

"After having deposited B. near her home, we went back to the Latin Quarter with the carriage. On reaching the Rue de Vaugirard, before the gate of the Luxembourg, I felt myself seized by a terror intense as it was absurd. The street was admirably lighted, there was not a single passer-by, and the Quarter at that hour (just about midnight) is perfectly safe. Moreover, this fright did not seem to depend on any cause. It was fear just for fear. 'It is absurd,' said I, 'I am frightened, very much frightened; it is certainly a trick of B.'s.' My friend laughed at me, and almost immediately, 'Why, it is taking hold of me also. I am trembling with fear. It is very disagreeable.' The impression lasted until we were in front of the gate of the Luxembourg Palace; we got out of the carriage at the corner of the Rue Soufflot and the Boulevard Saint-Michel. As soon as we set foot on the ground: 'Look,' said P., 'don't you see something white floating in the air, there, just in front of our eyes; it has gone.' I saw nothing, but I felt very strongly the *influence* of B.

"The next day I met her at the hospital. 'Well! you saw nothing?' I begged her to tell me what we ought to have seen. This was her answer: 'First, your driver lost his way— oh! not you, you felt nothing; he took you by all sorts of queer ways.' It is a fact that our carriage, from the Rue de Babylone, had gone by a very complicated way, and one which, at the time, did not seem to me the right one, but I should not like to say anything definite about it. 'After that you were frightened.' (Which of us?) 'You at first, M. P. afterwards.

Oh, yes! afraid of nothing at all, without any reason, but you were very frightened. Then you saw some white pigeons flying round you, quite near.' I had never heard her speak of this hallucination. As to the fright, that subject was familiar to her, and she has frightened me several times, deliberately, as I have related."

CHAPTER VI.

GENERAL CRITICISM OF THE EVIDENCE FOR SPONTANEOUS THOUGHT-TRANSFERENCE.

IF the reader has been able to accept my estimate of the evidence brought forward in the preceding chapters, the possibility of the transmission of ideas and sensations, otherwise than through the known channels of the senses, must be held to be proved by the experiments there recorded. That proof can be impugned only on the ground that the precautions taken against communication between agent and percipient by normal means were insufficient. For if the precautions are admitted to have been sufficient, there can be no question that the results were not due to chance. It is not necessary here to enter into nice calculations of the probabilities. If, for instance, the odds in favour of some other cause than chance for the results recorded on pp. 66-69 were to be expressed in figures, the total sum would compete with or outstrip the stupendous ciphers employed by the astronomer to denote the distance of Sirius, or the weight of the Sun. But the kind of evidence now to be considered—the coincidence of some spontaneous affection of the percipient with some event in the life-history of the person presumed to be the agent, as when one sees the apparition of a friend at the time of his death—is of inferior cogency in two ways. The coincidences are neither so numerous nor so exact; and the risk of error in the record is far greater. On the one hand, therefore, there is a greater probability that the percipient's affection, even if correctly described, was unconnected with the state of the person supposed to be the agent ; on the other hand we have, in most cases, less assurance that the description given of his experience is in its essential features accurate.   The part played by coincident hallucination in the question of telepathy may be illustrated from another branch of scientific inquiry.   For some years the "Germ Theory" rested mainly on observations of the distribution of certain diseases, their periodic character and their mode of propagation and development ; phenomena which, though sufficiently striking, are not in themselves susceptible of exact interpretation.   It was not until the minute organisms, whose existence had been so long suspected, had been actually isolated in the laboratory, and had been proved capable of repro-ducing the disease, that the connection of certain maladies with the presence of certain microbes in the body became, from a plausible hypothesis, an accepted conclusion of Science.   So here it is important to bear in mind that dreams, visions, and apparitions, however captivating to the imagination, do not form the main argument for believing in some new mode of communication between human minds.   If all the cases of the kind hitherto recorded could be shown one by one to be explicable by more familiar causes,— though the result would indeed be to add a remark-able chapter to the history of human error ; though it would be a singular paradox that so many intelli-gent witnesses should have been so mistaken, and with such undesigned unanimity ; and that a whole class of alleged phenomena should have sprung up without any substantial basis,—the grounds for the belief in telepathy would not be seriously affected ; we should merely have to modify our conceptions of its nature, and restrict its boundaries.   But in fact there is no reason to anticipate so lame a conclusion. The incidents, of which examples will be adduced in the succeeding chapters, though their value will be differently estimated by different minds, are yet in their aggregate not such as can plausibly be attributed to misrepresentation or chance coincidence. And, first, it is important to note that the cases must be considered in the aggregate. Separately, no doubt, each particular case is susceptible of more or less adequate explanation by some well-known cause; and in the last resort it would be unreasonable to stake the credit of any single witness, however eminent, against what Hume would call the uniform experience of mankind. But as a matter of fact the experience of mankind is not uniform in this matter; and when we are forced by the mere accumulation of testimony to go on adding one strained and improbable explanation to another, and to assume at last an epidemic of misrepresentation, perhaps even an organised conspiracy of falsehood, a point is at length reached in which the sum of improbabilities involved in the negation of thought-transference must outweigh the single improbability of a new mode of mental affection. If to any reader that point should seem not yet to have been reached— and the position could scarcely be held an unreasonable one—I would remind him that the cases quoted in this book form but a small part of the evidence so far accumulated; and I would ask that he should reserve his judgment until he has studied the whole of the evidence recorded in *Phantasms of the Living*, in the *Proceedings* of the American Society for Psychical Research, the scattered cases appearing from time to time in the pages of various English and Continental periodicals dealing with this subject, and the ever-growing mass of testimony printed in the *Proceedings* and *Journal* of the Society for Psychical Research in this country.[1] He will then perhaps be prepared to

[1] Of the *Proceedings* of the S.P.R., published by Kegan Paul, Trench, Trübner, & Co., three or four parts are published yearly. The *Journal*, which appears monthly, contains a record of recent cases of interest, unaccompanied, for the most part, by any critical com-

endorse the verdict of a shrewd and genial critic on the evidence presented in *Phantasms of the Living*, viz., that it "can only be rejected as a whole by one who is prepared to repeat at his leisure what David is reported to have said in his haste."[1]

It is of course not possible with our present knowledge to estimate with any precision the probabilities for the coincidence by chance of such a vision as that recorded by Dr. Dupré (No. 47), or such a dream as Mr. Hamilton's (No. 58), with the event represented. Neither the nature of the percipient's impression in these and similar cases, nor the event to which the impression corresponds, are sufficiently well defined to admit of any numerical argument being based upon them. We can only recognise that whilst dreams and mind's-eye pictures are not very uncommon experiences, dreams and visions which faithfully reflect external events of an unlikely kind occur, if rarely, with sufficient frequency to give us pause. The common sense which in such cases leads us to infer a connection between the event and the corresponding mental experience is our only guide. But one large class of our spontaneous evidences is susceptible of more exact treatment. Sensory hallucinations are affections at once well marked and unusual. If we can ascertain their relative frequency it is possible to calculate with more or less exactness the probabilities of the coincidence by chance with some definite event. Such a calculation has been attempted in Chapter IX. with regard to hallucina-

mentary, and is privately printed for circulation amongst members and associates of the Society. Any reader, however, desirous of studying the subject may procure any number of the *Journal* referred to in this book on application at the Rooms of the S.P.R., 19 Buckingham St., Adelphi, W.C. Of the foreign periodicals referred to in the text, perhaps the most important is the *Annales des Sciences Psychiques*, edited by Dr. Dariex, and published by Germer Baillière et Cie., Paris. Cases of interest are also to be found in *Sphinx*, a German periodical, to be obtained through Kegan Paul & Co.; in the *Revue Spirite* (Paris: 24 Rue des Petits-Champs); and elsewhere.

[1] Professor C. Lloyd Morgan in *Mind*, 1887, p. 282.

tions of a certain well-defined type coinciding with the death of the person represented. The conclusion there reached is that such coincidences are far too numerous to be ascribed to chance. This part of the evidence cannot therefore be summarily dismissed, as suggested by more than one recent critic, on the plea that hallucinations which coincide with a death may be set off against hallucinations which occur without any coincidence, and both alike be regarded as purely subjective and without significance. Our own estimate of the probabilities is, of course, provisional, and may ultimately prove to be wide of the mark. But, meanwhile, it is at least proof against assault by conjectural statistics or the *obiter dicta* of amateur psychologists.

But in fact the criticism commonly made is not that, happening as described, visions and hallucinations happened by chance; but that they did not happen as described. This objection deserves careful consideration. It must, I think, be admitted that a proportion, perhaps a large proportion, even of the cases obtained at first-hand are so far inaccurate as to have comparatively small value for scientific purposes; and of the residue, in which the central fact of an unusual subjective experience on the part of the percipient and its coincidence with some external event is fairly well established, it is possible that the details are frequently—and where the record is not made until some years after the event,· generally— untrustworthy. In order to estimate the nature and probable extent of these defects, it is proposed briefly to pass in review the various kinds of error to which testimony is liable, and to note their bearings on the question at issue.

Errors of Observation.

Errors of observation are here of very little importance. The thing to be observed is, of course, the

percipient's own sensations. In subsequent conversation he may exaggerate the exceptional nature
of the impression ; but he can hardly make a mistake
at the time in observing what is purely subjective.
If a man calls green what we call red, we may
conclude that he is colour-blind ; and if he asserts
that he sees a human figure where we see none, that
he is hallucinated ; but in neither case have we
warrant for saying that he is making an erroneous
statement about his own sensations.

Errors of Inference.

But his interpretation of what he sees is a different matter. Not indeed that the mistake commonly
made of taking a hallucination at the time for a figure
of flesh and blood, and subsequently for a hypothetical
entity of another kind, directly affects the percipient's
testimony. So long as the witness accurately describes what he saw, it matters little whether he
believes in telepathic hallucinations, or in black magic,
ghosts, or the Himalayan Brothers. But there are
one or two errors of inference of sufficient importance to deserve notice.

A real figure seen under exceptional circumstances
may at the time or in the light of subsequent events
be regarded as a hallucination. Such a mistake is, as
a rule, possible only out of doors ; and the commonest
form of it is when a figure is seen by the percipient
resembling some friend believed to be at a distance,
or in circumstances which make it difficult to suppose
that the figure was of flesh and blood. A curious
instance came under my notice recently. It was
reported to me that a lady had seen in a certain provincial town the ghost of a friend at about the time
of her death. The figure, accompanied by another
figure, was seen in broad daylight at a distance of
a few feet only ; it was clearly recognised, and the
proof of its non-reality lay in the complete absence of

recognition in return. It was subsequently ascertained that the friend in question had actually been present in the flesh, with a companion, at the spot where the figures were seen, but that for sufficient reasons she desired to avoid recognition. Her death within a few days of the encounter was merely an odd coincidence.

Another kind of erroneous inference is worth noting. Cases are not infrequently quoted, as presumably telepathic, of a dream or vision embodying information demonstrably not within the conscious knowledge of the percipient. The inference that he cannot have obtained the information by normal means is clearly unsound, unless it can be shown that it was impossible for the information to have been received unconsciously. For it is well established that intelligence, even of events closely affecting the percipient, may enter through the external organs of sense and lie latent for days before emerging into consciousness. It is obvious that, for instance, many of the cases quoted in which an invalid became aware of news (*e.g.*, of the death of a relative) which had been studiously withheld from him by those around may be thus explained. Whispers heard in sleep, or hints unconsciously received, may have betrayed the secret.[1]

Errors of Narration.

Of much greater importance than errors of observation or inference are those due to defects either in narration or memory. Deliberate deception amongst educated persons is no doubt comparatively rare, though it would perhaps be unwise to hold out any

---

[1] See the case recorded by Miss X. (*Proc. S.P.R.*, vol. v. pp. 507, 508). In this instance Miss X. saw in the crystal a notice of a friend's death in the form of an extract from the obituary column of the *Times*, in which journal she had almost certainly seen the news, without perceiving it, the day before. There is a dream recorded in *Phantasms of the Living*, vol. ii. pp. 687, 688, which may probably be explained as the emergence in dream of intelligence unconsciously received a few hours before.

pecuniary inducement for the production of evidence.
But there are those, like Colonel Capadose in Mr.
Henry James' story *The Liar*, who tell ghost stories
for art's sake, and on a slender basis of fact build up
a large superstructure of fiction. And there are many
more who, with a natural and almost pardonable
desire to appear as the hero, or at least the *raconteur*,
of a good story, or from the mere love of the marvellous, allow themselves to exaggerate the coincidences,
adjust the dates, elaborate the details, or otherwise
improve the too bare facts of an actual experience.
This kind of embellishment, however, is probably
more frequent in second-hand accounts, where the
narrator speaks with less sense of responsibility, and,
it may be added, of reality.

Again, a common form of inaccuracy is to quote as
the experience of a friend one of those weird stories
which are passed on from mouth to mouth in ordinary
society—the inconvertible currency of psychical research. We all know these old friends—at a distance,
for no one has ever succeeded in making their nearer
acquaintance. There is the ghost at No. 50 B——
Square; the driver of the dream-hearse, recognised a
year later in a lift, which fell straightway, with all its
passengers, to the bottom of the hotel; the Form
which accompanies the priest, or Quaker, or godly
merchant to save him from robbery on his lonely
nocturnal journeyings; the young lady who took part
in some *tableaux vivants* whilst her body was lying
cold in death—and all the rest of the phantom throng.
Only a few months ago I heard one of them—it was
the ghost of the lift—from the son of a doctor, who
assured me that the incident occurred to one of his
father's patients, and gave me the name of the foreign
hotel which had been the scene of the disaster.[1]

[1] I have before me as I write one case of the kind which will serve as
a sample. A told us the story, and induced B to write to us about it.
B informed us that he heard it from his brother C, a F.R.S., who had
received it from D, to whom it was told by E, who had it from the lips

Sometimes a story is improved by the narrator that it may the better serve for instruction and edification. This tendency is especially liable to distort the evidence in cases connected with death. It must be remembered that though we may view a coincident hallucination, for instance, as merely an instance of an idea transferred from a *living* mind, to the percipient it frequently represents the spirit of the dead. From a certain class of witnesses the account of such an incident is as little to be trusted as the text of an apocryphal gospel. It inevitably becomes a *Tendenzschrift*, which reflects not the facts as they occurred, but the narrator's conception of what the facts ought to have been.

It is not necessary to dwell on these sources of error, for they are probably apparent to all; and to give illustrative cases would be superfluous, and perhaps invidious. But it is important to observe that stories so improved, whether from a desire to reinforce some theological tenet, or from the mere love of sensation, are apt to betray their origin in many different ways. Narrators of this kind rarely content themselves with the finer touches; the added ornaments are apt to be gross and palpable; the "spirit" will be made to speak words of warning or comfort; to intimate his testamentary dispositions; or even—in somewhat bolder flight of fancy —to leave a solid memento behind him. Now the authentic phantom is seldom either dramatic or edifying.

of F, "who was a visitor at the house where the occurrence took place." We wrote to D, who referred us to two sources of information, G and H. G wrote in reply to our letter that he heard the story from a stranger at a dinner-party "about three years ago," and promised further inquiries. H referred us to J and K. Our letter to K was answered by his cousin L, who wrote that she had heard it from M, "who got it from some one who was present," and further inquiries were again promised. It is needless to add that in cases of this kind the story, like a will-o'-the-wisp, ever recedes as we advance, until it ends with the nameless stranger at some dinner long since gone "away in the Ewigkeit."

Errors of Memory.

More insidious and more difficult to guard against are errors of memory. There is a natural and almost inevitable tendency to dramatic unity and completeness which leads to the unconscious suppression of some details, and the insertion of others. Probably of all errors due to this cause a nice adjustment of the dates is the commonest. In perhaps the majority of second-hand cases, and in some of the more remote first-hand narratives, the coincidence is said to be exact to the minute. *"At that very moment my friend passed away"* is a common phrase. As a matter of fact, in the best attested recent cases it can rarely be shown that the coincidence is precise, and the impression frequently follows the death by some hours. But there is risk also of the actual transformation of the experience itself. A dream after the lapse of years will be recalled as a hallucination,[1] a vague feeling of discomfort as a vivid emotion, or even a mental vision; a hallucination not recognised at the moment will in the retrospect seem to have been identified with some person who died at about that time; and details, such as clothes worn or words spoken by the phantom, will be borrowed from later knowledge and read back into the image preserved in the memory. There will further be a gradual simplifying and rounding off of the incident, a deepening of the main lines, and a suppression of what is not obviously relevant or coherent. With many persons there can be no doubt that this process is almost, if not wholly, unconscious; and it need hardly be said that in that very fact lies the special danger against which we have to guard.[2]

[1] There is, as Mr. Gurney has pointed out, a converse error to be guarded against—viz., the gradual effacement of the lines of an impression, so that an actual waking hallucination has in some instances come to be regarded, after a long interval, as only a dream.

[2] A good illustration of this kind of embellishment, in a case recorded at second-hand, will be found in the footnote on a case in Chapter XII.

As an instance of the gradual approximation of dates, I may cite a case recorded in the *Proceedings of the American S.P.R.* (pp. 401, 527). The narrator wrote to Dr. Hodgson :—" I once dreamed that W. T. H. was dead ; and the same night he was thrown down several feet on to an engine, . . , when he was taken up it was thought he was dead." From later inquiries it was ascertained that the accident did indeed occur as alleged—but a week or ten days after the dream !¹ As an illustration of a different kind of metamorphosis, a case may be given which I recently received from a lady and her daughter—an account of a " ghost " seen twenty-five years ago by the latter and her nurse. The younger lady described to me the figure seen ; the mother told me that she had received a similar description from both nurse and daughter at the time of the incident. Both ladies were clear-headed and sensible witnesses, and it was impossible to doubt that they believed what they said. But in her childish diary, which the younger lady kindly unearthed for my inspection, the only entry referring to the matter—an entry written in pencil and obviously as an afterthought—ran : " Ellen saw a ghost." If the diarist had herself shared the experience, it is difficult to believe that even the modesty natural to her age and sex would have withheld her from recording the fact for her private glorification.

It would be easy to multiply cases of this kind. But those who demand most proof of the action of telepathy will probably be least exacting of evidence for the untrustworthiness of ancient memories. As a matter of fact, we have the evidence of statistics to

---

¹ So in a case given in the *Annales des Sciences Psychiques*, vol. ii. pp. 5-10, we have an extract from the log-book of the *Jacques-Gabriel*, which records that the captain, mate, and another man when at sea heard, on the 17th July 1852, the sound of a woman's voice crying. In a marginal note on the log-book the captain adds that on reaching port they learnt of the death of the mate's wife, " *on the same day and at the same hour.*" But the official register shows that the death took place on the 16*th June* 1852.

show that the imagination does tend after a certain lapse of time to magnify coincidences in matters of this kind, and even to invent coincidences where none existed. It will be shown in Chapter IX., in the discussion on the results obtained from an inquiry into the distribution of sensory hallucinations, that whereas non-coincidental hallucinations tend to be forgotten after the passing of a few years, the records of coincidental hallucinations—or at least of those which are alleged to have coincided with the death of the person seen—are proportionately more frequent ten years ago than at the present time, the inference being that a certain number of coincidences have been unconsciously improved or invented in the interval.

Pseudo-presentiment.

In a letter published in *Mind* (April 1888) Professor Royce, of Harvard, U.S.A., hazarded a hypothesis that there may occur "instantaneous and irresistible hallucinations of memory which make it seem to one that something which now excites or astonishes him has been prefigured in a recent dream, or in the form of some other warning." In support of that hypothesis Professor Royce appeals to the analogy of the well-known cases of double memory,—the impression of having at some previous time looked on a scene now present, or heard a conversation now taking place; and to two or three instances of undoubted hallucination of memory amongst the insane, recorded by Krafft-Ebing and Kraepelin. As regards the latter, it is sufficient to remark that the hallucinations occurred to persons whose minds were admittedly diseased; that the hallucinations themselves were apparently slow of growth, whereas the hypothesis requires that they should be more or less instantaneous; and that in other respects they do not present by any means a perfect parallel to the presumably telepathic cases with which he compares them. In default, therefore, of more precise analogies, the hypothesis of pseudo-presentiment must be regarded as, at best, a plausible guess. And even if it were fully substantiated it would only, as pointed out by Mr. Gurney (*Mind*, July 1888), apply to certain classes of telepathic cases, and those the weakest from the evidential standpoint. At most the theory would account for dreams and indefinite impressions of various kinds not mentioned beforehand. In some cases of this kind, and in a large class of so-called " prophetic " dreams, I am inclined to regard Mr. Royce's explanation as possibly true, in the modified form suggested by Dr. Hodgson (*Proc. American S.P.R.*, pp. 540 *et seq.*)—*i.e.*, if it is restricted to cases where there is a vague memory of some actual dream or other impression, bearing a more or less remote resemblance to the event; in other words, if we assume an illusion rather than a hallucination of memory. But it need hardly be said that no serious investigator would treat the uncorroborated accounts of dreams and vague feelings of this kind as evidence for anything whatever. To extend the hypothesis, as Professor Royce suggests, to cases where there is evidence that the percipient's experience was mentioned beforehand, is to suppose not one kind of pseudo-memory, but two,—a pseudo-memory on the part of the percipient that he has had a certain subjective experience, and a pseudo-memory on the part of some other person that this experience was mentioned to him before the news of the event to which it related. In recent cases, at any rate, the assumption of a double mistake of this kind seems unwarranted.[1] And to apply this explanation to

---

[1] That such a pseudo-memory on the part of a person not professing to be the actual percipient is possible after a long interval appears to be shown by the account just cited of the " ghost " seen by the nurse in a foreign hotel. But we have no evidence that a memory hallucination of this kind could be, as demanded by the theory, of instantaneous or very rapid growth ; or that any verbal suggestion could intercalate a false picture into a series of still recent and unimpaired memories.

cases of actual sense-hallucination involves even more violent improbabilities. It would require far more evidence than Professor Royce can offer to make it credible that a man on hearing of the death of a friend should straightway be capable of imagining that at a definite hour and in a particular place he had seen an apparition of that friend, when in fact he had had no experience of the kind. It is remarkable that Mr. Royce does not himself appear to have realised the distinction between the two kinds of impressions.

Precautions against Error.

We have now to consider by what methods the various defects incident to testimony on these matters may be best eliminated. As the evidence upon which reliance is placed will be illustrated by the examples quoted hereafter, it will not be necessary to dwell at length here upon the precautions taken. The testimony at first-hand of the actual witnesses, it need hardly be said, is to be desired in any investigation; but in the case of phenomena which are at once stimulating to the imagination, and, as being novel, have no recognised standard of probability by which narrator or auditor can check deviations from the truth, no other evidence is worthy of consideration.[1] It will be seen that in all the cases here quoted the witness, or one of the witnesses, has furnished an account of his experience written by himself;[2] and it

---

[1] Second-hand narratives have, however, a value of their own, as shown later; for by taking note of the features which occur commonly in such cases, but are absent from the best attested first-hand narratives, we obtain a valuable standard of comparison by which to check aberrations of memory.

[2] An apparent exception to this statement will be found in Nos. 45 and 46, Chapter VII., and elsewhere, where the account is furnished not by the actual percipient, but by a person to whom the percipient related his experience before he knew of its correspondence with fact. The evidence in such cases, it should be pointed out, is as good as first-hand; indeed, where, as in Nos. 45 and 46, the actual percipient was illiterate and the narrator educated, it may be regarded as better than first-hand.

is worth noting that the very act of writing such an account to serve the purpose of a systematic inquiry is calculated to inspire the percipient with a sense of responsibility, and to lead him to weigh his words with precision. I may add that by the courtesy of our informants we have in most cases been enabled to question them orally on the details of their experience.[1]

But, for reasons already given, no case should be suffered to rest upon a single memory. It is of the highest importance, therefore, to obtain the corroborative testimony of persons who were cognisant of the occurrence of the impression before the news of the corresponding event. When this is not to be obtained, evidence of some unusual action on the part of the percipient, such as the taking of a journey, or the putting on of mourning, may be accepted as collateral proof of the reality of his impression. But, as we have already seen, the evidence of the attesting witnesses is liable to the same errors which affect the testimony of the percipient; and the evidence most to be desired is of a kind exempt from these weaknesses—that of a letter or memorandum written before the news. In a large proportion of the narratives dealt with, it is asserted that such a letter was written, or such a memorandum made. Unfortunately, this alleged documentary evidence is rarely forthcoming. It is possible that in some cases this statement is merely a conventional dramatic tag,—an addition made unconsciously and in perfect good faith to round off the story.[2] It cannot, however, I

---

[1] This part of the work has been undertaken in this country by Professor and Mrs. Sidgwick, Mr. E. Gurney, Mr. F. W. H. Myers, myself, and others; in America, chiefly by Professor Royce and Dr. Hodgson.

[2] In the *Times* of the 6th January 1893 there appeared a letter from a well-known writer, narrating how in 1851 he had received a description of the sea-serpent from a lady who had watched its movements for some half-hour in a small bay on the coast of Sutherlandshire. So far the story is on a par with any of our own second-hand ghost stories. But

think, be regarded as surprising either that a letter or note was not written at the time, or that, if written, it should not have been preserved. Sensory hallucinations—to take the most striking instance—though unusual are not extremely rare experiences; most educated persons are perfectly familiar with the fact of their occurrence and regard them (in most cases rightly) as purely subjective, the products of some transient cerebral disturbance, as little worthy of record as a headache or a bilious attack. Often, probably, the telepathic hallucination is indistinguishable from the mass of purely subjective experiences of the same kind; and even should it be recognised at the time as exceptional, the want of leisure, the fear of ridicule, even the dislike of seeming to admit to himself the possibility of his experience having a sinister significance, would probably deter the percipient from writing about it.[1] It is much more likely that he would speak of it to an intimate friend, should opportunity occur. And when in the rare conjunction of an exceptional experience, adequate leisure, and a sympathetic correspondent, or the habit of writing a diary, the letter is actually written or the note made, the chances which militate against its preservation are many. Few persons will take a general and impersonal (in other words, a scientific) interest in occurrences of this kind. Their own isolated experience may possess a deep and abiding interest for themselves, and, less certainly, for their friends; an interest, however, which is quite compatible with the treatment of the attesting record as waste paper. But unless it can be used to illustrate or support a theory of a future life, they seldom regard

the writer goes on to say that the serpent had rubbed off some of its scales on the rocks; that a few of these scales, of the size and shape of scallop-shells, were for some years in his own possession, but that when he searched amongst his curios, in order to show these scales to Professor Owen, they were not to be found. The humble investigators of the S.P.R. have occasionally found themselves in the same position as the illustrious anatomist.

[1] See, for example, the case quoted in Chapter X., No. 63.

a " ghost story " as having any value other than that
derived from the personal environment. It appears,
indeed, to possess for most little more significance
than the recital of an extraordinary run of luck at
cards, or a fortunate escape from a railway accident,
between which it is commonly sandwiched. Again,
few persons realise the high value of contemporary
documentary evidence in matters of the kind ; there
are many who would probably share the views of
a courteous correspondent, who, after sending me
condensed copies of some contemporary memoranda,
wrote in answer to my inquiries :—" I have not got
the originals ; I destroyed them immediately I sent
them (*i.e.*, the copies) to you, because I knew they
would be more permanently preserved and · recorded ; being authenticated to Professor Barrett and
you, there was no further need of them." And
even when they escape immediate destruction the
letters may, as in cases reported to us, be "washed out"
or burnt ; or may survive the perils of flood and fire
only to be mislaid, so that they cannot be found without
a more thorough search than the courtesy of our correspondents can induce them to make. Notwithstanding
these various adverse chances, it will be found that
many of the narratives which follow are actually
attested by contemporary documentary evidence.

When the great mass of narratives has been carefully examined and tested in the light of the considerations above set forth, and when all those which
are remote in date, or for some other reason suspect,
have been eliminated, there will be found to remain
an important body of testimony. And of this sifted
residue, though we cannot predicate of any single
narrative that it accurately represents the facts, or
that the coincidence with which it deals was not
purely casual, yet looking at the cases as a whole, we
may feel a reasonable assurance that in their essential
features the facts are correctly reported, and that the
coincidences are not due to chance.

I may conclude this chapter by calling attention to an argument of a different kind, on which Mr. Gurney,[1] in reviewing the material amassed chiefly in this country, laid considerable stress, and in which he has been followed by an independent observer, Professor Royce, dealing with narratives received from correspondents in America.[2] Both these investigators have pointed out, and probably all who make an equally careful and dispassionate study of the evidence will agree with them, that the phenomena vouched for in the best-attested narratives form a true natural group. They are manifestly not the products of folk-lore, nor of popular superstition, nor of the mere love of the marvellous. They are singularly free from the more sensational and bizarre features—dramatic gestures or speech on the part of the phantasms, prophetic warnings, movement of objects, etc.—which are conspicuous in second-hand narratives. If these accounts were purely fictitious, it would be difficult to conceive by what process, coming from persons of widely separated social grades, of various degrees of education, and of different nationalities, they could have been moulded to present such strong internal resemblances; resemblances consisting not merely in the possession of many common features, but in the absence of others which, by their frequent occurrence in admittedly fictitious accounts, are proved to be the natural fruits of the unrestrained imagination. This undesigned unanimity is strong evidence that the restraint operating throughout has been the restraint of fidelity to fact, and that the narratives themselves owe little to the imagination, and much to their reflection of genuine experience.

[1] *Phantasms of the Living*, vol. i. pp. 164-166.
[2] *Proceedings American S.P.R.*, pp. 350, 351.

CHAPTER VII.

TRANSFERENCE OF IDEAS AND EMOTIONS.

BEFORE proceeding to give examples of the evidence for spontaneous thought-transference, it may be well to repeat something of what has been said in the preceding chapter. In the first place, the narratives quoted in this book are offered as samples only of the evidence of this kind actually accumulated. No single narrative can afford to stand alone. Each contains one or more elements of weakness ; and in the last resort chance coincidence, memory-hallucination, or even deliberate deception would be *in any single case* a more probable explanation than a new mode of mental affection. It is only, to borrow Mr. Gurney's metaphor, as a faggot, and not as a bundle of separate sticks, that the evidence can finally be judged. But, in the second place, it is not claimed that the evidence reviewed even in its entirety is by itself sufficient to demonstrate the possibility of the affection of one mind by another at a distance. The main proof of such affection is based on the experiments already described, to which the spontaneous evidence so far adduced must be regarded as illustrative and in some degree auxiliary.

It will be more convenient, as a matter of arrangement, that the spontaneous experiences first considered should be those which resemble most closely the results of direct experiment, though this classification has the disadvantage of placing in the forefront cases of the least definite and striking kind; cases, that is, which are most readily explicable as due to chance coincidence. It is on all grounds, therefore, expedient that the reader should reserve his final verdict until he has the whole case before him.

In the present chapter there will be adduced instances of the spontaneous transference of (1) simple sensations; (2) ideas and mental pictures; (3) emotional states; (4) impulses tending to action. The first two classes, and in some measure the last, resemble the results described in the first five chapters of this book; for the third probably no direct experimental parallel can be offered, for the sufficient reason that vivid and intense emotion cannot be evoked at will.

Transference of Simple Sensations.

We will begin by quoting two instances of the transference of simple sensation. The first we owe to the kindness of Mr. Ruskin. The percipient was Mrs. Severn, wife of the well-known landscape painter.

No. 41.—From MRS. ARTHUR SEVERN.

"BRANTWOOD, CONISTON,
October 27th, 1883.

" I woke up with a start, feeling I had had a hard blow on my mouth, and with a distinct sense that I had been cut and was bleeding under my upper lip, and seized my pocket-handkerchief, and held it (in a little pushed lump) to the part, as I sat up in bed, and after a few seconds, when I removed it, I was astonished not to see any blood, and only then realised it was impossible anything could have struck me there, as I lay fast asleep in bed, and so I thought it was only a dream !—but I looked at my watch, and saw it was seven, and finding Arthur (my husband) was not in the room, I concluded (rightly) that he must have gone out on the lake for an early sail, as it was so fine.

" I then fell asleep. At breakfast (half-past nine), Arthur came in rather late, and I noticed he rather purposely sat farther away from me than usual, and every now and then put his pocket-handkerchief furtively up to his lip, in the very way I had done. I said, 'Arthur, why are you doing that?' and added a little anxiously, 'I know you've hurt yourself! but I'll tell you why afterwards.' He said, 'Well, when I was sailing, a sudden squall came, throwing the tiller suddenly round, and it struck me a bad blow in the·mouth, under the upper lip, and it has been bleeding a good deal and won't stop.' I then said, 'Have you any idea what o'clock it was when it happened?' and he answered, 'It must have been about seven.'

"I then told what had happened to *me*, much to *his* surprise, and all who were with us at breakfast.

"It happened here about three years ago at Brantwood, to me.

"JOAN R. SEVERN."

Mr. Severn wrote to us on the 15th November 1883, giving an account of the trivial accident described by the percipient, and adding that after leaving the boat he

"walked up to the house, anxious of course to hide as much as possible what had happened to my mouth, and getting another handkerchief walked into the breakfast-room, and managed to say something about having been out early. In an instant my wife said, 'You don't mean to say you have hurt your mouth?' or words to that effect. I then explained what had happened, and was surprised to see some extra interest on her face, and still more surprised when she told me she had started out of her sleep thinking she had received a blow on the mouth! and that it was a few minutes past seven o'clock, and wondered if my accident had happened at the same time; but as I had no watch with me I couldn't tell, though, on comparing notes, it certainly looked as if it had been about the same time.

"ARTHUR SEVERN."

(Phantasms of the Living, vol. i. pp. 188, 189.)

So far as I know, this is a unique instance, if we limit ourselves to first-hand evidence, of the spontaneous transference of a sensation of pain to a waking percipient.[1] Impressions of the kind, indeed, unless more definite and intense than the analogy of experiment gives us warrant for anticipating, would

---

[1] Two other examples are referred to in *Phantasms*, vol. i. p. 189, but in neither case is the evidence obtainable at first-hand.

as a rule be quickly forgotten, or would be naturally ascribed to some other source than telepathy. We owe the record of the present instance to the fortunate chance that the agent and percipient met within an hour of the occurrence, and that the pain of the percipient, though slight, was not such as could be readily attributed to ordinary causes. In the next instance, also, where the impression belonged to a different sense, the agent and percipient were in the habit of meeting almost daily, otherwise it seems possible that the coincidence would have escaped notice.

No. 42.—From MISS X.

The percipient was Miss X.; the agent was her friend D., already referred to, who writes :—

"April 13th, 1888.

"In the spring of 1881, in the evening after dinner, I accidentally set fire to the curtains of a sitting-room, and put myself and several others into some danger. The next morning, on visiting X., I heard from her that she had been disturbed overnight by an unaccountable smell of fire, which she could not trace, but which seemed to follow her wherever she went. I was led to discover the fire, and so probably to save the house, by what seemed a chance thought of X. I had left the room, unconscious of anything wrong, and had settled to my work elsewhere, when I suddenly remembered I had not put away some papers I had been looking at, and which I had thought might wait for daylight, but a strong feeling that X. would insist upon order, had she been there, induced me to go back, when I found the whole place in flames."

Miss X., in describing the case, adds : " I took considerable trouble to ascertain the cause (of the smell of fire), and was quieted only by the assurance that it was imperceptible to the rest of the household." (*Proc. S.P.R.*, vol. vi. p. 367.)

When we leave these simple modes of feeling, and consider the affections of the higher senses of hearing and sight, we are confronted with a new problem.

Sensations of the first class are almost purely homo-
geneous, they owe little or nothing to memory and
imagination. Moreover, though generally due to an
external cause, they are in the case of smell or taste
occasionally, and in that of pain frequently, excited
by causes within the organism. It is not, therefore, a
matter calling for comment that in such cases the
transferred idea should assume a definitely sensory
form. But when the organs of sight or hearing are
sensibly affected, past experience has taught us to
look for an external cause; the line between *idea* and
sensation is here sharply drawn and clearly understood.[1] The line, indeed, as drawn by common use
may not correspond to any real distinction in the
nature of the experience itself. Ideas may be only
paler sensations, and a train of thought nothing else
than a series of suppressed hallucinations. But at
any rate the distinction, whether fundamental or not,
serves a useful purpose as a rough-and-ready means
of classing our mental experiences. A visual or
auditory image either is on the same level of intensity
as the series of impressions which represent for us
the external world, or it falls below that level. In
the former case we call it a sensation or percept, in
the latter, an idea. Sensations and percepts may be
again subdivided, as objective or hallucinatory, according as they do or do not correspond to a supposed
material cause. In the experiments described in the
first five chapters, it will have been observed that
when the transferred impression was of a visual
nature it generally remained ideal, rising occasionally,
however, as in some of the experiments with hypnotised percipients, and in Mr. Kirk's cases, to the level
of a complete sensory hallucination or quasi-percept.
In the present chapter it is proposed to deal with
auditory and visual phantasms which, so far as can

[1] Except, of course, in cases of rudimentary hallucinations, such as
after-images and bright spots in the eyes and singing in the ears, which
are caused by the physical condition of the external organ.

be judged, were of an ideal kind, though one or two of the cases cited may seem to approximate to sensory embodiment. The more striking hallucinatory effects will be reserved for later chapters.

Transference of Ideas.

There is one kind of coincidence, so common as to have passed into a proverb, which is often referred to as illustrating the action of telepathy; that is, the idea of a person coming into the mind shortly before the person himself actually approaches. In most of the cases cited the coincidence is too indefinite to call for attention, as it is obvious that the narrator has not taken the elementary precaution of noting the "misses" as well as the "hits." But if telepathy acts at all, there is no *à priori* unlikelihood of its acting in this direction as well as in others, and it is to be desired that persons who believe themselves susceptible to impressions of the kind would keep a full record of their occurrence. Two instances which happened in his own recent experience are recorded by Professor Richet (*Proceedings S.P.R.*, vol. v. p. 52). Leaving such cases, however, as too indefinite to have much evidential value, we may quote the following as an example of an impression of a more detailed kind.

No. 43.—From MISS X.

On the 12th October 1891, Miss X. wrote to Mr. Myers as follows:—

". . . I was much upset yesterday by the consciousness that a Master B. (son of A. B.) had arrived unexpectedly upon the scene . . . no nurse—doctor three miles off—husband away. Being Sunday, I could not telegraph, but the news as to hour and sex arrived this morning. My impression was at 2.30 onwards. He arrived at 3.30, and in the interval I heard her voice over and over again calling my name. All is well now, but these impressions are not always comfortable."

In a later letter Miss X. writes:—

"A.'s own account is that (about two, I think), when she was made aware of her danger, the thought passed through her mind how fortunate it was that the impossibility of telegraphing would prevent anxiety at home, and then—that any way *I* should know. No one expected to have any cause for anxiety for at least a week. Yes; I ought to have sent to Mrs. Sidgwick, but I was so wretchedly ill that—don't shudder—I never at the time even *thought* of the S.P.R. I had been dreadfully worried all that week, and was utterly worn out."

The coincidence is, no doubt, not of the strongest kind. But in estimating its value it should not be overlooked that the impression was sufficiently intense to produce a decided feeling of discomfort. And though Miss X. unfortunately omitted to send an account of her experience until after she had learnt of its partial correspondence with the event, she did not know at the time when the first letter was written that her impression was correct as regards the details of the absence of husband and nurse. Whatever the value of the coincidence, therefore, it seems clear that the account owes nothing to exaggeration or unconscious reading back of details. With this may be compared a narrative sent to me in December 1891, by the Rev. A. Sloman, Master of Birkenhead School. On the 12th of the month, whilst Mrs. Sloman was absent at a concert, a chimney in the school-house had caught fire, and Mr. Sloman had been summoned from his work to give directions for dealing with the mischief. On the matter being mentioned to Mrs. Sloman on her return, she at once explained that during the concert, just about the actual time of the fire, "I suddenly began to think what you would do if the house took fire, and I distinctly pictured you going into the kitchen and speaking about a wet blanket." The account was written down and signed by both Mr. and Mrs. Sloman on the day of the occurrence, and the coincidence in time between event and impression seems to be well established. It must be admitted that the apprehension of fire may not improbably have a more or less permanent place in the background of a housewife's consciousness; still, even a slight outbreak of fire is not in an ordinary household a matter of common occurrence.

The next case is interesting as presenting evidence of the transference of an auditory impression. The account was originally published in the *Spectator* of June 24th, 1882:—

No. 44.—From MRS. BARBER.

"FERNDENE, ABBEYDALE, near SHEFFIELD,
June 22nd, 1882.

"I had one day been spending the morning in shopping, and returned by train just in time to sit down with my children to our early family dinner. My youngest child—a sensitive, quick-witted little maiden of two years and six weeks old—was one of the circle. Dinner had just commenced, when I suddenly recollected an incident in my morning's experience which I had intended to tell her, and I looked at the child with the full intention of saying, 'Mother saw a big black dog in a shop, with curly hair,' catching her eyes in mine, as I paused an instant before speaking. Just then something called off my attention, *and the sentence was not uttered.* What was my amazement, about two minutes afterwards, to hear my little lady announce, 'Mother saw a big dog in a shop.' I gasped. 'Yes, I did!' I answered; 'but how did you know?' 'With funny hair,' she added, quite calmly, and ignoring my question. 'What colour was it, Evelyn?' said one of her elder brothers; 'was it black?' She said, 'Yes.'"

I called on Mrs. Barber in the spring of 1886, and heard full details of the incident from herself and Mr. Barber, who, though not himself present at the time, was conversant with the facts. The incident took place on January 6th, 1882, and Mrs. Barber allowed me to see the note-book in which the account (substantially reproduced in the *Spectator*) was written down on January 11th. Of course there is always the possibility in a case of this kind that the lips may have unconsciously begun to form the words, but in the present instance it seems unlikely that any indication of the kind would have escaped the notice of the others present at the table. Mrs. Barber has given us other accounts, extracted from her journal, of thought-transference, in which the same percipient was concerned. She writes on December 26th, 1886:—

"On Wednesday J. went to London, and on getting his breakfast at a little inn in C——, he found a 'blackclock' (*i.e.*, cockroach) floating in his coffee. He fished it out and supposed it was all right, but on pursuing the coffee he got one in his mouth! Next day, at breakfast, he said, 'What's the most horrible thing that could happen to any one at breakfast? I don't mean getting killed, or anything of that sort.' E. looked at him for a moment and said, 'To have a blackclock in your coffee!'

"She was asleep in bed when her father returned the night before, and they met at the breakfast-table for the first time the next morning, when the question was asked quite suddenly. When asked how she came to think of it, she said, 'I looked at the bacon-dish, and thought a blackclock in the bacon,—no, he would see that—it must have been in the coffee.'

"She has a special horror of 'blackclocks,' so the incident may merely have been one of the numerous instances of her unusually quick wit.

"CAROLINE BARBER."

Transference of Mental Pictures.

The next three narratives are interesting as illustrating three different stages in the externalisation of visual impressions. In the first case, which is quoted from the *Proceedings of the American S.P.R.* (pp. 444, 445), the impression seems to have been almost of the nature of an illusion—*i.e.*, the idea emerged into consciousness only when a somewhat similar image was presented to the external organ of vision.[1]

[1] See case No. 51, later; and compare Mr. Galton's observations in his lecture at the Royal Institution on "The Just Perceptible Difference" (reported in the *Times*, January 30th, 1893). Mr. Galton found that the ideal auditory impressions called up by reading the printed substance of a lecture enabled him to hear the lecturer's voice at a greater distance than when he had not the printed text before him; the ideal appears to have supplemented the real impression, as, in the case given in the text, the real reinforced the ideal.

No. 45.—From MR. HAYNES.

In a letter to Mr. Hodgson, Mr. Haynes writes :—

"BOSTON, *June* 25, 1887.

"The name of the prisoner alluded to has passed from my recollection. He belonged in East Boston, and was sentenced for life for an assault upon a woman. I think he was pardoned some years ago, but am not certain about it. He had but one child, a boy about five years old, who always came with his wife to visit him. He seemed very fond of the child, always held him in his arms during the visit, and showed a good deal of feeling at parting.

"The following is an account of the affair made at the time :—

"'The following very singular incident I can vouch for as having actually occurred. I refer to it, not to illustrate a supernatural or any other unusual agency, as I am a sceptic in such matters, but as a remarkable instance of hallucination or presentiment.

"'I received a message from the wife of one of our convicts, in prison for life, that their only child, a bright little boy five years old, was dead, he having accidentally fallen into the water and been drowned. I was requested to communicate to the father the death of the child, but not the cause, as the wife preferred to tell him herself when she should visit him a week or two later.

"'I sent for him to the guard-room, and after a few questions in regard to himself, I said I had some sad news for him. He quickly replied, "I know what it is, Mr. Warden; my boy is dead!" "How did you hear of it?" I asked. "Oh, I knew it was so; he was drowned, was he not, Mr. Warden?" "But who informed you of it?" I again asked. "No one," he replied. "How, then, did you know he was dead, and what makes you think he was drowned?" "Last Sunday," he said, "your little boy was in the chapel; he fell asleep, and you took him up and held him. As I looked up and caught sight of him lying in your arms, instantly the thought occurred to me that my boy was dead—drowned. In vain I tried to banish it from my mind, to think of something else, but could not; the tears came into my eyes, and it has been ringing in my ears ever since; and when you sent for me, my heart sunk within me, for I felt sure my fears were to be confirmed."

"'What made it more remarkable was the fact that the child was missed during the forenoon of that Sunday, but the body was not found for some days after.'

"The foregoing is copied from my journal, the entry made on the day of the interview, and I can assure you is strictly correct in every particular.

"GIDEON HAYNES."

In answer to inquiries as to the name and address of the percipient, Mr. Haynes writes :—

"His name was Timothy Cronan. He was pardoned in 1873 or 1874. Mr. Darling, the officer in the guard-room to-day, occupied the same position when I had the interview with Cronan. He was present, and remembers distinctly all the circumstances of the case, which were discussed by us at the time. Cronan served some ten or twelve years. . . . He has not been heard from at the prison since his discharge."

In this case it may perhaps be inferred, from the circumstances of its occurrence, that the impression was of a rudimentary visual character.

In the next case it seems clear that the percipient saw what she described, but the impression appears to have been of a purely inward nature.

No. 46.—From PROFESSOR RICHET.

"On Monday, July 2nd, 1888, after having passed all the day in my laboratory, I hypnotised Léonie at 8 P.M., and while she tried to make out a diagram concealed in an envelope I said to her quite suddenly: 'What has happened to M. Langlois?' Léonie knows M. Langlois from having seen him two or three times some time ago in my physiological laboratory, where he acts as my assistant. 'He has burnt himself,' Léonie replied. 'Good,' I said, 'and where has he burnt himself?' 'On the left hand. It is not fire: it is—— I don't know its name. Why does he not take care when he pours it out?' 'Of what colour,' I asked, 'is the stuff which he pours out?' 'It is not red, it is brown ; he has hurt himself very much—the skin puffed up directly.'

"Now, this description is admirably exact. At 4 P.M. that day M. Langlois had wished to pour some bromine into a bottle. He had done this clumsily, so that some of the bromine flowed on to his left hand, which held the funnel, and at once burnt him severely. Although he at once put his hand into water, wherever the bromine had touched it a blister was formed in a few seconds—a blister which one could not better describe than by saying, 'the skin puffed up.' I need not say that Léonie had not left my house, nor seen any one from my laboratory.

Of this I am *absolutely certain*, and I am certain that I had not mentioned the incident of the burn to any one. Moreover, this was the first time for nearly a year that M. Langlois had handled bromine, and when Léonie saw him six months before at the laboratory he was engaged in experiments of quite another kind." (*Proc. S.P.R.*, vol. vi. pp. 69, 70.)

In the next case the mental picture seems to have been much more vivid than the visions of distant familiar scenes, or faces, which most of us can summon up by an effort of will; in fact, the impression probably approached very nearly to a hallucination. It is noteworthy, however, that it did not apparently form part of the external order, but replaced it. We have no means therefore of measuring the degree of vividness.

No. 47.—From Dr. G. Dupré.

"REIMS, *July 6th*, 1891.

"One day in May 1890, I had just been visiting a patient, and was coming downstairs, when suddenly I had the impression that my little girl of four years old had fallen down the stone stairs of my house, and hurt herself.

"Then gradually after the first impression, as though a curtain which hid the sight from me were slowly drawn back, I saw my child lying at the foot of the stairs, with her chin bleeding, but I had no impression of hearing her cries.

"The vision was blotted out suddenly, but the memory of it remained with me. I took note of the hour—10.30 A.M.—and continued my professional rounds.

"When I got home I much astonished my family by giving a description of the accident, and naming the hour when it occurred.

"The circumstance made a great impression on me, and my memory of it is quite clear.

"Dr. G. Dupré."

In a further letter Dr. Dupré adds :—

"REIMS, *August 2nd*, 1891.

"The account which I have given you is exact in every point. Madame Dupré remembers it perfectly. As I had a great many visits to pay that day I did not return home at once, but continued my rounds. I took particular note of the time, however, and it was found to be exact.

"This phenomenon of perception seemed to me so curious that I noted all the particulars, in order to analyse them at my leisure.

"When I got home my first words were these, addressed to my wife, 'Loulou is hurt. Is it serious?' Madame Dupré exclaimed, 'Who told you?' 'No one,' I replied; 'I saw her fall,' and then while examining my little girl I told my wife about the vision.

"I did not relate the circumstance to any one else but my father-in-law, Dr. Bracon, and he did not take it very seriously. Indeed, I was not inclined to lay much stress upon the matter either, as I did not wish to be considered visionary or credulous."

Madame Dupré writes:—

"*25th September* 1891.

"My husband's account of his telepathic experience is perfectly correct. For my own part I was extremely surprised at the circumstances, for till then my attitude towards all questions of clairvoyance had been one of almost complete incredulity. Let me add, however, that my husband is of an excessively nervous temperament, and was liable to somnambulism in his youth. It is seldom that a night passes in which he does not talk in his sleep. It would be quite possible to hold a conversation with him for a few minutes whilst he is in this condition." (*Annales des Sciences Psychiques*, vol. i. pp. 324, 325.)

It seems permissible to conjecture that in this case Madame Dupré, as in the previous case Professor Richet, was the agent.

Transference of Emotion.

Sometimes the telepathic impulse appears to express itself in a vague feeling of alarm or distress. Of course, impressions of this sort, with no definite content, and not recognised at the time as having reference to any particular person, can do little to strengthen the proof of telepathy. But when it has been shown, by the mention of the experience beforehand, or by any unusual action consequent on its occurrence, that the emotion was unique in the history of the percipient, and when the coincidence with a serious crisis is clearly established, the telepathic explanation may be admitted as at least plausible. These conditions appeared to be fulfilled in the following case, which is quoted from the *Proceedings of the American S.P.R.* (pp. 474, 475).

No. 48.—From MR. F. H. KREBS.

The percipient in this case described his experience to Professor William James, of Harvard, who writes as follows :—

" Mr. Krebs (special student) stopped after the logic lesson of Friday, November 26, and told me the facts related in his narrative.

" I advised him to put them on paper, which he has thus done.

" His father is said by him to be too much injured to do any writing at present.

"WM. JAMES.

" *December* 1, 1886."

From MR. F. H. KREBS.

"On the afternoon of Wednesday, November 24, I was very uneasy, could not sit still, and wandered about the whole afternoon with little purpose. This uneasiness was unaccountable; but instead of wearing away it increased, and after returning to my room at about 6.45 it turned into positive fear. I fancied that there was some one continually behind me, and, although I turned my chair around several times, this feeling remained. At last I got up and went into my bedroom, looked under the bed and into the closet; finding nothing, I came back into the room and looked behind the curtains. Satisfied that there was nothing present to account for my fancy, I sat down again, when instantly the peculiar sensation recurred; and at last, finding it unbearable, I went down to a friend's room, where I remained the rest of the evening. To him I expressed my belief that this sensation was a warning sent to show me that some one of my family had been injured or killed.

"While in his room the peculiar sensation ceased, and, despite my nervousness, I was in no unusual state of mind ; but on returning to my room to go to bed it returned with renewed force. On the next day (the 25th), on coming to my grandfather's, I found out that the day before (the 24th), at a little past 12, my father had jumped from a moving train and been severely injured. While I do not think that this warning was direct enough to convince sceptics that I was warned of my father's mishap, I certainly consider that it is curious enough to demand attention. I have never before had the same peculiar sensation that there was some being besides myself in an apparently empty room, nor have I ever before been so frightened and startled at absolutely nothing.

"On questioning my father, he said that before the accident he was not thinking of me, but that at the very moment that it happened his whole family seemed to be before him, and he saw them as distinctly as if there.

"F. H. KREBS, JUN.

"*November* 29, 1886."

From MR. CHAUNCEY SMITH, JUN.

"I, the undersigned, distinctly remember that F. H. Krebs, Jun., came into my room November 24 and complained of being very nervous. I cannot remember exactly what he said, as I was studying at the time, and did not pay much attention to his talk.

"On the 25th he came into my room in the evening, and made a statement that his state the evening before was the consequence of an accident that happened to his father, and that he had the night before told me that he had received a warning of some accident to some one dear to him. This I did not contradict, because I consider that it is extremely probable that he said it, and that I did not, through inattention, notice it.

"CHAUNCEY SMITH, JUN."

The present case well illustrates the difficulties attendant on any efforts to procure reliable contemporary evidence for psychical events. Even when, as here, the percipient himself took the right course, from the standpoint of psychical research, his forethought was to a great extent frustrated by the shortcomings of his friend.

With this narrative may be compared three cases given in *Phantasms of the Living* (vol. i. pp. 280 *et seq.*) of the occurrence of exceptional distress to one twin at the time of the death of the other. Mr. Leveson Gower has sent us an account of a similar marked fit of depression, accompanied by "a vivid sense of the presence of death," which coincided with the quite sudden and unlooked-for death of a near relation, the late Lady Marion Alford. (*Journal S.P.R.*, May 1888.) Professor Tamburini records an analogous case. A lunatic died in the asylum at Reggio on the 21st May 1892. A letter of inquiry, dated the 22nd May, was received at the asylum from the husband, who had not previously written for more than a year; and it was ascertained that he was prompted to write the letter by a feeling of "great discomfort, as though some misfortune were about to befall him," experienced on the previous day, the day of the death.

No. 49.—From Dr N., of New York State.

The next case is specially interesting, because the emotion which was felt in the first instance was succeeded by a visual impression of a detailed kind. This case again comes to us from America (*Proc. Am. S.P.R.*, pp. 397-400). Dr. N., the percipient, writes to Professor Royce as follows:—

[Postmarked *Aug.* 16, 1886.]

" In the convalescence from a malarial fever during which great hyperæsthesia of brain had obtained, but no hallucinations or false perceptions, I was sitting alone in my room looking out of the window. My thoughts were of indifferent trivialities ; after a time my mind seemed to become absolutely vacant ; my eyes felt fixed, the air seemed to grow white. I could see objects about me, but it was a terrible effort of *will* to perceive anything. I then felt great and painful sense as of sympathy with some one suffering, who or where I did not know. After a little time I knew with whom, but how I knew I cannot tell ; for it seemed some time after this knowledge of personality that I saw distinctly, in my brain, *not* before my eyes, a large, square room, evidently in a hotel, and saw the person of whom I had been conscious, lying face downward on the bed in the throes of mental and physical anguish. I felt rather than heard sobs and grieving, and felt conscious of the nature of the grief subjectively ; its objective cause was not transmitted to me. Extreme exhaustion followed the experience, which lasted forty minutes intensely, and then very slowly wore away. Let me note :—

" 1st. I had not thought of the person for some time and there was no reminder in the room.

" 2nd. The experience was remembered with more vividness than that seen in the normal way, while the contrary is true of dreams.

"3rd. The natural order of perception was reversed, *i.e.*, the emotion came first, the sense of a personality second, the vision or perception of the person third.

"I should be glad to have a theory given of this reverse in the natural order of perception."

The agent, M., is well known to both Professor Royce and Dr. Hodgson. In the report it is stated that "there can be no doubt of his high character and general good judgment." He writes as follows :—

"BOSTON, *Nov.* 16*th*, 1886.

"Some years ago, perhaps eight or nine, while in a city of Rhode Island on business, my house being then, as now, in Boston, I received news which was most unexpected and distressing to me, affecting me so seriously that I retired to my room at the hotel, a large square room, and threw myself upon my bed, face downward, remaining there a long time in great mental distress. The acuteness of the feeling after a time abating, I left the room. I returned next day to Boston, and the day after that received a short letter from the person whose statement I enclose herewith, and dated at the town in Western New York, from which her enclosed letter comes. The note begged me to tell her without delay what was the matter with me 'on Friday, at 2 o'clock,'—the very day and hour when I was affected as I have described.

"This lady was a somewhat familiar acquaintance and friend, but I had not heard from her for many months previous to this note, and I do not know that any thought of her had come into my mind for a long time. I should still further add that the news which had so distressed me had not the slightest connection with her.

"I wrote at once, stating that she was right as to her impression (she said in her letter that she was sure I was in very great trouble at the time mentioned), and expressed my surprise at the whole affair.

"Twice since that time she has written to me, giving me some impression in regard to my condition or situation, both referring to cases of illness or suffering of some kind, and both times her impressions have proved correct enough to be considered remarkable, yet not so exact in detail or distinctness as the first time. I feel confident that I have her original letter, but have not been able to command the time necessary to find it.

"(Signed) M.

"P.S.—The three occurrences above detailed comprise all the experiences of this sort which I have had in my life."

12

Mr. M. has searched in vain for the original letter of Dr. N. referring to the incident. Two letters, however, referring to one of the later experiences mentioned by him have been found, and copies of them, made by Dr. Hodgson on June 6th, 1887, are given below.

(1.)

DR. N. to MR. M.

"DOCTOR'S OFFICE, *July* 24*th*,
(Year not given).

"If I don't hear from you to-morrow, I shall write you a letter! I am anxious about you.

"N."

(2.)

MR. M. to DR. N.

"BOSTON, *July* 26, 1883.

"What clairvoyant vision again told you of me Monday and Tuesday and Wednesday? Was it as vivid and real as the other time? It had, at least, a very closely related cause.

"It is past 1 A.M., but I will not go to bed till I have sent you a word. A letter will follow very soon. For two days I have been thinking of the way you wrote to me that time, and I should have written to you within twenty-four hours if I had not received the note from you. Please write to me as you proposed. This is only to tell you that I am alive and not ill, but tired, tired! Tell me of yourself. I have had a hard three months in the West, eighteen to twenty hours a day, scarce a respite— I am not ill; I am sure I am not, but I am *worked out*. I couldn't get to —— or write.

"I used the telegraph even with my sisters.

"I hope for a letter, and will surely send you one.

"Yours,

"M."

These letters, which apparently relate to the second of the three experiences mentioned by M., afford incidentally strong corroboration of the accuracy of the statements made as to the first and most remarkable experience.

Several instances have been already published

(*Phantasms of the Living,* vol. ii. pp. 365-370) of what appears to be telepathic affection, in which there was no apparent link to connect the agent and per-cipient. Thus intimation of the deaths of three dukes —Cambridge, Portland, and Wellington—was con-veyed to complete strangers. A similar impression is recorded (*Journal S.P.R.,* Nov. 1892) as affecting a stranger at the death of Lord Tennyson, and a somewhat similar instance is recorded (*Journal,* May 1892) in connection with the death of General the Hon. Sir Leicester Smyth. The Head-master of a Grammar School in Leicester saw in a vision the irrup-tion of water into the Thames Tunnel (*Phantasms, loc. cit.*). In all these cases, if we accept the incidents as telepathic, they recall, as Mr. Gurney remarks, "the Greek notion of φήμη, the Rumour which spreads from some unknown source, and far outstrips all known means of transport." The evidence so far adduced, however, is by no means sufficient to establish any such conclusion. But the following narrative, which comes from a lady well known to me, is worth con-sidering in this connection.

No. 50.—From MISS Y.

"PERTH, *19th January* 1890.

"One Sunday evening I was writing to my sister, in my own room, and a wild storm was raging round the house (in Perth). Suddenly an eerie feeling came over me, I could not keep my thoughts on my letter, ideas of death and disaster haunted me so persistently. It was a vague but intense feeling; a sudden ghastly realisation of human tragedy, with no 'where,' 'how,' or 'when' about it.

"I remember flying upstairs to seek refuge with my mother, and I remember her soothing voice saying, 'Nonsense, child,' when I insisted that I was sure '*lots* of people were dying.'

"We both thought it was a little nervous attack, and thought no more about it. But when we heard the news of the Tay Bridge disaster next day, we both noticed (we received the news separately from the maid when she came to wake us) that the time of the accident coincided with my strange experience of the evening before.

"We spoke of the 'coincidence' together, but did not attach much importance to it.

"I have never had any experience like it, before or since."

Mrs. Y., in a letter of the same date, corroborates her daughter's statement. Mrs. Y.'s account, it should be added, was written without previous consultation with Miss Y., and embodies her independent recollection of the incident.

"On the night of the Tay Bridge disaster A. was sitting alone in her room, when she suddenly came running upstairs to me, saying that she had heard shrieks in the air; that something dreadful must have happened, for the air seemed full of shrieks. She thought a great many people must be dying. Next morning the milk-boy told the servant that the Tay Bridge was down."

In a later letter, Miss Y. adds :—

"My mother says she cannot remember my having any other experience of the kind. It happened before 9 P.M., we think."

From the *Times* of December 29th, 1879 (Monday), it appears that the accident took place on the previous evening (28th). The Edinburgh train, due at Dundee at 7.15 P.M., crossed the bridge during a violent gale. It was duly signalled from the Fife side as having entered on the bridge for Dundee at 7.14. It was seen running along the rails, and then suddenly there was observed a flash of fire. The opinion was the train then left the rails and went over the bridge.

Motor Impulses.

Occasionally the telepathic impression manifests itself to consciousness as a monition or impulse to perform a certain action. There is no ground for thinking in such a case that the idea transferred from the agent has in itself any special impulsive quality. The impulse towards action is no doubt the result of the percipient's unconscious reasoning on the information supplied to him.

Sometimes the impulse to action, though strong, is vague and inarticulate. Thus Mrs. Hadselle, of Pittsfield, Mass., U.S.A., narrates (*Journal S.P.R.*, May

1891) that some years ago she experienced, when spending the evening with some friends, "a sudden and unaccountable desire to go home, accompanied by a dread and fear of something, I knew not what." She eventually yielded to her impulse, and at some inconvenience returned home, just in time to rescue her son, who was insensible through the smoke from a fire of wet sticks in his room. Professor Venturi (*Annales des Sci. Psy.*, vol. iii. pp. 331-333) relates that in July 1885, in obedience to an irresistible impulse, he made a sudden and quite unpremeditated journey from Pozzuoli to his home at Nocera, to find his child in serious danger from a sudden attack of croup. A case is recorded in the *Proc. Am. S.P.R.* (pp. 227, 228), in which a lady living in a Western State awoke in the night of January 30th-31st, 1886, with a strong feeling that her daughter in Washington was ill and needed her, and in the morning telegraphed to her son-in-law, offering to come at once. There had been no previous cause of anxiety on the mother's part, but as a matter of fact the daughter had been taken suddenly and seriously ill on that night. A letter and the telegram relating to the event have been preserved. In another case Lady de Vesci, in 1872, telegraphed on a sudden impulse from Ireland to a friend in Hong Kong. The telegram arrived less than twenty-four hours before the recipient's death, an event which Lady de Vesci had no reason to anticipate for some months (*Journal S.P.R.*, October 1891).

In another case, also recorded by Mrs. Hadselle (*loc. cit.*), the impulse took the form of a voice bidding her go to a certain town, where, as it appeared, an intimate friend stood in urgent need of her. The effect produced in this case was so strong that the percipient actually bought a fresh railway ticket and changed her route. In the following case the impulse found a more unusual mode of expression—viz., utterance on the part of the percipient.

No. 51.—From ARCHDEACON BRUCE.

"ST. WOOLOS' VICARAGE, NEWPORT,
MONMOUTHSHIRE, *July 6th,* 1892.

"On April 19th, Easter Tuesday, I went to Ebbw Vale to preach at the opening of a new iron church in Beaufort parish.

"I had arranged that Mrs. Bruce and my daughter should drive in the afternoon.

"The morning service and public luncheon over, I walked up to the Vicarage at Ebbw Vale to call on the Vicar. As I went there I heard the bell of the new church at Beaufort ringing for afternoon service at three. It had stopped some little time before I reached the Vicarage (of Ebbw Vale). The Vicar was out, and it struck me that I might get back to the Beaufort new church in time to hear some of the sermon before my train left (at 4.35). On my way back through Ebbw Vale, and not far from the bottom of the hill on which the Ebbw Vale Vicarage is placed, I saw over a provision shop one of those huge, staring Bovril advertisements—the familiar large ox-head. I had seen fifty of them before, but something fascinated me in connection with this particular one. I turned to it, and was moved to address it in these, my *ipsissima verba:* 'You ugly brute, don't stare at me like that: has some accident happened to the wife?' Just the faintest tinge of uneasiness passed through me as I spoke, but it vanished at once. This must have been as nearly as possible 3.20. I reached home at six to find the vet. in my stable-yard tending my poor horse, and Mrs. Bruce and my daughter in a condition of collapse in the house. The accident had happened—so Mrs. Bruce thinks—precisely at 3.30, but she is not confident of the moment. My own times I can fix precisely.

"I had no reason to fear any accident, as my coachman had driven them with the same horse frequently, and save a little freshness at starting, the horse was always quiet on the road, even to sluggishness. A most unusual occurrence set it off. A telegraph operator, at the top of a telegraph post, hauled up a long flashing coil of wire under the horse's nose. Any horse in the world, except the Troy horse, would have bolted under the circumstances.

"My wife's estimate of the precise time can only be taken as approximate. She saw the time when she got home, and took that as her zero, but the confusion and excitement of the walk home from the scene of the accident leaves room for doubt as to her power of settling the time accurately. The accident happened about 2¼ miles from home, and she was home by 4.10 ; but she was some time on the ground waiting until the horse was disengaged, etc.   "W. CONYBEARE BRUCE."

Archdeacon Bruce adds later :—

> "*May 20th*, 1893.
>
> " I think I stated the fact that the impression of danger to Mrs. Bruce was only momentary—it passed at once—and it was only when I heard of the accident that I recalled the impression. I did not therefore go home expecting to find that anything had happened. "W. CONYBEARE BRUCE."

Mrs. Bruce writes :—

> " The first thought that flashed across me as the accident happened was, ' What will W. say ?' My ruling idea then was to get home before my husband, so as to save him alarm."

The Rev. A. T. Fryer, to whom the incident was originally communicated by the percipient, ascertained independently from the Vicar of Ebbw Vale that the date of Archdeacon Bruce's visit to him was April 19th, 1892. It is worth noting that here, as in case 45, an external object appears to have acted as a *point de repère*, and to have thus aided in the development of the transferred idea. Another instance of a telepathic impulse leading to speech is to be found in the *Annales des Sciences Psychiques* (vol. i. p. 36). The Lady Superior of a convent was moved during the celebration of a service to pray for the safety of the children of a neighbour—a visitor to the convent—who was somewhat startled by the Superior's abrupt action. It subsequently appeared that at about the time of this prayer the two boys were involved in a carriage accident.

The most striking evidence, however, of telepathically induced action is to be found in automatic writing. Some experimental cases of the kind have been quoted in Chapter IV. The spontaneous cases are more numerous. Mr. Myers has recorded several instances in his article on Motor Automatism (*Proc. S.P.R.*, vol. ix. pp. 26 *et seq.*), and Mr. W. T. Stead has published, in the *Review of Reviews* and elsewhere, accounts of messages and conversations with friends at a distance written through his hand.

Generally speaking, however, where living persons are concerned, it is difficult, without full knowledge of all the circumstances, to feel assured that the facts recorded by this means are not such as might conceivably have been within the knowledge of the writer, or at least within his powers of conjecture. The best evidence, therefore, for spontaneous tele-pathic automatism is no doubt afforded by those cases in which some altogether unforeseen event, such as the death of the presumed agent, is communi-cated. Such is the case recorded by M. Aksakof (*Psychische Studien*, February 1889, quoted in *Proc. S.P.R.*, vol. v. pp. 434, etc.), in which Mademoiselle Emma Stramm, a Swiss governess at Wilna, on the 15th January 1887 wrote particulars of the death on the same day of a former acquaintance of hers, August Duvanel, in Canton Zurich. A similar instance is recorded by Dr. Liébeault (*Annales des Sciences Psychiques*, vol. i. pp. 25, 26). The automatic writer was in this case at Nancy, and the person whose death was announced was a young English lady resi-dent at Coblentz. Dr. Liébeault was shown the written message within an hour or two of the séance, and some days before news of the death was received. Other cases of the kind are recorded by M. Aksakof and others (*Revue Spirite*, August 1891, April 1892, etc.).

CHAPTER VIII.

COINCIDENT DREAMS.

SEEING that so large a part of our lives is spent in sleep, we should perhaps be warranted in looking amongst dreams for evidence of the transference of thought from one mind to another; especially as the quiescence and the absence of outward impressions characteristic of sleep are precisely the conditions indicated by our researches as favourable to such transmission. Nor do the actual results in this direction at all fall short of any reasonable expectation. Long before scientific attention was directed to the subject the coincidences reported between dreams and external events had won the special consideration of the superstitious, and had given to the dreamer of dreams high rank in the company of the prophets and soothsayers. And such coincidences appear to be not less frequent at the present time. My chief difficulty in writing this chapter has been the task of selection from the superabundant material at hand, much of it accumulated within the last five or six years; and this material is itself the carefully-sifted residuum of a much larger mass of testimony, inferior, if at all, by slight and various degrees. But notwithstanding this great accumulation, it cannot be contended that the proof of telepathy derived from a consideration of dream coincidences is at all comparable in cogency with that furnished by impressions received during waking life.

That some at least of the dreams quoted below owed their origin to ideas transmitted to the sleeper from another mind will no doubt be admitted as probable, but the probability depends perhaps not more on their intrinsic value than on the analogy of similar testimony from waking percipients. When (as in some of the cases to be given later, in Chapters X.-XIII.) a witness of integrity asserts that he saw in broad daylight a figure where no such figure was, resembling a friend, and coincident with that friend's death, we are justified in attaching great weight to the coincidence. But if the same witness had dreamt of the figure, instead of seeing it, the coincidence would deserve far less consideration. And yet the cerebral mechanism involved in both processes is no doubt very similar. A dream is a hallucination in sleep, and a hallucination is only a waking dream; though it is probable that the waking impression, seeing that it can contend on equal terms with the impressions derived from external objects, is more vivid than the common run of dreams. But the evidence of dream coincidence is defective, primarily, from the frequency of dreams; it is only a small proportion of educated persons, at any rate, who ever experience a hallucination, but everybody dreams occasionally, and some persons dream every night. Clearly there must be here a wide scope for coincidence. Secondly, whilst dream impressions are probably less vivid at the time, they are certainly more elusive in the memory. There is a serious risk, therefore, that after the event is known detailed correspondences may be read back into the indistinct picture preserved in the memory; or that a dream which at the time made but a slight impression may be charged retrospectively with emotional significance. Finally, as the dream does not enter into any organic series of impressions, and has no landmarks of its own, either in space or time, it becomes after the lapse of a few days, or even hours, a matter of difficulty to determine its date. Against

the last two sources of error it is indeed possible
to guard. Under ordinary circumstances no dream
should be regarded as having evidential value which
has not been either recorded in writing or mentioned
to some other person before the coincidence is known.
Mention of the dream immediately after the receipt
of the news, even with persons of proved accuracy, can
by no means be regarded as equivalent to mention
of it beforehand. For it is possible, as already
pointed out (p. 155), that some alleged coincident
and prophetic dreams may be due to hallucination
of memory, or still more probably to the embellishment and amplification of vague pre-existent
memories.

But however carefully dreams are noted and
described, the objection still holds good that with
impressions of such frequent occurrence chance alone
will account for a considerable number of coincidences. It is easy, however, on a superficial view
to exaggerate the probabilities of chance coincidence.
The great majority of dreams, vague at the time and
fugitive in the retrospect, are like footsteps in the
sand. Yet as, here and there, one set of footprints out
of the millions impressed upon the shore of a long-
forgotten sea has been preserved for us in sand now
turned to stone, so now and then one dream stands
out from all the rest, and leaves on the memory an
imprint which the daily reflux of the tide of consciousness cannot efface. If we strike out of the
account all the dreams which are too vague to leave
any permanent impress on waking, all those which
are purely inconsequent and fantastic, and all which
can be readily traced to some physical cause, we shall
find that the number which we have to deal with,—
the number, that is, of vivid and passably realistic
dreams, — though no doubt large, is perhaps not
beyond the range of definite calculation. It could
not, for instance, be plausibly contended that the
correspondence of a dream such as that of Captain

Campbell's, recorded below, with the death of the person portrayed, is on the same level as the prophetic vision of the City clerk, who, dreaming every other night of the success of some horse which he has backed, happens on some one occasion to dream of the future winner.

It will be observed that of the nine dreams which are given in full in this chapter, no less than four are concerned with death. Of the much larger number—149—of coincident dreams published in *Phantasms of the Living*, no less than 79 relate to a death. Now, as dreams of death or suggesting death do not form a large proportion of dreams in general, their startling preponderance amongst coincident dreams constitutes in itself an argument for ascribing such dreams to telepathy; for if any power exists whereby one mind can affect another, it would appear *à priori* probable that such a power would be exercised most frequently and effectually at times of exceptional crisis. As has been pointed out by Mr. Gurney (*Phantasms of the Living*, vol. i. p. 303), the preponderance amongst "true" dreams of dreams relating to death may indeed be explained on the assumption that such dreams are more frequently remembered than other "true" dreams. This assumption is no doubt in a measure justified, but the consequences of admitting its truth must not be overlooked; for it of course follows that a large number of coincident dreams are forgotten, *i.e.*, that the grounds furnished by dreams for believing in telepathy are much stronger than would at first sight appear.

Again, the frequency of coincident dreams of death offers a favourable opportunity for estimating the probabilities of their occurrence by chance. The problem is simplified in one direction by the consideration that death is at all events a unique event in the history of the agent. If we can ascertain the proportion which "true" bear to "not-true" dreams of death, we can calculate by means of the tables of mortality the probabilities for some other cause than chance. The problem was actually attempted by Mr. Gurney, who found that coincident dreams of death in the collection published in *Phantasms of the Living* were twenty-four times as numerous as chance would allow.[1]

Theoretically, dreams are of considerable interest as throwing light upon the nature of waking impressions; for it should be observed that dreams are of many kinds and of many degrees of vividness. Some in the vagueness and ideality of the impressions resemble closely the waking experiences recorded in the preceding chapter. Others in their extreme clearness and semi-externalisation approach nearly to the level of hallucinations. But whilst few persons above the level of the savage believe that their dream percepts correspond to actual external objects visibly present, there are some who think that the hallucinatory image of a dying friend which they see with their eyes open, and taking a place in the external order of things, must, just because they see it with open eyes, form a part of that external order. And if the percipient himself is not under any such misconception, the journalist who sneers at him for believing in

---

[1] *Phantasms*, vol. i. pp. 303-310. The statement in the text must not be regarded as having more weight than its author himself would have assigned to it. Mr. Gurney certainly regarded his estimate as little more than a guess—a guess indeed made by one who had carefully studied and weighed the facts, so far as they could be known, but because of our inevitable ignorance a guess still, rather than an estimate on the approximate accuracy of which it would be safe to rely. The calculation depends on several assumptions, one or two of which, at least, are highly controvertible; for instance, the accuracy of the 5187 persons who asserted that they had not within a given period of twelve years had an exceptionally vivid and distressing dream relating to the death of a friend; and the accuracy of the twenty-four persons who described themselves as having had within the same period a similar dream actually occurring within twelve hours of the death of the person represented. Probably the estimate given requires modification by large allowances being made in both directions for defects of memory. But even when thus discounted the coincidences will, it is thought, by any one who carefully studies the subject be found to be more numerous than can plausibly be attributed to chance.

"ghosts" is so, by his own confession. If once it is recognised that between dreams and hallucinations there is no essential difference, the chief obstacle to the acceptance, by two different classes of minds, of telepathy as the explanation of coincident hallucinations will have disappeared. It will become clear, on the one hand, that a belief in the significance of such hallucinations does not necessarily carry with it a belief in "ghosts"; and on the other, that the fact of an apparition taking its place as a fully externalised percept does not imply any substantial basis for the percept.

In dealing with dreams we will discuss first those which resemble most closely the experimental results and the cases considered in the last chapter, and proceed from these to dreams which include a definite representation of the agent. Finally, cases of somewhat aberrant type and clairvoyant dreams will be considered.

Simultaneous Dreams.

No. 52.—From MISS INA BIDDER.

"RAVENSBURY PARK, MITCHAM,
June 10*th*, 1890.

"The night before last a curious case of what I cannot but call telepathy occurred between myself and my sister. (We sleep in the same room.) For the last two years the whole family have been very much interested in some skeletons and flint instruments found in a gravel pit in one of the fields. They have never been properly excavated, and about ten days ago my sister and I had been amusing ourselves pulling out, bone by bone, one of these 'palæolithic men,' as we pleased to call them. He was a particularly interesting one, as we found a flint arrow-head in his hip-bone, but we only got to his ribs. On the night in question I dreamt that my father was excavating in a more approved method, taking off the top mould and leaving the bones in their original position in the brown earth, so that you could see the form of the man to whom they had belonged. In this way we lifted out the rest of the skeleton at which my sister and I had been working, and behold! when we got to the skull it had a snout. We were delighted to be able to prove this extraordinary fact respecting palæolithic man, and the doctors crowded down from town to see the creature; but my sister was nowhere about, and in my anxiety to tell her of our discovery I woke myself and nearly woke her. I stopped myself just in time, thinking what a shame it was to spoil her night's rest for a dream. Still wishing she were awake to hear, and thinking again of the curious effect of the black, earth-filled skull, with its projecting snout, and dreaming of my dream, I turned over and dropped into another. Before I had got well started in this, however, I was awakened by my sister trying to light the candle. 'What is it?' I said, 'what's the matter?' 'I've just had such a horrid dream,' she answered; 'it haunts me still.' But I do not think I need repeat her dream, which I believe she has written."

Miss M. Bidder writes as follows:—

"*June 9th*, 1890.

"I was sleeping last night with my sister, with whom I have shared a room all my life. I was sleeping soundly, and my dreams, of which I now retain only the vaguest recollection, took their most usual form of a confused repetition of all the events of the past day jumbled together without meaning or sequence, and without even much distinctness. The whole scene of the dream was hazy and confused, until I became suddenly conscious of the figure of a skeleton in the foreground, as it were, which disturbed me in my dream with a sense of incongruity. I first made a half-conscious effort to banish the figure—which struck me with great horror—from my dream, but instead of disappearing it grew more and more prominent and distinct, while all the rest of the scene and the people in it seemed fading away. The figure of the skeleton, which I can perfectly recall, presented one of the most vivid impressions I ever remember to have received in a dream. It appeared to stand upright before me, with what seemed to be a dark cloak hanging about its limbs and forming a kind of background as of a black hood behind the skull, which showed against it with extreme distinctness. It was on the skull, which was facing me full, that my attention was chiefly concentrated, and as I stared at it it slowly turned sideways, showing, to my horror, the profile of a very long, sharp nose in place of the hollow socket. The feeling of terror with which I perceived this (for the first time) was so intense as to awaken me, nor could I even then entirely banish it. So unpleasantly strong, indeed, was the impression of some horrible presence which still remained, that it was with difficulty that I resisted the desire to rouse my sister that she might help me to shake it off. Some movement of mine did in fact presently awake her, and I at once began to tell her of my horrible dream. Before, however, I had described it to her, she interrupted me to tell me of a dream which she had had."

Here it is perhaps permissible to conjecture that some common experience of their waking life might have suggested to both sisters the idea of a primeval skeleton with a snout. But it is remarkable, if such is the true explanation, that the common idea was elaborated into a dream by the two percipients almost simultaneously. It must be admitted, however, that such dreams, which have hitherto been reported only as occurring between persons whose lives are spent for the most part in the same surroundings, have little value as evidence. It is only those who believe, on evidence derived from other sources, in the reality of telepathy, who will be inclined to regard such cases as possibly due to its action, rather than to the spontaneous association of ideas in minds sharing the same experiences and moving to some extent in similar grooves.

Dreams coinciding with external events.

In the cases which follow the coincidence is of a more definite kind, and the question is now no longer of the correspondence of thought in closely associated minds, but of the correspondence of thought with an outward event—with something done or suffered by the person whose mind apparently affects that of the dreamer.

Transference of Sensation in Dreams.

The following case, quoted from the *Proc. of the Am. S.P.R.* (pp. 226, 227), offers a curious parallel to some of the cases recorded at the beginning of Chapter II. The narrator is a lady of Boston, whose good faith is vouched for by Professor Royce. She wrote from Hamburg on the 23rd of June 1887 to her sister, who was at that time in Boston, U.S.A. The following is an extract from this letter :—

No. 53.

" I very nearly wrote from the Hague to say that I should be very thankful when we had a letter from you of the 18th of June saying that you were well and happy. . . . In the night of the 17th I had what I suppose to be a nightmare, but it all seemed to belong to you . . . and to be a horrid pain in your head, as if it were being forcibly jammed into an iron casque, or some such pleasant instrument of torture. The queer part of it was my own dissociation from the pain, and conviction that it was yours. I suppose it was some slight painful sensation magnified into something quite severe by a half-asleep condition. It will be a fine example of what the Society for Psychical Research ought to be well supplied with—an *Ahnung* which came to nothing."

As a matter of fact the lady in Boston to whom this letter was addressed is shown, on the evidence of a dentist's bill, to have spent on the 17th June an hour and three-quarters in the operating chair, while a painful tooth was being stopped. The discomfort consequent on the operation, as was learnt from the patient herself, " continued as a dull pain for some hours, in such wise that during the afternoon of the 17th June the patient could not forget the difficulty at all. She slept, however, as usual at night. The nightmare in Europe followed the operation in Boston by a good many hours, but the pain of the tooth returned daily for some three weeks." As the letter was written from Europe six days after the nightmare there was of course no possibility of any communication having passed in the interval except by telegram.

In the next case also the coincidence was of a trivial nature, but appears to have been exact in point of time. The narrative is quoted here because the impression, though not described beforehand, was of a quite unusual kind, being in part, if not altogether, a *waking* experience. It is doubtful, indeed, whether it should be classed as a dream, and not rather as a " borderland " hallucination.

13

No. 54.—From MRS. HARRISON.

"*February 7th*, 1891.

" I reside with my husband at 15 Lupton Street, N.W. This afternoon I was lying on the sofa, sound asleep, when I suddenly awoke, thinking I heard my husband sigh as if in pain. I arose immediately, expecting to find him in the room. He was not there, and looking at my watch I found it was half-past three. At six o'clock my husband came in. He called my attention to a bruise on his forehead, which was caused by his having knocked it against the stone steps in a Turkish bath. I said to him, ' I know when it happened—it was at half-past three, for I heard you sigh as if in pain at that time.' He replied, ' Yes, that was the exact time, for I remember noticing the clock directly after.'

"The gentleman who appends his name as witness was present when this conversation took place.

"LOUISA E. HARRISON.

" Witness : Henry Hooton, 23 Bunhill Row, E.C."

This account was sent to the S.P.R. by Mr. Harrison on the day of the occurrence described. In an accompanying letter he writes: " Everything happened exactly as stated."

In the cases which follow, with one exception, the dream impression was of a well-marked visual nature. In the first three narratives the dream had reference to the death of the person represented. The mode of representation, however, it will be seen, differed in each case. In the first, the associated imagery was in part of a fantastic nature, and the dream, though sufficiently exceptional to leave a feeling of fatigue on the following morning, and to induce the percipient to write an account of it to his friends, resembled in other respects the motley crowd which throng through the gate of ivory. In the second case the surroundings of the central figure were such as the waking imagination of the dreamer would naturally have conjured up in picturing the deathbed of his friend.

No. 55.—From MR. J. T.

This case is recorded at some length in the *Proceedings of the Am. S.P.R.* (pp. 394-397) by Professor Royce. Professor Royce explains that Mr. E., the agent, died after a short illness in New York City, on Tuesday, February 23rd, 1886. Mr. J. T., who, though an acquaintance of Mr. E., had heard nothing of him for some time, and, as indeed appears from the letters quoted, knew of no special cause for anxiety, was on the day of the death, and for some time afterwards, in St. John, New Brunswick. In consequence of severe snowstorms, no mails had been received in St. John from the South for some days, and at the time when the letter, an extract from which we give below, was written, it was not possible for the writer to have known of Mr. E.'s death. The original letter, written by Mr. J. T. to his wife, and dated Wednesday, March 3rd, 1886, on paper headed Hotel Dufferin, St. John, N.B., has been seen by Professor Royce :—

"I have not heard of you for an age. The train that should have been here on Friday last has not arrived yet. I had a very strange dream on Tuesday night. I have never been in Ottawa in my life, and yet I was there, in Mr. E.'s house. Mrs. E., Miss E., and the little girls were in great trouble because Mr. E. was ill. I had to go and tell my brother [Mr. E.'s son-in-law], and, strange to say, he was down a coal-mine.

"When I got down to him I told him that Mr. E. was dead. But in trying to get out we could not do it. We climbed and climbed, but always fell back. I felt tired out when I awoke next morning, and I cannot account for the dream in any way."

Though the letter leaves it doubtful whether the dream actually occurred on the night of the death, or a week later, it appears from further correspondence that the percipient believes the dream to have taken place on the night of the 23rd February, the night of the death, and this is the most natural interpretation of the letter.[1] In any case, the dream preceded the news of the death.

In the next case, again, the dream is of a not uncommon type, but the impression made, it will be seen, was such as to wake the dreamer at the time,

[1] A man writing on Wednesday would almost certainly say "last night" if he meant to indicate the preceding night, whereas, having just before written of "Friday last," it was natural to describe the Tuesday in the previous week as simply "Tuesday."

and to induce him in the morning to take the unusual course of noting the dream in his diary.

No. 56.—From Mr. R. V. Boyle.

"3 STANHOPE TERRACE, W.,
July 30th, 1884.

"In India, early on the morning of November 2nd, 1868 (which would be about 10 to 11 P.M. of November 1st in England), I had so clear and striking a dream or vision (repeated a second time after a short waking interval) that, on rising as usual between 6 and 7 o'clock, I felt impelled at once to write an entry in my diary, which is now before me.

"At the time referred to my wife and I were in Simla, in the Himalayas, the summer seat of the Governor-General, and my father-in-law and mother-in-law were living in Brighton. We had not heard of or from either of them for weeks, nor had I been recently speaking or thinking of them, for there was no reason for anxiety regarding them. It is right, however, to say that my wife's father had gone to Brighton some months before on account of his health, though he was not more delicate than his elder brother, who is (1884) still living.

"It seemed in my dream that I stood at the open door of a bedroom in a house in Brighton, and that before me, by candle-light, I saw my father-in-law lying pale upon his bed, while my mother-in-law passed silently across the room in attendance on him. The vision soon passed away, and I slept on for some time. On waking, however, the nature of the impression left upon me unmistakably was that my father-in-law was dead. I at once noted down the dream, after which I broke the news of what I felt to be a revelation to my wife, when we thought over again and again all that could bear upon the matter, without being able to assign any reason for my being so strongly and thoroughly impressed. The telegraph from England to Simla had been open for some time, but now there was an interruption, which lasted for about a fortnight longer, and on the 17th (fifteen days after my dream) I was neither unprepared nor surprised to receive a telegram from England, saying that my father-in-law had died in Brighton on November 1st. Subsequent letters showed that the death occurred on the *night* of the 1st.

"Dreams, as a rule, leave little impression on me, and the one above referred to is the only one I ever thought of making a note of, or of looking expectantly for its fulfilment.

"R. VICARY BOYLE."

Mrs. Boyle writes as follows:—

"*6th August* 1887.

" I well remember my husband telling me one morning, early in November 1868, when at Simla, in India, that he had had a striking dream (repeated) in which my father, then at Brighton, seemed to be dying. We were both deeply impressed, and then anxiously awaited news from home. A telegram first reached us, in about a fortnight, which was afterwards confirmed by letters telling of my father's death having occurred on the same night when my husband had the dream.

"ELÉONORE A. BOYLE.

Mr. Gurney adds the following notes on the case:—

"The following entries were copied by me from Mr. Boyle's diary:—

"'Nov. 2. Dreamed of E.'s F[ather] early this morning.

"'Written before dressing.

"'Nov. 17. Got telegram from L[ouis] H[ack] this morning of his father's death on 1st Nov. inst.'

"The following notice of the decease of Mr. Boyle's father-in-law occurred in the *Times* for 4th November 1868:—

"'On 1st Nov., at Brighton, William Hack, late of Dieppe, aged 72.'

"Mr. Boyle informed me that he is a 'particularly sound sleeper, and very rarely dreams.' This dream was a very unique and impressive experience, apart from the coincidence.

"There was a regular correspondence between Mrs. Boyle and her mother, but for several mails the letters had contained no mention of her father, on whose account absolutely no anxiety was felt.   " E. G."

It appears that the death actually occurred at about 2 P.M. in England, which was, allowing for the difference in longitude, about nine hours before the dream.

In the next case the dream is of a more unusual character. The figure of the agent appears to have stood alone, whilst the impression made was such that the percipient is uncertain whether to class his experience as a dream or a vision. Indeed, in the absence of dream-background, and in the lifelike appearance of the figure, the dream bears a striking resemblance to a waking hallucination.

No. 57.—From CAPTAIN R. E. W. CAMPBELL (2nd Royal Irish Fusiliers).

"ARMY AND NAVY CLUB, PALL MALL, S.W.,
February 21*st*, 1888.

"I have much pleasure in enclosing you an account of a remarkable dream which occurred to me in the year 1886, together with three other accounts of the same, written by officers to whom the facts of the case are known. You are at liberty, in the interests of science, to make such use of them as you please.

"I was stationed at the Depôt Barracks, Armagh, Ireland, on the 30th November 1886, and on the night of the same date, or early in the morning of the 1st December (I cannot tell which, as I did not refer to my watch), I was in bed in my room, when I was awakened by a most vivid and remarkable dream or vision, in which I seemed to see a certain Major Hubbersty, late of my regiment, the 2nd Battalion Royal Irish Fusiliers, looking ghastly pale, and falling forward as if dying. He seemed to be saying something to me, but the words I could not make out, although I tried hard to understand him. The clothes he had on at the time appeared to me to have a thin red thread running through the pattern. I was very deeply impressed by my dream, and so much did I feel that there was something significant in it that on the 1st December, when at luncheon in the mess, I related it to three brother-officers, telling them at the same time that I felt sure we should soon hear something bad about Major Hubbersty. I had almost forgotten all about it when, on taking up the *Times* newspaper of the following Saturday on the Sunday morning following, the first thing that caught my eyes was the announcement of Major Hubbersty's death at Penzance, in Cornwall, on the 30th November, the very date on which I had the remarkable dream concerning him.

"My feelings on seeing such a remarkable fulfilment of my dream can be better imagined than described. Suffice it to say that on the return from church of Messrs. Kaye and Scott I asked them to try and recollect anything peculiar which had happened at luncheon on the 1st December, when, after a few moments' deliberation, they at once recounted to me the whole circumstances of my dream, as they had heard them from my lips on the 1st December 1886. On seeing Mr. Leeper a few days afterwards at his father's house, Loughgall, Co. Armagh, he at once remembered all I had told him about the dream on the 1st December, on my questioning him about it. I, of course, can assign no possible cause for the remarkable facts related, as apart from the difference of our standing in the service, the late Major Hubbersty and I were in no wise particularly friendly to one other, nor had we seen very much of each other. I had not seen him for eighteen months previously. A very curious fact in connection with the dream is that it occurred to me in the very same room in the barracks as Major Hubbersty used to occupy when stationed at Armagh, several years previously."

In answer to an inquiry, Captain Campbell writes, on February 29th, 1888 :—

" I do not dream much, as a rule, and cannot recall to my mind ever before having had a dream of a similar nature to that dreamt by me about the late Major Hubbersty."

Mr. A. B. R. Kaye, Lieutenant Third Royal Irish Fusiliers, writes on August 20th, 1887, from 62 Fitzwilliam Square, Dublin :—

" I was stationed in the barracks, Armagh Depôt, Royal Irish Fusiliers, in November and December 1886. On the 1st of December at lunch there were present Lieutenant R. E. W. Campbell (2nd R.I.F.), Lieutenant R. W. Leeper (2nd R.I.F.), Lieutenant T. E. Scott (4th R.I.F.), and myself. During our conversation Major Hubbersty's name was mentioned, and Campbell told us that he had a dream about him the night before, how he had seen a vision of Major Hubbersty looking very pale and seeming to be falling forward, and saying something to him which he could not hear ; also, he (Campbell) told us he was sure we would hear something about Major Hubbersty very soon.

" On the following Sunday, when Scott and I returned from church and went into the ante-room, Campbell, who was there, asked us both to try and remember anything peculiar that he had told us on the 1st. After a little time, we remembered about the dream, and he (Campbell) then showed us the *Times* newspaper of the day before, containing the notice of Major Hubbersty's death, at Penzance, on November 30th, 1886, the same date as that on which he had the dream ; also, I remember, he (Campbell) told us that in his vision he seemed to see the clothes which Major Hubbersty had on, and that there was a red thread running through the pattern of the trousers."

The two other friends mentioned by Captain Campbell, Messrs. Leeper and Scott, have written letters to the same effect.[1]

---

[1] These letters are omitted for want of space. They are given in full in the *Journal of the S.P.R.* for April 1888, pp. 255, 256.

From these letters there can be no doubt that the coincidence made a marked impression on each of those to whom the dream was related, and this fact, perhaps even more than Captain Campbell's own narrative, is a striking proof of the exceptional nature of the experience.

There is no reason in this case for supposing that the dream conveyed any other information than the fact of the agent's death. There is no evidence that the manner of death or the clothes worn by Major Hubbersty resembled what was seen in the dream. The clothes in which the figure appeared may have been a reminiscence of clothes which the percipient had actually seen worn on some occasion by the agent. But this explanation will hardly apply to the following case, where the dream included a representation, accurate in more than one particular, of the agent as he actually appeared at the time. It is true that we have to rely upon the percipient's memory after the interval of a fortnight for the details of the dream, but since the dream was sufficiently impressive to cause a note to be taken of it by a person not in the habit of making such notes, it seems not unreasonable to trust the memory to that extent.

No. 58.—From MR. E. W. HAMILTON, C.B.

"PARK LANE CHAMBERS, PARK LANE, W.,
April 6th, 1888.

"On Wednesday morning, March 21st, 1888, I woke up with the impression of a very vivid dream. I had dreamt that my brother, who had long been in Australia, and of whom I had heard nothing for several months, had come home; that after an absence of twelve years and a half he was very little altered in appearance, but that he had something wrong with one of his arms; it looked horribly red near the wrist, his hand being bent back.

"When I got up that morning the dream recurred constantly to my thoughts, and I at last determined to take a note of it, notwithstanding my natural prejudices against attaching any importance to dreams, to which, indeed, I am not much subject. Accordingly, in the course of the day, I made in my little Letts' diary a mark thus : X, with my brother's name after it.

"On the following Monday morning, the 26th March, I received a letter from my brother, which bore the date of the 21st March, and which had been posted at Naples (where the Orient steamers touch), informing me that he was on his way home, and that he hoped to reach London on or about the 30th March, and adding that he was suffering from a very severe attack of gout in the left arm.

"The next day I related to some one this curious incident, and I commented on the extraordinary coincidence of facts with the dream except in one detail, and that was, that the arm which I had seen in my dream did not look as if it were merely affected with gout: the appearance it had presented to me was more like extremely bad eczema.

"My brother duly reached England on the 29th, having disembarked at Plymouth owing to the painful condition of his arm. It turned out that the doctor on board ship had mistaken the case; it was not gout, but a case of blood poisoning, resulting in a very bad carbuncle or abscess over the wrist joint.

"Since my brother's return, I have endeavoured to ascertain from him the exact hour at which he wrote to me on March 21st. He is not certain whether the letter to me was written before noon or after noon of that day. He remembers writing four short letters in the course of that day—two before luncheon and two after luncheon. Had the note addressed to me been written in the forenoon, it might nearly have coincided in time with my dream, if allowance be made for the difference of time between Greenwich and Naples; for, having no recollection of the dream when I woke, according to custom, at an early hour on the morning of the 21st, I presume I must have dreamt it very little before eight o'clock, the hour at which I was called.

"I may add that, notwithstanding an absence of twelve years and a half, my brother has altered very little in appearance; and that I have not to my knowledge ever noted a dream before in my life."

On April 12th, 1888, Mr. Gurney inspected the diary with the entry (X, Clem) under Tuesday, March 20th, 1888, though, as Mr. Hamilton explained, "it was early the next morning that I had the dream, for I generally consider all that appertains to bed relates to the day on which one gets into it."

Mr. Gurney also saw the letter signed Clement E. Hamilton, and dated Naples, March 21st, 1888, which says "am suffering from very severe attack of gout in left arm."

The next case presents several points of interest. In part, at least, it seems to have been a waking experience, possibly the prolongation of a dream. In this respect it resembles Mrs. Harrison's case, already cited (No. 54), and if correctly described, the incident possesses therefore a higher evidential value than a mere dream, however vivid. I have here classed it as a dream, however, because the percipient himself so describes it in his letter written a few days after the experience. The utterance of words by the percipient finds a parallel in the case of Archdeacon Bruce (Chapter VII., No. 51). But in the present case there is the additional feature that the percipient is conscious not only of the sound of his own voice, but of another voice in reply. The incident, it will be seen, though remote, is attested by letters written immediately after the event, and by the percipient's recollection of action taken in consequence of the dream-warning.

No. 59.—From MR. EDWARD A. GOODALL, of the Royal Society of Painters in Water-Colours.

"*May*, 1888.

"At Midsummer, 1869, I left London for Naples. The heat being excessive, people were leaving for Ischia, and I thought it best to go there myself.

"Crossing by steamer, I slept one night at Casamicciola, on the coast, and walked next morning into the town of Ischia [Mr. Goodall then describes an accident to his hand, which prevented him from sketching.]

"It must have been on my third or fourth night, and about the middle of it, when I awoke, as it seemed, at the sound of my own voice, saying: 'I know I have lost my dearest little May.' Another voice, which I in no way recognised, answered: '*No,* not May, but your *youngest boy.*'

"The distinctness and solemnity of the voice made such a distressing impression upon me that I slept no more. I got up at daybreak, and went out, noticing for the first time telegraph-poles and wires.

"Without delay I communicated with the postmaster at Naples, and by next boat received two letters from home. I opened them according to dates outside. The first told me that my youngest boy was taken suddenly ill; the second, that he was dead.

" Neither on his account nor on that of any of my family had I any cause for uneasiness. All were quite well on my taking leave of them so lately. My impression ever since has been that the time of the death coincided as nearly as we could judge with the time of my accident.

" In writing to Mrs. Goodall, I called the incident of the voice a dream, as less likely perhaps to disturb her than the details which I gave on reaching home, and which I have now repeated.

" My letters happen to have been preserved.

" I have never had any hallucination of any kind, nor am I in the habit of talking in my sleep. I do remember once waking with some words of mere nonsense upon my lips, but the experience of the voice speaking to me was absolutely unique.

"EDWARD A. GOODALL."

Extracts from letters to Mrs. E. A. Goodall from Ischia :—

"WEDNESDAY, *August 11th*, 1869.

" The postman brought me two letters containing sad news indeed. Poor little Percy! I dreamt some nights since the poor little fellow was taken from us. . . ."

"*August 14th.*

" I did not tell you, dear, the particulars of my dream about poor little Percy.

" I had been for several days very fidgety and wretched at getting no letters from home, and had gone to bed in worse spirits than usual, and in my dream I fancied I said: 'I have lost my dearest little May.' A strange voice seemed to say: 'No, *not* May, but your youngest boy,' not mentioning his name."

Mr. Myers adds :—

" Mr. Goodall has given me verbally a concordant account of the affair, and several members of his family, who were present at our interview, recollected the strong impression made on him and them at the time."[1]

In the case which follows the agency is difficult to elucidate. The persons who were spectators of the scene represented in the dream can hardly be supposed to have been acquainted with the dreamer,

[1] *Proc. S.P.R.*, vol. v. pp. 453-455.

and assuredly would not willingly have revealed the secret. The dream appears to have been of a clairvoyant character. The account is taken from the *Proceedings of the Am. S.P.R.*, pp. 454 *et seq.*

No. 60.—From MRS. E. J.

"CAMBRIDGE (U.S.A.), *Nov.* 30, 1886.

"The dream I will endeavour to relate as clearly as possible.

"It occurred during the month of August, last summer, while we were boarding with Mrs. H., in Lunenburg, where I first met the Misses W. I am a perfectly healthy woman, and have always been sceptical as to hallucinations in any one, always before having felt the cause of the experience might be traced.

"In my dream I arrived unexpectedly at the house of the Misses W., in Cambridge, where I found everything in confusion, drawers emptied and their contents scattered about the floor, bundles unrolled, and dresses taken down from the closets. Then, as I stepped into one room, I saw some boys in bed,—three or four, I cannot distinctly remember. I saw their faces distinctly, as they sat up in bed at my approach, but the recollection of their faces has faded from me now. I could not reach the boys, for they disappeared suddenly, and I could not find them; but I thought, These cannot be the people whom the Misses W. trusted to care for their house in their absence; and I was troubled to know whether it was best to tell them when I should return to Lunenburg. This is all there was in the dream.

"Thinking only to amuse them, I related my dream at the breakfast-table the following morning, and I regretted doing so immediately, for anxiety showed itself in their faces, and the elder Miss W. remarked that she hoped my dream was not a forerunner of bad tidings from home. I laughed at the idea, but that morning the mail brought a letter telling them that their house had been entered, and when they went down they found almost the same confusion of which I had been a witness the night before—with everything strewn about the floor. It was a singular coincidence, surely."

Miss W. writes :—

"7 —— STREET, *Dec.* 4.

"I am not quite sure whether the incident to which you allude in your note is worthy your attention or not, but I will give you the facts, that you may judge for yourself of its value.

"The burglary, we suppose, took place on the night of the 17th or 18th of August, I being at the time, for the summer, in the town of Lunenburg, Mass.

"Coming down to breakfast on the morning of the 17th, a lady said to me that she had had a strange dream. She thought she went to our house, finding it in the greatest confusion, everything turned upside-down. As she entered one of the sleeping-rooms she saw two boys lying in the bed; but she could not see their faces, for as soon as they saw her they jumped up and ran off. I said, 'I hope that does not mean that we have been visited by burglars.'

"I thought no more about it, till the eleven o'clock mail brought a note from the woman in charge of the house saying that it had been entered,—that everything was in great confusion, many things carried off, and she wished we would come home at once. The policeman who went over the house with her said he had never seen a house more thoroughly ransacked.

"We found that in the upper attic room the bed had evidently been used, and there was, perhaps, more confusion in this room than in any other.

"The lady who had the dream was Mrs. E. J., of Cambridgeport. I was told that she had been suffering for about a year from nervous prostration, and she was evidently in a condition of great nervous excitement.

"I forbore to speak to her of the occurrence, as one of the ladies in the house told me that it had made an unpleasant impression on her mind.

"The whole thing seems rather curious to me, but I do not know that you will find it of any value in your investigations."

A dream presenting similar features is recorded in the *Journal of the S.P.R.* for June 1890. Mr. William Bass, farm bailiff to Mrs. Palmer, of Turnours Hall, Chigwell, on Good Friday, 1884, "awoke in violent agitation and profuse perspiration" from a dream that something was wrong at the stables. He was at first dissuaded by his wife from paying any attention to the dream, but subsequently, at about 2 A.M., dressed and proceeded to the stables (a third of a mile off) to find that a mare had been stolen. The case has been investigated by Mr. T. Barkworth, of West Hatch, Chigwell, and by Mr. J. B. Surgey, of 22 Holland Street, Kensington. In a dream recorded in *Phantasms of the Living* (vol. i. p. 369), Miss Busk, of 16

Montagu Street, W., dreamt that in a spot in Kent well known to her she stumbled over "the heads, left protruding, of some ducks buried in the sand, under some firs." The dream was mentioned at breakfast to Miss Busk's sister, Mrs. Pitt Byrne, and an hour later the ladies learnt from their bailiff that some stolen ducks had accidentally been found buried on the spot and in the manner described.

CHAPTER IX.

ON HALLUCINATION IN GENERAL.

BEFORE proceeding, in the chapters which follow, to cite instances of hallucinations which purport to have been telepathically originated, it seems needful to glance briefly at sensory hallucination in general. To most persons, no doubt, the word connotes disease. Their ideas of hallucination are probably derived from vague reports of asylum experience and *delirium tremens;* or at least from the cases of Goethe's butt, Nicolai, the Berlin bookseller, and the Mrs. A. whose experiences are described in Brewster's *Letters on Natural Magic,* both of whom are known to have been under medical treatment for illness of which the hallucinations were regarded as a symptom. Indeed, until recent years the tendency of even well-instructed opinion has been to regard a sensory hallucination as necessarily implying some physical or mental disorder. This misconception—for it is a misconception—has had some curious consequences. Since it does occasionally happen that a person admittedly sane and healthy reports to have seen the likeness of a human figure in what was apparently empty space, such reports have been by some perforce scouted as unworthy of credence, and by others regarded as necessarily indicating some occult cause —as testifying, in short, to the agency of "ghosts." There was indeed the analogy of dreams to guide us. Few educated persons would regard dreams, on the one hand, as a symptom of ill-health, or on the other as counterparts or revelations of any super-terrestrial world ; or, indeed, as anything else than purely sub-jective mental images. Yet dreams belong to the same order of mental phenomena as hallucinations, and are commonly so classed—such differences as exist being mainly due to the conditions under which the two sets of phenomena respectively occur. In fact, a hallucination is simply a hypertrophied thought —the last member of a series, whose intermediate terms are to be found in the mind's-eye pictures of ordinary life, in the vivid images which some artists can summon at will, and in the Faces in the Dark which many persons see before passing into sleep, with its more familiar and abundant imagery.

Of recent years, however, our knowledge of hallu-cinations has been largely augmented from two dis-tinct sources. On the one hand, a systematic attempt has been made to study the spontaneous non-recurrent hallucinations occurring amongst normal persons ; on the other hand, wider knowledge of hypnotism and the discovery of various processes for inducing hallucina-tions has afforded facilities for the experimental in-vestigation of their nature, mechanism, and genesis, both in the trance and in waking life. The hallucina-tions, indeed, of the ordinary hypnotic subject, with which the public has been familiarised by platform demonstrations, are possibly not sensory at all. When a hypnotised lad eats tallow-candle for sponge-cake, drinks ink for champagne, or professes to see a lighted candle at the end of the operator's finger, we may conclude, if the performance is a genuine one, that a false belief has been engendered in his mind ; but we have, in most cases, no evidence that this belief includes any sensory element. In many labor-atory experiments, however, there can be little ques-tion that a complete sensory hallucination is induced, and that what the subject professes to see and hear is as real to him as the furniture or the person of the operator. One or two such cases have been quoted in a previous chapter (Chap. III., p. 68). The nature and reaction of these hypnotic hallucinations have been investigated with much ingenuity by various Continental observers.[1]   MM. Binet and Féré, to quote the best-known series of experiments, have found, speaking generally, that the hallucinatory percept behaves under various conditions precisely as if it were a real percept.   Thus, if the subject is told to see a picture on a blank card, he will not only see the picture at the time, but he will be able subsequently to pick out the card, recognising it by means of the hallucinatory picture impressed on it, from a number of similar cards.   If the card is inverted, he will see the picture upside-down ; if a magnifying glass is interposed, he will see the picture enlarged ; viewed through a prism, it will appear doubled ; it will be reflected in a mirror ; and if the hallucinatory image consists of written or printed words, he will see the writing in the mirror inverted.   Hallucinatory colours will develop after-images of the complementary colour, precisely as if coloured surfaces were actually present to the eyes of the *halluciné ;* and a mixture of these hallucinatory colours will produce the appropriate third colour.   If other proof were needed of the sensory nature of the induced affection, MM. Binet and Féré find it in the observation that with cataleptic subjects who have lost the sensitiveness of the cornea and conjunctiva, this sensitiveness is restored when a visual hallucination is enjoined upon them.   M. Pierre Janet, in *L'Automatisme Psychologique*, has recorded a similar restoration of sensitiveness in a subject's arm by the imposition of a tactile hallucination.

It is right to point out that these experiments, by the authors' admission, succeed only occasionally, and that many of them have not yet been confirmed by other observers.   In fact, according to the evidence

[1] See *Animal Magnetism*, by Binet and Féré, in the International Science Series, and the references there given.

collected by the S.P.R., the results of applying such optical tests differ with each individual. Thus Mr. Myers succeeded by post-hypnotic suggestion in inducing two young men to see hallucinatory images in the crystal enlarged by the application of a magnifying glass (*S.P.R.*, viii. 462, 463), and Miss X. (*id.*, pp. 485, 486) reports that she sees hallucinatory pictures distorted in a spoon, reversed in a mirror, enlarged by a magnifying glass, and doubly refracted by Iceland spar. She believes herself also to have experienced complementary colours as the result of prolonged looking at a hallucinatory picture. But Mrs. Verrall (*id.*, p. 474) finds the crystal pictures vanish when the magnifying glass is applied; and Miss A. (*id.*, p. 500) finds that the superimposition of a magnifying glass does not affect the picture. In all these cases, it should be noted, the percipients were in their normal condition, and were more or less familiar with the nature of the optical effects following under similar circumstances with real percepts.

MM. Binet and Féré suppose that the appropriate reaction of the hallucinatory picture to the various tests described is due to the hallucination being built up round a fragment of actual percept, such as a mark on a card, which would conform to ordinary optical laws. This imaginary nucleus they name the *point de repère*. It is not improbable that in some cases this may be the true explanation. But experience leads us to infer that suggestion would be competent to produce all the observed effects in cases where the subject, either from previous knowledge of the instrument or process, from the behaviour of the investigators, or from his own observations at the time, was aware of the nature of the effect to be expected. And it is not clear that MM. Binet and Féré, and other investigators of this school, have been sufficiently on their guard against the abnormal receptivity of the hypnotised subjects with whom they have for the most part experimented. Miss X., it may be remarked, professes herself uncertain whether or not to ascribe the results which she has recorded to self-suggestion. But to choose between these alternative explanations is not important for our present purpose. To whatever cause we may attribute the results observed, there can be no doubt either of the sense of reality conveyed by the false percept, or of its appropriate behaviour under favourable conditions.

An instance may be quoted in detail which illustrates at once the apparent attachment of the hallucination to an external object, and its successful competition with the impressions of waking life. A lady of my acquaintance, Sister L., was put into the hypnotic state by Mr. G. A. Smith in the spring of 1892. Whilst she was entranced, Mr. Smith, at my request, handed to her several blank cards, and told her that one of them (which had been privately marked on the back) bore a portrait of himself, and that she was to look at it ten minutes after waking. A few minutes later, when engaged in conversation and apparently completely awake, Sister L. picked out the card in question from the little heap of similar cards and showed it to me, remarking that it was an excellent likeness. Some half-hour later, when Sister L. was about to take her departure, I handed her the card and said that Mr. Smith would be glad if she would accept the photograph. She looked at the card, expressed her thanks for the gift, and placed it in her pocket. When I met her a few days later I learnt that on her arrival at home she had searched in her pocket for the photograph, and had been much surprised to find there only a blank card. In this instance there can be little doubt that a complete sensory hallucination was induced, and that it persisted, or was capable of being revived, for some 30 minutes or more after the original impression had been established.

This last example, it will be seen, belongs to the important class of post-hypnotic hallucinations—*i.e.,* hallucinations enjoined on the subject in the hypnotic state, but realised only after waking. Special interest attaches to hallucinations of this kind, because the subject is in a condition which, if not fully normal, at least approaches in some cases very nearly to the normal, and is thus able to observe and describe his own sensations with care.[1]

A more striking form of the same experiment, the post-hypnotic production of a completely developed hallucination of the human figure, has been practised by Bernheim,[2] Beaunis,[3] Liegeois,[4] and others. Thus M. Liegeois, on the 12th October 1885, told a hypnotised subject that on the 12th October of the year following he would go to Dr. Liébeault's house, where he would also see M. Liegeois, and would thank them both for the good done to his eyes. He would then see a performing dog and monkey enter the consulting room, where they would perform many amusing tricks; ultimately he would see a gipsy enter with a

---

[1] In many cases the post-hypnotic performance of an enjoined action, or the experience of a post-hypnotic hallucination, is associated with the partial recurrence of the hypnotic trance, or of some condition closely allied to it. Mr. Edmund Gurney has carefully investigated the question (*Proc. S.P.R.*, iv. pp. 268-323. See also Delbœuf's article there quoted, "De la pretendue Veille Somnambulique," *Rev. Phil.*, Feb. 1887), and has shown that, with some subjects, during the performance of the enjoined action a further command can be given, or a further hallucination imposed, and that the whole incident will have passed from memory a few seconds later. In the case of some persons hypnotised by Dr. Bramwell, and bidden to see after waking an imaginary scene in a crystal, I have myself observed that they retained no recollection a few minutes later of the scene which they had been describing; and in at least one case the subject at the time of the hallucination was apparently insensible to pain. On the other hand, as Mr. Gurney has pointed out (*loc. cit.*, p. 270), "there are some cases in which no reason whatever appears for regarding the state in which the action is performed as other than normal," and the same remark apparently holds good of post-hypnotic hallucinations. And there are many persons who can see hallucinatory pictures in a crystal, a glass of water, etc., when in full health and in a perfectly normal condition. See Mr. Myers' article already referred to (*S.P.R.*, vol. viii.).

[2] *De la Suggestion*, p. 29.

[3] *La Somnambulisme provoqué*, p. 233.

[4] *Rev. de l'Hypnotisme*, November 1886, p. 148.

bear, to reclaim the dog and monkey, and would borrow two sous from M. Liegeois to give to the gipsy. On the 12th October 1886 the subject entered Dr. Liébeault's consulting room and thanked him and M. Liegeois as arranged. He then saw a dog and monkey enter the room, and ultimately a gipsy. The bear he did not see, and the two sous, which were duly borrowed, he handed to the imaginary dog. With these exceptions the hallucinations enjoined a year before were exactly realised. Some experiments of a similar nature are recorded by Mr. Gurney (*Proc. S.P.R.*, vol. v. pp. 11-13). The subject was a servant named Zillah, in the service of Mrs. Ellis, of 40 Keppel Street, Russell Square. In the first two experiments Zillah was told in the trance that at a certain hour on the following day she would see Mr. G. A. Smith. In each case the experiment succeeded.

The third and last experiment with this "subject" was made on Wednesday evening, July 13th, 1887. On this occasion S. told her, when hypnotised, that the next afternoon at three o'clock she would see me come into the room to her. She was further told that I would keep my hat on, and would say, "Good afternoon ;" that I would further remark, "It is very warm ;" and would then turn round and walk out. These hallucinations were suggested in another room, where Zillah was taken for the purpose, and neither Mrs. Ellis nor any other person, except S. and myself, knew their nature. Zillah, as usual, knew nothing about them on waking. On the second day after, the following letter was received from Mrs. Ellis:—

"40 KEPPEL STREET, RUSSELL SQUARE, W.C.,
July 14th.

"DEAR MR. SMITH,—Mr. Gurney did not ask me to write in case there was anything to communicate with respect to Zillah, but as I *suppose* you gave her a post-hypnotic hallucination, probably you will wish to hear of it. I will give you the story in her own words, as I jotted them down immediately afterwards—saying nothing to her, of course, of my doing so. She said : ' I was in the kitchen washing up, and had just looked at the clock, and was startled to see how late it was— five minutes to three—when I heard footsteps coming down the stairs—rather a quick, light step—and I thought it was Mr. Sleep' (the dentist whose rooms are in the house), 'but as I turned round, with a dish mop in one hand and a plate in the other, I saw some one with a hat on, who had to stoop as he came down the last step, and there was Mr. Gurney! He was dressed just as I saw him last night, black coat and grey trousers, his hat on, and a roll of paper, like manuscript, in his hand, and he said, 'Oh, good afternoon.' And then he glanced all round the kitchen, and he glared at me with an awful look, as if he was going to murder me, and said, 'Warm afternoon, isn't it?' and then, 'Good afternoon' or 'Good day,' I'm not sure which, and turned and went up the stairs again, and after standing thunderstruck a minute, I ran to the foot of the stairs, and saw like a boot just disappearing on the top step.' She said, 'I think I must be going crazy. Why should I always see something at three o'clock each day after the séance? But I am not nearly so frightened as I was at seeing Mr. Smith.' She seemed particularly impressed by the 'awful look' Mr. Gurney gave her. I presume this was the hallucination you gave her.

"AMELIA A. ELLIS."

It is important to note that in cases of this kind there is no discoverable *point de repère*, at least in the sense in which the phrase is understood by its authors; and the nature of the effect produced—a moving figure, apparently occupying a position in solid space —makes it very difficult to suppose that the hallucination is attached to any external object, which must necessarily be fixed. But the whole discussion about the necessity of external excitation or of *points de repère* seems beside the mark in such cases as these. For there can be no question that what in the first instance excites the hallucination is not a present sensation, but a memory. Whether for the full development of a sensory hallucination some external stimulus to the sense-organ is necessary is here a question of quite minor importance. The really interesting fact in its bearing on the question of telepathic hallucination is that some hallucinations are shown to be centrally, not peripherally, initiated. It should be further remarked that Zillah's astonishment at seeing the figure is typical, since in the case of post-hypnotic hallucinations in general neither the injunction to see the figure, nor indeed any other incident of his trance life, is remembered by the percipient in the normal state ; and he is therefore entirely ignorant of the chain of events which led up to the hallucination, and can only by inquiry and reflection ascertain that the apparition which he has seen is of his own manufacture.

From these experimental cases we may pass to the consideration of spontaneous hallucinations, and amongst them to that class with which we are more directly concerned, the occasional hallucinations of sane and healthy persons.   Owing, amongst other causes, to their comparative infrequency, and to the difficulty of obtaining accurate contemporary records (since their occurrence cannot, as in the hallucinations of disease, be foreseen), phenomena of this class have hitherto attracted little attention amongst psychologists.[1] Mr. Edmund Gurney, however, in 1884 and onwards conducted an inquiry, by means of a printed schedule of questions, amongst a circle of some 6000 persons ; and during the last four years, at the request of the Congress of Experimental Psychology which met at Paris in 1889, Professor Henry Sidgwick, with the aid of a Committee of members of the S.P.R., has carried on a similar investigation on a larger scale. 17,000 adult persons, for the most part resident in the United Kingdom, have been questioned as to their experience of sensory hallucinations.[2] In the result it

---

[1] Professor Sully, to quote a recent instance, in his work on *Illusions* in the International Scientific Series (ed. 1887), devotes less than a page and a half to the discussion of the sensory hallucinations of normal life, and sums up the subject by saying that "when not brought on by exhaustion or artificial means, the hallucinations of the sane have their origin in a preternatural power of imagination" (p. 117).

[2] The question, which was worded as follows:—*Have you ever, when believing yourself to be completely awake, had a vivid impression of seeing, or being touched by a living being or inanimate object, or of hearing a voice, which impression, so far as you could discover, was not due to any external physical cause?*—was printed at the top of a schedule containing twenty-five spaces for the names and other par-

appeared that 1684 out of 17,000, or 9.9 per cent.—to wit, 655 out of 8372 men, and 1029 out of 8628 women —had experienced a sensory hallucination at some time in their lives. In about one-third of the cases the percipient had more than one experience of the kind. The phenomenon, therefore, though not so common as dreaming, is less rare than is generally supposed, seeing that about one in every ten educated persons has such an experience in the course of his life. The inquiries of the Committee have revealed no general cause for the greater number of these isolated hallucinations. In a small proportion of the cases there was a slight degree of ill-health, and in a rather greater number there was a certain amount of anxiety or other emotional excitement, to which the hallucinatory experience might with some plausibility be attributed.[1] But in the great majority of the cases there was no obvious antecedent to be discovered either in the condition of the percipient or in the surrounding circumstances, and we are led to the conclusion that an isolated hallucination of this kind is as little incompatible with ordinary health as a blush or a hiccough. At the same time we are entitled to infer, from the relatively large proportion of cases occurring when the percipient is in bed, or alone, that quiescence and freedom from external stimuli are favourable conditions for the genesis of

---

ticulars of those answering. Collectors were instructed not to *select* those of whom the question was asked; and to record alike negative and affirmative answers. In the case of an affirmative answer being received, further particulars were sought. For a full discussion of the various sources of error incident to an inquiry of this nature, and the precautions taken to avoid them, and for details of the results obtained, the reader is referred to the Report of the Committee, presented in a condensed form to the Congress of Experimental Psychology which met in London in 1892, and to be published in full in the *Proc. S.P.R.*, vol. x., part 26 (forthcoming).

[1] There was ill-health alone in about 5 per cent., anxiety alone in about 11 per cent., and both ill-health and anxiety in about 1.7 per cent. of first-hand cases.

hallucinations.[1] They may, in short, be regarded as unusually vivid dreams, and have for the most part just so much interest and significance. The nature and variety of these casual hallucinations may be gathered from the table on the following page.

If we turn to the mechanism of hallucinations, we shall find that—like dreams—some are apparently originated by the condition of the bodily organs; others again appear to be mere automatic reverberations of recent sensation; whilst yet others cannot be referred.to any immediate external stimulus, and suggest the "spontaneous" activity of the higher cerebral centres. With the rudimentary hallucinations—singing in the ears, sparks and flashes of light, etc.—which are caused by transient conditions of the external organs of sense, we are probably all familiar. But experience shows that a small nucleus of actual sensation may enter into more fully developed hallucinations. Thus, to take the simplest case, it is known that "sparks" may develop into "Faces in the Dark," which are themselves on the border-line between mind's-eye pictures and hallucinations. (See *St. James's Gazette*, "Faces in the Dark," Feb. 10, 1882, and *Proc. S.P.R.*, vol. iii. p. 171.) And in another recorded case (*Proc. S.P.R.*, vol. i. pp. 102, 103) an artist was accustomed to see constantly at his studio the figure of a man, under circumstances which strongly suggest that a *point de repère* was furnished by those floating.motes in the eyeballs which are liable momentarily to cloud the vision when the position is abruptly changed after a period of immobility. And we find cases where the constructive impulse has so amplified and misinter-

---

[1] Hallucinations occurring in the ambiguous state between waking and sleeping are called by some writers *hypnagogic*. For the purposes of our investigation, coincident hallucinations occurring at times when it is doubtful whether the percipient is fully awake, *e.g.*, when he is in bed, are termed "borderland." Their evidential value is, of course, somewhat less than that of hallucinations occurring when the percipient is unquestionably awake. (See cases 57, 59, 65, 66, etc.)

HALLUCINATIONS CLASSIFIED ACCORDING TO THE SENSE AFFECTED AND ACCORDING TO THE KIND OF PERCEPT.

	Realistic Human Phantasms (1)(2)(3)			Incompletely developed apparitions (4)	Visions (i.e., scenes or pictures) (5)	Angels and religious phantasms (6)	Grotesque, horrible, or monstrous apparitions (7)	Animals (8)	Definite inanimate objects (9)	Lights (10)	Indefinite objects or touches (11)	Insufficiently described for classification (12)	TOTALS (13)	(14)
	of living¹ people	of dead people	un-recognised											
Visual	296	105	272	120	18	10	23	22	10	14	14	8	912	⎫
Visual and Auditory (vocal) ...	30	41	10	1	3	1	1	3	—	2	1	—	87	⎪
Visual and Auditory (non-vocal)	7	4	24	13	—	—	7	3	3	1	2	—	67	⎬ 1120
Visual and Tactile	13	7	4	5	—	1	2	—	1	—	—	—	31	⎪
Visual and Auditory (vocal) and Tactile ...	5	6	4	2	—	—	—	—	—	—	—	—	19	⎪
Visual and Auditory (non-vocal) and Tactile ...	1	—	1	2	—	4	—	—	—	—	—	—	4	⎭
Auditory (vocal)	172	57	144	—	—	—	—	2	2	—	—	—	377	⎫ 388
Auditory (vocal) and Tactile ...	6	4	1	—	—	—	—	—	—	—	—	—	11	⎭
Tactile	6	8	55	—	—	—	—	—	—	—	35	—	108	⎫ 114
Tactile and Auditory (non-vocal)...	—	—	5	—	—	—	—	—	—	—	1	—	6	⎭
Total	536	232	520	143	21	16	33	27	16	17	53	8	1622	1622

NOTE.—This Table does not include 510 cases, of which the details are given at second-hand in 320, and are not given at all in 190.

¹ Including apparitions of persons not dead more than twelve hours, and not known by the percipient to be dead.

preted the data of normal sensation that we hardly know whether to class the result as hallucination or illusion. Thus, in a case given in *Phantasms* (vol. ii. p. 28), a young girl sees the face of a friend growing out of a yellow pansy; and an account of a similar incident has recently been furnished to me by Mr. H. Smith, of the Central Telegraph Office. The reference in the first line of the following narrative is to a rumour of the house being haunted, the remembrance of which possibly gave a definite form to the apparition :—

" POST OFFICE, *3rd Dec.* 1892.

" I had a turn last night, and for the moment thought I had caught the spook of my predecessor, but, alas! it all ended in smoke instead of spook. It gave me a turn, though, and made cold water run rippling down my back. It happened thus:—I had paid a good-night visit to the room of a dear little friend, a Callithrix monkey, whose lodgings are in a side building which has a door opening into the entrance hall. There was no light in the room of my friend, but a side light shone in through the door from the hall. (I was smoking.) On going out I looked back before shutting the door, and was startled to see just behind me, in the dark shade, the face of a human being—apparently an old man with grey hair. The face was perfectly distinct in every detail for an appreciable interval, and the eyes seemed to look sadly at me, and I looked sadly at him. The face moved, and the appearance, though a bit out of shape, still remained. I, however, saw what it was, and gave a gasp of relief which blew the old man's countenance into the shapelessness of the last remains of an extra strong puff of tobacco smoke I had left behind me."

Hallucinations of this kind, whose origin we can trace with more or less probability to some external sensation, may be in some respects compared with the visions seen on blank cards by the subjects of MM. Binet and Féré. But there are other hallucinations which cannot with any plausibility be referred to peripheral excitation. Such, as already said, are many hypnotic hallucinations, and the majority of the fully-developed hallucinations of normal life would appear to fall under the same category. Hallucinations of this class, like what may be called hallucinatory[1] dreams, are no doubt due to the spontaneous activity of the higher cerebral centres; they are simply ideas which take on sensory colouring. And just as the hallucinations of hypnotism, for the most part, are due to external suggestion, so it would seem that amongst the centrally initiated hallucinations of normal life there are some which owe their origin not to the spontaneous activity of the percipient's brain, but to an idea intruded from without—a suggestion not verbal but telepathic.

The proof of this proposition—the proof, that is, of the operation in certain cases of some distant cause external to the percipient's organism—lies in a numerical comparison of those hallucinations which coincide with an external event—e.g., the death of the person seen—and those which do not. For when the relative frequency of hallucinations has been ascertained the probability of chance coincidence in such cases can be exactly calculated. And should it appear that coincidental hallucinations are more frequent than chance would allow, it is certain that some other cause has to be sought for. And here we are met at the outset by a serious difficulty. It would appear from the results of the census just described that hallucinations even of a vivid and interesting character tend very quickly to be forgotten. Thus, to take only the cases of *realistic* apparitions resembling a living person, we find 157 cases recorded as occurring during the last ten years, and only 166 as occurring more than ten years ago; although, as the average age of our informants is about 40, we might have anticipated that the latter number would be about three times as great as the former.[2] But the discrepancy becomes still more

---

[1] As opposed to "dream-illusions," which depend on various organic sensations, or on the stimulation of the external organs of sense. The distinction is made by Professor Sully, *loc. cit.*, p. 139.

[2] These figures do not include second-hand cases. There are besides 29 undated cases, most of which probably belong to the remote period. See column 1 of table on p. 218 (visual cases).

striking if the figures are examined in detail. The subjoined table gives the number of apparitions resembling the human form recorded for each of the last ten years :—

No. of Years Ago—	1 and under	b'tw'n—1 and 2	2-3	3-4	4-5	5-6	6-7	7-8	8-9	9-10	Total.
Realistic Human Apparitions } Living . . .	35	19	15	13	15	13	17	12	8	10	157
Dead . . .	12	10	7	1	7	6	6	2	8	3	62
Unrecognised	17	16	12	17	17	18	11	10	5	8	126
	64	45	34	31	39	32	34	24	21	21	345

It will be seen that the number of hallucinations recorded as occurring between nine and ten years ago is less than one-third of the number recorded for the last twelve months. Nay, if the analysis is carried still further, it is found that within the last year the number of hallucinations remembered decreases month by month as we recede further from the present. The inference is irresistible, that the great majority even of interesting hallucinations do not sufficiently impress the memory to be preserved for a few years. After a careful analysis of the figures the Committee are of opinion that the number of visual hallucinations actually experienced by their informants since the age of ten would be approximately secured by multiplying the recorded number by *four*.[1]

But if hallucinations in general are not remembered enough, coincidental hallucinations, at least those which coincide with the death of the person seen,[2] would appear to be remembered too well, as will appear from the following figures. There are 13 such cases recorded during the last ten years. Now if we assume that this figure accurately re-

[1] The calculation is based upon an analysis of the whole number of visual cases reported during the most recent month, which would indicate an annual rate of about 140. The figures for the most recent quarter indicate an annual rate of about 120.

[2] A hallucination which *coincides* with a death is defined, for the purposes of this inquiry, as a hallucination which occurs within twelve hours of the death.

presents the number of such coincidences that have occurred in the experience of our informants during the last ten years, then, since the average age of our informants in this particular case is 46, we should expect to find for the whole period since the age of ten years 47 such coincidences reported; that is on the assumption that no death-coincidence is ever forgotten, and that the liability to such hallucination is practically uniform during the entire period. We do actually find 65 cases; from which it should, the Committee think, be inferred, not only that few or no death-coincidences are forgotten,—a result which is probably not surprising,—but also that a certain number of cases which are not death-coincidences have by the lapse of time grown to appear so.[1] Nor is it difficult to conjecture the particular form of error. It is probable that in most of the 18—more or less —spurious death-coincidences, there was an actual phantasm and an actual death, but that the two events did not stand in close relation to each other. We have already (see Chap. VI.) seen reason to suspect a constant tendency to magnify the closeness of a coincidence of this kind. Seen from a distance the two events—like a binary star-system—are apt to coalesce into one; and a new spectral analysis is required to dissociate them.

Nor would it be safe to assume that the tendencies which have demonstrably operated to falsify the more remote records have been altogether inactive during the last ten years. The causes which tend to sophisticate narratives of this kind, as already shown, are many and difficult to detect; the kind of evidence required to place the alleged death-coincidence beyond

[1] There is another possible explanation—viz., that some of the recent death-coincidences have been withheld from us, on account of the painful associations connected with them. That some cases—and recent would be more affected than remote examples—have been withheld on this account seems certain; but the explanation given in the text must, it is thought, be held primarily responsible for the discrepancy in the figures.

reasonable doubt has in some cases never existed ; in others, through the destruction of documents, the death of friends, or the mere lapse of time, it is now unattainable. Of the 65 reported coincidences perhaps not more than one-fifth reach the evidential standard of the cases included in this volume. And whilst there is a strong presumption that some proportion of those, which from one or other of the causes suggested inevitably fall below the standard, yet represent facts with substantial accuracy, we have no test which will enable us to determine with precision what narratives and to what extent are worthy of credence. Many of the best-attested cases are printed in full in the Report already referred to, and any reader who is interested in the matter will be able to form an estimate for himself. Meanwhile, an attempt has been made, by means of a careful examination of each narrative in detail, to estimate its evidential value. In the result it would appear that about 44 narratives rest on evidence that may be regarded as fairly good. Of these 44 cases, however, 12 must be struck out, 3 as having been imported into the census,[1] and 9 because a certain amount of anxiety may be presumed to have existed, and may be supposed—though the evidence for such action is very slight—to have caused the hallucination. We thus have 32 cases remaining, in which we have evidence of the occurrence of a hallucination, without apparent cause, within twelve hours of the death of the person seen.

The total number of recognised apparitions of living persons recorded at first-hand as occurring in the circle of 17,000 persons from which these death-coincidences were drawn, is 322.[2] But if, in order

[1] Cases, that is, in which the collector is known or suspected to have asked the question of the narrator, because he knew that he was to receive an affirmative answer.

[2] The gross total of visual phantasms recorded at first-hand as representing a living human being, or part of a human being (*e.g.*, a hand or a face), is 381. This total includes cases given in columns 1, 4,

to allow for forgetfulness, as already indicated (p. 221), we multiply the number recorded by 4, we shall arrive at a total of 1288, as representing the probable number actually experienced by our informants since the age of ten. We have, therefore, 32 cases of hallucinations coinciding with the death of the person seen, in an estimated total of nearly 1300 recognised apparitions of living persons—or about 1 in 40. But the death-rate for England and Wales in the last completed decade being 19.15 per 1000 per annum, the average probability that any particular person will die on any particular day is $\dfrac{1000 \times 365}{19.15} =$ about 1 in 19,000. That is, there is one chance in 19,000 that a man will die on the day on which his apparition is seen and recognised, supposing there to be no causal connection between the two events. Or in other words, for every hallucination which coincides with the death of the person seen, we should have to find about 18,999 similar hallucinations (*i.e.*, recognised apparitions of living persons) which do not so coincide.

But after making due allowance for forgetful-

---

and 5 of the table on p. 218. From this total we have deducted 31 cases where the percipient has had other experiences but has not enumerated them, and 28 cases which are estimated to have occurred before the age of ten, leaving the total given in the text, 322.

Of the gross total of 381, 80 are alleged to have coincided with the death of the person represented. Deducting in like manner 7 cases where the percipient has had other unspecified experiences, and 8 where the experience is believed to have occurred before the age of ten, we reach the total of 65 given above.

As, however, more care was no doubt taken to procure first-hand evidence in the case of apparitions coinciding with a death than in other cases, it would perhaps lead to more accurate results if in the larger total were included the second-hand non-coincidental cases, 38 in number. The reader can, if he prefer, work out the result for himself on this basis. But it will, of course, be understood that it is not practicable to sum up in a few pages the results of a long investigation; and those readers who are interested in the nature and distribution of casual hallucinations, and their relations to telepathic apparitions, are referred to the forthcoming Report, from which the figures in the text are quoted.

ness on the one hand, and for the creative activity of the imagination on the other, we find the actual proportion to be 1 to 40. In the face of these figures it would be preposterous to ascribe the reported cases of hallucinations at the time of death to chance. And the argument for some causal connection between hallucinations and external events is of course considerably strengthened if, in addition to (*a*) the coincidences of visual hallucinations with death, we take account of (*b*) the coincidences of auditory hallucinations with death, and (*c*) the coincidences of both visual and auditory hallucinations with other events than death, and (*d*) the cases in which the coincidence of the apparition with the death is nearer than twelve hours, the limit assumed in the above calculations.

It may not be superfluous to repeat (see *ante*, p. 27, footnote) that the calculation above given does not purport to establish thought-transference as the cause of these coincidences. The cause may be a greater prevalence of exaggeration and memory-illusion than the Committee have allowed for. What the calculation does is to bring us face to face with the problem : Here are certain phenomena, demonstrably not due to chance: do they reveal a new mode of communication between human minds, or merely a new source of fallacy in human testimony? It will hardly be disputed that, in either event, to find an answer to the question will justify much labour spent upon the search.

CHAPTER X.

INDUCED TELEPATHIC HALLUCINATIONS.

IN the present chapter we revert once more to experimental evidence. The cases now to be discussed should, in the logical order, have been included in Chapter V., and for a proper appreciation of their theoretic bearings and evidential value they ought to be considered in connection with the instances of thought-transference at a distance there recorded. It seemed best, however, to separate these instances of the experimental production of hallucinations at a distance, and reserve them for subsequent treatment, with the view of anticipating as far as possible the misconceptions to which this class of evidence is peculiarly open. In brief, until some attempt had been made to elucidate the nature of sensory hallucination in general, it seemed unwise to introduce matter so controvertible as apparitions of the human figure. For we are here assailing the last fortress of superstition ; in discussing such matters even educated persons find it difficult to free themselves from the fetters of traditional modes of thought and speech. Men who would be ashamed to think of earth, air, fire, and water as elements, because they were so held a century ago and are now so styled in the language of the market-place, will often see no middle course between rejecting altogether evidence of the kind here dealt with, and accepting the existence of " ghosts." But those who have followed the argument of the preceding chapters will see, if the possibility of thought-transference is granted, that the narratives now to be presented fall naturally into place as illustrating one of its modes of manifestation. That A. by taking thought should cause an image of himself to appear to B. need provoke no more surprise than that by the same means he should cause B. to see No. 27, or the Queen of Hearts. No one demands a spiritual entity corresponding to the Queen of Hearts, why then should any one believe in the other case that A.'s spirit had left its fleshly tabernacle to interview B.? The hallucinatory figure induced post-hypnotically in certain subjects presents an even closer parallel. It is recognised by all in such a case that the figure seen is a *thought* fashioned by the subject's mind, with no more substance than any other thought. It is only the influence of an unrecognised animism which leads us to demand such a substantial basis when the figure seen represents a dying man. The impulse which led to the projection of the hallucination was in the one case conveyed by word of mouth, in the other by some process as yet not understood. But the mystery lies in the process rather than in the result.

The present chapter, then, will contain instances of the action of thought-transference in which the transmitted idea was translated in the percipient's mind, not, as in most of the cases described in previous chapters, into a simple feeling, or sensation, or dream, but into a hallucination representing the human figure. Readers of *Phantasms of the Living* will remember the accounts there given (vol. i. pp. 104-109) of some experiments made by a friend of ours, Mr. S. H. B. On several occasions Mr. B. succeeded by an effort of will in causing a phantom of himself to appear to acquaintances who were not aware of his intention to try the experiment. On one occasion the figure was seen by two persons simultaneously. As at that time results of the kind were almost unprecedented, we felt, notwithstanding our full confidence in Mr. B., some reluctance in publishing an account of his experiments, lest isolated marvels of the kind might prejudice our whole case. But fortunately, while *Phantasms of the Living* was actually passing through the press, we received from an independent source an account of successful experiments of the same kind (see below, case 63), and within a few weeks of its publication a friend of the present writer was induced by a perusal of Mr. B.'s narrative to make on his own account a similar trial, which completely succeeded. This gentleman wrote to me on 16th November 1886 as follows :—

No. 61.—From the Rev. CLARENCE GODFREY.

" I was so impressed by the account on p 105 that I determined to put the matter to an experiment.

" Retiring at 10.45 [on the 15th November 1886] I determined to appear, if possible, to a friend, and accordingly I set myself to work with all the volitional and determinative energy which I possess, to stand at the foot of her bed. I need not say that I never dropped the slightest hint beforehand as to my intention, such as could mar the experiment, nor had I mentioned the subject to her. As the 'agent' I may describe my own experiences.

" Undoubtedly the imaginative faculty was brought extensively into play, as well as the volitional, for I endeavoured to *translate myself*, spiritually, into her room, and to attract her attention, as it were, while standing there. My effort was sustained for perhaps eight minutes, after which I felt tired, and was soon asleep.

" The next thing I was conscious of was meeting the lady next morning (*i.e.*, in a dream, I suppose?) and asking her at once if she had seen me last night. The reply came, 'Yes.' 'How?' I inquired. Then in words strangely clear and low, like a well audible whisper, came the answer, 'I was sitting beside you.' These words, so clear, awoke me instantly, and I felt I must have been dreaming ; but on reflection I remembered what I had been 'willing' before I fell asleep, and it struck me, 'This must be a *reflex* action from the percipient.' My watch showed 3.40 A.M. The following is what I wrote immediately in pencil, standing in my night-dress :—'As I reflected upon those clear words, they struck me as being quite *intuitive*, I mean *subjective*, and to have proceeded *from within*, *as my own conviction*, rather than a communication from any one else. And yet I can't remember her face at all, as one can after a vivid dream !'

"But the words were uttered in a clear, quick tone, which was most remarkable, and awoke me at once.

"My friend in the note with which she sent me the enclosed account of *her own* experience, says :—'I remember the man put all the lamps out soon after I came upstairs, and that is only done about a quarter to four.'"

Mr. Godfrey received from the percipient on the 16th November an account of her side of the experience, and at his request she wrote it down as follows :—

"Yesterday—viz., the morning of November 16th, 1886—about half-past three o'clock, I woke up with a start and an idea that some one had come into the room. I heard a curious sound, but fancied it might be the birds in the ivy outside. Next I experienced a strange restless longing to leave the room and go downstairs. This feeling became so overpowering that at last I rose and lit a candle, and went down, thinking if I could get some soda water it might have a quieting effect. On returning to my room I saw Mr. Godfrey standing under the large window on the staircase. He was dressed in his usual style, and with an expression on his face that I have noticed when he has been looking very earnestly at anything. He stood there, and I held up the candle and gazed at him for three or four seconds in utter amazement, and then, as I passed up the staircase, he disappeared. The impression left on my mind was so vivid that I fully intended waking a friend who occupied the same room as myself, but remembering that I should only be laughed at as romantic and imaginative, refrained from doing so.

"I was not frightened at the appearance of Mr. Godfrey, but felt much excited, and could not sleep afterwards."

On the 21st of the same month I heard a full account of the incident given above from Mr. Godfrey, and on the day following from Mrs. ——. Mrs. —— told me that the figure appeared quite distinct and life-like at first, though she could not remember to have noticed more than the upper part of the body. As she looked it grew more and more shadowy, and finally faded away. Mrs. ——, it should be added, told me that she had previously seen two phantasmal figures, representing a parent whom she had recently lost.[1]

Mr. Godfrey at our request made two other trials, without, of course, letting Mrs. —— know his intention. The first of these attempts was without result, owing perhaps to the date chosen, as he was aware at the time, being unsuitable. But a trial made on the 7th December 1886 succeeded completely. Mrs. ——, writing on December 8th, states that she was awakened by hearing a voice cry, "Wake," and by feeling a hand rest on the left side of her head. She then saw stooping over her a figure which she recognised as Mr. Godfrey's.

In this last case the dress of the figure does not seem to have been seen distinctly. But in the apparition of the 16th November, it will be observed that the dress was that ordinarily worn in the day-time by Mr. Godfrey, and that in which the percipient would be accustomed to see him, *not* the dress which he was actually wearing at the time. If the apparition is in truth nothing more than an expression of the percipient's thought this is what we should expect to find, and as a matter of fact in the majority of well evidenced narratives of telepathic hallucination this is what we actually do find. The dress and surroundings of the phantasm represent, not the dress and surroundings of the agent at the moment, but those with which the percipient is familiar. If other proof were wanting, this fact would in itself seem a sufficient argument that we have to deal, not with ghosts but with hallucinations. It is to be regretted, however, that most recent experimenters in this direction have succeeded only in producing apparitions of themselves. But a crucial experiment of the kind desired is to be found in an account published in

[1] These details are taken from notes made by the writer immediately after the interview.

1822 by H. M. Wesermann, Government Assessor and Chief Inspector of Roads at Düsseldorf. He records five successful trials with different percipients, of which the fifth seems worth quoting in full.[1]

No. 62.—From H. M. WESERMANN.

" A lady, who had been dead five years, was to appear to Lieutenant ——n in a dream at 10.30 P.M. and incite him to good deeds. At half-past ten, contrary to expectation, Herr ——n had not gone to bed, but was discussing the French campaign with his friend Lieutenant S—— in the ante-room. Suddenly the door of the room opened, the lady entered dressed in white, with a black kerchief and uncovered head, greeted S—— with her hand three times in a friendly manner; then turned to ——n, nodded to him, and returned again through the doorway.

" As this story, related to me by Lieutenant ——n, seemed to be too remarkable from a psychological point of view for the truth of it not to be duly established, I wrote to Lieutenant S——, who was living six[2] miles away, and asked him to give me his account of it. He sent me the following reply :—

" ' . . . On the 13th of March, 1817, Herr ——n came to pay me a visit at my lodgings about a league from A——. He stayed the night with me. After supper, and when we were both undressed, I was sitting on my bed and Herr ——n was standing by the door of the next room on the point also of going to bed. This was about half-past ten. We were speaking partly about indifferent subjects and partly about the events of the French campaign. Suddenly the door out of the kitchen opened without a sound, and a lady entered, very pale, taller than Herr ——n, about five feet four inches in height, strong and broad of figure, dressed in white, but with a large black kerchief which reached to below the waist. She entered with bare head, greeted me with the hand three times in complimentary fashion, turned round to the left towards Herr ——n, and waved her hand to him three times; after which the figure quietly, and again without any creaking of the door, went out. We followed at once in order to discover whether there were any deception,

---

[1] *Der Magnetismus und die allgemeine Weltsprache.* A brief account of the five trials, quoted from the *Archiv für den thierischen Magnetismus*, vol. vi. pp. 136-139, will be found in *Phantasms of the Living*, vol. i. pp. 101, 102. In the other cases the impression was produced in a *dream*. The distance varied from ⅛ of a mile to 9 miles in the case quoted in the text.

[2] In Wesermann's book, as also in the account given in the *Archiv*, the account is headed " Fifth experiment at a distance of *nine* miles."

but found nothing. The strangest thing was this, that our night-watch of two men whom I had shortly before found on the watch were now asleep, though at my first call they were on the alert, and that the door of the room, which always opens with a good deal of noise, did not make the slightest sound when opened by the figure. "'S.

"'D——n, January 11th, 1818.'

"From this story (Wesermann continues) the following conclusions may be drawn:—

"(1) That waking persons, as well as sleeping, are capable of perceiving the ideas [*Gedankenbilder*] of distant friends through the inner sense as dream images. For not only the opening and shutting of the door, but the figure itself—which, moreover, exactly resembled that of the dead lady—was incontestably only a dream in the waking state, since the door would have creaked as usual had the figure really opened and shut it.

"(2) That many apparitions and supposed effects of witchcraft were very probably produced in the same way.

"(3) That clairvoyants are not mistaken when they state that a stream of light proceeds from the magnetiser to the distant friend, which visibly presents the scene thought of, if the magnetiser thinks of it strongly and without distraction."

More philosophic or more successful than recent investigators, Wesermann, it will be seen, varied the form of his experiment. In the first he caused his own figure to appear, but in each of the subsequent trials he chose a fresh image, meeting on each occasion with equal success. It should be observed, however, that though Wesermann seems to have been a careful as well as a philosophic investigator, he has omitted to record how often he made trials of this kind without producing any result, and it cannot fairly be assumed that there were no failures. But in comparing such cases as those here recorded with the experiments at close quarters described in Chapters II., III., and IV., it should be remembered that a failure which consists merely, as in Mr. Godfrey's second trial, in the absence of any unusual impression on the part of the percipient, detracts far less from the value of occasional success than failures attested by the production of wrong impressions; and further, that a sensory hallucination being a much rarer phenomenon than an idea, the improbability of chance-coincidence between a hallucination and the attempt (unknown to the percipient) to produce it is greater in the same proportion.

Later experience has not confirmed Wesermann's third inference, as to the stream of light proceeding from the agent; there are no grounds for regarding such an appearance as other than subjective, due to the percipient's preconceived ideas of what he ought to see.   But another feature in the narrative is more significant.   One is led to infer both from Herr S.'s description and from Wesermann's remarks in (1) that the figure seen resembled a deceased lady who was not known to either of the percipients.   If this interpretation is correct, the figure seen cannot have been subjective in the same sense as the hallucinations described in Chapter IX. and Mr. Godfrey's apparition may be supposed to have been.   The latter were, *ex hypothesi, autoplastic—i.e.,* they were hallucinations built up in the percipient's own mind on a nucleus supplied from without.   But what Herren S. and ——n saw was a *heteroplastic* image, a picture like that of a diagram or a card transferred ready-made from the agent's mind.   We should not of course be justified, on the evidence of a single narrative of somewhat doubtful import, in concluding that such an origin for a hallucination is possible.   But there are a few narratives to be cited later (Chapter XIII.) which also suggest such an interpretation.

In Mr. Godfrey's trials, as also in those made by Mr. S. H. B., the agent was asleep at the time of the experiment.[1]   In the two cases which follow the agent was in a hypnotic trance.   In the first instance, it will be seen, there appears to have been a reciprocal effect, the agent himself becoming aware at the time of the percipient's surroundings, and of the effect pro-

[1] Wesermann unfortunately does not record his own state at the time of the experiments.

duced on her by his influence. The account was sent
to us in January 1886.

No. 63.—From MR. H. P. SPARKS.

After describing various hypnotic experiments on
a fellow-student, Mr. A. H. W. Cleave, Mr. Sparks
continues:—

"Last Friday evening (January 15th, 1886) he expressed his
wish to see a young lady living in Wandsworth, and he also
said he would try to make himself seen by her I accordingly
mesmerised him, and continued the long passes for about 20
minutes, concentrating my will on his idea. When he came
round (I brought him round by just touching his hand and
willing him, after 1 hour and 20 minutes' trance) he said he had
seen her in the dining-room, and that after a time she grew
restless, and then suddenly looked straight at him and then
covered her eyes with her hands. Just after this he came
round. Last Monday evening (January 18th, 1886) we did the
same thing, and this time he said he thought he had frightened
her, as after she had looked at him for a few minutes she fell
back in her chair in a sort of faint. Her little brother was in the
room at the time. Of course, after this we expected a letter if
the vision was real; and on Wednesday morning he received
a letter from this young lady asking whether anything had
happened to him, as on Friday evening she was startled by
seeing him standing at the door of the room. After a minute
he disappeared, and she thought that it might have been fancy;
but on the Monday evening she was still more startled by seeing
him again, and this time much clearer, and it so frightened her
that she nearly fainted.

"This account I send you is perfectly true, I will vouch, for
I have two independent witnesses who were in the dormitory at
the time when he was mesmerised, and when he came round.
My patient's name is Arthur H. W. Cleave, and his age is
18 years. A. C. Darley and A. S. Thurgood, fellow-students,
are the two witnesses I mentioned.   "H. PERCY SPARKS."

Mr. Cleave writes, on March 15th, 1886:—

"H.M.S. *Marlborough*, PORTSMOUTH.

"Sparks and myself have, for the past eighteen months, been
in the habit of holding mesmeric séances in our dormitories.
For the first month or two we got no very satisfactory results,
but after that we succeeded in sending one another to sleep.
I could never get Sparks further than the sleeping state, but he

could make me do anything he liked whilst I was under the influence ; so I gave up trying to send him off, and all our efforts were made towards my being mesmerised. After a short time we got on so well that Sparks had three or four other fellows in the dormitory to witness what I did. I was quite insensible to all pain, as the fellows have repeatedly pinched my hands and legs without my feeling it. About six months ago I tried my power of will, in order, while under the influence, to see persons to whom I was strongly attached. For some time I was entirely unsuccessful, although I once thought that I saw my brother (who is in Australia), but had no opportunity of verifying the vision.

"A short time ago I tried to see a young lady whom I know very well, and was perfectly surprised at my success. I could see her as plainly as I can see now, but I could not make myself seen by her, although I had often tried to. After I had done this several times I determined to try and make myself seen by her, and told Sparks of my idea, which he approved. Well, we tried this for five nights running without any more success. We then suspended our endeavours for a night or two, as I was rather over-exerted by the continued efforts and got severe headaches. We then tried again (on, I think it was, a Friday, but am not certain), and were, I thought, successful ; but as the young lady did not write to me about it, I thought I must have been mistaken, so I told Sparks that we had better give up trying. But he begged me to try once more, which we did on the following Monday, when we were successful to such an extent that I felt rather alarmed. (I must tell you that I am in the habit of writing to the young lady every Sunday, but I did not write that week, it order to make her think about me.) This took place between 9.30 P.M. and 10 P.M. Monday night, and on the following Wednesday morning I got the letter which I have enclosed. I, of course, then knew I had been successful. I went home about a fortnight after this, when I saw the young lady, who seemed very frightened in spite of my explanations, and begged me never to try it again, and I promised her that I would not."

The two witnesses of the experiment last described write as follows:—

"I have seen Mr. Cleave's account of his mesmeric experiment, and can fully vouch for the truth thereof.
"A. C. DARLEY."

"I have read Mr. Cleave's statement, and can vouch for the truth of it, as I was present when he was mesmerised and heard his statement after he revived. "A. E. S. THURGOOD."

The following is a copy, made by Mr. Gurney, of the letter in which the young lady, Miss A——, described her side of the affair. The envelope bore the postmarks, " Wandsworth, Jan. 19, 1886," " Portsmouth, Jan. 20, 1886," and the address, " Mr. A. H. W. Cleave, H.M.S. *Marlborough*, Portsmouth."

"WANDSWORTH, *Tuesday morning.*

"DEAR ARTHUR,—Has anything happened to you? Please write and let me know at once, for I have been so frightened.

"Last Tuesday evening I was sitting in the dining [room] reading, when I happened to look up, and could have declared I saw you standing at the door looking at me. I put my handkerchief to my eyes, and when I looked again you were gone. I thought it must have been only my fancy, but last night (Monday), while I was at supper, I saw you again, just as before, and was so frightened that I nearly fainted. Luckily only my brother was there, or it would have attracted attention. Now do write at once and tell me how you are. I really cannot write any more now."

It will be seen that Miss A—— fixes the date of her first hallucination on *Tuesday*, whereas Mr. Sparks and Mr. Cleave speak of it as *Friday*. Mr. Gurney, in conversation with the experimenters, was unable to fix the actual date with any certainty, but there can be little doubt that if Tuesday was the day, it fell within the five days on which Mr. Cleave attempted to see Miss A——. Of the second coincidence there can be no doubt.

The next case is recorded by Mr. F. W. H. Myers (*Journal S.P.R.*, March 1891), who writes:—

No. 64.

"In 1888 a gentleman, whom I will call Mr. A., who has occupied a high public position in India, and whom I have known a long time, informed me verbally that he had had a remarkable experience. He awoke one morning, in India, very early, and in the dawning light saw a lady, whom I will call Mrs. B., standing at the foot of his bed. At the same time he received an impression that she needed him. This was his sole experience of a hallucination; and it so much impressed him that he wrote to the lady, who was in England at the time, and mentioned the circumstance. He afterwards heard from her that she had been in a trance-condition at the time, and had endeavoured to appear to him by way of an experiment.

"Mr. A. did not give me the lady's name, supposing that she did not desire the incident to be spoken of; nor did he find an opportunity of himself inquiring as to her willingness to mention the matter."

Subsequently, on July 13th, 1890, the agent, Mrs. B., wrote of her own accord to Mr. Myers. Mrs. B. began by stating that she had submitted herself to be experimented upon by a lady friend, with the view of acquiring clairvoyant faculties. She then described how in the course of one experiment in 1886 she lost consciousness of outward things, and saw the figure of a tall woman, whom she recognised as a friend of her mother's, standing by her. Then she goes on :—

"I find myself seriously debating within myself what I should do to prove to myself, and for my own satisfaction, if I am indeed the victim of hallucination or not. I decided in a flash on a man whom I knew to be possessed of the most work-a-day world common-sense; his views and mine regarding most things were at the antipodes, very unreceptive, who would be entirely out of sympathy with me in my present experiment and experiences, at which I knew he would only laugh, while regarding me as a simple tool in tricky hands. Such a man was, I decided, the most satisfactory for my trial. The grey lady here impressed me with a desire to will; in her anxiety she appeared to move towards me. I felt her will one with mine, and I willed with a concentrated strength of mind and body, which finally prostrated me, thus : I will that [Mr. A.] may feel I am near him and want his help ; and that, without any suggestion from me, he write to tell me I have influenced him to-night.

"The grey lady disappeared. I was seated in the chair, weary, but feeling naturally, and back in common-place life. We put down the date and the appearance of the grey lady, and I spoke to none of what had happened. Some weeks passed, when I received a letter from [Mr. A.], asking how had I been employed on a certain July evening at such and such an hour, mentioning to what hour it would answer in London—day, date, and hour were those on which I had made my proof trial— saying that he was asleep, and had dreamed something he would tell me, but that he awoke from the dream feeling I wanted something of him, and asking me to let him know if at the time he so carefully mentioned I had been doing anything which had any reference to him. I then, and then only, told him what I have here related."

Unfortunately Mr. A., on being again appealed to, refused to write an account of his own experience, on the ground that his memory for details might by lapse of time have become untrustworthy. The case is therefore defective, not merely by the length of time which passed between the incident and the agent's record of it, but by the absence of any direct testimony from the percipient. It will be seen that Mrs. B. writes of Mr. A.'s impression as a *dream*. It seems clear, however, that Mr. A. did not himself regard his experience as a dream.

An interesting account is given by Miss Edith Maughan (*Journal S.P.R.*) of a similar experiment made by her in the summer of 1888. She was reading in bed when the idea occurred to her of "willing" to appear to her friend, Miss Ethel Thompson, who occupied the adjoining room. After concentrating her attention strongly for a few minutes she "felt dizzy and only half-conscious." On recovering full consciousness she heard Miss Thompson's voice speaking in the next room. The time was about 2 A.M. As a matter of fact, Miss Thompson, who was fully awake, was disturbed between 2 and 3 A.M. by seeing at the bedside the figure of Miss Maughan, which disappeared instantly on a light being struck. It is not perhaps possible under the circumstances, in view of Miss Maughan's own statement that she was only semi-conscious during part of the experiment, absolutely to exclude the hypothesis that the figure seen was that of Miss Maughan in some state analogous to somnambulism, and the case is not therefore given in full; but it is important to note that both ladies—and we have reason to know that they are good observers—are convinced that the figure seen was not that of Miss Maughan in the flesh, and the rapidity of the disappearance is a further argument against such a supposition.

In the cases so far dealt with the agent, when his state is recorded, was asleep or entranced at the time of the experiment, whilst the percipient appears as a rule to have been awake. In the cases which follow the agent was awake, but the percipient, in two of the cases—if not also in the third—seems to have seen the hallucinatory figure in the borderland state on awaking from sleep. In two of the cases the agent, no doubt intentionally, chose a time when he had reason to believe that the percipient would be asleep; in the third case, whilst the experiments at night failed, success was obtained when the percipient had fallen asleep unexpectedly in the day-time. In view of the absence of any well-attested cases in which both agent and percipient are shown to have been fully awake immediately before and at the time of the experiment,—in case 62 (Wesermann) the state of the agent, and in case 66 (Wiltse) that of the percipient, is not clearly shown,—it is difficult to resist the conclusion that the condition of sleep or trance in one or both parties to the experiment is favourable to transference of this kind. That sleep, or rather the borderland which lies on either side of sleep, is peculiarly favourable to the production in the *percipient*, not only of hallucinations in general, but of telepathic hallucinations in particular, has already been shown. But the instances cited in the present chapter would seem to indicate that in the agent also sleep and trance (or possibly a trance self-induced in sleep or in waking) may facilitate such transmissions.

No. 65.—From DR. VON SCHRENCK-NOTZING.

We received the following case from Baron von Schrenck-Notzing, some of whose experiments have been already quoted (No. 9, p. 54). Dr. von Schrenck-Notzing first gave an account of the incident verbally to Professor Sidgwick at Munich, and subsequently, at his request, sent in June 1888 the following written narrative :—

"In the winter of 1886-87, I think it was in the month of February, as I was going along the Barerstrasse one evening at half-past 11, it occurred to me to make an attempt at influencing at a distance, through mental concentration. As I had had, for some time, the honour of being acquainted with the family of Herr ——, and thus had had the opportunity of learning that his daughter, Fräulein ——, was sensitive to psychical influences, I decided to try to influence her, especially as the family lived at the corner of the Barerstrasse and Karlstrasse. The windows of the dwelling were dark as I passed by, from which I concluded that the ladies had already gone to rest. I then stationed myself by the wall of the houses on the opposite side of the road, and for about five minutes firmly concentrated my thoughts on the following desire:—Fräulein —— shall wake and think of me. Then I went home. The next day when I met Fräulein ——'s friend on the ice, I learned from her (they shared a bedroom between them) that something strange had happened to the ladies during the preceding night. I remarked thereupon to Fräulein Prieger (such was the friend's name) that the time when the occurrence took place was between half-past 11 and 12; whereat she was greatly astonished. Then I obtained from the lady an account of the circumstance, as she herself has written it out on the accompanying sheet of paper. For me the success of this experiment was a proof that under certain circumstances one person can influence another at a distance.
"ALBERT FREIHERR VON SCHRENCK-NOTZING."

The percipient, Miss ——, writes on May 11th, 1888 :—

"There is not much to tell concerning the incident of which you ask me to give an account. It happened thus:—Baron Schrenck was returning home one night in March 1887 (or April, I am not sure as to the date), about 11.30, and stood for some time outside my bedroom window, which looked on-to the street. I was in bed at the time, lying with closed eyes, nearly asleep. It seemed to me as if the part of the room where my bed was had become suddenly light, and I felt compelled to open my eyes, seeing at the same time, as it appeared to me, the face of Baron Schrenck. It was gone again as quick as lightning. The next day I told my friend Fräulein Prieger of this occurrence; she went skating that same day, and met Baron Schrenck on the ice. They had scarcely conversed together five minutes before he asked Fräulein Prieger if I had seen 'anything last night. Fräulein Prieger repeated what I had told her, whereupon Baron Schrenck said that, at the time of my seeing him, he was standing outside my window, trying hard to impress his presence upon me. This never occurred again, and I believe Baron Schrenck did not have occasion to repeat the experiment."

In a further letter Miss —— adds (1) that the blinds of her room were drawn down, (2) that she has experienced no other hallucination of any kind.

Fräulein Prieger, whose account was enclosed in Dr. von Schrenck-Notzing's letter of June 1888, writes:—

" The winter before last, shortly after Christmas, I was suddenly awakened in the night, between 11 and 12 o'clock, by my friend ——, who asked me in an excited manner if I *also* saw Baron von Schrenck, who was close by her bed. On my objecting that she had been dreaming, and should now quietly go to sleep again, she repeated that she had been completely awake, and had seen Baron von Schrenck so close to her that she could have caught hold of his beard. By degrees she quieted herself, and we both went to sleep.

"The following day, on my way home from the ice, I told Baron von Schrenck of this exciting nocturnal scene, and noticed to my not slight astonishment that he seemed greatly rejoiced, as though over a successful experiment which had received its completion in what I communicated to him.

"LINA PRIEGER.

" Gubelsbergerstrasse, 15 I."

It is much to be regretted that none of the persons concerned thought it worth while to write down an account of the incident at the time. It will be observed that even in the comparatively short interval —little more than a year—which elapsed before this was done, one slight discrepancy, as to the time at which Fräulein Prieger was told of the impression, has crept into the narrative. But it seems clear that Miss —— told her experience before Fräulein Prieger met Baron von Schrenck-Notzing.

In the next two cases also the result here recorded

16

is one of many successful experiments in thought-transference made by the agent (see Chapter XV.).

No. 66.—From Dr. WILTSE, Skiddy, Kansas, U.S.A.

"*March* 16*th*, 1891.

"Some weeks ago several persons were passing the evening at my house, and two children, a little girl of eight years and a boy of six years, whose mother is stopping with us, had been put to bed in an adjoining room, the door between the rooms being closed. The company were engaged in games that did not interest me, and I took a seat some five feet from the bedroom door and began trying to make the boy see my form in the room at his bedside, he being on the front side of the bed. I knew the children were awake, as I could hear them laughing. After some ten or fifteen minutes, the boy suddenly screamed as if frightened, and, hurrying in there, I found the little fellow buried up in the bedclothes and badly frightened, but he seemed ashamed of his fright and would not tell me what was the matter.

"I kept the matter of my having tried an experiment a thorough secret, and after some two weeks it came out through the little girl that Charlie thought he saw a "great big tiger standing by his bed looking at him, and he could see Uncle Hime (myself) in the tiger's eyes." What was the tiger? I had not thought of any form but my own. The child lives in Cleveland, Ohio, and has seen the collections in Zoological Gardens, but has not been taught the different colours. I have just now shown him the plates in Wood's *Natural History*, and he pointed out a lion as the animal he saw, but as the plates are not coloured, they are little good for the purpose; but as I began at the back of the book and took through all sorts first, and the lion was the first and only animal designated by him as the one he had seen in the room, I conclude he was near enough to the classification for our purpose. No one but myself knew of my experiment until the children had told their story.

"A. S. WILTSE."

Dr. Wiltse writes later:—

"SKIDDY, MORRIS CO., KANSAS,
March 29*th*, 1891.

"I tried one more experiment of the same kind with the little boy, but failed, but I was conscious of wavering in mind during the whole course of the experiment, and besides this there were other unfavourable conditions. The child's mother was absent for the evening and the children with my own boy (aged fifteen) were making Rome howl in the way of untrammelled fun."

Mrs. Wiltse and Dr. Wiltse's son write as follows:—

> "SKIDDY, KANSAS,
> *March 28th*, 1891.

"I was present when Josie Skene told papa what her brother Charlie was scared about.

"She said that Charlie throwed the cover over his head and told her that he saw a tiger, and Uncle Hime, as he called papa, was in the tiger's eyes.

> "JASON WILTSE."

"I certify that the above statement is substantially correct, as I also heard the little girl relate it.

> "MRS. HAIDEE WILTSE."

Mrs. Charles Skene, the mother of the little boy, writes:—

> "153 PLATT STREET [CLEVELAND, OHIO],
> *April 9th*, 1891.

"Your letter dated the 6th came to hand to-day. I was on a visit to the Dr. and his family, and one evening he said he would try an experiment on my little boy; it was about seven o'clock and they had just been put to bed. The Dr. wanted to make him see him by his bedside, and him in the other room, and he did; he saw him in the form of a tiger and he also had tigers in his eyes. He commenced to shout, and said he was frightened, but did not say any more, he was so frightened. This is my daughter's statement as far as she can recollect.

"If there are any more questions you would like me to answer I will gladly do so. I was not at home the night this happened.

> "MRS. CHAS. SKENE."

Later she adds:—

> "*April 27th*, 1891.

"Your letter of the 17th came to hand. I do not know the date, but it was about the middle of February, on a Wednesday evening. My little boy is six years old; he remembers it well, and often talks of it."

Mrs. Skene added, in answer to a question, that the boy did not know that the experiment was being tried on him. It should be added that Mr. Rasero, who was present, wrote, on the 30th October 1891, to confirm Dr. Wiltse's statement that nothing was said beforehand about trying an experiment of any kind.

The tiger in this experiment appears to have been

a confused nightmare effect produced by the telepathic impression on the mind of the child percipient.
In the next case, it will be seen, the percept appears
to have been unusually clear and distinct.

No. 67.—From JOSEPH KIRK.[1]

Mr. Kirk has made several attempts to produce a
hallucination of himself. Writing to us on the 7th July
1890, he stated that without the knowledge of his friend
and neighbour, Miss G., he tried each night, from the
10th to the 20th of June, and once on the 11th in the
afternoon, to induce her to see a hallucination of himself. From casual conversation, however, with Miss
G. he gathered that no effect had been produced.
But on June 23rd Mr. Kirk learned that the trial
made on June 11th, the day and hour of which had
been noted at the time, had completely succeeded.
He thus describes the occasion :—

"2 RIPON VILLAS, PLUMSTEAD.

" . . . I had been rather closely engaged on some auditing
work, which had tired me, and as near as I can remember the
time was between 3.30 and 4 P.M. that I laid down my pencil,
stretched myself, and in the act of doing the latter I was seized
with the impulse to make a trial on Miss G. I did not, of
course, know where she was at the moment, but, with a flash,
as it were, I transferred myself to her bedroom. I cannot say
why I thought of that spot, unless it was that I did so because
my first experiment had been made there—*i.e.*, on the previous
night, the 10th June. As it happened, it was what I must call
a 'lucky shot,' for I caught her at the moment she was lightly
sleeping in her chair—a condition which seems to be peculiarly
favourable to receiving and externalising telepathic messages.

"The figure seen by Miss G. was clothed in a suit I was at
the moment wearing, and was *bareheaded*, the latter as would
be the case, of course, in an office. This suit is of a dark
reddish-brown *check* stuff, and it was an unusual circumstance
for me to have had on the *coat* at the time, as I wear, as a rule,
an office coat of *light* material. But this office coat I had, a
day or so before, sent to a tailor to be repaired, and I had,
therefore, to keep on that belonging to the dark suit.

"I tested the reality of the vision by this dark suit. I asked,

---

[1] See Nos. 37, 38, 39, Chapter V.

'How was I dressed?' (not at all a leading question). The reply of Miss G. was, touching the sleeve of the coat I was then wearing (of a *light* suit), 'Not this coat, but that dark suit you wear sometimes. I even saw clearly the *small check* pattern of it; and I saw your features as plainly as though you had been bodily present. I *could not* have seen you more distinctly.'"

Miss G.'s account is:—

"*June 28th*, 1890.

"A peculiar occurrence happened to me on the Wednesday of the week before last. In the afternoon (being tired by a morning walk), while sitting in an easy-chair near the window of my own room, I fell asleep. At any time I happen to sleep during the day (which is but seldom) I invariably awake with tired, uncomfortable sensations, which take some little time to pass off; but that afternoon, on the contrary, I was suddenly quite wide awake, seeing Mr. Kirk standing near my chair, dressed in a dark brown coat, which I had frequently seen him wear. His back was towards the window, his right hand towards me; he passed across the room towards the door, which is opposite the window, the space between being 15 feet, the furniture so arranged as to leave just that centre clear; but when he got about 4 feet from the door, which was closed, he disappeared.

.   .   .   .

"I feel sure I had not been dreaming of him, and cannot remember that anything had happened to cause me even to think of him that afternoon before falling asleep."

Mr. Kirk writes later:—

"I have only succeeded once in making myself visible to Miss G. since the occasion I have already reported, and that had the singularity of being only my features—my face in *miniature*, that is, about *three inches* in diameter."

In a letter dated January 19th, 1891, Mr. Kirk says as to this last appearance:—

"Miss G. did not record this at the time, as she attached no importance to it, but I noted the date (July 23rd) on my office blotting-pad, as it was at the office I was thinking of her. I say 'thinking,' because I was doing so in connection with another subject, and with no purpose of making an experiment. I had a headache, and was resting my head on my left hand. Suddenly it occurred to me that my thinking about her might probably influence her in some way, and I made the note I have mentioned."

Mr. Kirk enclosed in his statement to us the piece of blotting-paper on which the note of the second successful experiment had been made. The fact that the hallucination in the first case included a representation of the clothes actually worn by the agent at the time may have been a mere coincidence. But the case should be borne in mind in considering the possibility of heteroplastic hallucination.

CHAPTER XI.

SPONTANEOUS TELEPATHIC HALLUCINATIONS.

IN the last chapter we gave illustrations of telepathic hallucinations induced by an act of voluntary concentration on the part of the agent. The hallucinatory effects now to be described were produced without design, and in some cases, it would appear, without the conscious direction of the agent's thoughts to the person affected. They purport, in fact, to have been the spontaneous outcome of some emotional stress on the part of the person whom the hallucination represented.

Auditory Hallucinations.

We will begin by quoting two examples of auditory hallucination.

No. 68.—From MISS C. CLARK.

"1889.

"I heard some one sobbing one evening last August (1888) about 10 P.M. It was in the house in Dunbar, Scotland, as I was preparing to go to bed. Feeling convinced that it was my youngest sister, I advised another sister not to go into the next room, whence the sounds seemed to proceed. After waiting with me a few minutes this sister went into the dining-room, and returned to me saying that our youngest sister was in the dining-room, and not crying at all. Then I at once thought there must be something the matter with my greatest friend, a girl of twenty-four, then in Lincolnshire. I wrote to her next day, asking her if, and at what hour on the previous night, she had been crying. In her next letter she said, 'Yes, she was suffering great pain with toothache just at the time, and was unable to restrain a few sobs.' . . . This has been the only similar experience I have had."

I have seen the letter referred to, together with three others, extracts from which are given below. It will be seen that Miss Clark was mistaken in supposing that she wrote *next day*. The letter was actually begun three days after—on the Wednesday—and completed on the subsequent day, after the receipt of Miss Maughan's letter written on the Tuesday evening. In view, however, of the fact that Miss Clark wrote of her impression before the receipt of her friend's letter, the mistake seems not material.

From MISS CLARK.

"DUNBAR,
"Wednesday, *August 22nd*, 1888, 9 P.M.
"Were you crying on Sunday night near eleven o'clock? Because I *distinctly* heard some one crying, and supposed it was H. in the next room, but she was not there at all.
"Then I thought it must be something 'occult,' and that it might be you, and I felt so horrid."

"Thursday, *August 23rd*, 1888, 4.45 P.M.
"Thank you very much for your letter just come. I am so sorry your face was sore. Did it make you cry on Sunday night?"

From MISS MAUGHAN.

(The cover of this letter has been preserved, and bears the postmark, "Spilsby, Aug. 22nd, 1888.")

"Tuesday Evening, *Aug. 21st*, 1888.
"On Sunday we went to see Wroxham Broad. We had an immense amount of walking to do altogether, and I think I got a little cold in my face in the morning, and all night I suffered with it, and my face is swelled still."

In a second letter Miss Maughan writes:—

"Thursday, *August 23rd*, 11 P.M.
"I am putting poultices on my gums. I have never had such a huge swelling before, and it *won't* go down. It is so horribly uncomfortable."

"Saturday Afternoon.

"Thanks for letter. Yes, I was crying on Sunday night; only on account of the pain. It was awful, but I only cried quietly, as Edith was asleep. . . ."

From MISS CLARK.

"Monday, *August 27th*, 1888, 10.30 A.M.

"Thanks for your letter. I am sorry it was you crying. You don't seem at all struck. I was very much so. It was a subdued sort (*sic*) I heard, and thought H. was trying not to let it be heard. I shall always be afraid now of hearing things."

The sound here was of an inarticulate kind, nor was it immediately referred to the actual agent, and both these facts must be held to detract from the evidential value of the coincidence. In the next case, however, the voice, it will be seen, was at once recognised. The voice in this case awoke the percipient, and the impression should therefore be classed as a hallucination rather than as a dream, but it was of the "borderland" type. The uneasiness caused to the percipient, as attested by the letter and telegram sent, is sufficient proof that the impression was of a kind unusual in his experience.

No. 69.—From MR. WILLIAM TUDOR.

"AUBURNDALE, MASS., *July 11th*, 1890.

"Your favour[1] of the 30th ult., addressed to Mrs. Tudor, I will answer, as the incident more directly concerned me.

"Late in the evening of Monday, March 17th, near midnight, my nephew, Frederic Tudor, Jun., fell in front of an electric car going to Cambridge, was dragged some distance and so badly injured that for a time his life was in doubt, though he recovered with the loss of a foot. My wife heard of the accident on Tuesday afternoon and was much distressed all the night of Tuesday, and quite restless and wakeful.

"At this time I was in Gainesville, Florida, having important business there in connection with land purchases. On the night of Tuesday I went to bed rather early in a calm

---

[1] Mr. Tudor wrote to Dr. Hodgson in answer to a letter received from him.

state of mind. I slept soundly, as I usually do. About midnight, as I should judge, I heard my wife call my name quite distinctly and waked instantly broad awake. I sat up in bed, but soon remembering where I was, fell asleep again and waked no more until morning. The next day the incident of the night made me quite uneasy, also during the following day, and as I was obliged to leave on the afternoon of Friday for a rough journey in the country I telegraphed to my wife to know what was the matter. I usually receive a letter from home every day, and on these days no letter arrived, which added to my uneasiness. No answer was received to my first telegram, for the very good reason that it was never delivered. I was obliged to start, however, in the afternoon of this day, Friday the 21st, and in the morning of the 22nd, from a small town called New Branford, sent another telegram, of which the following is the substance:—' Shall be gone three days; what has happened? Answer Branford.' I had a strong impression that something serious had occurred, that my wife was possibly ill, or some of the children were ill, or that some accident or death had occurred to a near relation, not however involving my immediate family. The following extracts from my letters will illustrate this feeling :—

" Letter of March 19th :

"'I thought you called me last night. I waked up and was much worried ; I hope you are not ill.'

" Letter of March 22nd, from New Branford :

"'No answer comes to my telegram, although I left word to have it forwarded here. Surely some one would telegraph if you were ill. Surely you would let me know if anything had happened. I do not *feel* that anything serious has happened, and yet I cannot understand such a combination of circumstances. I have no confidence in these telegraph people, and daresay you never received my message.'

" Letter of March 24th, from Gainesville, after telegram giving account of accident was finally received :

"'I had a feeling that something was wrong but that you were all right.'

" Such I give as the substance of the facts in this case, which I trust may be interesting to the Society.

"WILLIAM TUDOR."

Mrs. W. Tudor writes :—

"AUBURNDALE, *July 29th*, 1890.

" My nephew's accident occurred on Monday night. Being out of town I heard of it on Tuesday afternoon. I immediately went to Boston and returned the same evening about nine o'clock, feeling greatly distressed. I wrote a letter to my husband after my return describing the accident and retired to bed rather late and passed a restless night. The telegram received from my husband rather surprised me, as he is not usually anxious when away from home. I believe this is all I know connected with this incident.　ELIZABETH TUDOR."

An account of a similar experience was sent to us in 1889 by the late Sir John Drummond Hay, K.C.B. He wrote that about 1 A.M. on some day in February 1879 he heard distinctly the voice of his daughter-in-law saying, "Oh, I wish papa only knew that Robert was ill." Sir John awoke Lady Drummond Hay to tell her what he had heard, and made a note of the incident in his diary. It was shortly ascertained that Mr. R. D. Hay had been taken seriously ill on that night, and that Mrs. Hay had used the words heard. Sir John's account is confirmed by Lady Hay and Mrs. R. D. Hay.

Visual Hallucinations.

The comparative frequency of auditory hallucinations, and especially the ease with which auditory illusions can be built up on a basis of real sound, render coincidences of the kind, even the best attested, of less service to support, however valuable as illustrating, the theory of telepathy. Visual hallucinations, however, present us with a much rarer type of impression, and one in which explanation by illusion is comparatively seldom possible. Telepathic hallucinations, like ordinary non-coincidental hallucinations, may assume various forms, and instances of grotesque and partially developed visual impressions are not wanting. Thus we have a case in which the face of a dying relative was recognised in the middle of a large ball of light like a firework (*Journal*, October 1891); and Mr. Sherer, of Amble, Northumberland, tells us that he saw reflected in a ship's compass the face of a young lady to whom he was engaged, at about the time of her death. In the following case the hallucination, though still far from complete, appears to have been more realistic and more fully developed.

No. 70.—From COUNTESS EUGENIE KAPNIST.

[Writing on June 24th, 1891, the percipient explains that in February 1889 she and her sister made the acquaintance at Talta of a Mr. P., who was at that time in an advanced stage of consumption. On one occasion, in the course of conversation, Mr. P. promised Countess Ina Kapnist, in the presence of the narrator, that should he die before her he would endeavour to appear to her. The Countess and her sister met Mr. P. occasionally after this conversation, and frequently saw him walking about in a nut-brown overcoat, which caused them some amusement. They left Talta, however, in May 1889, and in the course of a few months had completely forgotten Mr. P. and his wife, whom they regarded merely in the light of ordinary acquaintances. On the 12th March 1890 the two ladies, on their way home from the theatre, drove to the railway station with a friend who was to return at 1 A.M. to Tsarskoé.]

" On leaving the station," the Countess writes, "our servant went on before to find the carriage, so that on reaching the steps we found it had driven up and was waiting for us. My sister was the first to take her seat; I kept her waiting, as I descended the steps more slowly; the servant held the door of the landau open. With one foot on the step I suddenly stood still, arrested in the act of entering the carriage, and stunned with surprise. It was dark inside the carriage, and nevertheless, facing my sister and looking at her, I saw in a faint grey light which seemed unnatural, and which was clearest at the point on which my eyes were fixed, a face in profile, not so much vague as soft and transparent. This vision only lasted an instant, during which, however, my eyes noted the smallest details of the face, which seemed familiar to me; the rather sharp features, the hair parted a little on one side, the prominent nose, the sharp chin with its sparse, light brown beard. What strikes me when I think of it now is the fact that I could distinguish the different colours, though the greyish light which scarcely revealed the stranger would have been insufficient to enable me to distinguish them in ordinary circumstances. He had no hat, but wore a top-coat, such as is worn in the South, in colour a rather light nut-brown. His whole person had an air of great weariness and emaciation. The servant, much surprised that I did not enter the carriage but remained petrified on the step, thought I had trodden on my gown, and helped me to seat myself, while I asked my sister, as I took my place beside her, if it was really our carriage, so much was I confused and stupefied by seeing a stranger seated opposite her. It had not occurred to me that if a real person had been sitting there, neither my sister nor the footman would have remained so quietly face to face with him. When I was seated I no longer saw anything, and I asked my sister, 'Did you see nothing opposite you?' 'Nothing whatever, and what possessed you to ask as you got in if it was really our carriage?' she answered laughing. Then I told her what I have related above, describing my vision minutely. 'That familiar face,' said she, 'the hair parted at the side, the nut-brown coat, where have we seen it? Certainly nothing here answers to your description,' and we racked our brains without finding any clue. After we got home we related the incident to our mother; my description made her also remember vaguely a similar face. The next evening (March 12th) a young man of our acquaintance, Mr. Solovovo, came to see us. I told him also what had just occurred. We discussed it at some length, but fruitlessly. I still could not find the right name for the man of my vision, though I remembered quite well having seen a face exactly similar among my numerous acquaintances, but when and where? I could remember nothing, with my bad memory, which often fails me in this fashion. Some days later we were calling on Mr. Solovovo's grandmother. 'Do you know,' she said, 'what sad news I have just received from Talta? Mr. P. has just died, but I have heard no details.' My sister and I looked at each other. At the mention of this name the pointed face and the nut-brown top-coat found their possessor. My sister recognised him at the same time as myself, thanks to my minute description. When Mr. Solovovo entered I begged him to find the exact date of the death in the newspapers. The date of the death was given as the 14th of March, that is to say two days after my vision. I wrote to Talta for information, and learned that Mr. P. was confined to bed from the 24th November, and that from that time he was in a very feeble state, but sleep never left him. He slept so long and so profoundly, even during the last night of his life, that hopes were entertained of his improvement.

"We were much astonished that it was I who saw Mr. P., although he had promised to appear to my sister; but here I ought to add that before the occurrence mentioned above I had been clairvoyante a certain number of times; but this vision is certainly the one in which I distinguished details most clearly, even down to the colours of the face and dress.

" COMTESSE EUGENIE KAPNIST.
COMTESSE INA KAPNIST."

The second signature is that of the sister who was present at the time. The account above given, it should be explained, is a translation from the original French.

Our friend, Mr. Petrovo-Solovovo, through whom we obtained the account, writes :—

"I have much pleasure in certifying that the fact of Countess Kapnist's vision was mentioned, among others, to myself before the news of Mr. P.'s death came to St. Petersburg. I well remember seeing an announcement of his demise in the papers."

The narrative presents several points of interest. The deferred recognition is by no means without parallel (see case 68 and cases 26, 191, etc., in *Phantasms*), but in this case the interval which elapsed before the identification of the phantasm was unusually prolonged. Of course the fact that the vision was not identified beforehand is an element of weakness in the case, but as the deep impression left on the percipient by her vision seems well established, we have some warrant for assuming that the details have been accurately remembered. And if we may accept these details the case throws light upon the genesis of such hallucinations. That a dying man, whilst failing to impress the idea of his own personality upon the mind of a distant acquaintance, should succeed in calling up the image—to himself of quite secondary importance — of the clothes which he habitually wore, would seem at first sight a paradox. But the difficulty disappears if we recognise that the telepathic impression in such cases is probably received and the hallucination elaborated by a subconscious stratum of the intelligence, and that the picture is in due time flashed up thence fully formed to the ordinary consciousness. The image of the clothes worn by the agent, trivial and unessential to himself, would not improbably bulk more largely in the conception formed of him by an acquaintance, and might even find an echo in the percipient's consciousness when the image of the man himself had been obliterated by more recent memories. It is possible that the arrested development of the hallucination may have some connection with the imperfect recognition.

In the following case also the hallucination, though recognised, appears to have fallen short of complete embodiment.

No. 71.—From MISS L. CALDECOTT.

"February 11*th*, 1890.

"A sensation of faint glowing light in the darkest corner of the room made me first look in that direction (which happened to be next the door), and I then became aware of some one standing there, holding her hands outstretched as if in appeal. My first impression was that it was my sister, and I said, 'What's the matter?' but instantly saw who it was—a friend, who was at that time in Scotland. I felt completely riveted, but though my heart and pulses were beating unnaturally fast, neither much frightened nor surprised, only with a sort of impulse to get up and go after the figure, which I could not move to do. The form seemed to melt away into the soft glow, which then also died out. It was about half-past ten at night. I was at my home in ——. The date I am unable to fix nearer than that it was either August or September 1887.

"I was perfectly well. I was reading Carlyle's *Sartor Resartus* at the time. I was in no trouble or anxiety of any kind. Age about twenty-six.

"I had not seen my friend for about a year. I wrote to her the day after this happened, but, before my letter reached her, received one in which she told me of a great family trouble that was causing her much suffering, and saying that she had been longing for me to help her. Another letter in answer to mine then told me that her previous letter was written about 10.30 on the night I saw her, and that she had been wishing for my presence then most intensely. My friend died very shortly afterwards.

"No other persons were present at the time."

One of the agent's letters, written in reply to a letter from Miss Caldecott describing the apparition, has fortunately been preserved. The letter is dated

August 16th, 1888. The following extracts were written down by Mrs. Sidgwick from Miss Caldecott's dictation :—

" ' Your account is very strange, and I cannot quite make up my mind what to think of it. If it had not been that on that very Tuesday night I really was thinking of you very much, and wishing from the bottom of my heart that I could get at you, I should be inclined to say that your apparition was entirely subjective, and that you imagined you saw me. But if there is any connection between mind and mind, why should it not be so, and that it really was because I was wishing so hard I could be with you. You know that was the night I got back. I unpacked some of my things, and then began to write to you. It was then somewhere between eleven and twelve. At all events, I remember it struck twelve some time after I got into bed. . . . Tell me anything you can of my general appearance, and so forth. If you saw me as I was at the time it seems fairly conclusive it was my thinking of you caused you to see me, and not indigestion on your part, and entirely independent of me.' "

In conversation Mrs. Sidgwick learnt that the face and hands of the figure were seen most clearly. The hands appeared as if held out, palms upward. The dress was "rather indefinite. She looked as Miss Caldecott was accustomed to see her, but Miss Caldecott did not notice the dress particularly, and did not see the figure clearly at all below the knees." Miss Caldecott has had a visual hallucination on two other occasions, when she was in bed recovering from an illness. At the time of the vision above described she was in perfect health. It will be observed that the phantasm developed gradually, the percipient's attention having been first arrested by noticing the glow in the corner of the room. (Compare No. 84, Chapter XII., and the cases given in *Phantasms of the Living*, vol. i., chap. xii.) It will be seen that the percipient's recollection was at fault, both as to the date and the hour of the incident. But a discrepancy of this kind cannot be regarded as serious. Persons whose lives are not marked off—*e.g.*, by changes of residence or occupation—into distinct periods, frequently experience a difficulty in assigning to the right year even an event of importance. But in this case the incident in itself was trivial, and there was no land-mark by which to determine its relation, in point of time, to external events. A mistake in the date under such circumstances can scarcely be held to reflect upon the narrator's general accuracy.

In the next case also the apparition was pre-ceded and accompanied by a luminous effect. In this instance, however, the percipient appears to have been in bed, and the hallucination should be classed as a "borderland" case. It will be seen that the apparition preceded the actual death by several hours, but apparently coincided with a period of severe illness.

No. 72.—From Dr. Carat.[1]

"25 bis RUE VICTOR-HUGO, MALAKOFF,
PARIS, *July* 20*th*, 1891.

" My mother, from the time she was twenty-five years old, had suffered from an affection of the lungs, but she had kept her health, although she had gone through many troubles. There was nothing to indicate what happened on the 11th June 1877 —she succumbed in a few hours to an attack of inflammation of the lungs ; indeed, I had two days before that date received a letter from her in which she showed no anxiety about her health.

" On the night of the 10th June 1877 I had what might be called a telepathic hallucination. I cannot state the hour with absolute precision, but it was between ten o'clock and mid-night. About that time, ' between sleeping and waking,' I saw the end of my room lighted up, the darkness was illuminated by a silvery light (it is the only word I can think of), and I saw my mother gazing fixedly at me, with a sort of troubled expression. After a few seconds it all disappeared.

" Next day one of my friends—M. Laroche, now sub-director of the *Conservateur* Co., 18 Rue Lafayette—was breakfasting with me. I told him about my experience, and he too regarded it as a hallucination. At parting I said to him, ' Remember, Laroche, if anything happens, that I have told you this to-day.'

---

[1] *Annales des Sciences Psychiques*, July-August 1893, pp. 196, 197.

"Next day I received news of my mother's death.

"I have never on any other occasion experienced a hallucination, or anything approaching to it."

From M. LAROCHE.

[TO PROFESSOR RICHET.]

"SIR,—After an absence from home I have just returned and found awaiting me the letter which you did me the honour to write on the 7th inst., on the subject of a vision which my friend Dr. Carat had on the eve of his mother's death, at a time when he believed her to be in good health at Dunkirk. The circumstance was told me by Dr. Carat immediately after it occurred. You can make any use of my testimony you think fit.

"LAROCHE."

From the last case we pass, by an easy transition, to those completely externalised apparitions which cheat the senses by the life-like presentment of a human figure.

No. 73.—From MISS BERTA HURLY, Waterbeach Vicarage, Cambridge.

"*February* 1890.

"In the spring and summer of 1886 I often visited a poor woman called Evans, who lived in our parish, Caynham. She was very ill with a painful disease, and it was, as she said, a great pleasure when I went to see her; and I frequently sat with her and read to her. Towards the middle of October she was evidently growing weaker, but there seemed no immediate danger. I had not called on her for several days, and one evening I was standing in the dining-room after dinner with the rest of the family, when I saw the figure of a woman dressed like Mrs. Evans, in large apron and muslin cap, pass across the room from one door to the other, where she disappeared. I said, 'Who is that?' My mother said, 'What do you mean?' and I said, 'That woman who has just come in and walked over to the other door.' They all laughed at me, and said I was dreaming, but I felt sure it was Mrs. Evans, and next morning we heard she was dead.

"BERTA HURLY."

Miss Hurly's mother writes :—

"On referring to my diary for the month of October 1886, I find the following entry :—'19th. Berta startled us all after dinner, about 8.30 last evening, by saying she saw the figure of a woman pass across the dining-room, and that it was Mrs. Evans. This morning we hear the poor woman is dead.' On inquiring at the cottage we found she had become wandering in her mind, and at times unconscious, about the time she appeared to Berta, and died towards the morning.

" ANNIE ROSS.

" *February 25th*, 1890."

In this case the apparition, it will have been observed, was mistaken for a real person. We should not be justified, however, in concluding that the sensory effect produced was comparable in intensity to that which would have been caused had a real figure walked across the room. Perception is so largely a psychical process that it is difficult in any particular case to assign a definite value to the sensory element. And in a case of this kind, where, as appears to be generally the case with telepathic hallucinations, the vision is of brief duration, the difficulty is, of course, increased.

The hallucination in this, as in the previous case, occurred some hours before the death, and the evidential value of the coincidence is so far lessened. But it is perhaps worth while pointing out that we have no warrant in theory for concluding that in a case of death after prolonged illness the actual moment of dissolution is more favourable for the initiation of a telepathic impulse than any moment in the hours or days of illness preceding death ; nor, if due allowance be made for the tendency to exaggerate the closeness of coincidence, is it clear that there is sufficient evidence at present to support any such conclusion. On the other hand, in cases of accident or momentary illness, we have more than one case where the impression is shown, on good evidence, to have occurred within, at most, an hour of death.[1] In the narrative which follows, the vision, it will be seen, took place some days before the actual

---

[1] See, for instance, *Phantasms of the Living*, cases 28, 79, etc.

death, during the crisis of a serious illness, of which the percipient was not at the time aware.

No. 74.—From MRS. MCALPINE, Garscadden, Bearsden, Glasgow.

The following account was enclosed in a letter, dated April 12th, 1892. We had previously received a somewhat briefer account, dated May 7th, 1891, which agrees in all essential particulars with the one printed below:—

"On the 25th March 1891 my husband and I were staying at Furness Abbey Hotel, Barrow-in-Furness, with a friend of ours, the late Mr. A. D. Bryce Douglas, of Seafield Tower, Ardrossan. He was managing director of the 'Naval Construction Armament Company,' and had resided at Furness Abbey Hotel for some eighteen months or more. He had invited us, along with a number of other friends, to the launch of the *Empress of China*. We breakfasted with Mr. Bryce Douglas on the day of the launch, the 25th, and afterwards saw the launch, had luncheon at the shipyard, and returned to the hotel. He appeared to be in his usual health and spirits (he was a powerfully-built man, and justly proud of his fine constitution). The following day (Thursday) he left with a party of gentlemen, to sail from Liverpool to Ardrossan, on the trial trip of the *Empress of Japan* (another large steamer which had been built at his yard).

"We remained on at the hotel for some days with our son Bob, aged twenty-three, who was staying there, superintending work which Mr. McAlpine was carrying on at Barrow.

"On the Monday night, the 30th, I went upstairs after dinner. On my way down again I saw Mr. Bryce Douglas standing in the doorway of his sitting-room. I saw him quite distinctly. He looked at me with a sad expression. He was wearing a cap which I had never seen him wear. I walked on and left him standing there. It was then about ten minutes to eight. I told my husband and Bob. We all felt alarmed, and we immediately sent the following telegram, 'How is Mr. Bryce Douglas?' to Miss Caldwell, his sister-in-law, who kept house for him at Seafield. It was too late for a reply that night. On Tuesday morning we received a wire from her; it ran thus: 'Mr. Bryce Douglas dangerously ill.' That telegram was the first intimation of his illness which reached Barrow. As will be seen in the account of his illness and death in the *Barrow News*, he died on the following Sunday, and we afterwards ascertained from Miss Caldwell that he was unconscious on Monday evening, at the time I saw him.

"My husband and son can corroborate this, and I have also letters which bear out my statements."

Mrs. McAlpine enclosed a copy of the *Barrow News* for April 11th, 1891, containing a memoir of Mr. Bryce Douglas, and a full account of his last illness and death. It appears from this account that he left Barrow on Thursday, March 26th, to join the steamer *Empress of Japan.* He was noticed by his friends to be far from well on Wednesday, the previous day, on the occasion of the launch of the *Empress of China*, and was advised to go home. He did not do so, however, until the Sunday, when he was put ashore at Ardrossan, and walked home to Seafield—a distance of nearly two miles. His medical man was sent for the same day, and the case was considered serious from the first, and on the following Thursday the doctors pronounced it hopeless. He died on April 5th, at about 5 A.M.

From the evidence which follows it seems clear that if any anxiety as to his health was felt before he left Barrow, as suggested in the newspaper report, Mrs. McAlpine knew nothing of it.

Mr. Myers writes:—

"I discussed the incident connected with the death of Mr. Bryce Douglas with Mr. and Mrs. McAlpine and Mr. McAlpine, Jun., on February 24th, 1892. I believe that their evidence has been very carefully given. Mr. McAlpine knew Mr. Bryce Douglas intimately. Mr. Bryce Douglas was a robust and vigorous man, and disliked ever to be supposed to be ill. Mr. McAlpine therefore felt great unwillingness to telegraph to him about his health, but from his previous knowledge of phenomena occurring to Mrs. McAlpine, he felt sure that her vision must be in some sense veridical."

Mrs. McAlpine's husband and his son corroborate as follows:—

"*April* 1892.

"I was at Barrow on the 25th of March of last year (1891), and distinctly remember the incident of the following Monday night. I can bear testimony to the statements made by my wife and son.

"ROBERT McALPINE."

"GARSCADDEN HOUSE, *April 4th*, 1892.

"I was living for several months in the Furness Abbey Hotel, at Barrow-in-Furness, and I remember father and mother coming for a few days in order to see the launch of the *Empress of China* on the 25th of March 1891, and on the following day (Thursday) Mr. Bryce Douglas (who was then in his usual health) left with a party of friends on the trial trip of the *Empress of Japan*. I also distinctly remember that the following Monday night (30th) my father and I were sitting at the drawing-room fire after dinner, and mother came in looking very pale and startled, and said she had been upstairs and had seen Mr. Bryce Douglas standing at the door of his sitting-room (he had used this sitting-room for nearly two years). Both my father and I felt anxious, and after some discussion we sent a telegram to Mr. Bryce Douglas's residence at Ardrossan asking how he was, and the following morning had the reply, 'Keeping better, but not out of danger,' or words to that effect. I can assert positively that no one in Barrow knew of his illness until after the receipt of that telegram.

"ROBERT McALPINE, JUN."

Letters corroborating the above account have also been received from Miss Caldwell, sister-in-law to Mr. Bryce Douglas, to whom the telegram was sent, and who writes: "I was very much surprised at receiving it;" from Mrs. Scarlett, the wife of the proprietor of the Furness Abbey Hotel, and from Miss Charlton, of Barrow-in-Furness, both of whom were cognisant of the circumstances at the time.[1]

Mrs. McAlpine has had several other apparently telepathic experiences, one of them a vision coinciding with the death of the infant child of her brother.

In the next case the vision occurred about two hours after the actual death.

---

[1] These letters will be found in full in the account of the case published in *Proc. S.P.R.*, vol. x., part xxvi.

No. 75.—From MISS MABEL GORE BOOTH.

"LISSADELL, SLIGO, *February* 1891.

"On the 10th of April 1889, at about half-past nine o'clock A.M., my youngest brother and I were going down a short flight of stairs leading to the kitchen, to fetch food for my chickens, as usual. We were about half-way down, my brother a few steps in advance of me, when he suddenly said, 'Why, there's John Blaney; I didn't know he was in the house!' John Blaney was a boy who lived not far from us, and he had been employed in the house as hall-boy not long before. I said that I was sure it was not he (for I knew he had left some months previously on account of ill-health), and looked down into the passage, but saw no one. The passage was a long one, with a rather sharp turn in it, so we ran quickly down the last few steps and looked round the corner, but nobody was there, and the only door he could have gone through was shut. As we went upstairs my brother said, 'How pale and ill John looked, and why did he stare so?' I asked what he was doing. My brother answered that he had his sleeves turned up, and was wearing a large green apron, such as the footmen always wear at their work. An hour or two afterwards I asked my maid how long John Blaney had been back in the house? She seemed much surprised, and said, 'Didn't you hear, miss, that he died this morning?' On inquiry we found he had died about two hours before my brother saw him. My mother did not wish that my brother should be told this, but he heard of it somehow, and at once declared that he must have seen his ghost.

"MABEL OLIVE GORE BOOTH."

The percipient's independent account is as follows:—

"*March* 1891.

"We were going downstairs to get food for Mabel's fowl, when I saw John Blaney walking round the corner. I said to Mabel, 'That's John Blaney!' but she could not see him. When we came up afterwards we found he was dead. He seemed to me to look rather ill. He looked yellow; his eyes looked hollow, and he had a green apron on.

"MORDAUNT GORE BOOTH."

We have received the following confirmation of the date of death:—

"I certify from the parish register of deaths that John Blaney

(Dunfore) was interred on the 12th day of April 1889, having died on the 10th day of April 1889.

"P. J. SHEMAGHS, C.C.

"The Presbytery, Ballingal, Sligo,
"10*th February* 1891."

Mr. Myers originally received an account of the incident *viva voce* from Lady Gore Booth, and subsequently at his request the percipient and his sister, aged at the time ten and fifteen respectively, wrote the accounts given above.

Lady Gore Booth writes :—

"*May* 31*st*, 1890.

"When my little boy came upstairs and told us he had seen John Blaney, we thought nothing of it till some hours after, when we heard that he was dead. Then, for fear of frightening the children, I avoided any allusion to what he had told us, and asked every one else to do the same. Probably by now he has forgotten all about it, but it certainly was very remarkable, especially as only one child saw him, and they were standing together. The place where he seems to have appeared was in the passage outside the pantry door, where John Blaney's work always took him. My boy is a very matter-of-fact sort of boy, and I never heard of his having any other hallucination."

The interval in this case between the death and the vision may probably be explained as due to the telepathic influence received from the dying boy having remained latent in the percipient's mind, awaiting a favourable opportunity for emerging to consciousness. But it seems possible that the message may have come, not from the dying boy, but from some member of the household who was aware of the death. It is to be noted that Miss Gore Booth did not share her brother's experience.

Hallucinations Affecting Two Senses.

So far we have dealt with hallucinations of one sense only. In the next two cases, it will be seen, both sight and hearing appear to have been affected.

No. 76.—From the REV. MATTHEW FROST.

"BOWERS GIFFORD, ESSEX, *January 30th*, 1891.

"The first Thursday in April 1881, while sitting at tea with my back to the window and talking with my wife in the usual way, I plainly heard a rap at the window, and looking round I said to my wife, 'Why, there's my grandmother,' and went to the door, but could not see any one; and still feeling sure it was my grandmother, and knowing, though eighty-three years of age, she was very active and fond of a joke, I went round the house, but could not see any one. My wife did not hear it. On the following Saturday I had news my grandmother died in Yorkshire about half-an-hour before the time I heard the rapping. The last time I saw her alive I promised, if well, I would attend her funeral; that [was] some two years before. I was in good health [and] had no trouble, [age] twenty-six years. I did not know that my grandmother was ill."

Mrs. Frost writes :—

"*January 30th*, 1891.

"I beg to certify that I perfectly remember all the circumstances my husband has named, but I heard and saw nothing myself."

The house (seen by Mrs. Sidgwick) in which Mr. Frost was living when the event occurred stands some way back from the road in a garden, and the door into the garden opens out of the sitting-room, so that he must have got to the door much too quickly, if he went at once, for any one to have got away unseen by him.

Professor Sidgwick called on Mr. Frost in June 1892, and learned from him that he had last seen his grandmother in 1878, on which occasion she had promised, if possible, to appear to him at her death. On first seeing the figure Mr. Frost thought that his grandmother had actually come in the flesh to surprise him. It was full daylight, and had there been a real knock and a real presence Mrs. Frost must have both heard and seen. Mr. Frost had no cause for anxiety about his grandmother, and has had no other experience of this kind. News of the death came by letter, and Mrs. Frost remembers the letter, and that she noticed the coincidence at the time.

In the next case the order of perception is reversed; the visual preceded the auditory image. The narrative was procured for us by M. Aksakof, of 6 Nevsky Prospect, St. Petersburg, who also translated the original Russian into French, from which we have translated it into English.

No. 77.—From M. A——.

"It was at Milan, on the 10th (22nd) of October 1888. I was staying at the Hotel Ancora. After dinner, at about seven o'clock, I was seated on the sofa, reading a newspaper. My wife was resting in the same room on a couch, behind a curtain. The room was lighted by a lamp upon the table near which I was sitting reading. Suddenly I saw against the back-ground of the door, which was opposite me, my father's face. He wore as usual a black surtout, and was deadly pale. At that moment I heard quite close to my ear a voice which said to me, 'A telegram is coming to say your father is dead.' All this only took a few seconds. I started up and rushed towards my wife, but not to startle her I said nothing to her about it. To explain my sudden movement I exclaimed 'Look, do you not see that the kettle is boiling over!' . . . On the evening of the same day, about eleven o'clock, we were taking tea in the company of several other people, among whom were Madame Y., her daughter E. Y., formerly an actress at the Court Theatre, and Mademoiselle M., who is now living in Florence. All at once there was a knock at the door, and the *concierge* presented a telegram. Pale with emotion I immediately exclaimed, 'I know my father is dead; I have seen. . . .' The telegram contained these words, 'Papa dead suddenly.—Olga.' It was a telegram from my sister living at St. Petersburg. I learned later that my father had committed suicide on the morning of the same day.

"(Signed)   E. A."

Madame A. writes:—

"I was present at the time, and I testify to the accuracy of the account."

M. Aksakof wrote to us that he had seen the original telegram, which ran—

" Ricevuto il 22,[1] 1888.   Milano, Petersbourg, data 22,[1] ore e minute, 8.40. ' Papa mort subitement.—Olga.' "

Another case, in which the senses affected were those of touch and hearing, has been given to us by Mr. Malleson.   In 1874 or 1875 he went for a short sea voyage, taking with him his young son. On the night of his departure, while in a dreamy, half-conscious state, he imagined that his son had fallen overboard, and that he himself was bringing the sad news to his wife.   On his return home he learned that on that night Mrs. Malleson had been awakened by feeling some one leaning over her. She put out her arm and, as she thought, touched her husband's coat.   She had no doubt that it was her husband's bodily presence, spoke to him, and heard him answer, " Yes, I have come back."   But on her continuing, " Where is Eddy ? " she received no reply, and felt much alarmed.   There are several instances recorded of tactile hallucinations accompanying visual and auditory phantasms.[2]

[1] M. Aksakof explains that the name of the month (October) was omitted, through a mistake on the part of the telegraph clerk.

[2] *Phantasms of the Living*, vol. i. pp. 434-445; vol. ii. p. 134, etc.; and *Proc. S.P.R.*, etc.

CHAPTER XII.

COLLECTIVE HALLUCINATIONS.

WE have now to discuss that numerous class of cases in which the phantasm was perceived by two or more persons. The difficulties of interpretation which such cases present are enhanced for us by the various defects to which the evidence is here peculiarly liable. Many so-called cases of collective apparition, especially when the figure is seen out-of-doors, were probably real men and women.[1] In others we have to deal with a collective illusion, a quasi-hallucinatory super-structure built up by each witness, aided by hints from the others, on a common sensory basis. Such, for instance, appears to us the most probable interpreta-tion of the following singular case.

From MRS. ALDERSON.

" My son and I were staying in the town of Bonchurch (Isle of Wight) last Easter vacation (1886). Our lodgings were close to the sea, and the garden of our house abutted on the beach, and there were no trees or bushes in it high enough to intercept

---

[1] Thus we have a case, regarded by the narrator as hallucinatory, in which three persons saw a figure ascending the staircase of a country rectory. The occurrence took place shortly after the return of the family from church, and the figure was supposed to be that of the rector, until it was ascertained that he was at the time in another part of the house. As, however, it was dark and the head of the figure could not be seen, the identification could hardly have been complete, and as no search was made in the upper part of the house, it seems possible that the figure was that of some person who had gained entrance to the house during the absence of the family at church.

our view. The evening of Easter Sunday was so fine that when Miss Jowett (the landlady's daughter) brought in the lamp, I begged her not to pull down the blinds, and lay on the sofa looking out at the sea, while my son was reading at the table. Owing to a letter I had just received from my sister at home, stating that one of the servants had again seen ' the old lady,' my thoughts had been directed towards ghosts and such things. But I was not a little astonished when, on presently looking out of the window, I saw the figure of a woman standing at the edge of the verandah. She appeared to be a broad woman, and not tall (Mrs. A. is tall), and to wear an old-fashioned bonnet, and white gloves on her closed hands. As it was dark the figure was only outlined against the sky, and I could not distinguish any other details. It was, however, opaque, and not in any way transparent, just as if it had been a real person. I looked at it for some time, and then looked away. When, after a time, I looked again, the woman's hands had disappeared behind what appeared to be a white marble cross, with a little bit of the top broken off, and with a railing on one side of the woman and the cross, such as one sometimes sees in graveyards.

"After looking at this apparition, which remained motionless, for some time, about twenty minutes, perhaps, I asked my son [then an undergraduate at B.N.C.] to come and to look out of the window, and tell me what he saw. He exclaimed, ' What an uncanny sight!' and described the woman and the cross exactly as I saw it. I then rang the bell, and when Miss J. answered it, I asked her also to look out of the window and tell me what she saw, and she also described the woman and the cross, just as they appeared to my son and myself. Some one suggested that it might be a reflection of some sort, and we all looked about the room to see whether there was anything in it that could cause such a reflection, but came to the conclusion that there was nothing to account for it."

Mr. Alderson writes:—

" Staying at B. (Isle of Wight) during the Easter vacation of 1886, I remember distinctly seeing an apparition in the form of a woman with her hands clasped on the top of a cross. The cross looked old and worn, as one sees in churchyards. My mother drew my attention to the figure, and after we had watched it for some time we rang the bell and asked the servant if she saw the figure. She said she did. I then went out to the verandah (where the figure was), and immediately it vanished.

" E. H. ALDERSON."

A corresponding account of the incident has been received from Miss Jowett, the landlady's daughter. We owe the accounts of the incident to Mr. F. Schiller, who investigated the matter for the Oxford Phasmatological Society.

The persistency of the vision in this case is a feature very rarely found in cases of undoubted hallucination, and the fact that it was only seen through glass suggests that the whole appearance was due to a reflection of some kind, although it must be admitted that this explanation, which was considered and rejected by the percipients at the time, cannot be accommodated to the facts without difficulty.

In the epidemics of religious hallucination so common in the Middle Ages, and still occurring from time to time in Catholic countries, it would appear that as a rule there is no objective basis for the perception. When, as at Knock, in Ireland, a few years ago, the figure of the Virgin or a Saint is said to have been seen by a large number of persons simultaneously, it seems probable that in those who really saw the figure the hallucination was due to repeated verbal suggestions acting on minds which, under the influence of strong emotion, were temporarily in a state analogous to that of trance. The nearest analogy to such cases is no doubt to be found in hypnotism. A collective hallucination can be imposed upon a whole roomful of hypnotised persons by the mere command of the operator. But not the most explicit verbal suggestion—*si vera est fabula*—could make the courtiers in the fairy tale see the king's clothes; and there is no evidence that with normal persons in full possession of their ordinary faculties any hints derivable from look, word, or gesture could suffice to originate an instantaneous hallucination. Still, the possibility of such an explanation under certain conditions should perhaps be kept in view. (See later, Chapter XVI.)

A possible explanation of a different kind has

been already illustrated by the story quoted on page 153, where it was shown that a solitary hallucination had grown in the course of five-and-twenty years into a collective vision. The narrator in this case was a child at the time of the alleged experience. Children and uneducated persons generally, who are not prone to analyse their own sensations, seem liable after a certain interval to mistake the image called up by another's recital for an actual experience of their own; and this is especially likely to occur when the auditor was present at the time of the experience or familiar with the scene of the occurrence. Indeed, most persons who visualise with moderate facility are probably liable to this form of mistake on a small scale. I had about five years since an example of this in my own case. A friend had described to me minutely some simple apparatus of his own invention. About a year later he brought the apparatus to London and offered to show it to me. I replied that I had already seen it; but on being confronted with it I found the proportions and general appearance of the actual object quite unlike my mental image of it. I had in fact never seen the object, but the image which I had mentally constructed to enable me to follow my friend's description a year before remained so vivid as to lead me to believe that it was founded on actual sensation. But a sensory hallucination is too striking and unusual an experience to be readily feigned, and it is very improbable that the memory of educated persons, at any rate, would be untrustworthy as regards their recent experiences of the kind. As already explained, the accounts of this and other forms of telepathic affection included in this book have in almost all cases been written down within ten years of the event.

When the fullest allowance has been made for all possible explanations we find a considerable number of cases remaining of which no other account can be given than that they are apparitions, due to no ascertained cause, which are perceived by two or more persons simultaneously. That the collective perception proves the objective, or—to use a less ambiguous word—the *material* existence of the thing perceived, is probably held now by few persons outside the ranks of professed mystics. Apart from the theoretical difficulties of such a hypothesis—difficulties which have by no means been surmounted by the invocation of fixed ether, intercalary vortex rings, space of four dimensions, and other subtler forms of the theory evolved in recent times,—it is to be noted that no facts of any significance have been adduced to support it. There is at present no trustworthy evidence that an apparition has ever been weighed or photographed,[1] or submitted to spectroscopic or chemical analysis. But, indeed, the theory betrays its own origin in a prescientific age; and without formal destruction by argument it has shared in the euthanasia which has overtaken many other, pious opinions found inadequate to the facts. The phenomena which it professes to explain are paralleled in all their essential features by other phenomena, for which even its supporters would hardly be rash enough to claim substantial reality; and as the phantasms now to be discussed bear in all points a close resemblance to those already described as occurring to solitary percipients, probably no one who accepts the one class of appearances as hallucinatory will hesitate to accept the other.

But when the hallucinatory character of collectively-perceived, or, as they may be styled for brevity, "collective" phantasms is recognised, there are difficulties of interpretation to be dealt with. On the telepathic hypothesis there are two modes in which a collective hallucination may be conceived to originate: (*a*) it may be communicated direct from a third person to each of the percipients; or (*b*) it may be communi-

---

[1] See the article on Spirit Photographs by Mrs. Henry Sidgwick, *Proc. S.P.R.*, vol. vii. pp. 268-289.

cated by telepathic infection from one percipient to another. The first explanation involves in most cases, as Mr. Gurney has pointed out (*Phantasms of the Living*, vol. ii. pp. 171, 172), serious theoretical difficulties. For on the view to which we are led by a review of all the evidence, a telepathic hallucination, like any other, is, as a rule, the work of the percipient's mind, and is not transferred ready made from the agent. As such it is frequently of slow growth, and there are grounds for believing that it is sometimes not externalised for the percipient's senses until some hours after the receipt of the original telepathic impulse. We should hardly expect, therefore, to find two percipients independently developing similar hallucinations, and at the same moment. But in most of the cases of collective hallucination hitherto reported, the hallucinations have been, so far as could be ascertained, similar and simultaneous, so as indeed to suggest a real figure rather than a hallucination. Moreover, in well-attested recent narratives it rarely happens that a connection between the hallucination and any unusual state of the person represented is clearly established; whilst in many, perhaps most cases, the hallucination has not been recognised as resembling any person known to either percipient, and has in some instances been purely grotesque. In most cases, therefore, it seems easier to believe that we have to deal with a contagious hallucination, which, whether initiated by a telepathic impulse, or purely subjective in its origin, has been transferred telepathically from the original percipient to others in his company at the time. In some cases, indeed, it is no doubt permissible, as suggested by Mr. Gurney, to conjecture that the minds of all the percipients may have been directly influenced by the agent, and that subsequently an overflow from the mind of one of the percipients may have served to reinforce the original impulse, and determine the exact moment of the explosion in his co-percipients, just as the current

18

regulates the exact hour of striking in electrically synchronised clocks. Or again, the mind of each percipient may react upon the others. There are, however, a few cases where the percipients appear to have had experiences relating to the same event neither precisely similar nor simultaneous, which seem to require the hypothesis of an impulse in each case directly derived from the person represented. Some cases of the kind are given in *Phantasms of the Living* (vol. i. p. 362 ; vol. ii. 173-183), and others will be cited in the latter part of this chapter. It will be more convenient, however, to begin by giving examples of the ordinary type of collective hallucination.

Collective Auditory Hallucinations.

No. 78.—From MR. C. H. CARY.

"SECRETARY'S OFFICE, GENERAL POST OFFICE,
29th March 1892.

"At Bow, London, on the 8th March 1875, at about 8.30 P.M., I heard a voice say, 'Joseph, Joseph.' I was talking with my father and cousin (Joseph Cary) about the battle of Balaclava. I was in good health, etc. My age was nearly thirteen. All three of us heard the voice, which we suppose to have been that of Joseph's grandmother."[1]

In conversation, Mr. Cary explained to me that the voice was not recognised by any of those who heard it. It was indeed at first mistaken for the voice of Mrs. Cary (Mr. C. H. Cary's mother), who was at the time in an adjoining room, but who had not spoken. A telegram announcing the grandmother's death was received on the day following, and Mr. Joseph Cary then said that the voice must have been that of his grandmother. Mr. C. H. Cary had never seen this lady.

[1] This account was originally written in answer to a series of questions on a "census" form. A few connecting words have been inserted in order to make it read consecutively.

Mr. R. H. Cary writes from 49 Gladsmuir Road, London, N. :—

"*March 31st*, 1892.

"With reference to your inquiry concerning the voice which was heard at the time of the late Mrs. Victor's death, I am able to state that my son, my nephew, and myself were sitting together, and we all heard it distinctly. This occurred about fourteen years ago. The account given by my son exactly coincides with my own recollection.   "R. H. CARY."

We have ascertained from the Registrar-General that Mary Victor, widow of Thomas Victor, farmer, died at Linwood, Paul, Penzance, on March 8th, 1875, from bronchitis.

Mr. C. H. Cary adds that though Mrs. Victor was known to be ill, her death was not thought to be imminent. He has himself had other auditory hallucinations—viz., the hearing of footsteps on two or three occasions at about the time of the death of a relation.

In the next case the voice heard did not correspond with any external event. It was, as it were, "the after-image" of a voice once familiar in the house.

No. 79.—From MISS ANNIE NEWBOLD.

"*May 7th*, 1892.

"Florence N., a little child of under four years old, to whom I was very much attached, died on May 23rd, 1889. She lived in the house where I have my studio, and during the daytime was invariably with me. There were no other children in the house, and she was a general pet. I was ill for some time after her death, and one morning in July 1889 I went to see Mrs. N. We were sitting talking in her room on the ground-floor when I suddenly heard the child's voice distinctly call 'Miss Boo' (her name for me). I was about to answer, when I remembered that it could be no living voice and so continued my sentence, thinking that I would say nothing about the occurrence to her mother. At that moment Mrs. N. turned to me and said, 'Miss Newbold, did you hear that?' 'Yes,' I replied, 'what was it?' And she said, 'My little child, and she called "Miss Boo."' We both noticed that the sound came from below, as if she were standing in the kitchen doorway underneath the room in which we were sitting. There was no possibility of its being another child, as there was not one in the house. The upper floors were empty, too, at the time. I can vouch for the accuracy of this account.

"ANNIE NEWBOLD."

Mrs. N. writes:—

"Miss Newbold came to see me one morning in July 1889, about two months after my only child's death. We were in my room talking when I distinctly heard my little girl's voice call 'Miss Boo.' I asked Miss Newbold if she had heard anything and she said 'Yes. What was it?' I replied, 'My little child, and she said "Miss Boo."'   "LIZZIE N."

In answer to questions, Miss Newbold writes:—

"1. Mrs. N. never heard her little girl's voice on any other occasion.

"2. We were not talking about the little girl at the time, nor upon any subject connected with her. I, however, had a box of roses on my knee, which I was mechanically sorting, and putting all the white ones on one side to send to the little child's grave.

"3. Mrs. N. has never heard any other voices, either before or since. Neither have I; but I have three or four times in my life been conscious of a presence without being able to explain definitely what it was I felt. I have never seen anything."[1]

---

[1] With this may be compared an incident recorded by William Bell Scott (*Autobiographical Notes*, vol. ii. pp. 117, 118). The account is perhaps worth quoting, though the length of time which has elapsed, and the fact that it rests upon a single memory, leave to the narrative little value other than that derived from its literary associations. It should be added, however, that Mr. Scott's claim to a rational scepticism in these matters appears to be borne out by other passages in the book.

"I have so repeatedly expressed my unbelief in all the vulgar or popular forms of supernaturalism (says Mr. Scott), that I feel a little hesitation in recording a circumstance resembling that class of things which began the very evening after his [*i.e.*, Rossetti's] departure. I could now get a little peace to revise my *Dürer Journal*, and my German friend Mr. Reid, who had given me an hour, stayed to dinner. Rossetti's habit, when composing or even correcting for the press, was to retire after dinner to the room above, the drawing-room of the old house, to read aloud to himself, when by himself. This he did in a voice so loud that we in the dining-room beneath could almost hear his words. Well, as we were sitting after dinner, when he must have been approaching London in the train, what could it be we heard? The usual voice reading to itself in the usual place over our heads! I looked at A. B.; she was listening intently till she could bear it no

Collective Visual Hallucinations.

Passing to visual phantasms, we will begin by citing a case in which there can be little doubt that the hallucination was purely subjective; a better case for illlustrating the hypothesis of the infectious character of casual hallucination could hardly be found. It is to be noted indeed that the second percipient saw the apparition on the first occasion only after a distinct *verbal* suggestion, but, as already stated, there is no evidence that a single verbal suggestion can produce a hallucination in a healthy person in full possession of his normal faculties.

No. 80.—From MRS. GREIFFENBERG and MRS. ERNI-GREIFFENBERG.

Mr. F. C. S. Schiller, through whom the account was obtained, tells us that he heard the story in October 1890 from the two percipients. The following account was put together by him from an account (which he also sent us) written by Mrs. Erni-Greiffenberg, and various conversations which he had with both ladies on the subject. He afterwards obtained their signatures to it. Neither of them has had any other hallucinatory experience.

longer, and left the room. Our learned priest found me, I fancy, to be rather *distrait*, so he rose, saying it was about his time, and besides, he continued, ' I hear Miss Boyd has some friend in the drawing-room, so I won't go up. Give her my good-bye and respects.' I joined her at once, but of course we heard nothing in the room itself. Such is the circumstance as it took place. Mr. Reid, who knew nothing of the habit of D. G. R., hearing the voice as well as we did, although it sounded to him like talking rather than reading, was a sure evidence we were not deceiving ourselves. Next night it was the same, and so it went on till I left. When we tried to approach it it was not audible, or when the doors of the drawing-room and its small ante-room communicating with the staircase were left open, we could make nothing of it. It gradually tapered off when Miss Boyd was left by herself; by-and-by the whole establishment was bolted and barred for the winter. Next season it had entirely ceased."

"December 14th, 1890.

"In the beginning of the summer of 1884 we were sitting at dinner at home as usual, in the middle of the day. In the midst of the conversation I noticed my mother suddenly looking down at something beneath the table. I inquired whether she had dropped anything, and received the answer, 'No, but I wonder how that cat can have got into the room?' Looking underneath the table, I was surprised to see a large white Angora cat beside my mother's chair. We both got up, and I opened the door to let the cat out. She marched round the table, went noiselessly out of the door, and when about half-way down the passage turned round and faced us. For a short time she regularly stared at us with her green eyes, then she dissolved away, like a mist, under our eyes.

"Even apart from the mode of her disappearance, we felt convinced that the cat could not have been a real one, as we neither had one of our own, nor knew of any that would answer to the description in the place, and so this appearance made an unpleasant impression upon us.

"This impression was, however, greatly enhanced by what happened in the following year, 1885, when we were staying in Leipzig with my married sister (the daughter of Mrs. Greiffenberg). We had come home one afternoon from a walk, when, on opening the door of the flat, we were met in the hall by the same white cat. It proceeded down the passage in front of us, and looked at us with the same melancholy gaze. When it got to the door of the cellar (which was locked), it again dissolved into nothing.

"On this occasion also it was first seen by my mother, and we were both impressed by the uncanny and gruesome character of the appearance. In this case, also, the cat could not have been a real one, as there was no such cat in the neighbourhood."

A very striking example of a collective hallucination, apparently of the same type, was given to us by Mrs. Ward. She and her husband, the late E. M. Ward, R.A., in 1851 saw in their bedroom two small pearshaped lights which, when touched, broke into small luminous fragments. (*Phantasms of the Living,* vol. ii. p. 193.) We have also a case in which our informant, when a girl of fifteen, with another girl, saw in the middle of the room, at a dancing class, a hallucinatory chair. Yet another case is recorded by Miss Foy, a careful observer, who had been troubled for some time with a hallucinatory skeleton, the subjective character of which she fully recognised. On one occasion when in hospital the hallucination recurred, and appears to have been seen also by the patient in the adjoining bed, to whom no hint of any kind had been given.   In both these cases, however, the evidence depends upon a single memory. We have another case in which a singular luminous body—apparently a hallucination of a rudimentary kind—was perceived by two witnesses coincidently with the death of a near relative of one of them. The Rev. A. T. S. Goodrick, from whom I originally received the account *viva voce*, was walking with a friend across a moor in Sutherlandshire

"when there suddenly arose, to all appearance out of the road between our feet as we walked, a ball of fire, about the size of an 18lb. cannon ball. It was of an orange-red colour, and there seemed to be a kind of rotatory motion in it, not unlike a firework of some description. . . . It seemed to move forward with us, at a distance of not more than 6 inches in front, and at the same time rose pretty swiftly breast high . . . and then disappeared and left no trace."

Mr. Goodrick adds that a light rain was falling; but there was no thunderstorm.

From uneducated witnesses such an account no doubt would have but little value.   A will-o'-the-wisp in an adjoining marsh, or even a flash of lightning, might in such a case form a sufficient basis for the story.   And even assuming that the account here given accurately describes what was seen, it is difficult to feel certain that the appearance was hallucinatory.   But if it were of a physical nature, it is certainly not easy to conjecture what it could have been, and the coincidence with the death is an additional argument for regarding the phenomenon as hallucinatory.

In the next case the phantasm seems to belong to a not unusual type of subjective hallucinations, the "after-image" of a familiar figure.   There are no grounds for ascribing the apparition to any "agency" on the part of the person whose image was seen. If the incident is correctly described, the *prima facie* explanation is that a casual hallucination was communicated by telepathic suggestion to a second person in the company of the original percipient. At our request the two accounts which follow were written independently.

No. 81.—From MRS. MILMAN.

"17 SOUTHWELL GARDENS, S.W.,
March 20th, 1888.

"About three years ago I was coming out of the dining-room one day, after lunch, with my sister. My mother had, as I supposed, preceded us upstairs, as usual. The library door, which faces the dining-room, stood wide open, and looking through it as I crossed the hall, I saw my mother in the library, seated at the writing-table, and apparently writing. Instead, therefore, of going upstairs, as I had intended, I went to the library door, wishing to speak to her, but when I looked in the room was empty.

"At the same moment, my sister, who had also been going towards the stairs in the first instance, changed her direction, and, crossing the hall, came up to the library door behind me. She then exclaimed, 'Why, I thought I saw mamma in the library, at the writing-table.' On comparing notes, we found that we had both seen her seated at the writing-table, and bending over it as if writing. My mother was never in the habit of writing in the library.

"I recollect her dress perfectly, as the impression was quite distinct and vivid. She had on a black cloak, and bonnet with a yellow bird in it, which she generally wore.

"It is the only time anything of the kind has happened to me.   "M. J. MILMAN."

From MISS CAMPBELL.

"17 SOUTHWELL GARDENS, S.W.,
March 21st, 1888.

"My sister and mother and myself, after returning from our morning drive, came into the dining-room without removing our things, and had luncheon as usual, during which my sister and I laughed and cracked jokes in the gayest of spirits. After a time my mother rose and left the room, but we remained on for a few minutes. Finally we both got up and went into the passage, and I was about to go upstairs and take off my things when I saw my sister turn into my father's study (which was directly opposite the dining-room), with the evident intention, as I supposed, of speaking to my mother, whom I distinctly noticed seated at my father's desk in her cloak and bonnet, busily absorbed in writing. The door of the study was wide open at the time. I turned round and followed her to the door, when, to my surprise, my mother had completely disappeared, and I noticed my sister turned away too, and left the room as if puzzled. I asked her, with some curiosity, what she went into the room for? She replied that she fancied she saw my mother bending over the desk writing, and went in to speak to her. Feeling very much startled and alarmed, we went upstairs to see after her, and found her in her bedroom, where she went immediately on leaving the dining-room, and had been all the time. "E. J. CAMPBELL."

In the next case the apparition was recognised by one of the percipients only, as resembling a relative who had been dead some years. Neither percipient appears to have seen the face.

No. 82.—From MRS. J. C.

"*August 20th*, 1893.

"Seven years ago my husband and I had the following curious experience :—

"In the middle of the night I awoke with the feeling that some one was near me, and at once saw a figure moving from the side of my bed towards the wardrobe where I kept jewellery. My supposition was that it was a burglar, and I refrained from waking my husband (whose bed was two feet from mine), as I thought the burglar would be armed, and I knew my husband would certainly attack him and be at his mercy. I therefore lay perfectly still.

"The apparition having passed the foot of my bed, then came opposite my husband's, when, to my astonishment, I saw my husband sit up in bed gazing at the figure. In a moment or two he lay down again, and the figure apparently passed to the door.

"We neither of us spoke one word that night.

"In the morning I asked my husband to look if the doors were locked (of which there are three in the room). They were all secure. I also examined the beds to see if they by any possibility could have touched, and so I unconsciously have awakened him, but they were quite separate. I then asked if he remembered anything happening in the night, and he replied, 'Yes, a strange thing : I thought I saw my father go out of that door.' Not till then did I tell him that I thought the figure was a burglar, and how frightened I had been at the thought of his struggling with an armed man, and had therefore remained silent.

"The gas was burning, and I could see quite across the room."

I received a full account of the incident orally from Mrs. C. on the 20th August 1893. She told me that she never saw the face of the figure, and could not see, or cannot now recollect, the dress. She had no doubt at the time that it was a burglar. Mrs. C. has had no other hallucination of any kind.

Mr. C. writes on the 21st August 1893:—

" I have read my wife's account, and endorse it.

" To my recollection I was not dreaming previously to sitting up in bed, when I believed I saw my father going towards the door. My mind had not been specially active about his affairs at that time, although I was rather anxious about some matters of business.

" The figure I supposed to be my father (and I had no thought it was any one else) moved noiselessly across the room and disappeared through the doorway. I should have treated it as a dream only, if my wife had not recalled my attention to it in the morning by asking me if I remembered sitting up in bed.

" Although I am certain my eyes were open at the time of the apparition, I did not see the face, but recognised the figure as that of my father by the general appearance as I remembered him.

" I have had no other similar waking experience, but have previously seen my father distinctly in a dream after his decease."

Mr. C. told me that he was positive the figure could not have been that of a real man : the doors were found locked on the inside in the morning. Moreover, his recognition of the figure, though he could not see the face, was unmistakable.

We have many similar accounts of collective phantasms which appear to have differed from subjective hallucinations of the ordinary type in no other particular than the fact of their occurrence to two persons simultaneously. Thus, to quote a few instances, Mrs. Willett, of Bedales, Lindfield, Sussex, sent us an extract from her diary describing a figure seen by her daughter and a visitor,—a fair-haired child running along a gallery. The account is confirmed by the visitor, Miss S. From Mrs. and Miss Goodhall we have an account of a tall figure seen by them when driving in a country lane. Miss C——— and two of her sisters saw in a bedroom in a London house the figure of a young man of middle height wearing a peaked cap and dark clothes. · Mrs. Y. and her niece saw the figure of a child in a long grey dressing-gown running down a lighted staircase. In this last case the figure was mistaken for Mrs. Y.'s daughter, but in the other cases the phantasm bore no resemblance to any one with whom the percipients were acquainted. In no instance does it seem possible except by violently straining the probabilities to suppose the figure seen to have been that of a human being.

In the next case the phantasm, which was recognised, occurred within a short time of the death of the person represented. The narrator is a decorator and house-painter, of Uniontown, Kentucky, U.S.A.

No. 83.—From MR. S. S. FALKINBURG.

"*September* 12*th*, 1884.

"The following circumstance is impressed upon my mind in a manner which will preclude its ever being forgotten by me or the members of my family interested. My little son Arthur, who was then five years old, and the pet of his grandpapa, was playing on the floor, when I entered the house a quarter to seven o'clock, Friday evening, July 11th, 1879. I was very tired, having been receiving and paying for staves all day, and it being an exceedingly sultry evening, I lay down by Artie on the carpet, and entered into conversation with my wife—not, however, in regard to my parents. Artie, as usually was the case, came and lay down with his little head upon my left arm, when all at once he exclaimed, 'Papa! papa! Grandpa!' I cast my eyes towards the ceiling, or opened my eyes, I am not sure which, when, between me and the joists (it was an old-fashioned log-cabin), I saw the face of my father as plainly as ever I saw him in my life. He appeared to me to be very pale, and looked *sad*, as I had seen him upon my last visit to him three months previous. I immediately spoke to my wife, who was sitting within a few feet of me, and said, 'Clara, there is something wrong at home; father is either dead or very sick.' She tried to persuade me that it was my imagination, but I could not help feeling that something was wrong. Being very tired, we soon after retired, and about ten o'clock Artie woke me up repeating, 'Papa, grandpa is here.' I looked, and believe, if I remember right, got up, at any rate to get the child warm, as he complained of coldness, and it was very sultry weather. Next morning I expressed my determination to go at once to Indianapolis. My wife made light of it and over-persuaded me, and I did not go until Monday morning, and upon arriving at home (my father's), I found that he had been buried the day before, Sunday, July 13th.

"Now comes the mysterious part to me. After I had told my mother and brother of my vision, or whatever it may have been, they told me the following :—

"On the morning of the 11th July, the day of his death, he arose early and expressed himself as feeling unusually well, and ate a hearty breakfast. He took the Bible (he was a Methodist minister), and went and remained until near noon. He ate a hearty dinner, and went to the front gate, and, looking up and down the street, remarked that he could not, or at least would not be disappointed, some one was surely coming. During the afternoon and evening he seemed restless, and went to the gate, looking down street, frequently. At last, about time for supper, he mentioned my name, and expressed his conviction that God, in His own good time, would answer his prayers in my behalf, I being at that time very wild. Mother going into the kitchen to prepare supper, he followed her and continued talking to her about myself and family, and especially Arthur, my son. Supper being over, he moved his chair near the door, and was conversing about me at the time he died. The last words were about me, and were spoken, by mother's clock, 14 minutes of 7. He did not fall, but just quit talking and was dead.

"In answer to my inquiries, my son Arthur says he remembers the circumstances, and the impression he received upon that occasion is ineffaceable.

"SAMUEL S. FALKINBURG."

We have procured a certificate of death from the Indianapolis Board of Health, which confirms the date given.

Mrs. Falkinburg writes to us, on September 12, 1884 :—

" In answer to your request, I will say that I cheerfully give my recollection of the circumstance to which you refer.

" We were living in Brown County, Indiana, fifty miles south of Indianapolis, in the summer of 1879. My husband (Mr. S. S. Falkinburg) was in the employ of one John Ayers, buying staves.

" On the evening of July 11th, about 6.30 o'clock, he came into the room where I was sitting, and lay down on the carpet with my little boy Arthur, complaining of being very tired and warm. Entering into conversation on some unimportant matter, Arthur went to him and lay down by his side. In a few moments my notice was attracted by hearing Arthur exclaim : ' Oh, papa, grandpa, grandpa, papa,' at the same time pointing with his little hand toward the ceiling. I looked in the direction he was pointing, but saw nothing. My husband, however, said : ' Clara, there is something wrong at home ; father is either dead or very sick.' I tried to laugh him out of what I thought an idle fancy ; but he insisted that he saw the face of his father looking at him from near the ceiling, and Arthur said, ' Grandpa was come, for he saw him.' That night we were awakened by Artie again calling his papa to see ' grandpa.'

" A short time after my husband started (Monday) to go to Indianapolis, I received a letter calling him to the burial of his father ; and some time after, in conversation with his mother, it transpired that the time he and Artie saw the vision was within two or three minutes of the time his father died.

" CLARA T. FALKINBURG."

Asked whether this was his sole experience of a visual hallucination, Mr. Falkinburg replied that it was. Occasionally, however, since that time, he has had auditory impressions suggestive of his father's presence.

Here again, in the absence of evidence to the contrary, it seems more probable that Mr. Falkinburg's hallucination was telepathically originated, than that the casual remark of a child of five could produce an effect hitherto observed only as the result of hypnotic influence or some other equally potent disturbing cause.

In the following case, which again comes to us from

the United States, the vision was of a more complicated kind, and part only of the original percipient's experience was shared. The occurrence of the apparition within a few hours of the death of a person to whom it bore some resemblance seems to be established; but in estimating the value of the coincidence, it should be borne in mind that the phantasm was not at the time referred to the deceased, and that there are numerous chances of the coincidence of an unrecognised hallucination with a death amongst a doctor's circle of acquaintance.

No. 84.—From DR. W. O. S.,

who wrote to Dr. Hodgson from Albany, New York, on the 10th September 1888, enclosing the following account :—

"I am a physician, have been in practice about eleven years; am in excellent health, do not use intoxicants, tobacco, drugs, or strong tea or coffee. Am not subject (in the least) to dreams, and have never been a believer in apparitions, etc.

"On Monday last, September 3rd, 1888, I went to bed about 11 P.M., after my day's work. Had supper, a light one, about 7 P.M.; made calls after supper.

"My bedroom is on the second floor of a city block house, and I kept all my doors locked except the one leading to my wife's room, next to mine, opening into mine by a wide sliding door, always left wide open at night. The diagram opposite will illustrate the relation of the rooms.

"I occupy room 1 and my wife room 2. Her room has but one window, and a door opening only into my room. My room has three doors (all bolted at night) and one window. Both windows in our rooms have heavy green shades, which are drawn nearly to the bottom of the window at night, shutting out early daylight. No artificial lights command the windows, and the moonlight very seldom.

"I undressed and went to bed about 11, and soon was asleep. In the neighbourhood of 4 A.M. I was awakened by a strong light in my face. I awoke and thought I saw my wife standing at Fig. 3, as she was to rise at 5.30 to take an early train. The light was so bright and pervading that I spoke, but got no answer. As I spoke, the figure retreated to Fig. 4, and as gradually faded to a spot at Fig. 5. The noiseless shifting of the light made me think it was a servant in the hall and the light was thrown through the keyhole as she moved.   That could not be, as some clothing covered the keyhole.   I then thought a burglar must be in the room, as the light settled near a large safe in my room.   Thereupon I called loudly to my wife, and sprang to light a light.   As I called her name she suddenly awoke, and called out, 'What is that bright light in your room?'   I lit the gas and searched (there had been no light in either room).   Everything was undisturbed.

"My wife left on the early train.   I attended to my work as usual.   At noon, when I reached home, the servant who answers the door informed me that a man had been to my office to see about a certificate for a young lady who had died suddenly early that morning from a hemorrhage from the lungs. She died about one o'clock—the figure I saw about four o'clock.

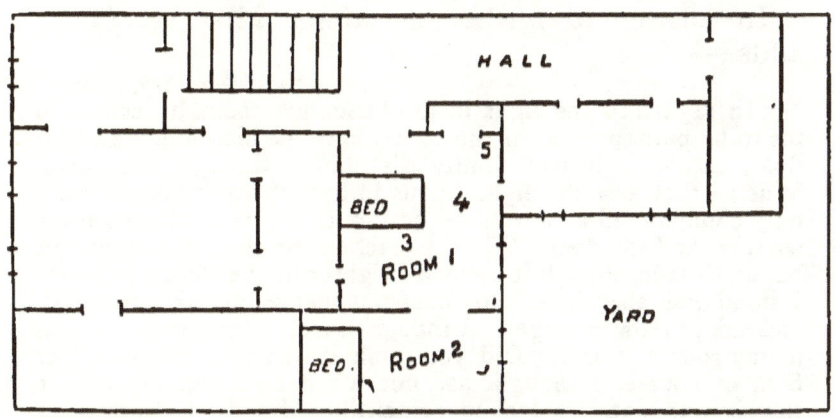

There was but little resemblance between the two, as far as I noticed, except height and figure.   The faces were not unlike, except that the apparition seemed considerably older.   I had seen the young lady the evening before, but, although much interested in the case, did not consider it immediately serious. She had been in excellent health up to within two days of her death.   At first she spit a little blood, from a strain.   When she was taken with the severe hemorrhage, and choked to death, she called for help and for me.

"This is the first experience of the kind I have ever had, or personally have known about   It was very clear—the figure or apparition—at first, but rapidly faded.   My wife remarked the light before I had spoken anything except her name.   When I awake I am wide awake in an instant, as I am accustomed to answer a telephone in the hall and my office-bell at night."

From MRS. W. O. S.

"ALBANY, *September 27th*, 1888.

"On the morning of September 4 I was suddenly awakened out of a sound sleep by my husband's calling to me from an adjoining room. Before I answered him I was struck with the fact that although the green shade to his window was drawn down, his room seemed flooded by a soft yellow light, while my chamber, with the window on same side as his, and with the shade drawn up, was dark. The first thing I said was, 'What is that light?' He replied he didn't know. I then got up and went into his room, which was still quite light. The light faded away in a moment or two. The shade was down all the time. When I went back to my room I saw that it was a few moments after four."

In answer to further questions, Mrs. W. O. S. adds :—

"*October 16th*, 1888.

"In regard to the light in my husband's room, it seemed to me to be perhaps more in the corner between his window and my door, although it was faintly distributed through the room. When I first saw the light (lying in bed) it was brilliant, but I only commanded a view of the corner of his room, between his window and my door. When I reached the door the light had begun to fade, though it seemed brighter in the doorway where I stood than elsewhere. My husband seemed greatly perplexed, and said, 'How strange! I thought surely there was a woman in my room.' I said, 'Did you think it was I?' He said, 'At first, of course, I thought so, but when I rubbed my eyes I saw it was not. It looked some like Mrs. B——' (another patient of his,—not the girl who died that night). He, moreover, said that the figure never seemed to look directly at him, but towards the wall beyond his bed; and that the figure seemed clothed in white, or something very light. That was all he said, except that later, when he knew the girl was dead, and I asked him if the figure at all resembled her, he said, 'Yes, it did look like her, only older.'"[1]

---

[1] *Proc. American S.P.R.*, pp. 405-408. The reader may be interested in comparing the ragged and possibly commonplace account given in the text with the following spirited version of the same incident quoted from the *Arena*, March 1892. The writer of the account states that "the story, as I tell it, was given me by the wife." But he does not, it will be observed, quote it as in Mrs. W. O. S.'s words. After describing how the doctor was awakened by a strong light in the room and saw the figure of a woman, whom

So far the instances quoted belong to what may be called the normal type of collective hallucination. In the last case, indeed, one percipient saw less than the other, but that may have been due merely to the fact that she awoke later.   In the three cases which follow the impressions produced upon the percipients were diverse, and there is no evidence that they were simultaneous.   In the first of the three cases, indeed, the circumstances strongly suggest that the mind of one percipient was influenced by the other.   But in the last case, where the percipients were far apart, and their impressions markedly different, it seems reasonable to conjecture—their interest in the agent being equal—that the results produced were in each case directly referable to the dying man.

he at first mistook for his wife, the writer in the *Arena* proceeds as follows :—

" By this time he was broad awake, and sat upright in bed staring at the figure.   He noticed that it was a woman in a white garment; and looking sharply, he recognised it, as he thought, as one of his patients who was very ill.   Then he realised that this could not be so, and that if any one was in the room, it must be an intruder who had no right to be there.   With the vague thought of a possible burglar thus disguised, he sprang out of bed and grasped his revolver, which he was accustomed to have near at hand.   This brought him face to face with the figure, not three feet away.   He now saw every detail of dress, complexion, and feature, and for the first time recognised the fact that it was not a being of flesh and blood.   Then it was that, in quite an excited manner, he called his wife, hoping that she would get there to see it also.   But the moment he called her name, the figure disappeared, leaving, however, the intense yellow light behind, and which they both observed for five minutes by the watch before it faded out.

"The next day it was found that one of his patients, closely resembling the figure he had seen, had died a few minutes before he saw his vision,—had died *calling for him.*

" It will be seen that this story, like the first one in this article, *is perfectly authentic in every particular.   There is no question as to the facts.*"

That, no doubt, is how the thing ought to have happened.   A revolver and a watch are essential to a properly upholstered ghost-story.   There ought to have been the dramatic confrontation of the living man with his spectral visitant; there ought to have been the instant recognition and as instant disappearance.   Above all, there ought to have been the exquisite adjustment in the times of vision and death.

The narrative which follows was originally printed in July 1883, in an account written by the Warden, entitled "The Orphanage and Home, Aberlour, Craigellachie." It will be observed that the account, though written in the third person, is actually first hand.

No. 85.—From the REV. C. H. JUPP, Warden.

"In 1875 a man died leaving a widow and six orphan children. The three eldest were admitted into the Orphanage. Three years afterwards the widow died, and friends succeeded in getting funds to send the rest here, the youngest being about four years of age. [Late one evening, about six months after the admission of the younger children, some visitors arrived unexpectedly; and] the Warden agreed to take a bed in the little ones' dormitory, which contained ten beds, nine occupied.

" In the morning, at breakfast, the Warden made the following statement:—'As near as I can tell I fell asleep about eleven o'clock, and slept very soundly for some time. I suddenly woke without any apparent reason, and felt an impulse to turn round, my face being towards the wall, from the children. Before turning, I looked up and saw a soft light in the room. The gas was burning low in the hall, and the dormitory door being open, I thought it probable that the light came from that source. It was soon evident, however, that such was not the case. I turned round, and then a wonderful vision met my gaze. Over the second bed from mine, and on the same side of the room, there was floating a small cloud of light, forming a halo of the brightness of the moon on an ordinary moonlight night.

"'I sat upright in bed, looking at this strange appearance, took up my watch and found the hands pointing to five minutes to one. Everything was quiet, and all the children sleeping soundly. In the bed, over which the light seemed to float, slept the youngest of the six children mentioned above.

"'I asked myself, "Am I dreaming?" No! I was wide awake. I was seized with a strong impulse to rise and touch the substance, or whatever it might be (for it was about five feet high), and was getting up when something seemed to hold me back. I am certain I heard nothing, yet I *felt* and perfectly understood the words—" No, lie down, it won't hurt you." I *at once* did what I *felt* I was told to do. I fell asleep shortly afterwards and rose at half-past five, that being my usual time.

"'At six o'clock I began dressing the children, beginning at the bed furthest from the one in which I slept. Presently I came to the bed over which I had seen the light hovering. I took the little boy out, placed him on my knee, and put on some of his clothes. The child had been talking with the others; suddenly he was silent. And then, looking me hard in the face with an extraordinary expression, he said, " Oh, Mr. Jupp, my mother came to me last night. Did you see her ? " For a moment I could not answer the child. I then thought it better to pass it off, and said, " Come, we must make haste, or we shall be late for breakfast." '

" The child never afterwards referred to the matter, we are told, nor has it since ever been mentioned to him. The Warden says it is a mystery to him; he simply states the fact and there leaves the matter, being perfectly satisfied that he was mistaken in no one particular."

In answer to inquiries, the Rev. C. Jupp writes to us :—

> "THE ORPHANAGE AND CONVALESCENT HOME,
> ABERLOUR, CRAIGELLACHIE,
> *November* 13*th*, 1883.
>
> " I fear anything the little boy might now say would be un-reliable, or I would at once question him. Although the matter was fully discussed at the time, it was never mentioned in the hearing of the child; and yet when, at the request of friends, the account was published in our little magazine, and the child read it, his countenance changed, and looking up, he said, ' Mr. Jupp, that is me.' I said, ' Yes, that is what we saw.' He said, ' Yes,' and then seemed to fall into deep thought, evidently with pleasant remembrances, for he smiled so sweetly to himself, and seemed to forget I was present.
>
> " I much regret now that I did not learn something from the child at the time.
>
> "CHAS. JUPP."

In answer to inquiries, Mr. Jupp says that he has never had any other hallucination of the senses ; and adds :—

> " My wife was the only person *of adult age* to whom I mentioned the circumstance at the time. Shortly after, I mentioned it to our Bishop and Primus."

Mrs. Jupp writes, from the Orphanage, on June 23, 1886 :—

> " This is to certify that the account of the light seen by the Warden of this establishment is correct, and was mentioned to me at the time "—*i.e.*, next morning.

It is to be regretted that it is not now possible
to ascertain whether the child's experience were
of the nature of a dream or a borderland hallucination. But the ambiguity does not affect either the
interpretation or the significance of the incident.

In the next case the two apparitions were not only
different, but were seen in different rooms. The time
in each case appears to have been within an hour of
midnight. It will be noticed that each percipient
is doubtful whether to class her experience as a
dream or a waking vision. If dreams, they were
certainly of an unusual type, since they included
in each case an impression of the room in which
they occurred.

No. 86.—From SISTER MARTHA.

Account, signed by herself, which Sister Martha
(Sister of the Order of Saint Charles) gave to M.
Ch. Richet at Mirecourt—

"On Friday, 6th March 1891, I was called to nurse M.
Bastien. At night, when I had been dozing for about five
minutes, I had the following dream—if I may call it a dream;
I think I was sleeping. A light, a sound came from the fire-
place, and a woman stepped out whose appearance I did not
recognise, but who had a voice like Madame Bastien's. I saw
her as distinctly as I see you. She approached the bed where
Cécile was sleeping, and taking her hand, said, 'How sweet
Cécile is!' I followed her—in my dream, crossing myself as
I went. She opened the door and vanished.

"I cannot say the exact hour, but it was early in the night,
between 11 P.M. and 1 A.M.—I do not know exactly, for I had
not a watch. I awoke immediately after this dream. I did not
waken Cécile, for I did not want to say anything to her about
it, but as the dream impressed me very much, I told it to her the
following morning when I awoke. I can give no further details
about the dream except that the lady carried a candle and had
coloured spots on her garments.

"I have never had a similar dream except once, when I
thought I saw my dead mother and heard her say, 'You do not
remember me in your prayers.'"

Madame Houdaille writes:—

"MIRECOURT, 20*th March*, 1891.

" During my father's illness the Sister kept watch on the first floor, and my brother and I passed the evening on the ground floor. About ten o'clock I left my brother and went upstairs to bed. Between eleven o'clock and midnight (I do not know whether I was waking or sleeping, probably between the two) I perceived, near my bed, a white shadow like a phantom, which I had not time to recognise. I gave a loud cry of terror which startled my brother, who was just going up to bed. He hastened to my room, and found me gazing wildly around. The rest of the night passed quietly.

" Next morning Cécile told me about the Sister's dream.

" She, Cécile, had seen or heard nothing. I was almost angry with her and her tale, and treated it as a silly dream, so terrified was I at the occurrence of the two apparitions the same night, and probably at the same hour. Cécile and the Sister knew nothing of my dream. I did not tell it to the Sister till two days after M. Richet and Octave[1] had visited the hospital."[2]

In the next case, as already said, the two percipients were many miles apart. The impression in the first narrative should probably be classed as a dream; in the second as an auditory hallucination.

No. 87.—From SIR LAWRENCE JONES.

"CRANMER HALL, FAKENHAM, NORFOLK,
April 26th, 1893.

" On August 20th, 1884, I was staying at my father-in-law's house at Bury St. Edmunds. I had left my father in perfectly good health about a fortnight before. He was at home at this address. About August 18th I had had a letter from my mother saying that my father was not quite well, and that the doctor had seen him and made very light of the matter, attributing his indisposition to the extreme heat of the weather.

" I was not in any way anxious on my father's account, as he was rather subject to slight bilious attacks.

" I should add, though, that I had been spending that day, August 20th, at Cambridge, and should have stayed the night there had not a sort of vague presentiment haunted me that possibly there would be a letter from home the next morning.

---

[1] M. Octave Houdaille.
[2] *Annales des Sciences Psychiques*, vol. i. pp. 98, 99.

My wife, too, had a similar feeling that if I stayed the night at Cambridge I might regret it. In consequence of this feeling I returned to Bury, and that night woke up suddenly to find myself streaming with perspiration and calling out: 'Something dreadful is happening; I don't know what.' The impression of horror remained some time, but at last I fell asleep till the morning.

"My father, Sir Willoughby Jones, died very suddenly of heart disease about 1 A.M. on August 21st. He was not in his room at the moment, but was carried back to his room and restoratives applied, but in vain.

"My brother Herbert and I were the only two of the family absent from home at the time. The thoughts of those present (my mother, brother, and three sisters) no doubt turned most anxiously towards us, and it is to a telepathic impression from them in their anxiety and sorrow that I attribute the intimations we received.

"LAWRENCE J. JONES."

Lady Jones writes :—

"I have a vivid remembrance of the occurrence related above by my husband. I was sound asleep when he awoke, and seizing me by [the] wrist, exclaimed: 'Such a dreadful thing is happening,' and I had much difficulty in persuading him that there was nothing wrong.

"He went to sleep again, but was much relieved in the morning by finding a long letter from Sir Willoughby, posted the day before, and written in good spirits. Having read this and gone to his dressing-room, however, he soon returned with the telegram summoning him home at once, and said as he came in: 'My impression in the night was only too true.'

"EVELYN M. JONES."

Mr. Herbert Jones, the other percipient, describes his experience as follows :—

"KNEBWORTH RECTORY, STEVENAGE.

"Recollections of August 20th, 1884.

"I had spent the day at Harpenden, and returned home about 8 P.M., and went to bed about 10.30.

"I woke at 12 o'clock, hearing my name called twice, as I fancied. I lit my candle, and, seeing nothing, concluded it was a dream—looked at my watch, and went to sleep again.

"I woke again and heard people carrying something downstairs from the upper storey, just outside my room. I lit my candle, got out of bed, and waited till the men were outside my door. They seemed to be carrying something heavy, and came down step by step.

"I opened my door, and it was pitch dark. I was puzzled and dumbfounded. I went into my sitting-room and into the hall, but everything was dark and quiet. I went back to bed convinced I had been the sport of another nightmare. It was about 2 A.M. by my watch. At breakfast next morning on my plate was a telegram telling me to come home.

"This whole story may be nothing, but it was odd that I should have twice got up in one night, and that during that night and those hours my father was dying.

"H. E. JONES.

"*April 4th,* 1893."

Sir Lawrence Jones adds:—

"My brother was then a curate in London, living at 32 Palace Street, Westminster, where the above experience took place.

"L. J. J."

A case somewhat resembling this last is recorded by Professor Richet (*Proc. S.P.R.*, vol. v. pp. 163, 164). On the night of the 14-15th November 1887, when his physiological laboratory in Paris was burnt, two of his intimate friends, M. Ferrari and M. Héricourt, dreamt of fire ; and on the evening of the 15th Madame B. (the hypnotic subject referred to in Chapter V.) was hypnotised by M. Gibert at Havre and "sent on a journey" [*i.e.,* in imagination] to Paris to visit, amongst others, M. Richet. Shortly afterwards she awoke herself by crying out in great distress, "It is burning." Unfortunately, those present contented themselves with calming her excitement, and did not at the time inquire into the nature of her impression. But the triple coincidence is certainly remarkable.

A case which may perhaps be referred to the same category is recorded by the Rev. A. T. Fryer in the *Journal* of the S.P.R. for June 1890. Mr. C. Williams died at Plaxtol, Sevenoaks, on Sunday, April 28th, 1889, having been confined to his bed with pleuro-pneumonia since the preceding Tuesday. On Friday the 26th his figure was seen in the street by

Mr. Hind at about 10.40 A.M., and on the day following at about 1 P.M. by two ladies, Miss Dalison and Miss Sinclair, simultaneously. None of the percipients were aware of Mr. Williams' illness. It was impossible that the figure seen could have been the real man, and, as Mr. Fryer shows that a mistake of identity was under the circumstances extremely improbable, it seems not unlikely that we have here to deal with a case of two telepathic hallucinations originated independently and at a considerable interval by the same agent.

CHAPTER XIII.

SOME LESS COMMON TYPES OF TELEPATHIC HALLUCINATION.

THE hallucinations so far dealt with belong to classes numerically strong, and the narratives quoted could be paralleled over and over again from our records by other narratives equally well attested. And this fact furnishes in itself a strong presumption of the substantial accuracy of the accounts given. For as there is little in the kind of incident described—the bare occurrence of a hallucination coincidently with an external event or with another hallucination—to suggest the work of the imagination, there is little warrant for ascribing this consensus of testimony among the narratives to any other cause than a common foundation in fact. The episodes consist, indeed, of such simple elements as to leave small room for embellishment. Moreover, by those who accept the theory of telepathy an additional argument for the authenticity of these narratives may be found in the consideration that in that theory they receive a simple and sufficient explanation. But we meet occasionally with accounts of hallucinatory experiences which do not fall readily under any of the comparatively simple categories already discussed. The mere difficulty of explaining the genesis of hallucinations of such aberrant types would not, in the present stage of our knowledge, be an argument against their authenticity. But it serves to rob them of the support which they might otherwise have received from their affiliation with better known forms of hallucination; whilst the recent first-hand evidence actually available is not sufficient in itself to substantiate them. Whilst, therefore, such cases should be duly recorded and may legitimately be discussed, it seems best to await the receipt of further evidence before a final judgment is passed upon them. But in some instances there is a further reason why the question should at most be held unproven. Some of the features which distinguish these cases from ordinary telepathic hallucinations, whilst occurring rarely in well-attested recent narratives, are to be found more commonly in remote, uncorroborated, and traditional stories. This circumstance is, of course, a strong argument against their genuineness, since it proves that the imagination tends to create such features. But it is not a conclusive argument. The imagination may itself have been inspired in the first instance by fact; it may have copied, not bettered, nature. That the legendary epics of the older world have invented winged dragons is clearly not an argument that can weigh against positive evidence for the existence in a still more remote past of pterodactyls.

Reciprocal Cases.

These considerations apply with full force to the first of the dubious types here to be considered. In publishing seven first-hand "reciprocal" cases in 1886 (*Phantasms*, vol. ii. p. 167) Mr. Gurney pointed out that the evidence then available was "so small that the genuineness of the type might fairly be called in question." Still, regarding it as probably genuine, he anticipated that we should ultimately obtain more well-attested specimens of it. In the eight years which have elapsed since Mr. Gurney wrote this anticipation has met with only partial fulfilment. We have met with but two recent well-attested cases which clearly fall under the same category as those already

given. One of these cases has already been quoted
(No. 63), and was indeed included in the supplementary chapter of *Phantasms of the Living;* the other is
as follows :—

No. 88.—From the REV. C. L. EVANS.

"FORTON, GARSTANG.
(Received on the 18th of September 1889.)

"Two years ago I had occasion to undergo a course of
magnetism, under the treatment of Miss ——. I was under her
treatment for six weeks, and derived considerable benefit from
her treatment. A warm friendship sprang up between us, as
she had wonderfully improved my sight. I went up to St.
Edmund Hall, Oxford, at the commencement of the October
term, as my eyes were so much stronger. One afternoon, as I
had just come in from the river, being rather tired, I sat down
for a minute before I changed, when, to my great surprise, the
door opened, and Miss —— appeared to walk in.

"She was looking rather pale at the time, and looked intently
at me for about a minute, then left the room as slowly as she had
walked in. I was much alarmed, as I fancied that something
must have happened to her, and I immediately sat down and
wrote off two letters, one to Miss ——, asking if she was well,
and another to my mother, telling her of the strange occurrence.
The next day I had back the two replies. My mother said
that on that very afternoon she had called on Miss ——, and
naturally they had been discussing my case. She said that my
description of Miss ——'s dress, etc., was perfectly accurate. I
then read Miss——'s note. She stated that my mother had called,
and had left at about half-past four, she then had lain down for a
few minutes, and was thinking and wishing to see me. She had a
distinct impression that she saw me during this sleep, or trance,
but when she awoke the impression was not very vivid. The
time exactly coincided, and she said that my description of her
was very accurate. At the time that she appeared to me I was
not thinking in the least of her.

"CHARLES LLOYD EVANS."

I called on Mr. Evans on the 20th April 1892, and
had a long conversation with him. The following
notes of my interview were made at the time and
written out a few days later :—

"The occurrence took place in November 1887. It would
be about 4.15 P.M. He was resting in his chair—in boating

clothes—with the door ajar. Heard a knock or sound as of some one entering ; turned round and saw Miss —— come into the room and walk towards him. She was dressed in red bodice and dark silk skirt (a not unfamiliar dress), but with a silver filigree cross hanging from a chain round her neck which he had never seen before. Learnt afterwards that the cross had been given by General —— only a few days before the incident.

"The figure looked him straight in the face, then seemed to fade away bit by bit.

"He was himself perfectly well and not a bit sleepy.

"He has had no other hallucinations. His age at the time was twenty."

Mr. Evans's mother writes :—

"*April 27th*, 1892.

"In reply to the questions you asked me about the apparition of Miss —— to my son, when at Oxford, I can fully verify his statement. He wrote to me the same afternoon, begging me to call upon Miss —— and see if she was ill, detailing me the account of what he had seen, and also describing her dress minutely and the cross she was wearing. I called upon Miss —— the following day, and read her my son's letter, giving the hour at which she had appeared to him. She told me that she had not been feeling well, and was lying down on the couch thinking, too, of my son, and that she went off into a sort of trance, and she saw him distinctly looking at her and he was very pale. This made a deep impression upon me, for I must own myself that I hardly believed it to be possible. However, Miss —— told me that my son had at once written to her, fearing that she must be ill, and told her the circumstances under which she appeared to him. When I saw Miss —— she was then wearing the same dress and filigree cross which Charlie had described to me in his letter, and which he had never seen her wearing before. I fear that I cannot now find my son's letter, but should I come across it I will forward it to you. Miss ——, however, can corroborate all that I have said.

"MARY E. EVANS."

Afterwards I saw Miss ——. The following notes of the interview were made the same day :—

"*July 17th*, 1892.

"Her account of the matter is that Mrs. Evans (percipient's mother) called on her on the afternoon of the vision and talked much about her son. After Mrs. Evans left—probably about 5.30 P.M.—Miss ——, as usual, lay down to sleep for a few minutes; woke about 6 P.M. with the recollection of having seen

Mr. C. L. Evans. Can recall no details of appearance—merely the recollection of having been in the same room with him.

"The next day she received a letter from Mr. C. L. Evans telling of his vision, and on the same day another visit from his mother.

"Miss —— was wearing the dress and filigree cross described. The cross, as stated, had been given to her only a few days before.

"Miss —— has kept Mr. Evans's letter.[1] She has had many visions and dreams in her life, but she cannot recall another relating to Mr. Evans.

"She is not sure of the time at which her vision or dream occurred. It may have been earlier than 6 P.M., her hours being very irregular.

"She had compared notes with Mr. Evans, and was under the impression that their experiences coincided. But I think that her first statement—6 P.M.—is probably correct. If so, her dream would have come one and a half to two hours after Mr. Evans's vision."

If the above account correctly describes what took place—and I know of no ground for doubting either the accuracy or the good faith of the narrators—it seems clear either that Mr. Evans and Miss —— reciprocally affected each other, or that Mr. Evans, whilst impressing Miss —— with the idea of his presence, was able himself to attain to a supernormal perception of her surroundings. For the latter explanation, however, we have no support in analogy, and it seems less unwarrantable provisionally to regard this case and others like it as being reciprocally telepathic. It should, perhaps, be pointed out, as bearing upon the extreme rarity of cases of the kind, that there may be instances of reciprocal affection of which, from the very nature of the case, we could not hope to obtain evidence. It is conceivable, for instance, that in the ordinary case of an apparition at death, the dying man may himself have been a percipient as well as an agent, since circumstances rarely permit of his side of the experience being recorded. It is conceivable also that in cases of collective

---

[1] She was, however, unable to find it.

hallucination the effect may really be a reciprocal one, the two persons concerned simultaneously affecting and being affected by each other, until the force so generated explodes into hallucination. But in the present state of our knowledge it would be premature to speculate further.

A Misinterpreted Message.

The next case also seems susceptible of more than one explanation. The account which follows was written in 1890.

No. 89.—From MISS C. L. HAWKINS-DEMPSTER, 24 Portman Square, W.

" I ran downstairs and entered the drawing-room at 7.30 P.M., believing I had kept my two sisters waiting for dinner. They had gone to dinner, the room was empty. Behind a long sofa I saw Mr. H. standing. He moved three steps nearer. I heard nothing. I was not at all afraid or surprised, only felt concern as [to] what he wanted, as he was in South America. I learnt next morning that at that moment his mother was breathing her last. I went and arranged her for burial, my picture still hanging above the bed, between the portraits of her two absent sons.

" I was in the habit of hearing often from [Mr. H.], and was not at that moment anxious about Mrs. H.'s health, though she was aged. I had had twenty-five days before the grief of losing an only brother. No other persons were present at the time."[1]

In answer to further inquiries, we learnt from Miss Hawkins-Dempster that the above incident occurred on New Year's Eve, 1876-77; the room was lighted by "one bright lamp and a fire," and the figure did not seem to go away, she merely "ceased to see it." She used to see Mrs. H. often, and was in no anxiety as to her health at the time. Mrs. H. was very old, but not definitely ill. Miss Hawkins-Dempster corrected her first statement as to the exactness of the coincidence

[1] It should be explained that this account was written on a "census" form, in the limited space provided for answers to our printed questions.

by informing us that Mrs. H. died in the morning of the same day on which the apparition was seen.

Miss Hawkins-Dempster mentioned what she had seen to her sister, who thus corroborates:—

"July 15th, 1892.

" I heard of my sister Miss C. L. Hawkins-Dempster's vision of Mr. H. in the drawing-room at 7.30 P.M. on New Year's Eve, 1876-77, immediately after it happened, and before hearing that Mrs. H. died the same day, the news of which reached us later that evening.

" H. H. DEMPSTER."

We have verified the date of death at Somerset House.

Miss Hawkins-Dempster has had one other experience—an apparition seen also by her sister and their governess. They were children at the time, aged about fourteen and twelve respectively.

Mr. Myers had an interview with the Misses Hawkins-Dempster on July 16th, 1892, and writes as follows the next day:—

" Miss C. Hawkins-Dempster's veridical experience is well remembered by both sisters. The decedent was a very old lady, who was on very intimate terms with them, and had special reasons for thinking of Miss C. Hawkins-Dempster in connection with the son whose figure appeared. He was at the other side of the world, and most certainly had not heard of his mother's death at the time.

" The figure was absolutely life-like. Miss Hawkins-Dempster noticed the slight cast of the eye and the delicate hands. The figure rested one hand on the back of a chair and held the other out. Miss Hawkins-Dempster called out, ' What can I do for you?' forgetting for the moment the impossibility that it could be the real man. Then she simply ceased to see the figure.

" She was in good health at the time, and her thoughts were occupied with business matters."

We have a parallel case amongst our records. Miss V. saw in church the hallucinatory figure of an acquaintance looking at her, and subsequently learned that he was at the time at the deathbed of his mother. A few other cases are given in *Phantasms of the*

Living. I should be disposed to explain these narratives as instances of the misinterpretation of a telepathic message. I should conjecture, that is, that the impulse received from the dying woman, instead of giving rise, as in an ordinary case, to a hallucination of herself, called up in the percipient's mind, whether through the operation of associated ideas or from some other cause, the image of a near relative. Indeed, seeing how potent is the influence of associated ideas, it is perhaps a matter for wonder that such miscarriages do not more often occur. It should be stated that, beyond their rarity, there is no special reason to mistrust stories of this type. Their distinguishing feature is not apparently of a kind which appeals readily to the imagination. Indeed, by most persons the want of precise correspondence would probably be regarded as a serious blemish in the story. Certainly cases of the kind occur rarely, if at all, among second-hand and traditional narratives.

Heteroplastic Hallucinations.

But another possible explanation of the incident suggests itself. It has already been conjectured that in some cases of hallucination or other impression, the percipient's vision may have originated not in the mind of the person primarily concerned, but in that of some bystander.[1] Conversely, the image seen in the narrative just cited may have been flashed directly from the dying woman's mind. In the case which follows a picture of the past preserved in the memory of one of two friends appears to have been spontaneously transferred to the mind of the other.

The case was sent to Dr. Hodgson on the 18th May 1888, and was published in the *Arena* for February 1889.

[1] See, for instance, Nos. 47, 75, 87, etc.

No. 90.—From MRS. G——.

" . . . For nearly two weeks I have had a lady friend visiting us from Chicago, and last Sunday we tried the cards and in every instance I told the colour and kind; but only two or three times was enabled to give the exact number. . . .

" I must write you of something that occurred last night. After this lady, whom I have mentioned above, had retired, and almost immediately after we had extinguished the light, there suddenly appeared before me a beautiful lawn and coming toward me a chubby, yellow-haired little boy, and by his side a brown dog which closely resembled a fox. The dog had on a brass collar and the child's hand was under the collar just as if he was leading or pulling the dog. The vision was like a flash, came and went in an instant. I immediately told my friend, and she said, ' Do you know where there are any matches?' and began to hurriedly clamber out of bed. I struck a light, she plunged into her trunk, brought out a book, and pasted in the front was a picture of her little boy and his dog. They were not in the same position that I saw them, but the dog looked exceedingly familiar. Her little boy passed into the beyond about four years ago. . . ."

Mrs. F. corroborates as follows:—

"*May 18th,* 1888.

" I wish to corroborate the statements of Mrs. N. G. relative to . . . and her wonderful vision of my little boy, and my old home. Mrs. G. never saw the place, or the little child, and never even heard of the peculiar-looking dog, which was my little son's constant companion out of doors. She never saw the photograph, which was pasted in the back of my Bible and packed away.

"(Signed)   I. F."

In this case, it will be noted, the vision was the direct sequel of some partially successful experiments in thought-transference ; and the transferred impression fell short of actual hallucination. In the following case there is no evidence of any special rapport between the percipient and the person who, on this hypothesis, acted as the agent; and the percipient's impression took the form of a completely externalised hallucination.

No. 91.—From FRANCES REDDELL.

"ANTONY, TORPOINT,
December 14th, 1882.

"Helen Alexander (maid to Lady Waldegrave) was lying here very ill with typhoid fever, and was attended by me. I was standing at the table by her bedside, pouring out her medicine, at about four o'clock in the morning of the 4th October 1880. I heard the call-bell ring (this had been heard twice before during the night in that same week), and was attracted by the door of the room opening, and by seeing a person entering the room whom I instantly felt to be the mother of the sick woman. She had a brass candlestick in her hand, a red shawl over her shoulders, and a flannel petticoat on which had a hole in the front. I looked at her as much as to say, 'I am glad you have come,' but the woman looked at me sternly, as much as to say, 'Why wasn't I sent for before?' I gave the medicine to Helen Alexander, and then turned round to speak to the vision, but no one was there. She had gone. She was a short, dark person, and very stout. At about six o'clock that morning Helen Alexander died. Two days after, her parents and a sister came to Antony, and arrived between one and two o'clock in the morning ; I and another maid let them in, and it gave me a great turn when I saw the living likeness of the vision I had seen two nights before. I told the sister about the vision, and she said that the description of the dress exactly answered to her mother's, and that they had brass candlesticks at home exactly like the one described. There was not the slightest resemblance between the mother and daughter.
"FRANCES REDDELL."

Frances Reddell fortunately described her vision to her mistress, Mrs. Pole-Carew, of Antony, Torpoint, Devonport, within a few hours of its occurrence, and before her encounter with the original. Mrs. Pole-Carew writes as follows :—

"*31st December* 1883.

"In October 1880, Lord and Lady Waldegrave came with their Scotch maid, Helen Alexander, to stay with us. [The account then describes how Helen was discovered to have caught typhoid fever, and pending the arrival of a regular nurse, was nursed for several days by Frances Reddell. On the Sunday week, Mrs. Pole-Carew continues], I allowed Reddell to sit up with Helen again that night, to give her the medicine and food, which were to be taken constantly. At about 4.30 that night, or rather Monday morning, Reddell looked at her watch, poured out the medicine, and was bending over the bed to give it to Helen when the call-bell in the passage rang. She said to herself, 'There's that tiresome bell with the wire caught again.' (It seems it did occasionally ring of itself in this manner.) At that moment, however, she heard the door open, and looking round, saw a very stout old woman walk in. She was dressed in a nightgown and red flannel petticoat, and carried an old-fashioned brass candlestick in her hand. The petticoat had a hole rubbed in it. She walked into the room and appeared to be going towards the dressing-table to put her candle down. She was a perfect stranger to Reddell, who, however, merely thought, 'This is her mother come to see after her,' and she felt quite glad it was so, accepting the idea without reasoning upon it, as one would in a dream. She thought the mother looked annoyed, possibly at not having been sent for before. She then gave Helen the medicine, and turning round, found that the apparition had disappeared, and that the door was shut. A great change, meanwhile, had taken place in Helen, and Reddell fetched me, who sent off for the doctor, and meanwhile applied hot poultices, etc., but Helen died a little before the doctor came. She was quite conscious up to about half-an-hour before she died, when she seemed to be going to sleep.

"During the early days of her illness Helen had written to a sister, mentioning her being unwell, but making nothing of it, and as she never mentioned any one but this sister, it was supposed by the household, to whom she was a perfect stranger, that she had no other relation alive. Reddell was always offering to write for her, but she always declined, saying there was no need, she would write herself in a day or two. No one at home, therefore, knew anything of her being so ill, and it is, therefore, remarkable that her mother, a far from nervous person, should have said that evening going up to bed, 'I am sure Helen is very ill.'

"Reddell told me and my daughter of the apparition, about an hour after Helen's death, prefacing with, 'I am not superstitious or nervous, and I wasn't the least frightened, but her mother came last night,' and she then told the story, giving a careful description of the figure she had seen. The relations were asked to come to the funeral, and the father, mother, and sister came, and in the mother Reddell recognised the apparition, as I did also, for Reddell's description had been most accurate, even to the expression, which she had ascribed to annoyance, but which was due to deafness. It was judged best not to speak about it to the mother, but Reddell told the sister, who said the description of the figure corresponded exactly with the probable appearance of her mother if roused in the night; that they had exactly such a candlestick at home, and that there was a hole in her mother's petticoat produced by the way she always wore it. It seems curious that neither Helen nor her mother appeared to be aware of the visit. Neither of them, at any rate, ever spoke of having seen the other, nor even of having dreamt of having done so.

"F. A. POLE-CAREW."

[Frances Reddell states that she has never had any hallucination, or any odd experience of any kind, except on this one occasion. The Hon. Mrs. Lyttelton, of Selwyn College, Cambridge, who knows her, tells us that "she appears to be a most matter-of-fact person, and was apparently most impressed by the fact that she saw a hole in the mother's flannel petticoat, made by the busk of her stays, reproduced in the apparition."]

The simplest explanation of this incident, and that which involves the least departure from known forms of telepathy, is that the figure seen by Frances Reddell was due to thought-transference from the mind of the dying girl. And this explanation has some direct evidence in its favour. There is, of course, abundant proof of the transference from agent to percipient of a real or imaginary scene. (See the cases described in Chapters II., III., XIV., and XV.) But in these cases the percipient's impressions appear rarely to have risen to the level of hallucination, and in the absence of direct evidence it would not perhaps have been safe to assume that a detailed impression, such as a scene or a human figure, transferred from another mind, would be capable of taking complete sensory embodiment in the mind of the percipient. The frequency, however, of collective hallucinations of an apparently casual character seems to require such an assumption (see *ante*, p. 273). Moreover, a case has been recorded (*Proc. S.P.R.*, vol. vi. pp. 434, 435) in which a hypnotically induced hallucination appears to have been reproduced in another hypnotised subject by telepathic suggestion from the original percipient. In the experiments recorded by Dr. Gibotteau (pp. 368, 369) the ideas mentally suggested by him appear in some cases to have assumed a hallucinatory form in the subject; and, finally, Wesermann (Chapter X., p. 233), in his fifth experiment succeeded in calling up a recognisable hallucination of a lady personally unknown to the percipients. We have, therefore, experimental parallels for our suggested interpretation of Frances Reddell's experience ; and when once the possibility of thought-transference in this form is recognised, many so-called "ghosts" or phantasms of the dead find a simple and satisfactory explanation. The following case may be instanced :—

No. 92.—From MR. JOHN E. HUSBANDS, Melbourne House, Town Hall Square, Grimsby.

"*September* 15*th*, 1886.

"The facts are simply these. I was sleeping in a hotel in Madeira in January 1885. It was a bright moonlight night. The windows were open and the blinds up. I felt some one was in my room. On opening my eyes, I saw a young fellow about twenty-five, dressed in flannels, standing at the side of my bed and pointing with the first finger of his right hand to the place I was lying in. I lay for some seconds to convince myself of some one being really there. I then sat up and looked at him. I saw his features so plainly that I recognised them in a photograph which was shown me some days after. I asked him what he wanted; he did not speak, but his eyes and hand seemed to tell me I was in his place. As he did not answer, I struck out at him with my fist as I sat up, but did not reach him, and as I was going to spring out of bed he slowly vanished through the door. which was shut, keeping his eyes upon me all the time.

"Upon inquiry I found that the young fellow who appeared to me died in that room I was occupying.

"If I can tell you anything more I shall be glad to, if it interests you.

"JOHN E. HUSBANDS."

The following letters are from Miss Falkner, of Church Terrace, Wisbech, who was resident at the hotel when the above incident happened :—

"*October* 8*th*, 1886.

"The figure that Mr. Husbands saw while in Madeira was that of a young fellow who died unexpectedly months previously, in the room which Mr. Husbands was occupying. Curiously enough, Mr. H. had never heard of him or his death. He told me the story the morning after he had seen the figure, and I recognised the young fellow from the description. It impressed me very much, but I did·not mention it to him or any one. I loitered about until I heard Mr. Husbands tell the same tale to my brother; we left Mr. H. and said simultaneously, 'He has seen Mr. D.'

"No more was said on the subject for days; then I abruptly showed the photograph.

"Mr. Husbands said at once, 'This is the young fellow who appeared to me the other night, but he was dressed differently'—describing a dress he often wore—'cricket suit (or tennis) fastened at the neck with sailor knot.' I must say that Mr. Husbands is a most practical man, and the very last one would expect 'a spirit' to visit.

"K. FALKNER."

"*October* 20*th*, 1886.

"I enclose you photograph and an extract from my sister-in-law's letter, which I received this morning, as it will verify my statement. Mr. Husbands saw the figure either the 3rd or 4th of February 1885.

"The people who had occupied the rooms had never told us if they had seen anything, so we may conclude they had not.

"K. FALKNER."

The following is Miss Falkner's copy of the passage in the letter:—

"You will see at back of Mr. du F——'s photo the date of his decease [January 29th, 1884]; and if you recollect 'the Motta Marques' had his rooms from the February till the May or June of 1884, then Major Money at the commencement of 1885 season. Mr. Husbands had to take the room on February 2nd, 1885, as his was wanted.

"I am clear on all this, and remember his telling me the incident when he came to see my baby."

At a personal interview Mr. Gurney learnt that Mr. Husbands had never had any other hallucination of the senses. (*Proc. S.P.R.*, vol. v. p. 416.)

It is, of course, conceivable that before his experience Mr. Husbands may have heard of the death of Mr. D. and have forgotten the circumstance. But this supposition will hardly account for the recognition of the photograph. In any case, however, there can be no justification for invoking other than terrestrial agencies to explain the vision. Until such agencies are proved inadequate to account for the facts a narrative of this kind can scarcely be held to raise a presumption, much less to afford a proof, of the action of the dead. Miss Falkner and her brother had known the dead man; no fact about him was communicated which was not within their knowledge; and there is nothing to negative the supposition that some echo of their thoughts or dreams may have given rise to the vision. A very similar case is quoted in the same volume (*Proc.*, vol. v. p. 418). Mr. D. M. Tyre, of St. Andrews Road, Pollokshields, Glasgow, stayed for some time in a lonely house in Dumbartonshire. On several occasions during their occupancy of the house Miss L. Tyre saw the figure of an old woman lying on the bed in the kitchen. The figure lay with the face turned to the wall, and the legs drawn up as if from cold. On her head was a "sow-backed mutch," *i.e.*, a white frilled cap of a peculiar shape common in the Highlands. The others who were present did not see the figure. It was subsequently ascertained from a neighbour that the description given correctly represented the dress and attitude of a former occupant of the house, who had died there some years before under painful circumstances. M. Richet (*Proc.*, vol. v. p. 148) gives an account of some spiritualist séances at which the promise was given that his grandfather, M. Charles Renouard, would appear. A figure resembling M. Charles Renouard was actually seen some days later, not by any of those present at the séance, but by an English lady staying in the house, who was believed to know nothing of the expected apparition.

A similar explanation may perhaps apply to the following account, which was communicated verbally to Mr. Myers on the 12th October 1888 by the percipient, Mr. J., a gentleman well known in the scientific world. Mr. Myers explains that the account which follows was written out by him from his notes of the conversation, and was subsequently revised and corrected by Mr. J. himself.

No. 93.—From MR. J.

" In 1880 I succeeded a Mr. Q. as librarian of the X. Library. I had never seen Mr. Q., nor any photograph or likeness of him, when the following incidents occurred. I may, of course, have heard the library assistants describe his appearance, though I have no recollection of this. I was sitting alone in the library one evening late in March 1884, finishing some work after hours, when it suddenly occurred to me that I should miss the last train to H., where I was then living, if I did not make haste. It was then 10.55, and the last train left X. at 11.5. I gathered up some books in one hand, took the lamp in the other, and prepared to leave the librarian's room, which communicated by a passage with the main room of the library. As my lamp illumined this passage, I saw apparently at the further end of it a man's face. I instantly thought a thief had got into the library. This was by no means impossible, and the probability of it had occurred to me before. I turned back into my room, put down the books, and took a revolver from the safe, and, holding the lamp cautiously behind me, I made my way along the passage—which had a corner, behind which I thought my thief might be lying in wait—into the main room. Here I saw no one, but the room was large and encumbered with bookcases. I called out loudly to the intruder to show himself several times, more with the hope of attracting a passing policeman than of drawing the intruder. Then I saw a face looking round one of the bookcases. I say looking *round*, but it had an odd appearance as if the *body* were *in* the bookcase, as the face came so closely to the edge and I could see no body. The face was pallid and hairless, and the orbits of the eyes were very deep. I advanced towards it, and as I did so I saw an old man with high shoulders seem to *rotate* out of the end of the bookcase, and with his back towards me and with a shuffling gait walk rather quickly from the bookcase to the door of a small lavatory, which opened from the library and had no other access. I heard no noise. I followed the man at once into the lavatory ; and to my extreme surprise found no one there. I examined the window (about 14 in. × 12 in.), and found it closed and fastened. I opened it and looked out. It opened into a well, the bottom of which, 10 feet below, was a sky-light, and the top open to the sky some 20 feet above. It was in the middle of the building, and no one could have dropped into it without smashing the glass nor climbed out of it without a ladder—but

·

no one was there. Nor had there been anything like time for a man to get out of the window, as I followed the intruder instantly. Completely mystified, I even looked into the little cupboard under the fixed basin. There was nowhere hiding for a child, and I confess I began to experience for the first time what novelists describe as an 'eerie' feeling.

"I left the library, and found I had missed my train.

"Next morning I mentioned what I had seen to a local clergyman, who, on hearing my description, said, 'Why, that's old Q.!' Soon after I saw a photograph (from a drawing) of Q., and the resemblance was certainly striking. Q. had lost all his hair, eyebrows and all, from (I believe) a gunpowder accident. His walk was a peculiar, rapid, high-shouldered shuffle.

"Later inquiry proved he had died at about the time of year at which I saw the figure." (*Proc. S.P.R.*, vol. vi. p. 57.)

Mr. J. states that he has seen but one other hallucination, a figure representing his mother, which appeared to him at the time of the birth of one of his sisters.

A hallucination of another kind was seen independently in the same library by Mr. R., the principal assistant, and a clerk, Mr. P. Mr. R. writes in 1889 :—

"A few years ago I was engaged in a large building in the ——, and during the busy times was often there till late in the evening. On one particular night I was at work along with a junior clerk till about 11 P.M., in the room marked A on the annexed sketch. All the lights in the place had been out for hours except those in the room which we occupied. Before leaving, we turned out the gas. We then looked into the fireplace, but not a spark was to be seen. The night was very dark, but being thoroughly accustomed to the place we carried no light. On reaching the bottom of the staircase (B), I happened to look up ; when, to my surprise, the room which we had just left appeared to be lighted. I turned to my companion and pointed out the light, and sent him back to see what was wrong. He went at once and I stood looking through the open door, but I was not a little astonished to see that as soon as he got within a few yards of the room the light went out quite suddenly. My companion, from the position he was in at the moment, could not see the light go out, but on his reaching the door everything was in total darkness. He entered, however, and when he returned, reported that both gas and fire were completely out. The light in the daytime was got by means of a glass roof, there being no windows on the sides of the room, and the night in question was so dark that the moon shining through the roof was out of the question. Although I have often been in the same room till long after dark, both before and since, I have never seen anything unusual at any other time."

Mr. P. endorses this :—

" I confirm the foregoing statement."

In subsequent letters Mr. R. says :—

" The bare facts are as stated, being neither more nor less than what took place. I have never on any other occasion had any hallucination of the senses, and I think you will find the same to be the case with Mr. P."

This incident took place after Mr. J.'s vision, but Mr. J. had mentioned his own experience only to his wife and one other friend, and no hint of it appears to have reached the assistants in the library, so that the two visions would appear to have been independent.

To extend the theory of thought-transference from living minds to cover a case such as that just quoted may seem to some extravagant. But if there is anything beyond chance in the occurrence—and it would be a very remarkable coincidence that three persons should independently be the subject of hallucination in the same house, and that one of the hallucinations should resemble a former occupant of the house, unknown to the percipient—some explanation is required, and an explanation which involves no novel or unproved agency is, *ceteris paribus,* to be preferred. As regards the apparently local character of the visitation, Mr. Gurney has suggested, with regard to some cases quoted in *Phantasms of the Living* (vol. ii. pp. 267-269), where the link between agent and percipient appears to have been of a local and not of a personal character, that a similarity of immediate mental content between the percipient and agent may have been the condition of the telepathic action. In the ordinary case of an apparition, *e.g.,* of a dying mother to her son, the condition of the appearance to that particular percipient rather than to the man in the street should on this hypothesis be sought in the community of intellectual and emotional experiences which may be presumed to exist between near relatives who have passed a large part of their lives in the same environment. In the cases now under consideration the substitute for such far-reaching community is to be found in the transitory occupation of both percipient and agent—the one in present sensation, the other in memory—with the same scene. Such partial community of perception, by a kind of extended association of ideas, tends under the hypothesis towards more complete community, and the agent thus imports into the sensorium of the percipient the image of his own or some other's presence in the scene which forms part of the present content of both minds. On this view Mr. J. saw the figure of Mr. Q. in the library, because some friend of Mr. Q.'s was at that moment vividly picturing to himself the late librarian in his old haunts.

Cases, such as the three last quoted, of the solitary appearance of a phantasmal figure, subsequently identified by description, photograph, or—as in Frances Reddell's case—actual encounter with the original, are rare; and experience shows how easy it may be for the somewhat vague image preserved in the memory to take on definite form and colour during the process, occasionally prolonged, of "recognition." The type cannot, therefore, be regarded as well established. As, however, such narratives have in some instances been regarded as affording evidence of the action of disembodied spirits, it seemed well to suggest that, if the facts are accepted, they are susceptible of another interpretation.

Haunted Houses.

But there are numerous cases to which the hypothesis of telepathic infection may be applied with perhaps less hesitation. The form which so-called "ghost stories" most commonly assume is the appearance of an unrecognised phantasmal figure. When the appearance is to one person only, or when, in the intervals of its appearance to others, the matter has been freely discussed amongst the members of the household, and the details of the figure described, we should probably be justified, on the analogy of hypnotic and epidemic religious hallucinations, in regarding the original appearance as purely subjective and the later ones as due to verbal suggestion and expectancy. But there are cases where, from the definite statements of the witnesses and the surrounding circumstances, it appears at all events extremely improbable that any mention was made of the original hallucination. In such cases it seems permissible to conjecture that the later apparitions, or some of them, may have been due to telepathic suggestion from the original percipient, to whom his solitary experience would naturally be a subject of frequent and vivid reflection.

I received the following account from the ladies concerned after a personal interview with one of them on February 27th, 1889, in the course of which I examined the scene of the apparition, the landing of a moderate-sized London house. The landing, though narrow, is well lighted, and it seems impossible that the appearance could have been a real person. The first experience, it will be seen, is a collective hallucination, of a type discussed in the preceding chapter.

No. 94.—From MRS. KNOTT.

"LONDON, S.W.,
March 5th, 1889.

"The incident I relate occurred at this address early in February 1889. I have lived in this house four years, and constantly *felt* another presence was in the drawing-room besides myself,

but never *saw* any form until last month. My cousin Mrs. R.
and myself returned from a walk at 1.30 P.M. The front door
was opened for us by my housekeeper, Mrs. E. I passed upstairs before my cousin, and on turning to my bedroom, the door
of which is beside the drawing-room door [*i.e.*, at right angles to
it], I saw, as I thought, Mrs. E. go into the drawing-room. I
put a parcel into my room and then followed her to give some
order, and found the room empty! My cousin was going up
the second flight of stairs to her room, and I called out, 'Did
you open the drawing-room door as you passed?' 'No,' she
replied, 'Mrs. E. has gone in.' Mrs. R. had seen the figure more
distinctly than I; it seemed to pass her at the top of the stairs,
and she thought, 'How quietly Mrs. E. moves! 'I inquired of
Mrs. E. what she did after opening the door for us, and she
said, 'Went to the kitchen to hasten luncheon, as you were in a
hurry for it.' The day was bright, and there is nothing on the
stairs that could cast a shadow. I quite hope some day I may
see the face of the figure."

From MRS. R., Malpas, Cheshire.

"*March 1st*, 1889.

"In answer to your letter on the subject of the figure seen
at C. Terrace, Mrs. K. and I had just come in at about half-past
one o'clock. Mrs. E. (the housekeeper) had opened the door.
We went upstairs, and on the first landing are two rooms, one
the drawing-room, the other Mrs. K.'s bedroom. She went into
her room while I stood a minute or two talking to her. Just as
I turned to go up the next flight of stairs I thought I saw Mrs.
E. pass me quickly and go into the drawing-room. Beyond
seeing a slight figure in a dark dress I saw nothing more, for
I did not look at it, but just saw it pass me. Before I
got upstairs Mrs. K. called out, 'Did you leave the drawing-
room door open?' I answered, 'I did not go in; I saw Mrs.
E. go in.' Mrs. K. answered, 'There is nobody there.' We
asked Mrs. E. if she had been up; she, on the contrary, had
gone straight down. Also, as she said, she would not have
passed me on the landing, but have waited until I had gone
upstairs; and as it struck me *afterwards*, she could not have
passed me on such a small landing without touching me, but
I never noticed that at the time. I do not know if a thought
ever embodies itself, but my idea was, and is, that as Mrs. E.
ran downstairs her thought went up, wondering if the drawing-
room fire was burning brightly. The figure I saw went into the
room as if it had a purpose of some sort. I have never seen
anything of the sort before."

In a later letter Mrs. R. adds:—

"*March* 10*th*, 1889.

"I am afraid I cannot give any very definite reply to your questions.

"(1) 'Had I any idea of the house being haunted?' No; and I do not think it is supposed to be haunted. Mrs. K. has said that at times it has seemed to her as if there was some one else in the room beside herself, but I think that is a feeling that has come to most people some time or other.

"(2) 'Did we see it simultaneously?' That I cannot exactly say, but I should think yes, for we neither of us said anything until Mrs. K. called out to me to know if I had been in the drawing-room."

In commenting on the story in November 1889 (*Proc. S.P.R.*, vol. vi. p. 250), I wrote, "Here we may almost see the story of a haunted house in the making. The essential elements are there. We have the visionary figure seen by two persons at once, and the mysterious feeling of an alien presence in the room. It is quite possible that the latter circumstance would have passed unrecorded, and even unnoticed, but for the subsequent phantasm, through which it gained a retrospective importance." My comments have met with unexpected justification. On April 7th, 1893, Mrs. Knott again wrote to me as follows:—

"On Saturday, the 18th March, at 1.50 P.M., Mrs. H. and I were going upstairs to the drawing-room, she first, I following with some flowers, *not looking up*. I heard her say, 'Mrs. E., don't go down until you have seen my screen.' (Mrs. H. had just finished painting one.) I said, 'Mrs. E. isn't here.' Mrs. H. replied, 'Yes, she is in the drawing-room.' Then I heard her say, 'Where *has* the woman gone?' for no one was visible in the room, and Mrs. H. said she *distinctly* saw a figure go in, and felt sure it was Mrs. E. This is exactly the same impression that Mrs. R. and I had when we each saw the figure go into the drawing-room four years ago, in February, and it was about the same hour of the day."

In a later letter Mrs. Knott explains that Mrs. H. had heard of the earlier apparition on the same spot, but adds that the story "most certainly did not stay in her mind." We shall probably be justified in assuming, however, that Mrs. H.'s hallucinatory experience was due to a subconscious reminiscence of her friend's ghost-story.

In the case which follows, however, there is strong evidence that the phantasms were seen independently by each percipient. The narrators are unwilling that their names or that of the house should appear. Mr. Gurney, however, fully discussed the circumstances with them at a personal interview.

No. 95.—From MRS. W.

"*February* 19*th*, 1885.

"In June 1881 we went to live in a detached villa just out of the town of C——. Our household consisted of my husband and myself, my step-daughter, and two little boys, aged nine and six, and two female servants. The house was between ten and twenty years old. We had been there about three weeks,

SKETCH PLAN OF THE GROUND-FLOOR OF THE HOUSE.

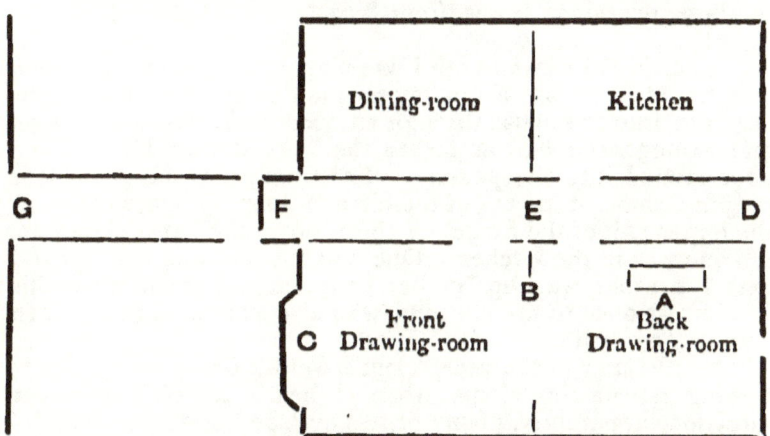

A Piano.　B First position of figure.　C Second position of figure.
D Garden door.　E Baize door.　F Front door and porch.
G Front gate.

when, about 11 o'clock one morning, as I was playing the piano in the drawing-room, I had the following experience:—I was suddenly aware of a figure peeping round the corner of the folding-doors to my left; thinking it must be a visitor, I jumped up and went into the passage, but no one was there, and the hall door, which was half glass, was shut. I only saw the upper half of the figure, which was that of a tall man, with a very pale face and dark hair and moustache. The impression lasted only a second or two, but I saw the face so distinctly that to this day I should recognise it if I met it in a crowd. It had a sorrowful expression. It was impossible for any one to come into the house without being seen or heard. I was startled, but not the least frightened. I had heard no report whatever as to the house being haunted; and am certainly not given to superstitious fancies. I did not mention my experience to any one at the time, and formed no theory about it. In the following August, one evening about 8.30, I had occasion to go into the drawing-room to get something out of the cupboard, when, on turning round, I saw the same face in the bay-window, in front of the shutters, which were closed. I again saw only the upper part of the figure, which seemed to be in a somewhat crouching posture. The light on this occasion came from the hall and the dining-room, and did not shine directly on the window; but I was able perfectly to distinguish the face and the expression of the eyes. This time I *was* frightened, and mentioned the matter to my husband the same evening. I then also told him of my first experience. On each of these occasions I was from 8 to 10 feet distant from the figure.

" Later in the same month I was playing cricket in the garden with my little boys. From my position at the wickets I could see right into the house through an open door, down a passage, and through the hall as far as the front door. The kitchen door opened into the passage. I distinctly saw the same face peeping round at me out of the kitchen door. I again only saw the upper half of the figure. I threw down the bat and ran in. No one was in the kitchen. One servant was out, and I found that the other was up in her bedroom. I mentioned this incident at once to my husband, who also examined the kitchen without any result.

"A little later in the year, about 8 o'clock one evening, I was coming downstairs alone, when I heard a voice from the direction, apparently, of my little boys' bedroom, the door of which was open. It distinctly said, in a deep sorrowful tone, ' I can't find it.' I called out to my little boys, but they did not reply, and I have not the slightest doubt that they were asleep; they always called out if they heard me upstairs. My step-daughter, who was downstairs in the dining-room with the door open, also heard the voice, and thinking it was me calling, · cried out, 'What are you looking for?' We were extremely puzzled. The voice could not by any possibility have belonged to any member of the household. The servants were in the kitchen, and my husband was out.

"A short time after I was again coming downstairs after dark in the evening when I felt a sharp slap on the back. It startled but did not hurt me. There was no one near me, and I ran downstairs and told my husband and my step-daughter.

"I have never in my life, on any other occasion, had any hallucination of sight, hearing, or touch."

The following is Miss W.'s account :—

"*February 19th*, 1885.

"In July, 1881, I was sitting playing the piano in our house in C——, about 11.30 in the morning, when I saw the head and shoulders of a man peeping round the folding-doors, in just the same way as they had appeared to my mother, but I had not at that time heard of her experience. I jumped up, and advanced, thinking it was an acquaintance from a few yards off. This impression, however, only lasted for a second; the face disappeared, but recalling it, I perceived at once that it was certainly not that of the gentleman whom I had for a second thought of. The resemblance was only that they were both dark. The face was pale and melancholy, and the hair very dark. I at once went to Mrs. W. in the dining-room, and asked if any one had called. She said, 'No'; and I then told her what I had seen. I then for the first time heard from her what *she* had seen, and our descriptions completely agreed. We had even both noticed that the hair was parted in the middle, and that a good deal of shirt-front showed.

"A few weeks later, about 11 P.M., Mrs. W. and I were play-ing bézique in the dining-room. Mr. W. was out, and the servants had gone to bed. The door of the room was open, and I was facing it. I suddenly had an impression that some one was looking at me, and I looked up. There was the same face, and the upper half of the figure, peeping round into the room from the hall. I said, 'There's the man again!' Mrs. W. rushed to the door, but there was no one in the hall or passage ; the front door was locked, and the green baize door which com-municated with the back part of the house was shut. The figure had been on the side of the dining-room door nearest to the front door, and could not have got to the green baize door without passing well in our sight. We· were a good deal frightened, and we mentioned the occurrence to Mr. W. on his return. He went all over the house as usual before going

21

to bed, and all windows were fastened, and everything in order.

"A few weeks after this, about 11.30 A.M., I was upstairs playing battledore and shuttlecock with my eldest brother in his bedroom. The door was open. Stepping back in the course of the game, I got out on to the landing; I looked sideways over my shoulder, in order to strike the shuttlecock, and suddenly saw the same face as before, and my brother called out at the same moment, 'There's a man on the landing.' I was startled myself, but to reassure the child I said there was no one—that he had made a mistake—and shut the door and went on with the game. I told my father and Mrs. W. of this as soon as I saw them.

"Later in the autumn I was sitting alone in the dining-room one evening, with the door open. Mrs. W. had been upstairs, and I heard her coming down. Suddenly I heard a deep, melancholy voice say, 'I can't find it.' I called out, 'What are you looking for?' At the same time the voice was not the least like Mrs. W.'s. She then came in and told me she had heard exactly the same thing. My father was out at the time, but we told him of the circumstance on his return.

"In September of 1882 I was for a week in the house with only the two children and the servants. It was about 7.30 on Sunday evening, and nearly dark. The others were all out in the garden. I was standing at the dining-room window, when I caught a glimpse of a tall man's figure slipping into the porch. I must have seen if anybody had approached the porch by the path from the front gate, and I should certainly have heard the latch of the gate, which used to make a considerable noise, and I should also have heard footsteps on the gravel-path. The figure appeared quite suddenly; it had on a tall hat. I was very much astonished, but ran to the door, thinking it might possibly be my father. No one was there; I went to the gate, and looked up and down the road. No one was in sight, and there was no possibility that anybody could have got so suddenly out of view.

"I have never at any other time in my life had any hallucination whatever, either of sight or hearing.

"I remember Mrs. W. telling me of her experience of the slap as soon as she came downstairs.

"I ought to add that at the time when we were negotiating about the house, the landlady of the lodgings where my father and I were staying told me that all the villas of the row in which our house was situated, ten in number, were haunted. I was with my father when I heard this. Mrs. W. was not with us. I am certain that the remark made no impression whatever on me, and that it did not even recur to my mind till I saw what I have described. I did not even mention the remark to Mrs. W."

Mrs. W. adds—

"I distinctly remember my step-daughter coming to me immediately after her first sight of the figure, and telling me about it. I then told her for the first time of my own experience (I had then only had one), and our descriptions completely tallied. I distinctly remember our agreeing about the parting of the hair in the middle, and about the amount of white shirt-front. We could neither of us remember whether his tie was white or black. We agreed that we should know the face if we ever met it. And subsequently, at an evening party, we both pitched on the same individual as more like our strange visitor than any one else we knew. The resemblance, however, was not extremely close.

"I distinctly remember, also, my step-daughter exclaiming, 'There's that man again!' when we were playing bézique. I rushed at once into the hall and found the door closed as she has described.

"I also remember her telling me at once about what she had seen, and what her brother had exclaimed when they were playing at battledore and shuttlecock.

"She told me about what she had seen in the porch when Mr. W. and I returned from town on the next (Monday) morning."

The following is Surgeon-Major W.'s confirmation :—

"I was told of these various occurrences by my wife and daughter at the times which they have specified. I only heard from my wife of her *first* experience after she had told me of her *second*. After she had seen the figure during the game of cricket, I went into the kitchen, but found everything as usual. On my return home, after my daughter's seeing the figure peeping round the dining-room door, I went all over the premises as my custom was, and found windows secured and everything in order.

"My wife and daughter are as unlikely as any one I know to suffer from causeless frights. They are completely free from nervousness, and though these experiences were startling and bewildering to them, they did not in the least worry themselves in consequence.

"It seems possible that the voice may have been that of one of the children talking in sleep, and the slap some effect of imagination, but it is not easy to account for the apparitions by any such known causes."

In this case it seems unlikely that Mrs. W., the original percipient, was mistaken in supposing that she had not mentioned her first experience, and that Miss W. was also mistaken in her statement that she had not heard of what Mrs. W. had seen until after the apparition to herself. And it is still more unlikely that either lady would have allowed any hint of the matter to reach the ears of the children. Whilst, therefore, in the absence of contemporary notes, or of any identification of the figure, the degree of resemblance between the apparitions seen by the two ladies may have been exaggerated, we are still confronted with the problem that three persons living in the same house are credibly reported to have seen independently the hallucinatory figure of a man, and that in the two instances in which the apparitions were compared they were found to exhibit certain resemblances. That the first figure was a subjective hallucination, and that the later apparitions were reproductions of that hallucination by means of telepathic suggestion, is a solution which is, at any rate, worthy of consideration. We have in our records many cases of the kind, in which hallucinatory figures, in some cases presenting strong resemblances, are alleged to have been seen by two or more independent witnesses in the same house or locality. Thus we have accounts from Miss Kathleen Leigh Hunt, Miss Laurence, and Mr. Paul Bird, of a woman's figure seen independently by each of them in 1881 (*Proc. S.P.R.*, vol. iii. pp. 106 *et seq.*). In another case (*Proc. S.P.R.*, vol. vi. pp. 270 *et seq.*) a doctor in a provincial town, his two daughters, and a young lady visitor saw the figure of a young child. In other cases different hallucinatory figures have been seen independently by successive occupants of the same house, the later percipients appearing not to have heard of the earlier apparitions. Thus we have accounts of figures seen during the period from 1861 to 1875 by three different families in an old Elizabethan manor-house (*Proc. S.P.R.*, vol. iii. p. 118);

and in a quite modern house in the South of England various phantasmal figures were seen between 1882 and 1888 by two successive sets of occupants. (*Proc. S.P.R.*, vol. vi. pp. 256 *et seq.*[1])

---

[1] Those desiring to study further the evidence on this subject are referred to the paper on "Phantasms of the Dead," *Proc. S.P.R.*, vol. iii., by Mrs. Henry Sidgwick, and the papers on "Recognised Apparitions occurring after Death," and on "Phantasms of the Dead," by Messrs. Gurney, Myers, and the present writer respectively, in Proc. v. and vi., and the "Record of a Haunted House," in Proc. viii. Many cases of the kind are also printed in the monthly journal of the Society; and there are one or two striking cases in the *Annales des Sciences Psychiques.*

CHAPTER XIV.

ON CLAIRVOYANCE IN TRANCE.

THE word "clairvoyance" was used by the older mesmerists to denote somewhat heterogeneous phenomena. It was applied in the first place to a supposed faculty by which the subject was enabled to ascertain facts not within human knowledge,[1] and in the second place to a power of discerning facts within the knowledge of some living mind. Of "clairvoyance" in the first sense there is not at present so much evidence as need cause hesitation in appropriating the name for other uses; and it is obvious that if such a faculty could be shown to exist, a discussion of it would find no place in a work which treats only of the affection of one human mind by another. But we have abundant evidence of clairvoyance in the second sense, that is, of a form of telepathy in which the

---

[1] For instance, Gregory and others record that the clairvoyant subjects of a certain Major Buckley were able to read the mottoes enclosed in nuts (the equivalent of the modern Christmas crackers) purchased at random from a confectioner's shop, and still unopened. The recent evidence of the kind is quite inconsiderable, and is perhaps hardly sufficient to allow of the existence of a faculty of independent clairvoyance being treated as an open question. Experiments with Mrs. Piper in this direction have yielded negative results, and Professor Richet's trials with Madame B. (*Proc. S.P.R.*, vol. v. pp. 77 and 149) are neither sufficiently numerous nor sufficiently striking to justify any conclusions being drawn from them. Some curious results have, however, been obtained by M. J. Ch. Roux (*Annales des Sciences Psychiques*, vol. iii. pp. 198 *et seq.*), and somewhat similar results have been obtained in this country by two Associates of the S.P.R. But it is possible that all these instances may be susceptible of another explanation. See, however, Mr. Myers' article on "Sensory Automatism," *Proc. S.P.R.*, vol. viii. pp. 436 *et seq.*

transmitted idea seems to reach the mind of the percipient no longer as the meagre result of a serious
crisis, or of a direct and often prolonged effort of
attention on the part of the agent, but spontaneously,
with great fulness of detail, and often with remarkable
ease and rapidity, as the outcome of a special receptivity on the part of the percipient. Such clairvoyance—and the word must be understood to include
the impressions of other senses than sight—occurs in
its most striking form with hypnotised percipients;
and in the present chapter I propose to deal with
results obtained in hypnotism and analogous states,
reserving for the following chapter instances of what
appears to be the same faculty occurring in the normal
state.[1]

MRS. PIPER.

The phenomena of clairvoyance, as thus defined,
have been observed with great care in the case of an
American lady, Mrs. Piper. Mrs. Piper had been
known for some years in the United States as a clairvoyante and spirit medium, and her trance utterances
had been carefully studied by Professor James and
Dr. Hodgson. In the winter of 1888-89 she spent
two months and a half in this country, at the invita-
tion of certain members of the S.P.R. She came to
England as a complete stranger, and was met on her
landing at Liverpool by Professor Lodge, and during

[1] The definition of clairvoyance given in the text differs somewhat
from that adopted by Mrs. Sidgwick (*Proc. S.P.R.*, vol. vii. p. 30)—
viz., "A faculty of acquiring supernormally, but not by reading the
minds of persons present, a knowledge of facts such as we normally
acquire by the use of our senses." Whether such a faculty exists or not,
it is certain that the phenomena which suggest it occur under the same
conditions and inextricably mingled with others which can, with some
plausibility, be explained as due to thought-transference from the conscious or unconscious memory of persons actually present. And as
the two sets of phenomena are found together in fact, it seemed best as
a matter of practical convenience that they should not be separated
in discussion. Moreover, the suggested application of the word finds
ample justification in popular usage.

the whole period she stayed either in the houses of
Professor Sidgwick or Mr. Myers at Cambridge, in
Professor Lodge's house at Liverpool, or in rooms in
London selected by Dr. Leaf. Neither at Cambridge
nor Liverpool were there any opportunities of her
acquiring knowledge of the histories and circumstances of the persons who visited her for experiments, other than those afforded during the actual
progress of the experiment, or by inquiries of servants
and children, the examination of books and photograph albums, or from the newspapers and private
correspondence. Practically she was under close and
almost continuous surveillance during the whole
period, and, independently of the special precautions
taken to guard against the acquisition of knowledge
by any of the means above indicated (*Proc. S.P.R.*,
vol. vi. pp. 438-440, 446-447, etc.), it is important to
note that the sitters were in almost every instance introduced to Mrs. Piper under an assumed name; that
some of them, and those not the least successful, were
persons in no way connected with the S.P.R., whose
admission was due to circumstances more or less
accidental; and that on several occasions she stated
facts which were not within the conscious knowledge
of any person present, and which could not conceivably have been discovered by any process of private
inquiry.[1]

The actual method of experiment was as follows:
Mrs. Piper would sit in a room partially darkened,
holding the hands of the sitter, whilst some other
person (generally Mr. Myers, Dr. Leaf, Professor
Lodge, or a shorthand writer) would be present to
take notes. Mrs. Piper would presently go off into

---

[1] It should be added that during the progress of similar investigations in the United States of America, Dr. Hodgson employed private
detectives to shadow Mr. and Mrs. Piper for some weeks, and that
nothing was discovered to intimate that any steps were taken by either,
whether by personal inquiry or by correspondence, to ascertain facts
relating to the history of actual or possible sitters. Mr. Piper did not
accompany his wife to this country.

a trance, attended at its outset by slight convulsive movements resembling those of an epileptic attack, and would after a brief interval assume the voice, gestures, and phraseology of a man.   In this guise she gave herself out as one " Dr. Phinuit," a medical man who had studied medicine in Paris in the first quarter of the present century.   In the impersonation of this character Mrs. Piper used occasionally broken English, pronounced some words, proper names especially, with a French accent, and was admittedly sometimes very successful in diagnosing and prescribing for the complaints of her sitters and their friends. "Dr. Phinuit" would then pour out a more or less coherent flood of conversation, questions, and remarks about the relatives and friends of those present, their past history and personal affairs generally, some of which was apparently mere padding, some obviously chance shots, or "fishing" for further information; whilst, in the midst of all the irrelevancy and incoherence, there would occasionally be clear, detailed statements on intimate matters of which it is inconceivable that Mrs. Piper could have attained any knowledge by normal means; just as, to quote the apt metaphor of Professor Lodge, in listening at a telephone "you hear the dim and meaningless fragments of a city's gossip, till back again comes the voice obviously addressed to you, and speaking with firmness and decision."   In regard to the trance itself, it has no doubt close analogy with the hypnotic trance, though Mrs. Piper is not readily amenable to hypnotism by ordinary means, and when hypnotised her condition is described by Professor James as very different from that of the "medium trance." (*Proc.*, vol. vi. p. 653; viii. p. 56.)   In the latter state Mrs. Piper is, occasionally at least, anæsthetic in certain senses, and analgesic in various parts of the body (viii. pp. 4-6), and her eyes are closed, with the eyeballs turned upwards.

There is no reason to suppose that the simulacrum

of "Dr. Phinuit" is anything else than an impersonation assumed by Mrs. Piper's subconsciousness. Such impersonations are very common amongst "spirit mediums" everywhere, and in all forms of spontaneously induced trance.[1] Nor is "Dr. Phinuit" the only form assumed by Mrs. Piper's secondary consciousness. It frequently happened in the trance that "Dr. Phinuit" gave place to an impersonation, often recognised as life-like and characteristic, of some deceased relative of the sitter's, as in the case of "Uncle Jerry," mentioned below.[2] Probably in many cases the basis of these representations was supplied by unguarded remarks of the sitters themselves, or by skilful guesses on the part of "Phinuit," sometimes possibly eked out by telepathic drafts on the sitters' memories. As regards Mrs. Piper's conscious share in the matter, the persons who have observed her most closely, both in this country and in America, agree in believing that she is a woman of transparent simplicity, and with a marked absence of inquisitiveness or even ordinary interest in matters outside her domestic concerns, and that she is incap-

[1] Independently of the fact that "Dr. Phinuit" is as obviously untrustworthy as Mrs. Piper in her natural state is apparently the reverse, the inquiries which have been made have entirely failed to corroborate the accounts, in themselves not always concordant, which "Dr. Phinuit" has given of his birth, his education, and other circumstances in his "earth-life." His knowledge of his native language is confined to a few simple phrases and a slight accent, frequently found useful in disguising a bad shot at a proper name; and the careful investigations conducted by Dr. Hodgson into Mrs. Piper's antecedents as a "medium" have made it almost certain that "Dr. Phinuit" is an invention, borrowed from the person through whose agency Mrs. Piper first became entranced, and who purported himself to be controlled by a French doctor named Albert Finnett (pronounced Finné). It should be added that "Dr. Phinuit" possesses apparently no knowledge of the medical names of drugs, nor any more intimate acquaintance with their properties than could be gathered from a manual of domestic medicine. (Vol. viii. pp. 47, 50, 51, etc.)

[2] At the present time (May 1894) "Dr. Phinuit" has, I understand, almost entirely ceased to "control" Mrs. Piper; his place being taken by the *soi-disant* spirit of a young American, recently deceased, who has given remarkable proofs of his identity.

able, morally and intellectually, of carrying on a prolonged and systematic deception, and must by all impartial persons be fully acquitted of responsibility for "Dr. Phinuit's" proceedings. As is almost invariably the case with entranced persons, in the normal state she appears to know nothing of what goes on in the trance, and to share none of the information supernormally acquired by her secondary consciousness. As to whether "Dr. Phinuit" is equally ignorant of Mrs. Piper's thoughts and of knowledge acquired normally by her, it is impossible to speak with equal confidence. There can be little doubt either that he is, or that he wishes, for the sake of effect, to produce the impression that he is. But, as is not infrequently the case, the second personality is markedly inferior in its moral character to the normal consciousness. Its ruling motive in this case appears to be a prodigious vanity, which drives "Dr. Phinuit," when telepathy fails, into shuffling, equivocation, and all manner of contemptible devices for eliciting information, and passing it off as supernormally acquired. Like the Strong Man of the music-halls, to make good his bragging he is forced continually to eke out what is genuinely abnormal by artifices at once disingenuous and transparent.[1]

The following is a summary of the proceedings at two of the more successful sittings. Mrs. Piper was at the time staying in Liverpool, with Professor Lodge, who introduced to her on the morning of December 23rd, 1888, under the pseudonym of Dr. Jones,[2] a medical man practising in the city. Notes

[1] I am glad to be able to append the following testimonial to Phinuit's good qualities. An investigator who has had unusual facilities for observing both Dr. Phinuit and Mrs. Piper, after reading the account given in the text, writes to me: "I suppose the account of Phinuit is true as far as it goes, but all the same . . . I suppose because he is more sympathetic, I am rather fond of Phinuit."

[2] At the evening sitting a servant unfortunately introduced the sitters by their real names, but the circumstance will hardly, I think, be held materially to affect the evidence.

were taken throughout by Professor Lodge, who was himself ignorant of nearly all the details given. The conversation was practically a monologue, as Dr. C. himself remained almost entirely silent, assenting, "with a grunt, to wrong quite as much as to right statements." It will be observed that here, as throughout, "Dr. Phinuit" appears to gain his information in an auditory form.

No. 96.

Sitting No. 42. Monday morning, December 23rd.

Present: Dr. C. (introduced as Dr. Jones) and O. J. L.

[The following is an abstract of the correct, or subsequently corrected or otherwise noteworthy, statements.]

"You have a little lame girl, lame in the thigh, aged thirteen; either second or third. She's a little daisy. I do like her. Dark eyes, the gentlest of the lot; good deal of talent for music. She will be a brilliant woman; don't forget it. She has more sympathy, more mind, more—quite a little daisy. She's got a mark, a curious little mark, when you look closely, over eye, a scar through forehead over left eye. The boy's erratic; a little thing, but a little devil. Pretty good when you know him. He'll make an architect likely. Let him go to school. His mother's too nervous. It will do him good. [This was a subject in dispute.] You have a boy and two girls and a baby; four in the body. It's the little lame one I care for. There are two mothers connected with you, one named Mary. Your aunt passed out with cancer. You have indigestion, and take hot water for it. You have had a bad experience. You nearly slipped out once on the water." [Dangerous yacht accident last summer. Above statements are correct except the lameness. See next sitting.]

Sitting No. 43. Monday evening, December 23rd.

Present: Dr. and Mrs. C. and O. J. L. [Statements correct when not otherwise noted.]

"How's little Daisy? She will get over her cold. But there's something the matter with her head. There's somebody round you lame and somebody hard of hearing. That little girl has got music in her. This lady is fidgety. There are four of you, four going to stop with you, one gone out of the body. One got irons on his foot. Mrs. Allen, in her surroundings, is the one with iron on leg. [Allen was maiden name of mother of lame one.] There's about 400 of your family. There's Kate ; you call her Kitty. She's the one that's kind of a crank. Trustworthy, but cranky. She will fly off and get married, she will. Think's she knows everything, she does. [This is the nurse-girl, Kitty, about whom they seem to have a joke that she is a walking compendium of information.] (An envelope with letters written inside, N—H—P—O—Q, was here handed in, and Phinuit wrote down B—J—R—O—I—S, not in the best of tempers.) A second cousin of your mother's drinks. The little dark-eyed one is Daisy. I like her. She can't hear very well. The lame one is a sister's child. [A cousin's child, the one *née* Allen, really.] The one that's deaf in her head is the one that's got the music in her. That's Daisy, and she's going to have the paints I told you of. [Fond of painting.] She's growing up to be a beautiful woman. She ought to have a paper ear. [An artificial drum had been contemplated.] You have an Aunt Eliza. There are three Maries, Mary the mother, Mary the mother, Mary the mother. [Grandmother, aunt, and granddaughter.] Three brothers and two sisters your lady has. Three in the body. There were eleven in your family, two passed out small. [Only know of nine.] Fred is going to pass out suddenly. He married a cousin. He writes. He has shining things. *Lorgnettes.* He is away. He's got a catchy trouble with heart and kidneys, and will pass out suddenly." [Not the least likely.]

NOTES.—The most striking part of this sitting is the prominence given to Dr. C.'s favourite little daughter, Daisy, a child very intelligent and of a very sweet disposition, but quite deaf; although her training enables her to go to school and receive ordinary lessons with other children. At the first sitting she is supposed erroneously to be lame, but at the second sitting this is corrected and explained, and all said about her is practically correct, including the cold she then had. Mrs. Piper had had no opportunity whatever of knowing or hearing of the C. children by ordinary social means. We barely know them ourselves. Phinuit grasped the child's name gradually, using it at first as a mere description. I did not know it myself.

The following is a summary of the false assertions :—

ERRONEOUS STATEMENTS.

At Sitting 42 :—

" Your lady's Fanny; well, there is a Fanny. [No.] Fred has light hair, brownish moustache, prominent nose. [No.] Your thesis was some special thing. I should say about lungs." [No.]

At Sitting 43 :—

"Your mother's name was Elizabeth. [No.] Her father's lame. [No.] Of your children there's Eddie and Willie and Fannie or Annie and a sister that faints, and Willie and Katie (no, Katie don't count) [being the nurse], and Harry and the little dark-eyed one, Daisy. [All wrong except Daisy.] One passed out with sore throat. [No.] The boy looks about 8. [No, 4.] Your wife's father had something wrong with leg; one named William. [No.] Your grandmother had a sister who married a Howe—Henry Howe. [Unknown.] There's a Thomson connected with you [no], and if you look you will find a Howe too. Your brother the captain [correct], with a lovely wife, who has brown hair [correct], has had trouble in head [no], and has two girls and a boy." [No, three girls.]

In this case it will be seen that no details were given which could not have been derived from the conscious knowledge of the sitter. Apart from the fact that the agent made no effort to impress his thought, it resembles a case of ordinary telepathy. Of much the same character are the following details, quoted from Professor James's account of his interviews with Mrs. Piper (*Proc. S.P.R.*, vol. vi. pp. 658, 659):—

No. 97.—From Professor W. JAMES.

"The most convincing things said about my own immediate household were either very intimate or very trivial. Unfortunately the former things cannot well be published. Of the trivial things, I have forgotten the greater number, but the following, *raræ nantes*, may serve as samples of their class : She said that we had lost recently a rug, and I a waistcoat. [She wrongly accused a person of stealing the rug, which was afterwards found in the house.] She told of my killing a grey-and-white cat, with ether, and described how it had 'spun round and round' before dying. She told how my New York aunt had written a letter to my wife, warning her against all mediums, and then went off on a most amusing criticism, full of *traits vifs*, of the excellent woman's character. [Of course no one but my wife and I knew the existence of the letter in question.] She was strong on the events in our nursery, and gave striking advice during our first visit to her about the way to deal with certain 'tantrums' of our second child, 'little Billy-boy,' as she called him, reproducing his nursery name. She told how the crib creaked at night, how a certain rocking-chair creaked mysteriously, how my wife had heard footsteps on the stairs, etc., etc. Insignificant as these things sound when read, the accumulation of a large number of them has an irresistible effect. And I repeat again what I said before, that taking everything that I know of Mrs. P. into account, the result is to make me feel as absolutely certain as I am of any personal fact in the world that she knows things in her trances which she cannot possibly have heard in her waking state, and that the definitive philosophy of her trances is yet to be found. The limitations of her trance-information, its discontinuity and fitfulness, and its apparent inability to develop beyond a certain point, although they end by rousing one's moral and human impatience with the phenomenon, yet are, from a scientific point of view, amongst its most interesting peculiarities, since where there are limits there are conditions, and the discovery of these is always the beginning of an explanation.

"This is all that I can tell you of Mrs. Piper. I wish it were more 'scientific.' But, *valeat quantum!* it is the best I can do."

But there are many cases (Professor Lodge enumerates forty-one instances, *Proc. S.P.R.*, vol. vi. pp. 649, 650) in which details were faithfully given by "Phinuit," which had either been forgotten by the sitters, or could not at any time have been within their knowledge. The instances clearly falling under the last head are perhaps too few to justify any inference being founded on them, although in view of some of the cases to be quoted later, telepathy from persons at a distance from the percipient seems a not impossible explanation. The following case, given by Professor Lodge, which at first sight seems to involve some such hypothesis, may perhaps be explained by the telepathic filching from his mind of the memories of incidents heard in his boyhood and long forgotten. It is right to say that Professor Lodge has no recollection of ever having heard of these incidents, and regards this explanation (or indeed any other which has been suggested) as extremely improbable. (*Proc. S.P.R.*, vol. vi. pp. 458-460.)

No. 98.—From PROFESSOR LODGE, F.R.S.

"It happens that an uncle of mine in London, now quite an old man, and one of a surviving three out of a very large family, had a twin brother who died some twenty or more years ago. I interested him generally in the subject, and wrote to ask if he would lend me some relic of this brother. By morning post on a certain day I received a curious old gold watch, which this brother had worn and been fond of; and that same morning, no one in the house having seen it or knowing anything about it, I handed it to Mrs. Piper when in a state of trance.

"I was told almost immediately that it had belonged to one of my uncles—one that had been mentioned before as having died from the effects of a fall—one that had been very fond of Uncle Robert, the name of the survivor—that the watch was now in possession of this same Uncle Robert, with whom he was anxious to communicate. After some difficulty and many wrong attempts Dr. Phinuit caught the name, Jerry, short for Jeremiah, and said emphatically, as if a third person was speaking, 'This is my watch, and Robert is my brother, and I am here. Uncle Jerry, my watch.' All this at the first sitting on the very morning the watch had arrived by post, no one but myself and a shorthand clerk who happened to have been introduced for the first time at this sitting by me, and whose antecedents are well known to me, being present.

"Having thus ostensibly got into communication through some means or other with what purported to be a deceased relative, whom I had indeed known slightly in his later years of blindness, but of whose early life I knew nothing, I pointed out to him that to make Uncle Robert aware of his presence it would be well to recall trivial details of their boyhood, all of which I would faithfully report.

"He quite caught the idea, and proceeded during several successive sittings ostensibly to instruct Dr. Phinuit to mention a number of little things such as would enable his brother to recognise him.

"References to his blindness, illness, and main facts of his life were comparatively useless from my point of view; but these details of boyhood, two-thirds of a century ago, were utterly and entirely out of my ken. My father was one of the younger members of the family, and only knew these brothers as men.

"'Uncle Jerry' recalled episodes such as swimming the creek when they were boys together, and running some risk of getting drowned; killing a cat in Smith's field; the possession of a small rifle, and of a long peculiar skin, like a snake-skin, which he thought was now in the possession of Uncle Robert.

"All these facts have been more or less completely verified. But the interesting thing is that his twin brother, from whom I got the watch, and with whom I was thus in a sort of communication, could not remember them all. He recollected something about swimming the creek, though he himself had merely looked on. He had a distinct recollection of having had the snake-skin, and of the box in which it was kept, though he does not know where it is now. But he altogether denied killing the cat, and could not recall Smith's field.

" His memory, however, is decidedly failing him, and he was good enough to write to another brother, Frank, living in Cornwall, an old sea captain, and ask if he had any better remembrance of certain facts—of course not giving any inexplicable reasons for asking. The result of this inquiry was triumphantly to vindicate the existence of Smith's field as a place near their home, where they used to play, in Barking, Essex; and the killing of a cat by another brother was also recollected ; while of the swimming of the creek, near a mill-race, full details were given, Frank and Jerry being the heroes of that foolhardy episode.

" Some of the other facts given I have not yet been able to get verified. Perhaps there are as many unverified as verified. And some things appear, so far as I can make out, to be false. One little thing I could verify myself, and it is good, inasmuch as no one is likely to have had any recollection, even if they had any knowledge, of it. Phinuit told me to take the watch out of its case (it was the old-fashioned turnip variety) and examine it in a good light afterwards, and I should see some nicks near the handle which Jerry said he had cut into it with his knife.

" Some faint nicks are there. I had never had the watch out of its case before ; being, indeed, careful neither to finger it myself nor to let any one else finger it.

" I never let Mrs. Piper in her waking state see the watch till quite towards the end of the time, when I purposely left it lying on my desk while she came out of the trance. Before long she noticed it, with natural curiosity, evidently becoming conscious of its existence then for the first time."[1]

There are many other cases of clairvoyance on record of the same type as Mrs. Piper's, but none

[1] It is impossible by means of a few short extracts to give a fair idea either of the strength of the evidence for telepathy afforded by the phenomena observed with Mrs. Piper, or of the variety and complexity of the problems there presented. Readers who are interested in the subject are referred to the record of the observations made by the S. P. R., occupying nearly 400 closely-printed octavo pages. (*Proc.*, vol. vi. pp. 436-660 ; vol. viii. pp. 1-167.) Further observations have been made during the year 1893 in the United States by Dr. Hodgson and others, the records of which have not yet been published.

which have been studied by so many observers with equal care, and through so prolonged a period. In the more usual form of trance clairvoyance, however, the percipient's impressions are of a visual character. He describes scenes which he appears to himself to *see*. In the pages of the *Zoist* and elsewhere vision of the kind is commonly called "travelling clairvoyance," it having generally been suggested to the hypnotised subject that he was actually present at the scene which he was desired to describe. It is possible that this suggestion, almost universally given, may have had some influence in determining the pictorial form which the telepathic impressions assume in such cases, as it has certainly led the percipient himself and the bystanders in many cases to believe in an extra-corporeal visitation of the scenes described. Often no details are given which were not within the knowledge, if not consciously present to the thoughts, of one of the bystanders. Such, for instance, is the case quoted by Dr. Backman, of Kalmar, in his paper on clairvoyance (*Proc. S.P.R.*, vol. vii. pp. 205, 206; viii. 405-407), in which the Director-General of Pilotage for Sweden, M. Ankarkrona, records how, when absent from home, he received from a maid-servant hypnotised by Baron Von Rosen an extremely detailed description of the interior of his own house and its inmates. Hardly a detail was incorrect, but no single detail was given which could not have been extracted from M. Ankarkrona's mind. To such a case there is no difficulty in applying the telepathic explanation.

No. 99.—From A. W. DOBBIE.

In the case to be next quoted, however, the information given by the hypnotised subject transcends the conscious knowledge, at all events, of those present. The account comes from Mr. A. W. Dobbie, of Adelaide, South Australia, who has for some years studied the phenomena of hypnotism on a number of subjects, and has observed some striking manifestations of telepathy and clairvoyance. I quote from a letter written to me in July 1886, containing a copy of his notes made at the time of the experiment, "the moment the words were uttered." The Hon. Dr. Campbell, M.L.C., who had lost a gold sleeve-link, brought its fellow on the 28th May 1886 to Mr. Dobbie, who placed it in the hand of one of his subjects. Then

"Miss Martha began by first accurately describing Dr. Campbell's features, then spoke of a little fair-haired boy who had a stud, or sleeve-link, in his hand, also of a lady calling him 'Neil'; then said that this little boy had taken the link into a place like a nursery where there were some toys, especially a large toy elephant, and that he had dropped the link into this elephant through a hole which had been torn or knocked in the breast; also that he had taken it out again, and gave two or three other interesting particulars. We were reluctantly compelled to postpone further investigation until two or three evenings afterwards.

"On the next occasion (in the interval, however, the missing sleeve-link had been found, but left untouched), I again placed the link in her hand and the previous particulars were at once reproduced; but as she seemed to be getting on very slowly, it occurred to Dr. Campbell to suggest placing his hand on that of the clairvoyant, so I placed him *en rapport* and allowed him to do so, he simply touching the back of her hand with the points of his fingers. As she still seemed to have great difficulty (she is always much slower than her sister) in proceeding, it suddenly occurred to me that it would be an interesting experiment to place Miss Eliza Dixon *en rapport* with Miss Martha, so I simply joined their disengaged hands, and Miss Eliza immediately commenced as follows, viz.:—

"'I'm in a house, upstairs, I was in a bathroom, then I went into another room nearly opposite, there is a large mirror just inside the door on the left hand, there is a double-sized dressing-table with drawers down each side of it, the sleeve-link is in the corner of the drawer nearest the door. When they found it they left it there. I know why they left it there, it was because they wanted to see if we would find it. I can see a nice easy-chair there, it is an old one, I would like it when I am put to sleep, because it is nice and low. The bed has curtains, they are a sort of brownish net and have a fringe of darker brown. The wall paper is of a light blue colour. There is a cane lounge there and a pretty Japanese screen behind it, the screen folds up. There is a portrait of an old gentleman over the mantelpiece, he is dead, I knew him when he was alive, his name is the same as the gentleman who acts as Governor when the Governor is absent from the colony,[1] I will tell you his name directly —it is the Rev. Mr. Way. It was a little boy who put the sleeve-link in that drawer, he is very fair, his hair is almost white, he is a pretty little boy, he has blue eyes and is about three years old. The link had been left on that table, the little boy was in the nursery, and he went into the bedroom after the gentleman had left. I can see who the gentleman is, it is Dr. Campbell. Doesn't that little boy look a young Turk, the link is quite a handful for his little hand, he is running about with it very pleased; but he doesn't seem to know what to do with it. (A.)

[Dr. Campbell was not present from this point.]

"'Now I can hear some one calling up the stairs, a lady is calling two names, Colin is one and Neil is the other, the other boy is about five years old and is darker than the other. The eldest, Colin, is going downstairs now, he is gone into what looks like a dining-room, the lady says, "Where is Neil?" "Upstairs, ma." "Go and tell him to come down at once." The little fair-haired boy had put the link down; but when he heard his brother coming up, he picked it up again. Colin says—"Neil, you are to come down at once." "I won't," says Neil. "You're a goose," replies Colin, and he turned and went down without Neil. What a young monkey! now he has gone into the nursery and put the link into a large toy elephant, he put it through a hole in front, which is broken. He has gone downstairs now, I suppose he thinks it is safe there.

"'Now that gentleman has come into the room again and he wants that link; he is looking all about for it, he thinks it might be knocked down: the lady is there now too, and they are both looking for it. The lady says, "Are you sure you put it there?" The gentleman says, "Yes."

"'Now it seems like next day, the servant is turning the carpet up and looking all about for it; but can't find it.

"'The gentleman is asking that young Turk if he has seen it, he knows that he is fond of pretty things. The little boy says, "No." He seems to think it is fine fun to serve his father like that.

"'Now it seems to be another day and the little boy is in the nursery again, he has taken the link out of the elephant, now he has dropped it into that drawer, that is all I have to tell you about it, I told you the rest before.'"

---

[1] Chief Justice Way is the gentleman who acts as Deputy for his Excellency when absent from the colony.—A. W. D.

Dr. Campbell, after reading through the above account, writes :—

"ADELAIDE, *July 9th,* 1886.

"At the point (A) the séance was discontinued till the next sitting, when I was absent. The conversation reported as passing between the children is correct. The description of the room is accurate in every point. The portrait is that of the late Rev. James Way. The description of the children and their names are true. The fact that the link was discovered in the drawer, in the interval between one sitting and the final one, and that the link was left there, pending the discovery of it by the clairvoyant, is also correct, as this was my suggestion to Mrs. Campbell when she showed it to me in the corner of the drawer. In fact, every circumstance reported is absolutely correct. I know, further, that neither of the clairvoyants has ever been inside of my door. My children are utterly unknown to them, either in appearance or by name. I may say also that they had no knowledge of my intention to place the link in their possession, or even of my presence at the séance, as they were both on each occasion in the mesmeric sleep when I arrived."

In a later letter, dated December 16th, 1887, Dr. Campbell writes:—

"With respect to the large toy elephant, I certainly knew of its existence, but was not thinking of it at the time the clairvoyant was speaking. I did not know even by suspicion that the elephant was so mutilated as to have a large opening in its chest, and on coming home had to examine the toy to see whether the statement was correct. I need hardly say that it was absolutely correct."

Mr. Dobbie tells us that "neither he nor his clairvoyants had any opportunity, directly or indirectly, of knowing any of the particulars brought out by the clairvoyant." He afterwards saw the room described, and says "the description is simply perfect in every particular."

This narrative presents us, at any rate, with a case of thought-transference of a very remarkable kind, an accurate and detailed description being given of a room wholly unknown to the clairvoyantes. But it is doubtful whether even here more was stated by the percipients than could have been extracted from the minds of those present. The statement as to the child placing the sleeve-link in the toy elephant could not, unfortunately, be verified, and the conversation described was natural enough under the circumstances, and may have been the result of a happy conjecture. It is unfortunate that a detailed description of the room was not given until the second sitting, since that lessens the improbability, in any case considerable, that some information as to the details given might have reached the ears of the clairvoyantes.[1] The most remarkable feature in the case is the statement, subsequently verified, as to the hole in the front of the elephant. We must suppose either that this detail was derived from the mind of the child, or that Dr. Campbell had once observed the hole but had forgotten its existence at the time of the experiment. Mr. Dobbie gives other instances of clairvoyance, by one of which the hypothesis of thought-transference from a distant and unknown person is strongly suggested. (*Proc. S.P.R.*, vol. vii. p. 63, etc.)

No. 100.—From DR. WILTSE.

We next quote two cases out of several recorded by Dr. A. S. Wiltse, of Skiddy, Kansas (*Proc. S.P.R.*, vol. vii. pp. 72 *et seq.*). The percipient was Fannie G., a servant of about fifteen years, who was frequently hypnotised by Dr. Wiltse in the summer of 1882, and developed clairvoyant powers of a very remarkable kind. Dr. Wiltse unfortunately took no notes at the time of the experiments, but he appears to be an accurate reporter, and it will be seen that his account of the incidents quoted is confirmed in each case by other observers. The first experiment was recorded with others in 1886, in a paper read before the Owosso Academy of Medicine; the second was not apparently written down until the account was sent to us in 1890:—

---

[1] It is hardly necessary to say that such an interpretation in no way reflects upon the good faith of the hypnotics. Hints derived from conversation overheard unconsciously might be quite sufficient.

"Miss Florence F., now Mrs. R., a neighbour, was invited to attend one evening with tests which she was to arrange during the day. She came and told the subject to go to her kitchen and tell her what she saw. It was about twenty rods to Miss F.'s kitchen. Subject was led to suppose she had gone to the kitchen, and being asked what she saw, readily answered: 'The table sits in the centre of the room, and upon it is a box covered with a cloth.' 'What is in the box, Fannie?' I asked. 'Oh, I daren't look in the box! Miss Florence might be mad.' 'Miss Florence is willing you should look; raise the cloth, Fannie, and tell me what is there.' She immediately answered, 'There are seven loaves of bread and sixteen biscuits in it.' (Correct.)

"I set this down as telepathy because Miss Florence F. was in the room, and undoubtedly the facts were prominently in her mind, having been purposely so arranged by her for a test; but what follows is not so plainly telepathy.

"Miss Florence asked Fannie to tell her what was in her stable. She answered, 'Two black horses, one grey horse, and one red horse' (meaning a bay horse). Miss Florence: 'That is wrong, Fannie; there are only my black horses in the stable.' Ten or fifteen minutes later, a brother of Miss Florence came to the house and told Miss Florence that there were travellers at the house, and upon inquiry we learned that the grey and 'red' horse belonged to them, and that they had been in the stable half-an-hour when Fannie's clairvoyant eye scanned it."

Mrs. Roberts, the Miss Florence F. of the narrative, writes to Dr. Wiltse:—

"CARDIFF, TENN., *January* 13*th*, 1891.

"Your letter was received late last night, and I hasten to reply. Your statement[1] is correct as far as it goes. But if you remember we asked, or rather you asked Fannie, to go into our store-room and see what was in there, and she said a hind quarter of beef, which was true, we had got it late that evening. You also asked her to go in the kitchen and see how many loaves of bread she could find, which she told, and on counting them after returning home, she was correct. It was in the winter of '81 or '82, I think, either December '81, or in the January or February of '82, I cannot remember the month; I know it was cold weather If you remember when old Julian

---

[1] The statement sent to Mrs. Roberts was substantially a copy of the last nine lines only of the preceding account. No reference was made to the visit to the kitchen.

Scott was drowned, it was about that time, for if I remember
right you were trying that same night to get her to find his
body. I think, as well as I remember, that she located his
saddle, and a few days after it was found in a place that she
described, but she could not find the body.

" MRS. FLORENCE F. ROBERTS."

In the second of the incidents above described, and
in the account which follows, the percipient's statements included facts which were not within the knowledge of any of those present, and we are forced to
the conclusion that the percipient in some way derived
her knowledge from persons at a distance. The case
presents a curious experimental parallel to the dream
(No. 60) recorded in Chapter VIII., and to case No.
107 below. In the present instance, however, the persons whom we may perhaps call the agents, though
unconscious of their agency in the matter, do not
appear to have been personally unknown to the
percipient.

No. 101.—From DR. WILTSE.

" Mr. Howard lived six miles from me. He had just built
a large frame house; our subject had never seen the house,
although, I presume, she may have heard it talked of. Mr.
Howard had not been home for some days, and asked that
Fannie should go there and see if all were well. She exclaimed
at the size of the house, but railed at the ugliness of the front
fence, saying she would not have ' such an old torn-down ' fence
in front of so nice a house. 'Yes,' said Howard, laughing, ' my
wife has been worrying the life out of me about the fence and
the front steps.' 'Oh,' interrupted Fannie, 'the steps are nice
and new !' 'She is off there,' said Howard, 'the steps are
worse than the fence.' 'Don't you see,' exclaimed Fannie,
impatiently, 'how new and nice the steps are? Humph!'
(And she seemed absolutely disgusted, judging by the tone.)
' I think they are real nice.'

"Changing the subject, Howard asked her how many
windows were in his house. Almost instantly she gave a
number (I think it was twenty-six). Howard thought it was
too many, but upon carefully counting, found it exact.

"From my house he went directly home, and, to his great
surprise, found that during his absence his wife had employed

a carpenter who had built new front steps, and they had been completed a day or two before Fannie had scanned the premises for him with her invisible telescope.

"Mr. Howard's son, a youth, had gone into an adjoining county and was not expected back for some days. Fannie was acquainted with the young man (Andrew). Mr. Howard, having business back at the station, was with us again the next night. His faith in our 'oracle' had assumed larger proportions, and he suggested a visit home by means of Fannie's wonderful faculty. She described the rooms excellently, even to a bouquet on one of the tables, and said that several young people were there. Asked who they were, she replied that she did not know any of them except Andrew. 'But,' I said, 'Andrew is not at home.' Fannie : 'Why, don't you see him ?' Q. 'Sure, Fannie?' F. 'Oh, don't I know Andrew? Right there, he is.' Mr. Howard returned home the next morning, where he found that Andrew had returned late the day before, and that several young people in the neighbourhood had passed the evening with him."

The following are copies of questions addressed to Mr. Howard, and his replies to them :—

"'Did she describe your new doorsteps to you before you knew they were built ?' 'Yes.'

"*Question.*—'Did she describe your house and tell you Andrew was there when you thought he was away, and, if so, was he actually at home as she stated ?'

"*Answer.*—'Yes.'

"*Question.*—'From what you saw, were you satisfied that Fannie had, when mesmerised, powers of imparting knowledge unknown to others about her ?'

"*Answer.*—'Yes.'

"WILLIAM HOWARD,
Kismet, Tenn., Morgan Co."

"We testify to these questions, asked William Howard, to be facts. We were present at the same time Mr. Howard was when Miss G. was mesmerised by Dr. A. S. Wiltse. We further state that when any of us would prick the doctor with a pin, she would flinch with the same part of her body. Miss G. was not in the habit of the use of tobacco. The doctor was in a different room, with a wall between them. When he would smoke, she grew nauseated and seemed to taste the same as he did.

"W. T. HOWARD AND LIZZIE HOWARD."

No. 102.—From MR. WILLIAM BOYD.

A remarkable case has been recorded, from contemporary knowledge, by Mr. William Boyd, of Peterhead, N.B. (*Proc. S.P.R.*, vol. vii. pp. 49 *et seq.*). The events occurred as far back as 1850, but a full account of them was contributed by Mr. Boyd to the *Aberdeen Herald* for May 8th and 18th of that year, from which it appears that the statements made by the percipient were written down and communicated to Mr. Boyd and others before their correspondence with the facts was known. The incident attracted much notice at the time, from its connection with the whaling fleet, the chief topic of local interest. The following is an extract from the original notes made by Mr. Reid, the hypnotiser, published in the *Aberdeen Herald*, May 18th, 1850:—

"On the evening of April 22nd I put John Park, tailor, aged twenty-two, into a state of clairvoyance, in presence of twelve respectable inhabitants of this town. (Here follows a description of certain statements regarding the fate of Franklin's expedition and the ships *Erebus* and *Terror*, which in the light of information subsequently received proved to have been inaccurate.) He (the clairvoyant) then visited Old Greenland, as was desired, and having gone on board the *Hamilton Ross*, a whale-ship belonging to this port, saw David Cardno, second mate, getting his hand bandaged up by the doctor in the cabin, having got it injured while sealing. He was then told by the captain that they had upwards of 100 tons of oil. I again, on the evening of the 23rd, put him into a clairvoyant state. (Here follow some further particulars regarding Sir John Franklin's expedition, which also are proved to have been inaccurate.) I again directed him to Old Greenland, and he again visited the *Hamilton Ross*, and found Captain Gray, of the *Eclipse*, conversing with the captain about the seal fishing being up.

"(Signed)   WILLIAM REID."

It appears from the *Herald* of May 8th that the *Hamilton Ross* did come to port first out of eleven ships, that she brought 159 tons of oil, that Cardno had injured his hand, and arrived with his arm in a sling, and that on the 23rd April the captain of the *Hamilton Ross* was conversing with the captain of the *Eclipse*. Mr. Boyd points out, however, that Cardno had some years before lost the tip of one finger, so that the clairvoyant's statement of the accident may have been simply a reminiscence. It is worth noting that here, as generally in visions of the kind, the false was mingled with the true, and that the percipient appears quite unable to distinguish between pictures which are obviously the work of his own imagination, and those which are apparently due to inspiration from without.

The next case is also remote in date, but we have received the evidence of several persons still living who were conversant with the facts at the time of their occurrence, and the account given below is taken from contemporary notes. "Jane" was the wife of a pit-man in County Durham, who for many years, from 1845 onwards, was hypnotised for the sake of her health by Mrs. T. Myers, of Twinstead Rectory, Mrs. Fraser, her sister, and other members of the same family. In the hypnotic sleep she appears to have been sensible to telepathic influences of the same kind as those described at the beginning of Chapter III. But she also gave remarkable demonstrations of "travelling clairvoyance," and frequently described correctly the interior of houses she had never seen. Occasionally she went beyond this, and stated facts not within the knowledge of those present, and opposed to their preconceptions. A good instance is the following, taken from notes made in the summer of 1853:—

No. 103.—From Dr. F.[1]

"Before commencing the sitting, I fixed to take her to a house, without communicating my intentions to any of the

---

[1] Dr. F., who is still living, is disinclined to have his name published, as he does not wish to be troubled with correspondence on the subject.

parties present. In the morning of the day I stated to a patient of my own, Mr. Eglinton, at present residing in the village of Tynemouth, that I intended to visit him. He stated that he would be present between 8 and 10 P.M. in a particular room, so that there might be no difficulty in finding him. He was just recovering from a very severe illness, and was so weak that he could scarcely walk. He was exceedingly thin from the effects of his complaint.

"After the usual state had been obtained, I said, 'We are standing beside a railway station, now we pass along a road, and in front of us see a house with a laburnum tree in front of it.' She directly replied, 'Is it the red house with a brass knocker?' I said, 'No, it has an iron knocker.' I have since looked, however, and find that the door has an old-fashioned brass handle in the shape of a knocker. She then asked, 'Shall we go up the steps? Shall we go along this passage, and up these stairs? Is this a window on the stair-head?' I said, 'You are quite right, and now I want you to look into the room upon the left-hand side.' She replied, 'Oh, yes, in the bed-room. There is no one in this room; there is a bed in it, but there is no person in it.' I was not aware that a bedroom was in the place I mentioned, but upon inquiry next day I found she was correct. I told her she must look into the next room, and she would see a sofa. She answered, 'But there is here a little gallery. Now I am in the room, and see a lady with black hair lying upon the sofa.' I attempted to puzzle her about the colour of her hair, and feeling sure it was Mr. Eglinton who was lying there, I sharply cross-questioned her, but still she persisted in her story. The questioning, however, seemed to distract her mind, and she commenced talking about a lady at Whickham, until I at last recalled her to the room at Tynemouth, by asking whether there was not a gentleman in the room. 'No,' she said; 'we can see no gentleman there.'

"After a little she described the door opening, and asked, with a tone of great surprise, 'Is that a gentleman?' I replied, 'Yes; is he thin or fat?' 'Very fat,' she answered; 'but has he a cork leg?' I assured her that he had no cork leg, and tried to puzzle her again about him. She, however, assured me that he was very fat and had a great corporation, and asked me whether I did not think such a fat man must eat and drink a great deal to get such a corporation as that. She also described him as sitting by the table with papers beside him, and a glass of brandy and water. 'Is it not wine?' I asked. 'No,' she said, 'it's brandy.' 'Is it not whisky or rum?' 'No, it is brandy,' was the answer; 'and now,' she continued, 'the lady is going to get her supper, but the fat gentleman does not take any.' I requested her to tell me the colour of his hair, but she only answered that the lady's hair was dark. I then inquired if he had any brains in his head,[1] but she seemed altogether puzzled about him, and said she could not see any. I then asked her if she could see his name upon any of the letters lying about. She replied, 'Yes'; and upon my saying that the name began with E, she spelt each letter of the name 'Eglinton.'

"I was so convinced that I had at last detected her in a complete mistake that I arose, and declined proceeding further in the matter, stating that, although her description of the house and the name of the person were correct, in everything connected with the gentleman she had guessed the opposite from the truth.

"On the following morning Mr. E. asked me the result of the experiment, and after having related it to him, he gave me the following account :—He had found himself unable to sit up to so late an hour, but wishful fairly to test the powers of the clairvoyante, he had ordered his clothes to be stuffed into the form of a figure, and to make the contrast more striking to his natural appearance, had an extra pillow pushed into the clothes so as to form a 'corporation.' The figure had been placed near the table, in a sitting position, and a glass of brandy and water and the newspapers placed beside it. The name, he further added, was spelt correctly, though up to that time I had been in the habit of writing it 'Eglington,' instead of as spelt by the clairvoyante, 'Eglinton.'"

In this case it will be seen that the only person from whom knowledge of the facts given could have been derived was personally unknown to the percipient, the only apparent link of connection being their common acquaintance with Dr. F.

In the last case to be mentioned there are again some indications of thought-transference from the mind of a person at a distance. On April 8th, 1890, Dr. Backman, at Kalmar, received a letter from Dr. Kjellman, at Stockholm, asking that on the following day Dr. Backman should request one of his subjects, Alma Radberg, to "find" Dr. von B. (known to Alma), and describe the apartment (Dr. Kjellman's own) in which he would be sitting, adding that something would be hung on the chandelier for her to describe. The percipient in the trance gave a

---

[1] On a previous occasion she had described a skull in a surgery as a head, but "not a live head, and with no brains in it."

description of the room, and when asked to look at the chandelier she said there was no chandelier, something more like a lamp, and described something long and narrow, of white metal, hanging from it, with some red stuff round it. When awake she said that what she saw was probably a pair of scissors for cutting paper, or a paper-knife. Dr. Backman sent his notes to Dr. Kjellman, who replied, showing that the description of the room, though in some respects accurate (*e.g.*, she mentioned a long stuffed easy-chair, a glass bookcase, three doors in the lobby, etc.), was in other features incorrect, and should on the whole be regarded as inconclusive. "But," he adds, "her statement that the object was hanging in a lamp, not a chandelier, was right. It is both a lamp and a chandelier, and the lamp was drawn down a long way under the chandelier," and that the object hanging there was "a large pair of paper scissors, fixed by an india-rubber otoscope, and with a tea-rose and some forget-me-nots in one of the handles of the scissors." It will thus be seen that on the one point to which her attention had been specially directed, the hypnotic's description was strikingly accurate; and the articles described were hardly within the range of conjecture.

Dr. Backman has made other experiments with the same subject, in which he obtained further indications of clairvoyance of this kind. (*Proc. S.P.R.*, vol. vii. p. 207, etc.)

CHAPTER XV.

ON CLAIRVOYANCE IN THE NORMAL STATE.

THERE is probably no sharp line to be drawn between the cases just described and those to be dealt with in the first part of the present chapter. Both present the common feature that the percipient receives a clear and detailed telepathic impression of an incident or scene in the experience of some other person, and in both the condition of that impression is manifestly not an effort of attention or an exceptional state on the part of the person whose experience is thus represented, but a specially stimulated receptivity on the part of the percipient. But in some cases the conditions of this special receptivity are found in trance, whilst in others the percipient is apparently in the normal state. This would seem indeed to constitute only a superficial difference, for in the majority of cases hitherto observed the waking clairvoyance does not occur spontaneously, but requires special preparation for its induction, and sometimes the percipient appears to pass into a state resembling the earlier stages of a hypnotic trance. Thus Mr. Keulemans, the well-known scientific draughtsman, who has had many experiences of telepathic clairvoyance,[1] has noticed in the course of his work, which consists largely of making drawings of birds for lithographic reproduction, that, in his own words,

---

[1] Several instances of Mr. Keulemans' telepathic experiences are given in *Phantasms of the Living* (cases 21, 38, 56, 184).

" Whenever strong impressions had got hold of my mind they had a tendency to develop themselves into a vivid mind-picture as soon as my eye and attention were concentrated upon the eye in the drawing; and that whenever I began darkening the iris, leaving the light speck the most prominent part, I would slowly pass off into a kind of dream-state. The mere act of drawing the eye is not enough to bring me into this state, or I should experience such a state at least once a day, which I do not. But if a strong mental impression takes hold of me I begin drawing an eye. . . . The drawing will then convey to me the news, either in the form of a vague, imperfect representation of the person indicated in the impression, or by a correct hallucinatory picture of the event as it actually occurred, both as regards the person and the surroundings. Sometimes I cannot get at the vision at once; other thoughts and scenes interfere. But when I begin to feel drowsy I know I shall have it right in a second; and here I lose normal consciousness. That there is an actual loss of consciousness I know from the fact that on one occasion my wife had been in the room talking to me, and not receiving a reply thought that something was wrong with me and shook my shoulder. The shake brought me back to my waking state." (*Proc. S.P.R.*, vol. viii. p. 517.)

But this would seem to be an extreme case, as under ordinary circumstances there is no apparent loss of consciousness; and the essential condition appears to be freedom from interruption and preoccupation. But the percipient generally finds it helpful, if not absolutely necessary, to employ a crystal, or some other object, for the full development of the impression. The exact part played by the crystal, glass of water, shell, or other object, in facilitating the hallucination, it is not easy to determine. In some cases, no doubt, it acts by furnishing a *point de repère*, or nucleus of actual sensation, round which the hallucination may develop. It is probable also that the mere act of fixing the eyes on one particular point may, by shutting out other sources of sensation, help to bring about the state of quietude necessary for the experiments; and yet again it is likely that the intrinsic virtue of the act, whatever that may be, is enhanced by the self-suggestion that it will prove beneficial; if indeed its virtue may not in some cases be altogether due to that cause. It should be remembered in this connection that fixation of the eye on a small bright object is one of the readiest means of inducing hypnosis.[1]

Induced Clairvoyance.

No. 104.—From MISS X.

Miss X., some of whose experiments have already been quoted, has been amongst the most constant and successful of crystal seers. The bulk of her visions, as she has pointed out (*Proc. S.P.R.*, vol. v. p. 505), consist either of mere after-images, recrudescent memories of things seen and heard, or of fancy pictures built out of a rearrangement of existing materials. But occasionally there occur visions of events then taking place, or representations of the past experience of some friend. Space will not permit of illustrations being given of the first two classes, though the first especially has some bearing on our researches. The following account of what appears to have been a telepathic vision is included by Mr. Myers in a paper on the subliminal consciousness (*Proc. S.P.R.*, vol. viii. p. 491). D. is the friend mentioned in Chapter V., p. 122.

---

[1] It should perhaps be said that there is nothing in the experience of the many persons who have so far tried crystal gazing, at the instance of the S.P.R., to indicate risk of injury to health. It is no doubt not advisable for an invalid, or for any one suffering from headache, or undue fatigue, to try the experiment. Indeed, the experience of Mrs. Verrall and others is that success under such conditions is unattainable. But with ordinary care to avoid straining the eyes, no evil effect, it is thought, need be apprehended; and there is probably no form of experiment which at the cost of so little trouble may be expected to yield results of so great interest and value. There is of course no magic in the crystal; a glass paper-weight, a mirror, or a glass of water will serve the purpose equally well. Records of experiments will be welcomed by Mr. F. W. H. Myers, from whose suggestive article many of the illustrations quoted in the text are taken. (See *Proc.*, vol. viii. p. 436, etc.)

"On August 10th of this year [1892] D. went with her family to spend the autumn at a country house which they had taken furnished, and which neither of us had ever seen. I was also away from home, the distance between us being at least 200 miles.

"On the morning of the 12th I received a pencil note from her, evidently written with difficulty, saying that she had been very fiercely attacked by a savage dog, from which she and our own little terrier had defended themselves and each other as best they could, receiving a score or so of wounds between them before they could summon any one to their assistance. She gave me no details, assuming that, as often happens between us, I should have received intimation of her danger before the news could reach me by ordinary methods.

"D. was extremely disappointed on hearing that I had known nothing. I had not consulted the crystal on the day of the accident, and had received no intimation. Begging her to tell me nothing further as to the scene of her adventure, I sought for it in the crystal on Sunday, 14th, and noted the following details :—The attacking dog was a large black retriever, and our terrier held him by the throat while D. beat at him in the rear. I saw also the details of D.'s dress. But all this I knew or could guess. What I could not know was that the terrier's collar lay upon the ground, that the struggle took place upon a lawn beyond which lay earth—a garden bed probably—overshadowed by an aucuba bush.

"On September 9th I had an opportunity of repeating all this to Mr. Myers, and on the 10th I joined D. at their country house. The rest of the story I give in her own words :—

From D.

"'As we were somewhat disappointed that no intimation of the accident which had occurred to me had reached Miss X., she determined to try to call up a mental picture of the scene where it had occurred, and if possible to verify it when visiting us later on.

"'On the night of her arrival at C——, we were not able to go over the whole of the grounds alone, and it was therefore not until the following morning that we went together for the special purpose of fixing on the exact spot. Miss X. was in front, as I feared some unconscious sign of recognition on my part might spoil the effect of her choice. The garden is a very large one, and we wandered for some time without fixing on a spot, the sole clue given by Miss X. being that she "could not get the right place, it wanted a *light* bush." I pointed out several, silver maples, etc., in various directions, but none would do, and she finally walked down to the place where the accident had occurred, close to a large aucuba (the *only* one, I believe, in the shrubbery), and said, " This must be it; it has the path and the grass and the bush, as it should, but I expected it to be much farther from the house."

" ' I may add that I was not myself aware of this bush, but as I was studying them all at the time we were attacked by the dog, and as this one is close to the spot where I was knocked down, it seems possible that it was the last I noticed, and it may therefore have influenced ne more than I knew.' "

Mr. Myers adds :—

" I understand that there are a good many acres of ground round the house in question, and that the dog's attack was made within fifty yards of the house—plainly an unlikely place for a struggle so long protracted without the arrival of help."

As the crystal picture was described to Mr. Myers before its verification, there was no room for the reading back of details from the actual scene.

No. 105.—From MISS X.

Miss X. has also succeeded on several occasions in obtaining telepathic information by holding a shell to her ear. Of one such case she writes (*ibid.*, p. 494) :—

"On Saturday, June 11th, Mr. G. A. Smith spent some time with us attempting some thought-transference experiments, which were fairly successful, and interested me greatly. Mr. Smith left the house soon after seven. After dinner, I took up the shell which had played some part—not very successfully— in our experiments. What occurred is best given in the following extracts :—

" ' [*June 11th*, 1892] *Saturday Evening*, 8.30. [X. to G. A. S.]

" ' Why—when the shell was repeating to me just now what you said about clambering over rocks at Ramsgate—did it stop suddenly to ask, still in your voice, " Are you a vegetarian then?" . . . Perhaps you dined at [your next appointment], and declined animal food? Do tell me whether you are responsible for this irrelevance.'

" ' *June 13th, Monday.* [G. A. S. to X.]

" ' . . . Without doubt the shell spoke the truth. . . . As you know, I left you soon after seven. After walking fifteen minutes

I suddenly met Mr. M. . . . I was thinking about points in connection with the experiments we had been engaged in, and am afraid I did not follow his remarks very closely . . . but he made some allusion to little dishes at a vegetarian restaurant somewhere, and immediately feeling an interest in the question whether he was a champion of the vegetarian cause, I interrupted him with "*Are you a vegetarian then?*" I believe these are the exact words I used. He will be sure to remember this, and must be questioned.'

"'*June 23rd.* [G. A. S. to X.]

"' I have to-day walked over the course which I took on June 11th, from [Miss X.'s house] to the spot where I met Mr. M. It took just eleven minutes. If I left you at 7.15, it was probably about 7.30, or a very few minutes later, that I put the query to Mr. M.'"

Mr. M. was away from home, and though at once applied to for corroboration, did not send a written statement till June 22nd, when he writes to Mr. Smith (after failing to recall the exact particulars of the previous conversation) :—

"The main fact remains that you asked me, to the best of my belief—bearing on my strong praise of the cooking at the Oxford Street Café—whether ' I was a vegetarian.' That is the core of the whole matter, and that is *sound*."

From Mr. Smith's statement it would appear that the voice in the shell reproduced words actually spoken about three-quarters of an hour before. That is, as is very generally the case, the clairvoyante perceived, not the events actually happening at the moment, but events already passed and chronicled in the memories of those who took part in them. This fact, which seems to have been commonly overlooked by the earlier writers on the subject, is in itself a very strong argument for the telepathic explanation of clairvoyance. Knowledge of a contemporaneous scene might be conceived as due to independent vision on the part of the percipient; knowledge of what is already past can most readily be explained as derived from other minds.[1]

[1] Of course in this case there is an alternative explanation—viz., that Miss X. received the impression at the time the words were spoken, and that the shell merely developed it for her conscious self.

No. 106.—From DR. BACKMAN.

This explanation is very clearly indicated in the following case, quoted from the paper already referred to (*Proc. S.P.R.*, vol. vii. p. 216). Dr. Backman, after describing how occasionally he asked his subject, while awake, to look in the crystal, writes :—

"I told the clairvoyant, Miss Olsen, to see in the crystal what Miss ——, who was present, had been doing the night before. After a few moments she said that she saw a meadow in the crystal, and in it a certain number (giving the number correctly) of ladies and gentlemen, who were dancing and drinking champagne. This seemed to her very improbable, because it was then November, a season that is not chosen in this country [Sweden] for picnics. She described minutely several other things which were not written down, but were quite correct, according to what Miss —— said later on."

In a letter dated December 19th, 1890, Dr. Backman adds :—

"Several persons were present. No notes were taken, but the story made so much sensation that it has not been forgotten. Miss —— supplemented the account to-day by reminding me that on looking into the crystal Miss Olsen first gave a perfect description of a lady with whom Miss —— had talked on meeting her in the street the day before; she described her face, her dress, etc., very accurately, and said besides that she had two gold rings on the fourth finger of her left hand (a sign of marriage). After that Miss Olsen suddenly began to laugh and said : ' Miss —— is in a merry company—they are dancing— the corks of the champagne bottles are jumping,' etc. Miss —— cannot remember that any wrong detail was given by Miss Olsen, except that she thinks the number of persons present was not correctly given."

With Dr. Backman's permission we wrote to Miss —— asking for her confirmation of these incidents, and she replied as follows, on March 8th, 1891 :—

"I am very willing to give you a description of what I saw and heard at Dr. Backman's the day he has mentioned in his letter to you.

"When I came to him, he made a hypnotic experiment with Miss Olsen, who should endeavour to find some papers lying somewhere in Dr. Backman's apartment, and, to my great surprise, she succeeded in finding them. After her being awakened, Dr. Backman gave her a large glass button and asked her to look in it and see if she could find out what I had done the day before. She succeeded even in this to an astonishing degree."

No. 107.—From Sir Joseph Barnby.

In the next case, however, the vision appears to have been as nearly as possible contemporaneous with the event. Miss A. is a lady who has had many telepathic experiments of a striking kind. She is extremely short-sighted and a bad visualist, but her crystal visions she describes as being clear and well defined, as if she were looking on a real scene through strong glasses. The following account of an incident in Miss A.'s experience is given by Sir Joseph Barnby, who was a witness before the verification. His account has been revised throughout by Lady Radnor, who has interpolated an explanatory note. Sir Joseph writes, in November 1892 :—

"I was invited by Lord and Lady Radnor to the wedding of their daughter, Lady Wilma Bouverie, which took place August 15th, 1889.

"I was met at Salisbury by Lord and Lady Radnor and driven to Longford Castle. In the course of the drive, Lady Radnor said to me : 'We have a young lady staying with us in whom, I think, you will be much interested. She possesses the faculty of seeing visions, and is otherwise closely connected with the spiritual world. Only last night she was looking in her crystal and described a room which she saw therein, as a kind of London dining-room. [The room described was not in London but at L., and Miss A. particularly remarked that the floor was in large squares of black and white marble—as it is in the big hall at L., where family prayers are said.—H. M. Radnor.] With a little laugh, she added, 'And the family are evidently at prayers, the servants are kneeling at the chairs round the room and the prayers are being read by a tall and distinguished-looking gentleman with a very handsome, long grey beard.' With another little laugh, she continued: 'A lady just behind him rises from her knees and speaks to him. He puts her aside with a wave of the hand, and continues his reading.' The young lady here gave a careful description of the lady who had risen from her knees.'

"Lady Radnor then said: 'From the description given, I cannot help thinking that the two principal personages described are Lord and Lady L., but I shall ask Lord L. this evening, as they are coming by a later train, and I should like you to be present when the answer is given.'

"The same evening, after dinner, I was talking to Lord L. when Lady Radnor came up to him and said: 'I want to ask you a question. I am afraid you will think it a very silly one, but in any case I hope you will not ask me why I have put the question?' To this Lord L. courteously assented. She then said: 'Were you at home last night?' He replied, 'Yes.' She said: 'Were you having family prayers at such a time last evening?' With a slight look of surprise he replied, 'Yes, we were.' She then said: 'During the course of the prayers did Lady L. rise from her knees and speak to you, and did you put her aside with a wave of the hand?' Much astonished, Lord L. answered: 'Yes, that was so, but may I inquire why you have asked this question?' To which Lady Radnor answered: 'You promised you wouldn't ask me that!'"

In commenting on the account, Mr. Myers adds :—

"This incident has been independently recounted to me both by Lady Radnor and by Miss A. herself. Another small point not given by Sir J. Barnby is that Miss A. did not at first understand that family prayers were going on, but exclaimed : 'Here are a number of people coming into the room. Why, they're smelling their chairs !' This scene may have been exactly contemporaneous." (*Proc. S.P.R.*, vol. viii. pp. 502, 503.)

Spontaneous Clairvoyance.

This incident was unquestionably very odd, but its evidential value is not lessened by that fact. Instances of a similar detailed perception of events at a distance are occasionally found to occur spontaneously. Two or three cases coming under this category have indeed already been quoted in Chapters VII. and VIII. The type, however, is interesting and important, and it is perhaps worth while citing a few more illustrative cases. It should be noted, however, that whereas in the cases of induced clairvoyance so far considered there is little evidence of any active contribution on the part of other persons to the percipient's impression, in the majority of the spontaneous instances the central figure in the vision was undergoing, or had just emerged from, some unusual experience, and his condition appears to have contributed to bring about the result. In the case which follows the vision represented a dying man. It is noteworthy that, as in other cases already given (*e.g.*, No. 46), the percipient's impression presented a substantially accurate picture of the scene of the drama, but of a scene which preceded its telepathic representation by some hours. It seems probable, therefore, that the vision was merely the reflection of the thoughts of one of the bystanders. And, indeed, in any case it would be difficult to attribute the impression to the mind of the dying man, who could scarcely be supposed to have a mental picture of himself in the act of falling overboard. In the present instance it does not appear that the percipient was personally acquainted with any of the witnesses of the scene, amongst whom, on this interpretation, the agent must be sought, and in this respect the case presents a parallel to Miss A.'s vision.

No. 108.—From MRS. PAQUET.

The case comes to us through the American Branch of the S.P.R. The evidence has been prepared by Mr. A. B. Wood, who received an account of the incident from Mrs. Paquet at a personal interview. Mr. Wood writes on April 29th, 1890:—[1]

"On October 24th, 1889, Edmund Dunn, brother of Mrs. Agnes Paquet, was serving as fireman on the tug *Wolf*, a small steamer engaged in towing vessels in Chicago Harbour. At about 3 o'clock A.M., the tug fastened to a vessel, inside the piers, to tow her up the river. While adjusting the tow-line Mr. Dunn fell or was thrown overboard by the tow-line, and drowned."

Mrs. Paquet's Statement.

"I arose about the usual hour on the morning of the accident, probably about six o'clock. I had slept well throughout the night, had no dreams or sudden awakenings. I awoke feeling gloomy and depressed, which feeling I could not shake off. After breakfast my husband went to his work, and, at the proper time, the children were gotten ready and sent to school, leaving me alone in the house. Soon after this I decided to steep and drink some tea, hoping it would relieve me of the gloomy feelings aforementioned. I went into the pantry, took down the tea canister, and as I turned around my brother Edmund—or his exact image—stood before me and only a few feet away. The apparition stood with back towards me, or, rather, partially so, and was in the act of falling forward—away from me—seemingly impelled by two ropes or a loop of rope drawing against his legs. The vision lasted but a moment, disappearing over a low railing or bulwark, but was very distinct. I dropped the tea, clasped my hands to my face, and exclaimed, 'My God! Ed. is drowned.'

"At about 10.30 A.M. my husband received a telegram from Chicago, announcing the drowning of my brother. When he arrived home he said to me, 'Ed. is sick in hospital at Chicago; I have just received a telegram,' to which I replied, 'Ed. is drowned; I saw him go overboard.' I then gave him a minute description of what I had seen. I stated that my brother, as I saw him, was bareheaded, had on a heavy, blue sailor's shirt, no coat, and that he went over the rail or bulwark. I noticed that his pants' legs were rolled up enough to show the white lining inside. I also described the appearance of the boat at the point where my brother went overboard.

"I am not nervous, and neither before nor since have I had any experience in the least degree similar to that above related.

"My brother was not subject to fainting or vertigo.

"AGNES PAQUET."

Mr. Paquet's Statement.

"At about 10.30 o'clock A.M., October 24th, 1889, I received a telegram from Chicago, announcing the drowning of my brother-in-law, Edmund Dunn, at 3 o'clock that morning. I went directly home, and, wishing to break the force of the sad news I had to convey to my wife, I said to her: 'Ed. is sick in hospital at Chicago; I have just received a telegram.' To which she replied: 'Ed. is drowned; I saw him go overboard.' She then described to me the appearance and dress of her brother as described in her statement; also the appearance of the boat, etc.

"I started at once for Chicago, and when I arrived there I found the appearance of that part of the vessel described by my wife to be exactly as she had described it, though she had never seen the vessel; and the crew verified my wife's description of her brother's dress, etc., except that they thought that he had his hat on at the time of the accident. They said that Mr. Dunn had purchased a pair of pants a few days before the accident occurred, and as they were a trifle long before, wrinkling at the knees, he had worn them rolled up, showing the white lining as seen by my wife."

Visions of this kind are of rare occurrence with waking percipients. The preoccupations of the day-time are probably in themselves sufficient to prevent the emergence of telepathic impressions under ordinary circumstances. But in the present instance it will be observed that the vision occurred in an interval of comparative rest after a period of active occupation. The feeling of gloom and depression mentioned by Mrs. Paquet may have marked the period of incubation, so to speak, of a latent impression of calamity. But a comparison of the case with those which follow suggests that this feeling of depression may have been not the effect, but the necessary condition of the transmission of the agent's thought, and that a slight degree of fatigue or ill-health may under certain circumstances facilitate the emergence of impressions of this kind. It is, at all events, noteworthy that in two of the three cases quoted the percipient was suffering from unusual fatigue or depression, and in the third was recovering from a long illness. In the next two cases the percipient's experience may have been actually synchronous with the events perceived.

No. 109.—From MR. F. A. MARKS.

The accounts, from which extracts are given below, were published in the *Oneida Circular* (U.S.A.) for January 19th, 1874. The percipient, Mr. F. A. Marks, writes :—

W. C., *January 14th*, 1874.

"You wish the simple facts of my dream. They are these:—
One afternoon in October [1873], being tired, I lay down to rest.
I soon fell asleep; at least I have no reason for thinking that I
did not sleep. I was not on the bed more than a few minutes.
During this time I dreamed of being near a large body of
water. I knew it to be the Oneida Lake. The wind was blowing
violently, and the waves ran exceedingly high. While standing
near the lake I felt under a strong disposition to sleep. My
eyes were heavy, they would close themselves. It was with an
exertion that I kept them open. I was like a man under nightmare; struggling to rouse myself, yet only partially successful.
Darkness was settling over me. Suddenly, when the wind was
blowing a gale and the waves seemed rolling one over the other,
a small sail-boat broke upon my sight, driven wildly before the
storm. For the moment it seemed as if it would be lost. It
appeared to be at the mercy of the waves, for they rose high
above its sides and almost concealed it at times. It was
manned by two persons—one in the after part; the other *trying
to pull down the sail!* Their situation was critical. At this
moment a feeling of horror shot through me as I recognised in
the man whose full length I saw standing near the mast and
struggling with the sail my brother Charles! The man in the
stern I did not recognise. In the time of the greatest peril,
something—I can scarcely tell what; I dare not call it an
apparition—gave me the impression that good beings were
interested and watchful over the voyagers.

"The shock I received on seeing my brother did not allow me
to sleep long. On awaking I was troubled, and thought I would
immediately write to Charles, entreating him to be careful.
Afterwards, thinking it merely a dream, I turned my attention
from writing, but I mentioned to Frank Smith that I had a
troubled dream about Charles. After this experience, perhaps
three or four days, a letter was received from Mrs. Mallory
giving an account of Charles' condition when he returned to the
Joppa station.

"This letter recalled the dream; and the coincidence of time
and circumstances made a deep impression on me, though I was
unable then, and am now, to accurately identify the time of my
vision with the time of actual peril described in Mrs. Mallory's
letter. (The letter, however, came so soon as to make it certain
that the peril and the vision were nearly, if not exactly, *simultaneous*.)"

Mr. C. R. Marks explains that on a beautiful day
in October he and a friend sailed eighteen miles down
the lake in a small open boat. They started for the

return voyage on the day following, at 2.45 P.M., in threatening weather. They had gone but a short distance when a violent storm came on, and they were in a position of considerable peril :—

" To add to our apprehensions it began raining, and the wind instead of slacking was evidently increasing. We had gone about two miles when I was startled by a cry from Arthur to 'look out for the sail !' as it was shifting to the other side. I lay down to let the sail pass over me, and got on to the other side of the boat to counteract the effect of the sail. This is told in a few words, but the actual event seemed to take a long time. When down in the boat I heard and felt the swash of the waves coming in, and for a moment I had the impression that Arthur was already in the water and that it would soon be my turn. But on looking round I saw he was still in his place, and also that we had shipped considerable water. The next thing was to take in sail, and that quickly. I let go the halyards, but the sail would not come down, as it was held by a miserable toggle at the top. In the excitement of the moment I jumped upon the seat at the imminent risk of capsizing the boat, and pulled down the sail as far as it would go, which left it about six feet high. This was still dangerous, as the slack of the sail was distended, looking like a huge bag. This was remedied by cutting away the rings in the lower part of the sail and winding up the lower yard. After this, with considerable baling, we got along tolerably well."

Appended is an extract from a letter written by Mr. B. Bristol, with whom Mr. F. A. Marks was working at the time of the vision, corroborating the accounts given above:—

" I was living in Wallingford at that time, raising small fruit. My principal helper was a young man named Frederic Marks, a graduate of Yale Scientific School. Frederic had a brother named Charles, who was living then in Central New York, near Oneida Lake. One rainy afternoon Frederic went upstairs to his room and lay down on a lounge. An hour or so after he came back and said he had just seen his brother Charles in vision, he thought, as he was not conscious of having been asleep. Charles was in a small sail-boat, and a companion with him, who sat in the stern steering. There seemed to be a wild storm prevailing, for the sea ran high. Charles stood in the bow grasping the mast with one arm, with the other he had hold of the boom, which appeared to have broken loose. His dangerous position so frightened Frederic that he awoke, or the vision departed."

In the next case the coincidence was not of itself a striking one, nor, as the account was not sent to the American S.P.R. until six years after the event, is the evidence as good as in the last narrative. But as an incident in itself trivial has remained in the memories of the other persons concerned, as well as in that of the percipient, it may be presumed to have made some impression at the time. The case is quoted from the *Proceedings of the American S.P.R.* (pp. 464-467).

No. 110.—From MRS. L. Z.

"*June 6th*, 1887.

"About the end of March 1881, after recovering from severe illness, while I was yet confined to my bed, I had the following experience. I was staying at the time at 172 Benefit Street, Providence, R.I.

"I had been asleep and suddenly became, as it were, half awake, being conscious of some of the objects in the room. I then heard a voice as if from the room adjoining, and made an effort to see the speaker, but I found myself unable to move. Then appeared, as though in a mist, an ordinary sofa, and behind it the vague outline of a woman's figure. I did not recognise the figure, but I recognised the voice which I heard: it was the voice of my hostess, Mrs. B., who was at that time not in the house. She was saying, 'I am ill and all worn out. Mrs. Z. has been so nervous, and in such a peculiar mental state, that it has quite affected my health' (or words to that effect), 'but I wouldn't for the world have her know it.' I then made a stronger effort to distinguish the figure, and woke completely to find myself in my room with my nurse. I inquired of the nurse who was in the other room, which was used as a sleeping-room by my child and her nurse. She said that no one was there; but I was so convinced that the voice had come from there that I insisted upon her going and looking. She went, but found no one there, and the door into the hall was latched. I then looked at the clock, which was opposite my bed. It was about 5 P.M. In the evening, about 8 P.M., Mrs. B. came up to see me, and I asked her where she had been that afternoon at 5 o'clock. She said that she had been at Mrs. G.'s (about two miles off). I said, 'You were talking about me.' She said,

'Yes, I was,' looking very much surprised. I repeated to her what I had seemed to hear her say, word for word. She was much astonished, and was very curious as to what else I had heard or seen. I told her that it was all very vague, except the appearance of the sofa, which I described in detail as being covered with a peculiar striped linen cloth, green stripes about two inches wide, alternating with pale-drab stripes, somewhat wider, which appeared to be the natural colour of the unbleached linen. She said that she had spoken the words which I had heard, and that she was at the time reclining on a sofa, but she said that the sofa was covered with green velvet.

"Next day Mrs. G. paid me a visit, and after hearing my story she exclaimed, 'You're right. The sofa had at the time the covering which you describe; it had just been put on. There is green velvet under the covering. I suppose Mrs. B. didn't notice the cover.'"

Mrs. B. writes :—

"In the year 1881, while living in Providence, on Benefit Street, No. 272, Mrs. Z. was with me, and during the winter of 1880 and the spring of 1881 she was in a peculiar mental state, and on two occasions read my thoughts and heard my voice. I remember distinctly on one occasion, when I returned from a visit to a friend, Mrs. Z. repeated the conversation that had passed between my friend and myself, and spoke of my lying on a lounge that had a striped covering. I said, 'No, it was a green plush,' but found afterwards she was right, as the summer covering had been put on.

"ELIZABETH L. B.

"BROOKLYN, N.Y., *June* 1887."

Mrs. G. writes from Providence, July 12th, 1887 :—

"When I received your note I could not at all recall the circumstances of the vision you referred to, but afterwards Mrs. B. refreshed my memory upon the subject, and I distinctly recalled it. It was as Mrs. Z. related it to you. At the time it occurred, I remember, I thought it quite marvellous.

"Sickness had prevented my writing you these few lines before. "C. B. Y. G."

Even if the conversation was correctly reported, it is probably not beyond the range of conjecture by a morbidly sensitive invalid; but the details given of the appearance of the sofa cover seem to indicate a telepathic faculty, like Dr. Phinuit's, of drawing on the agent's unconscious perceptions. Mrs. L. Z. gives also an account of a voluntarily induced clairvoyant dream, in connection with the same friend, which occurred about this time, and this account also Mrs. B. is able to corroborate. The whole case is interesting as serving to indicate that some conditions of disease may be favourable to this form of telepathy, and as being the only case which I am able to quote of spontaneous clairvoyance in which the impressions transferred were of quite trivial incidents. Mrs. Z. appears to have been in a state between sleeping and waking.

The next case occurred in a dream at night. The dream, it will be noted, caused the percipient to awake.

No. 111.—From MRS. FREESE.

"GRANITE LODGE, CHISELHURST,
March 1884.

"In September 1881 I had another curious dream, so vivid that I seemed to *see* it.

"My two boys of eighteen and sixteen were staying in the Black Forest, under the care of a Dr. Fresenius. I must say here that I always supposed the boys would go everywhere together, and I never should have supposed that in that lonely country, so new to them, they would be out after dark. My husband and I were staying at St. Leonards, and one Saturday night I woke at about 12 o'clock (rather before, as I heard it strike) having just seen vividly a dark night on a mountain, and my eldest boy lying on his back at the bottom of some steep place, his eyes wide open, and saying, 'Good-bye, mother and father, I shall never see you again.' I woke with a feeling of anxiety, and the next morning when I told it to my husband, though we both agreed it was absurd to be anxious, yet he would write and tell the boys we hoped they would never go out alone after dark. To my surprise my eldest boy, to whom I wrote the dream, wrote back expressing his great astonishment, for on that Saturday night he was coming home over the mountains, past 11 o'clock; it was pitch dark, and he slipped and fell down some 12 feet or so, and landed on his back, looking up to the sky. However, he was not much hurt, and soon picked himself up and got home all right. He did not say what thoughts passed through his mind as he fell."

In answer to inquiries, Mrs. Freese adds :—

"*Before* my son wrote about his fall in the Black Forest, I related my dream to my husband, and as he seemed a little moved by it, I wrote an account of it to my boy, saying his father did not wish them to be out after dark alone. I had not told my boy *when* it was, deeming that immaterial, but when in his letter, received days after, he said, 'Was it Saturday night, because then so-and-so ?' I remembered what I should not otherwise have noted, that it was Saturday night ; for on the Sunday morning my husband, being much worried about some business matter, elected to spend the morning with me in the fields instead of going to church, and as much to divert his mind as anything I related to him my dream of the night before."

Mrs. Freese sent us the letter from her son, which contained the following passage :—

" With regard to your dream : did you dream it on September 3rd ? if so it was on that night, coming home rather late, that I fell down a precipice of 8 feet, or perhaps more, in the dark, and might have broken my neck, but didn't. However, I don't think you will find me walking about after dark more than I can help, as the roads are very dark, and the fogs in the village awful.

"FRED. E. FREESE."

[September 3rd, 1881, was a Saturday.]

Mr. Freese wrote on March 7th, 1884, to confirm his wife's account of the dream.

An account by Dr. Gibotteau, given in the *Annales des Sciences Psychiques*, Nov.-Dec. 1892, deserves consideration in this connection. It is the record of a series of unusually successful experiments in the transfer of visual images. But the success obtained was apparently due to a condition of spontaneous clairvoyant perceptivity on the part of the subject. The percipient, who was throughout in a state not clearly distinguishable from that of normal wakefulness, was a head-nurse at the hospital to which Dr. Gibotteau was attached. The occurrence took place in 1888. Madame R. has now remarried and Dr. Gibotteau has lost sight of her, so that her testimony cannot be obtained, and unfortunately Dr. Gibotteau appears not to have committed the incident to writing until 1892. The account therefore represents merely the general impression left after the lapse of some years upon the memory of a trained observer by a very unusual and striking experience. Briefly, Dr. Gibotteau reports that he succeeded in inducing in Madame R., by the mere silent will, an immense number of striking hallucinatory, or rather semi-hallucinatory mental pictures. The ideas thus transferred included transformations and imaginary movements of objects actually present in the room ; the appearance of human figures and animals, a serpent, a rabbit, a dog, horses, a bear rampant ; and the disappearance of Dr. Gibotteau himself, leaving behind him an empty arm-chair. The séance lasted for nearly three hours, with very few failures of any kind, and left the narrator much exhausted.[1]

The experience, as described, it will be seen, was of an almost unprecedented kind. It is by no means clear that under a natural classification either this or others of the somewhat heterogeneous phenomena described in the present and preceding chapters would be grouped under the same genus, or that any of them are rightly called telepathic. They are provisionally ascribed to telepathy, in the sense already explained (p. 326, Chapter XIV.), because if we accept the facts at all, that appears to be the cheapest solution. The writer is not committed to telepathy as the true explanation ; he has adopted it provisionally, as an alternative to some hypothetical faculty of direct intuition beyond the range of sense. If to any reader who accepts the writer's estimate of the alleged facts as beyond chance or misrepresentation, the hypothesis of telepathy appears in such cases to be strained, it may be replied that when the choice of

---

[1] A translation of Dr. Gibotteau's account is given by Mr. Myers, *Proc. S.P.R.*, vol. viii. pp. 468, 469.

explanation seems to lie between telepathy and some faculty even more dubious and more remote from ordinary analogies, it is right that the hypothesis of telepathy should be strained—if necessary, to the breaking-point—before we invoke a stage-deity to cut the knot.

CHAPTER XVI.

THEORIES AND CONCLUSIONS.

CONSIDERATION more or less adequate has now been given to the various phenomena in which there is proof apparent of the action of telepathy. The experimental evidence has shown that a simple sensation or idea may be transferred from one mind to another, and that this transference may take place alike in the normal state and in the hypnotic trance. It has been shown also that the transferred idea may be reproduced in the percipient's organism under various disguises; at one time, for instance, it may cause vague distress or terror, or a blind impulse to action; under other circumstances it may inspire definite and complicated movements, as those involved in writing. Again, it may induce sleep or even more deep-seated organic effects, such as hysteria or local anæsthesia. Once more, it may be embellished with imagery presumably furnished by the percipient's own mind, and may appear as a dream or hallucination representing the distant agent. And these various results may be obtained either by deliberate experiment; as the result of some crisis affecting another mind; or, lastly, as following on some peculiar state of receptivity established, under conditions not yet clearly ascertained, in the percipient's mind.

But it would not be reasonable to infer that the few hundreds or thousands of examples collected during the last twelve years by a few groups of investigators exhaust the possibilities or indicate the limits of telepathic action. By those, at least, who accept the demonstration of telepathy as a real agency it will hardly be anticipated that its action should be confined to the comparatively few cases which present a coincidence sufficiently striking to be quoted as ostensive instances. That the distribution, indeed, of telepathic sensitiveness at the present time should be sporadic—as the distribution of a musical ear or the power of visualisation is sporadic—may appear not improbable. But we should be prepared to find instances of its presumptive operation which fall below the level of demonstration, and might with almost equal plausibility be referred to some other cause. And such instances we do certainly find, in simultaneous dreams and in vague presentiments, and in innumerable coincidences of thought and expression in ordinary life. And the suggestion that the same power may serve as an auxiliary to more completely systematised modes of expression, though incapable of proof, may yet be thought worthy of consideration. It is conceivable, for instance, that it may aid the intercourse of a mother with her infant child, that the influence of the orator may be due not only to the spoken word, and that even in our daily conversation thoughts may pass by this means which find no outward expression. The personal influence of the operator in hypnotism may perhaps be regarded as a proof presumptive of telepathy. When all the phenomena of "mesmerism" were attributed, by the few who believed in them, to the passage of a fluid from the mesmerist to his patient, it was easy to credit the successful operator with as large an endowment of available fluid as the facts might seem to require. But from those who assert that the results are not merely explicable, but are in practice to be explained, as due to suggestion alone, no entirely satisfactory explanation has ever been forthcoming of the observed differences between one operator and another. It is difficult to believe that Liébeault, Bernheim, Schrenck-Notzing, Van Eeden, Lloyd

Tuckey, Bramwell, etc., have succeeded where so many others have failed, merely through the exercise of greater patience, or the possession of an established reputation, which after all is based on the successes which it is now invoked to explain.[1] And the fact that a large proportion of well - known hypnotists have acted as agents in successful telepathic experiments of an unusual kind is a further argument in the same direction. There are, moreover, some more dubious beliefs, for the most part discredited by educated persons, yet persisting with a singular vitality, which receive in telepathy a simple and perhaps sufficient explanation. It has already been shown that some of the marvels of Dr. Dee and the Specularii have been paralleled by recent visions in "the crystal," revealing events then passing at a distance unknown to the seer; and that the nucleus of fact in some legends of ghosts and haunted houses is probably to be sought in a telepathic hallucination. And many of the alleged wonders of witchcraft and of ancient magic in general, when disentangled from the accretions formed round them by popular myth and superstition, present a marked resemblance to some of the facts recorded in this book. It is obvious, for instance, that the same power which inhibited Mr. Beard's utterance (p. 83) could have prevented the witch's victim from repeating the Lord's Prayer. And Mr. Godfrey (p. 228), in the sixteenth century, might have found that to appear in two places at once would be perilously strong evidence of unlawful powers.[2]

---

[1] The fact that most, if not all, the medical men quoted would themselves reject the explanation hinted at in the text, and would regard their own success as due rather to skill and patience than to any specific endowment, should, of course, have due weight, but cannot be regarded as decisive.

[2] See also the account given by Dr. Gibotteau in the *Annales des Sciences Psychiques* of the power possessed by *Berthe* (see *ante*, p. 139) of causing people to stumble or lose their sense of direction. Mr. Andrew Lang has recently drawn attention to the remarkable resemblances between accounts of medieval magic, etc., and modern telepathic phenomena (see, *e.g.*, his article in *Cont. Review*, Sept. 1893).

But there are two special kinds of marvels, whose occurrence has been widely vouched for within quite recent times by men of proved ability and trained in the experimental methods of the modern laboratory, which deserve to be considered in this connection—the influence of metals and magnets on the human organism, and the physical phenomena of Spiritualism. Baron von Reichenbach in the last generation published the results of numerous observations on various sensitives, who alleged that they could see flame-like emanations from crystals, from the poles of a magnet, from the bodies of the sick, and from newly-made graves, and that they experienced various sensations from contact with magnets and metals. On the evidence of Reichenbach's prolonged and laborious researches the existence of this supposed magnetic sense obtained a certain degree of credence. Accordingly the S.P.R., shortly after its foundation in 1882, conducted a series of control experiments on a number of persons with a powerful electro-magnet, which was alternately magnetised and demagnetised by a commutator in an adjoining room. Of forty-five persons tested three professed to see luminous appearances on the poles of the magnet; and on two or three occasions they were able to indicate with surprising accuracy throughout a whole evening the exact moment at which the current was switched on or off—the light, as they alleged, appearing or disappearing simultaneously. But these isolated successes were not repeated, and the very conditions of the experiment implied that it was known to some of those present whether or not the magnet was charged. Now it is obvious that unless special precautions are taken to guard against the telepathic[1] communication of this knowledge all experiments of the kind must be inconclusive ; and other investigators have failed

---

[1] It is possible that we need not go so far as telepathy for an explanation. Slight indications unconsciously apprehended may have furnished the necessary clue in all cases, as they almost certainly did in some.

to detect any trace of the so-called magnetic sense.[1]

Within the last few years this supposed sensitiveness has appeared in another form. M. Babinski of the Salpetrière claims to have shown that certain ailments—such, for example, as hemiplegia and hysterical mutism—can be transferred by the influence of a magnet from one side of the body to another, or from one patient to another. MM. Binet and Féré[2] find that unilateral hallucinations can be shifted by the same influence from one side of the body to the other, and that in general memories and sensations—real or imaginary—can be modified and destroyed by the magnet. And MM. Bourru, Burot, Luys, and others have published whole treatises dealing with the alleged influence of various drugs and metals on certain patients. A few drops of laurelwater enclosed in a flask and brought near to the patient, will, according to these writers, induce ecstasy; ipecacuanha will cause vomiting; alcohol intoxication, and so on; each drug, though securely stoppered and sealed, giving rise to the appropriate physical symptoms in the patient. However, MM. Bernheim,[3] Delboeuf,[4] and Jules Voisin[5] showed some time since, and Mr. Ernest Hart[6] has lately repeated the demonstration, that the same results can be made to follow if the patient is led to believe that an inert piece of wood is a magnet, or that an empty flask contains a powerful drug. It may be fairly assumed therefore that when special precautions are not shown to have been taken—and there is little

---

[1] See *Proc. S.P.R.*, vol. i. p. 230, vol. ii. p. 56; *Phil. Mag.*, April 1883; *Proc. Amer. S.P.R.*, p. 116.

[2] *Animal Magnetism* (International Science Series), pp. 264 *et seq.* Cf. Ottolenghi and Lombroso, in *Rev. Phil.*, Oct. 1889, on polarisation of hallucinations by magnets.

[3] *Rev. de l'Hypnotisme*, Dec. 1887.

[4] *Ibid.*, June 1887.

[5] *Rev. des Sciences Hypnotiques*, 1887-88, p. 111.

[6] *Brit. Med. Journal*, Jan. 1893.

evidence that such precautions were as a rule taken—
suggestion by word or look would be sufficient to
account for the phenomena observed. But it is
obvious that negative experiments of this kind are
not in themselves conclusive; and it is difficult to
believe that all the results recorded by investigators
of such experience as Babinski, Féré, and others
could have been due simply to carelessness on their
part, or hypnotic cunning on the part of the subject.
Indeed, in commenting on the counter experiments
made by M. Jules Voisin, MM. Bourru and Burot
expressly state that if the results obtained by them
are to be attributed to suggestion, as he proposes, it is
"*une suggestion sans parole, sans geste, sans pensée
même.*"[1] But a suggestion without word, gesture, or
conscious thought is an accurate description of one
form of telepathic suggestion; and if such suggestion
has indeed been at work we have an explanation of
the otherwise inexplicable reliance placed by these
French investigators upon experiments so much con-
troverted, and their faith in an interpretation so little
supported by scientific analogy.

That in general the so-called physical phenomena
of Spiritualism are due to self-deception and exaggeration on the one hand, and to fraud on the
other, is a proposition which to most readers, it is
likely, will seem to need little demonstration. And
there are of course many cases, such as the recent
experiments with Eusapia Palladino[2] at Milan, where,
though competent observers—Richet, Schiaparelli,
Lombroso, Brofferio—have seen things beyond their
power to explain, yet the line between what was
possible to fraudulent ingenuity and what was not

---

[1] *Rev. des Sciences Hypnotiques*, 1887-88, p. 151. See also *Force
Psychique et Suggestion Mentale*, by Dr Claude Perronnet, pp. 21-26,
who shows clearly how thought-transference may vitiate many hypnotic
experiments.
[2] *Annales des Sciences Psychiques*, Jan.-Feb. 1893; *Proc. S.P.R.*,
vol. ix. p. 218.

possible cannot be drawn with sufficient sharpness to warrant the invocation of any new agency. But there are other records which cannot be so summarily dismissed. Thus Mr. Crookes, F.R.S.,[1] has described the movements of a balance, specially constructed for the purpose of the experiments, in the presence of himself and other observers, under conditions which seemed to render it impossible for the effects to have been produced by the muscular force of any of those present. Lord Lindsay has testified to having seen Home's stature elongated to the extent of 11 inches, and heavy tables and other articles of furniture rise in the air without visible support, and to having himself, at Home's instance, handled, and seen others handle, red-hot coals with impunity. Other witnesses of repute have testified to the appearance of strange luminous bodies, the raining down of liquid scent, the production of inexplicable musical sounds and other phenomena equally marvellous.[2]

Now it is difficult to believe that Mr. Crookes and those with him could in their normal senses have imagined movements of a self-registering balance which never really took place, or have failed to detect actual movements on Home's part ; or that Home could have seemed to Lord Lindsay and others to add some fraction of a cubit to his stature or to float unsupported in the air, when he was really only stretching cramped muscles, or supporting himself on a captive balloon, or by unseen wires ; or that when he was seen to carry hot coals about the room, and to place them, still glowing, upon the bare head of Mr. S. C. Hall, he relied upon the observers overlooking such inconspicuous objects as a pair of tongs and an asbestos

---

[1] *Proc. S. P. R.*, vol. vi. p. 98.
[2] See, for instance, the *Report on Spiritualism of the London Dialectical Society;* Experiences of Mr. Stainton Moses in *Proc. S. P. R.,* vol. ix. p. 245 ; and article, "Spiritualism," in the *Encyclopædia Britannica,* by Mrs. Henry Sidgwick, and in *Chambers' Encyclopædia,* by Alfred Russel Wallace, F. R. S.

skull-cap—alternatives which must have been at
least as obvious at the time to the observers who,
by recording these things, have imperilled their
reputation for scientific acumen, and even for common sense, as now to their irresponsible critics.
But it is certainly not less difficult to believe, on
such grounds as these, in the discovery of a new
physical force—or rather new forces ; for the energy
which could move a balance cannot properly be
assumed to be identical with the energy which
could increase Home's stature, or restrain the
action of fire ; or, as elsewhere recorded, bring
delicate flowers uninjured through closed doors.
But fortunately we are not compelled to choose
between the alternatives of such almost incredible
stupidity and a multiplicity of new modes of
energy. It has been plausibly suggested that the
observers in such cases are the subjects of a
collective hallucination. It is true that we have
no precise analogy to support such a hypothesis.
The hallucinations of hypnotism can be imposed
upon several subjects simultaneously by dint of
repeated verbal suggestions. But here there were
none of the recognised preliminaries to the hypnotic
trance : in many of the recorded cases the observers
did not know what to expect, and it is clear that
verbal suggestion was not essential to the results;
while there is no trace of that break in the continuity
of consciousness which elsewhere marks the passage
from the hypnotic to the normal state. Moreover,
in some of the best-attested cases it was the presumed operator, and not the witnesses, who was
entranced. Assuredly if the phenomena described
were due to hypnotic hallucination, it was hallucination without any of the characteristic features of
hypnotism. But if we assume—as in the absence
of any evidence to the contrary we are entitled,
if not bound, to assume—that the observers were
in their normal state, we can find no nearer parallel

to this supposed hallucination than the collective telepathic hallucinations of which examples have been given in Chapter XII.[1]

It is true that the parallel is by no means exact. The hypothesis requires us to suppose not merely that investigators of spiritualistic phenomena are liable to see, by hallucination, things which are not there, but also that they are occasionally withheld, by hallucination, from seeing actual movements and objects. For Mr. Crookes' automatic balance recorded a real movement; flowers and other objects have actually been brought into locked rooms; furniture has been demonstrably displaced, or has even moved before the eyes of the investigators, and been found at the conclusion of the experiment in its new position; an actual blister was raised on Lord Lindsay's skin by the touch of a live coal which Home held in a hand apparently bare. Now if these results were due to the action of known forces, muscular and other, it seems clear that some of the medium's movements and appliances escaped observation. We have, however, no record, so far as I know, of collective negative hallucination telepathically caused. But it may be pointed out that whilst it is only in unusual circumstances that a hallucination of the kind could attract sufficient attention to be recorded, negative hallucinations can be imposed without difficulty on a hypnotic subject. So that their telepathic origination in the circumstances suggested presents no greater *à priori* difficulty than that of positive hallucinations. There are, however, other differences between the col-

---

[1] It need hardly be said that the oft-quoted story of the European who came late and unobserved to the performance of an Indian Fakir, and from a distant tree saw him cutting up a pumpkin when the crowd saw him cutting up a child, is merely *ben trovato*. Nor, indeed, until we have contemporaneous accounts of these performances from carefully trained observers is there need of any such hypothesis to explain the feats of Indian jugglery. See Mr. Hodgson's article in *Proc. S.P.R.*, vol. ix. p. 354.

lective hallucinations recorded in Chapter XII. and those which the hypothesis requires. For the former were for the most part vague and transitory, and were rarely shared by more than two persons ; whilst the hypothetical hallucinations of the spiritualistic séance are persistent, and may affect several persons simultaneously and to an equal extent. It may be suggested, however, that the different conditions in the latter case—the common expectancy, the attunement of the minds of all present to a common mood, the absence of external solicitation to the senses—may be sufficient to account for the differing characteristics of the phenomena observed.

It may be objected that the problem does not require the intervention of such a *Deus ex machina* as collective hallucination ; that fraud and malobservation are adequate to account for all the facts reported. I confess that I am unable so lightly to set aside the deliberate testimony of men of proved scientific distinction, whose word is still regarded as authoritative in observations not less delicate, and for results to the layman hardly less dubious. But I do not suggest that the phenomena, however interpreted, are likely to add anything to the proof of telepathy. I would merely urge that, as until the possibility of thought-transference in its various forms has been patiently and rigorously excluded, odylic flames and magnetic influences must remain unproven, so, in dealing with that residuum of evidence for the physical phenomena called spiritualistic which appears inexplicable by fraud and malobservation, the possibility of collective hallucination telepathically caused should be kept in view.[1]

It should be observed that the treatment of tele-

---

[1] The explanation suggested in the text for the physical phenomena of Spiritualism is worked out in some detail by Von Hartmann, the philosopher of the unconscious, in a little treatise on *Spiritism*, which has been translated into English by "C.C.M.," 1885. But Von

pathy by those responsible for the word involves as little of theory as Newton's conception of gravitation. What Newton did was to find the simplest general expression for the observed facts by saying that the heavenly bodies acted upon each other with a certain measurable force. He did not attempt to explain the mode of this action. And whilst succeeding astronomers have for the most part been content to follow Newton's example, the science has, nevertheless, advanced in a steady and continuous progression. So the conception of telepathy simply colligates the observed facts of spontaneous and experimental thought-transference, as instances of the action of one mind upon another. The nature of the action the theory does not discuss; it merely defines it negatively, as being outside the normal sensory channels. In accordance with this view, Mr. Gurney, and the English investigators generally, have consistently employed psychical terms in their discussion of the subject: they have spoken of the transmission of ideas, not neuroses, and of the affection of mind by mind, rather than of brain by brain.[1] This treatment involves no prejudgment of the question. Whatever may be the nature of the cause, we know the effects at present only in their psychical aspect, and in default of a physical theory, as psychical it seemed convenient to discuss them. This mode of speech is of course as legitimate as the popular usage which permits us, when the sun's rays strike upon our retina, to ignore the intervening physical processes, and to express only the psychical result, " I see the sun." But Mr. Gurney and his colleagues were further influenced in adopting and maintaining this usage by a conviction that the advancement of the subject has

Hartmann believes that some of the phenomena are produced by a hypothetical nerve-force under the direction of the somnambulic self of the medium—a prodigality of hypotheses which in the circumstances is surely superfluous.

[1] See *Phantasms of the Living*, vol. i. pp. 110-113.

not hitherto been dependent upon the discovery of physical correlates for the observed psychical action, and that the energy which would be diverted to the search for explanations, could be more fruitfully employed on the still imperfect demonstration that there is something to be explained.

But it is obvious that this attitude of reserve cannot be maintained indefinitely. Since Mr. Gurney wrote the sum-total of observations and experiments has steadily increased, and there is hardly any longer room for doubt that we have something here which no physical processes at present known can adequately account for. It is not possible to observe facts without speculating on the underlying law : it is the law indicated by the facts, more than the facts themselves, which is of permanent interest to the human mind. Nor indeed can any fruitful observation be long maintained, which is not accompanied, guided, and stimulated by theoretical speculation. Professor Lodge has called upon us, in this matter, to " press the doctrine of ultimate intelligibility ;" [1] and in so saying he has at once given articulate expression to an impulse from whose blind urgency no student of nature can escape, and has formulated what is after all the *differentia* of the scientific mind. The average man accepts things as they are ; the man of science presses the doctrine of ultimate intelligibility.

But however legitimate at the present stage of the inquiry theoretical speculation might seem, such speculation has for the most part been conspicuously wanting in the treatment of the subject by those best qualified to deal with it. At any rate the attitude of most continental investigators, like that of their English colleagues, has been a purely positive one. They have contented themselves with describing in psychical terms the psychical phenomena which they

[1] Presidential Address to the Section of Mathematics and Physics of the British Association, August 1891.

have observed. There are, indeed, some competent inquirers at the present time who incline to attribute thought-transference to the direct action of mind upon mind, or to some process yet more transcendent, just as in the last generation there were some who thought they were able to discern, in such instances as came under their notice, proof of the agency of disembodied spirits. And Von Hartmann, boldly accepting the facts wholesale, ascribes them to a communication between finite minds effected through the intermediation of the Absolute.[1] But until we have exhausted the resources of the world which we know, we should perhaps conclude, with Mistress Quickly, that there is no need to trouble ourselves with any such thoughts yet.

Any attempt at a physical explanation is, of course, beset with many difficulties. To begin with, there is no sense-organ for our presumed new mode of sensation; nor at the present stage of physiological knowledge is there likelihood that we can annex any as yet unappropriated organ to register telepathic stimuli, as the semicircular canals are supposed to register the movements of the body in space. In lacking an elaborate machinery specially adapted for receiving its messages and concentrating them on the peripheral end of the nerves, telepathy would thus seem to be on a par with radiant energy affecting the general surface of the body. But the sensations of heat and cold are without quality or difference, other than difference of degree; whereas telepathic messages, as we have seen, purport often to be as detailed and precise as those conveyed by the same radiant energy falling on the organs of vision.

---

[1] "If all individuals of higher or lower order are rooted in the Absolute, retrogressively in this they have a second connection among themselves, and there is requisite only a restoration of the *rapport* or telephonic junction (*Telephonanschluss*) between two individuals in the Absolute, by an intense interest of the will, to bring about the unconscious interchange between them without sense-mediation." (*Spiritism*, by Ed. von Hartmann, trans. C.C.M., p. 75.)

As regards the mode of transmission, we find first the theory of a fluid, which owes its origin to Mesmer, and was in vogue at a time when fluids were still fashionable in scientific circles. Dr. Baréty[1] has recently revived this theory in a new form. He alleges that there is a nerve-energy (*force neurique rayonnante*) which radiates from the eyes, the fingers, and the breath of the operator, and is capable of producing various effects upon hypnotised subjects. He finds that a knitting-needle acts as a conductor for this force, and water as a non-conductor; that the nerve-rays can be focussed by a magnifying-glass, refracted by a prism, and reflected from a mirror or other plane surface at an angle equal to the angle of incidence. Dr. Baréty has omitted to state whether in the latter case the rays are polarised, nor has he shown whether the force varies inversely to the square of the distance. But the consideration of these remarkable results need hardly detain us long, since they can all readily be explained by suggestion, verbal or telepathic.

If we leave fluids and radiant nerve-energy on one side, we find practically only one mode suggested for the telepathic transference—viz., that the physical changes which are the accompaniments of thought or sensation in the agent are transmitted from the brain as undulations in the intervening medium, and thus excite corresponding changes in some other brain, without any other portion of the organism being necessarily implicated in the transmission. This hypothesis has found its most philosophical champion in Dr. Ochorowicz, who has devoted several chapters of his book, *De la Suggestion mentale*, to the discussion of the various theories on the subject. He begins by recalling the reciprocal convertibility of all physical forces with which we are acquainted, and

---

[1] *Des Propriétés physiques d'une force particulière du corps humain,* 1882.

especially draws attention to what he calls the law of reversibility, a law which he illustrates by a description of the photophone. The photophone is an instrument in which a mirror is made to vibrate to the human voice. The mirror reflects a ray of light, which, vibrating in its turn, falls upon a plate of selenium, modifying its electric conductivity. The intermittent current so produced is transmitted through a telephone, and the original articulate sound is reproduced. Now in hypnotised subjects—and M. Ochorowicz does not in this connection treat of thought-transference between persons in the normal state—the equilibrium of the nervous system, he sees reason to believe, is profoundly affected. The nerve-energy liberated in this state, he points out, " cannot pass beyond" the subject's brain "without being transformed. Nevertheless, like any other force, it cannot remain isolated; like any other force it escapes, but in disguise. Orthodox science allows it only one way out, the motor nerves. These are the holes in the dark lantern through which the rays of light escape. . . . Thought remains in the brain, just as the chemical energy of the galvanic battery remains in the cells, but each is represented outside by its correlative energy, which in the case of the battery is called the electric current, but for which in the other we have as yet no name. In any case there is some correlative energy—for the currents of the motor nerves do not and cannot constitute the only dynamic equivalent of cerebral energy—to represent all the complex movements of the cerebral mechanism." [1]

Considered purely in its physiological aspect, such a theory appears to present no special difficulty; or rather, to put the matter more exactly, our ignorance of the ultimate nature of nerve-processes is so nearly complete as to permit us to theorise *in vacuo*,

---

[1] *De la Suggestion mentale*, Paris, 1887, pp. 511, 512.

25

with little risk of encountering any insuperable obstacle. It is true that Professor G. Stanley Hall,[1] in commenting on such physical theories of telepathy, maintains that they contravene well-established physical laws:—"The law of 'isolated conductivity,' formulated fully by Johannes Müller, which Helmholtz compares in importance to the law of gravity, first brought order into the field of neurology by insisting that impressions never jump from one fibre to another. . . . Is it likely that a neural state should jump from one brain to another, through a great interval, when intense stimuli on one nerve cannot affect another in the closest contact with it?" But it is clear that the "law" in question is merely a generalisation from observed facts, and from facts, moreover, not of the same order as those now under discussion. For the question here is not of the affection of another nerve-fibre in the same organism, but of a nerve-centre in another organism. And whilst it must have seemed *à priori* probable that between nerves belonging to the same system induction would not take place, because the alternative could hardly fail to be injurious to the organism, and that the susceptibility to such induction, if originally present, would have been eliminated in the course of evolution, it is at least theoretically conceivable that between different organisms induction might have persisted as innocuous, or even have been developed as positively beneficial.

In current theories it is assumed that there are changes in brain-substance correlated with psychical events, and that these changes, in their ultimate analysis, are of the nature of vibrations. That these vibrations should be capable of in some way propagating themselves through the surrounding medium would seem therefore a natural corollary. The real objections to such physical theories appear to be of a

[1] *American Journal of Psychology*, vol. i., No. i.

more general kind—viz., the improbability that any
such capacity of nervous induction should have
remained unobserved until now; and the difficulty of
supposing vibrations so minute to be capable of
producing effects at so great a distance, and to have
a selective capacity so finely adjusted that out of all
the thousands of persons within the radius, say, of
such a brain-wave as that set a-going by Mr. Cleave
(p. 234), only one set of brain-molecules should be
stirred to sympathetic vibration.   The first difficulty
in its psychical aspect has already been touched upon
at the commencement of this chapter, and need not
here be further considered.   The second is more
serious.   It is difficult to find an exact parallel for
the transmission across a considerable intervening
space of energy at once so minute in quantity and so
highly specialised.   Mr. W. H. Preece has indeed
shown that a current can be induced in a closed
circuit at a distance of some three miles or more,
and Professor Lodge has reminded us (*loc. cit.*)
that "all magnets are sympathetically connected,
so that, if suitably suspended, a vibration from one
disturbs others, even though they be distant ninety-
two million miles."   But the forces engaged are in
the one case on a commercial, in the other on a
cosmic scale.   Yet the difficulty is not, perhaps,
insuperable.   The amount of energy which has been
proved capable, at the distance of half a mile, of
inducing sleep in a French peasant woman may be
readily conceived as not more attenuated than those
"sweet influences" which are yet potent enough to
summon up before us the vision of the Pleiades or
the glowing nebula of Orion.   Nor need the difficulty
of selection trouble us much; for, after all, one of
the chief characteristics of organic life in general
is the power—a power ever more differentiated in
the higher organisms—of reacting only to selected
stimuli.   In short, it is too soon to say that any
physical communication between living beings of

the kind suggested is inconceivable. We shall be justified in affirming or denying its possibility on the day when we have guessed the secret of our own existence, and are able to explain how some fraction of a millegramme of albumen can contain not merely the promise of life, but the germ of a particular and individual organism, which shall reveal its own pedigree and contain in itself an epitome of life on our planet.

Until, therefore, we know more of the nature of the cerebral changes which are presumed to be the physical concomitants of thought, we are at most entitled to suggest that some kind of vibrations, propagated somehow through a conjectural medium from an unspecified nerve-centre, may possibly explain the transference of thought. Our main justification at the present time for discussing theories which aim at some solution is that they may indicate the lines on which experiment and observation may be usefully directed. Thus, it is not known how far the results depend on the state of health of the parties to the experiments, on their occupations and state of consciousness at the time ; whether blood-relationship or familiar intimacy between agent and percipient is conducive to success ; or whether the transmission is in any way affected by the introduction of more than one agent. And though some progress has been made in tracing the development of the transmitted idea after it has reached the percipient's mind, observations on the relation of the agent's impression to that of the percipient are at present few and isolated. The difficulties of systematic experiment in this direction are considerable, as will be apparent to any one who carefully studies the reports of the Brighton experiments (pp. 65-80); but it would seem that further investigation might be expected to throw light upon such questions as whether the percipient's original impression is necessarily of the same kind as the agent's; whether in the case of visual impressions lateral inversion or complementary colours can be detected, and so on.

Once more, but little has been learnt of the purely mechanical conditions under which the transmission is effected. There are indeed indications that contact facilitates the transference;[1] but from the difficulty of discriminating, when contact is permitted, between thought-transference and muscle-reading, even thus much can hardly be affirmed with certainty. On the analogy of the known physical forces it is of course to be anticipated that the difficulty of effecting telepathic communication would increase very rapidly with the distance. Yet even here experimental verification is difficult to obtain. It is obvious, indeed, in our experiments, that an increased interval between agent and percipient, especially if a wall or floor is made to intervene, has affected the results prejudicially. But it is by no means clear, as already said, how far the observed effects are to be attributed, not to the physical obstacle of the intervening space, but to the psychical effect produced thereby on the parties to the experiment.

There is, however, a difference, already referred to, in the characteristics of the ideas transferred at close quarters, and those transferred at a distance, which is so marked and so general as to call for some explanation of this kind. In the experiments conducted in the same room or house, and in most of the spontaneous cases at close quarters, the idea transferred corresponds to a mental image consciously present to the mind of the agent. But the cases, whether experimental or spontaneous, of such detailed transference at a distance of more than a mile or two are very few—too few to justify any valid generalisation. For in most cases of thought-transference at a distance the idea transferred is one not consciously present to the agent's mind at all—the idea of his own personality.

[1] See, for instance, Professor Lodge's paper in *Proc. S.P.R.*, vol. vii. p. 374.

To some critics indeed (see *Mind*, 1887, p. 280) this difficulty has seemed so serious as to suggest doubts of the propriety of referring the two sets of results to a common category; and Von Hartmann, whilst claiming, as already said, connection through the Absolute as the explanation of the results obtained at a distance, is content to postulate some kind of nervous induction in the case of experiments at close quarters. But if we examine the facts more closely we find, as has already been shown in some of the trials conducted by MM. Gibert and Pierre Janet in inducing sleep at a distance, and in a few other cases (*e.g.*, Nos. 40, 53, 58), that the idea of the personality of the agent may be transferred to the percipient, together with the specific idea present to the agent's mind. Moreover, in the recorded cases of thought-transference at close quarters, with hardly any exception, the presence of the agent was known to the percipient, and no evidence for the telepathic transmission of the idea of him can therefore be furnished. But since the idea of self is probably always present as part of the permanent substratum of consciousness, and since we have actual evidence that in some cases that idea may be communicated to the percipient, together with the idea consciously willed by the agent, it seems permissible to conclude that it may form an element in every case of transference. And if this be admitted, not merely will the difficulty referred to disappear, but some progress will have been made towards obtaining experimental verification of the physical effects of distance on telepathic transmission. For it would seem to follow that the telepathic energy, which at close quarters is able to effect the transference even of the trivial and momentary contents of the agent's mind, is competent when acting at a distance to convey only those continuous and more massive vibrations which may be presumed to correspond to his conception of his own personality. That the agent is not consciously "thinking of himself" need not prevent us from accepting this view. Nor would a like unconsciousness on the part of the percipient be a serious objection. For, as we have already seen (Nos. 24, 25, 27, etc.), ideas can be transferred from the subconscious to the subconscious; and indeed there is some ground for thinking that, outside of direct experiment, the intervention of the conscious mind in the telepathic transmission of thought is exceptional. Even in some of the most striking experimental cases it has been shown that either agent or percipient, or both, were asleep or entranced at the time. (See Chapter X., p. 239.)

This close connection of the activity of thought-transference with the subliminal consciousness, the consciousness which appears in hypnosis, and occasionally in dream - life and in spontaneous trance and automatism, may perhaps offer a clue to the origin of the faculty. For the future place of telepathy in the history of the race concerns us even more nearly than the mode of its operation; and we are led therefore to ask whether the faculty as we know it is but the germ of a more splendid capacity, or the last vestige of a power grown stunted through disuse. By those who view the matter simply as a topic of natural history the latter alternative will be preferred. The possible utility of telepathy as a supplement to gesture, etc., at a time when speech and writing were not yet evolved, is too obvious for comment. Whilst, on the other hand, such a faculty can with difficulty be conceived as originating by any physical process of evolution in our modern civilisation. But more direct evidence of the place of telepathy in our development is not wanting. For there are indications that the consciousness which lies below the threshold, with which the activity of telepathy is constantly associated, may be regarded as representing an earlier stage in the consciousness of the individual, and even it may be an earlier stage in

the history of the race. The readiest means of
summoning into temporary activity this subterranean consciousness is in the hypnotic trance.
Now the consciousness displayed by the hypnotised subject includes, as a rule, the whole of the
normal consciousness, and also extends beyond it.
That is, the hypnotised subject is aware not only
of what goes on in the trance but also of his
normal life: when awaked the events of the trance
have passed from his memory and are not revived
until the next period of trance. Our work-a-day
consciousness would appear to be, in fact, a selection from a much larger field of potential consciousness. Or, to put it in another way, the pressure on
the narrow limits of our working consciousness is so
great that ideas and sensations are continually being
crowded out and forced down below the threshold.
The subliminal consciousness thus becomes the receptacle of lapsed memories and sensations; and up
to a certain point in the history of each individual
these lapsed ideas can be temporarily revived. Long
forgotten memories of childhood, for instance, can be
resuscitated in the hypnotic trance, and ideas which
have demonstrably never penetrated into consciousness at all can be brought to light by crystal-vision,
planchette-writing, or other automatic processes.

Again, one of the most marked characteristics
of the subliminal consciousness, whether in dream,
hypnosis, spontaneous trance, or in crystal vision and
other automatism, is its power of visualisation—a
power which, as Mr. Galton has shown, and our daily
experience proves, tends to become aborted in later
life. And beyond these indications of memories lost
and imagery crowded out in the lifetime of the
individual, we come across traces of faculties which
have long ceased to obey the guidance or minister
to the needs of civilised man—the psychological
lumber of many generations ago. Such at least, it
may be suggested, is a possible interpretation of the

control frequently exercised by the hypnotic over the processes of digestion and circulation and the functions of the organic life generally. And the more doubtful observations, which seem to indicate the possession by the subconscious life of a sense of the passage of time and of a muscular sense superior to that of the waking state, may be held to point in the same direction.

From such facts and such analogies as these it may be argued that telepathy is perchance the relic of a once-serviceable faculty, which eked out the primitive alphabet of gesture, and helped to bind our ancestors of the cave or the tree in as yet inarticulate community. Dr. Jules Héricourt,[1] indeed, goes further, and suggests that we find here traces of the primeval unspecialised sensitiveness which preceded the development of a nervous system — a heritage shared with the amœba and the sea-anemone.

On the other hand, it may be urged that our present knowledge, either of telepathy itself or of the subconscious activities with which it is sought to link it, cannot by any means be held sufficient to support such an inference as to the probable origin of the faculty; and further, that the absence of mundane analogies, and the difficulties attending any such explanation yet suggested, forbid us to assume that the facts are capable of expression in physical terms.

It is further urged that whilst the dependence of telepathy on any material conditions is not obvious, it is constantly associated not only in popular belief, but in testimony from trustworthy sources, with phenomena which seem to point to supernormal faculties, such as clairvoyance, retro-cognition, and prevision, themselves hardly susceptible of a physical explanation. This view has found its ablest exponent in Mr. F. W. H. Myers.[2]

[1] *Annales des Sciences Psychiques,* vol. i. p. 317.
[2] See his articles on the "Subliminal Consciousness," etc., *Proc. S.P.R.,* vol. vii. p. 298; vol. viii. p. 333, pp. 436 *et seq.*

And though Mr. Myers would himself readily admit that the evidence for these alleged super-normal faculties is not on a par with the evidence for telepathy, yet he maintains that such as it is it cannot be summarily dismissed. No doubt if it should appear with fuller knowledge that there are sufficient grounds for believing in faculties which give to man knowledge, not derivable from living minds, of the distant, the far past, and the future, it would be more reasonable to regard telepathy as a member of the group of such supernormal faculties, operating in ways wholly apart from the familiar sense activities, and not amenable, like these, to terrestrial laws.

Such considerations may at any rate be held to justify a suspension of judgment. We are not yet, it may be said, called upon to decide whether tele-pathy is a vestigial or a rudimentary faculty; whether its manifestations are governed by forces correlative with heat and electricity, or whether we are justified in discerning in them the operation of some vaster cosmic agencies. But there is another aspect of the question. The first stage of our inquiry is not yet complete. It would be futile for us to debate what manner of new agency we propose to believe in until it is generally admitted by competent persons that the facts are not to be attributed to such recognised, if insufficiently familiar, causes as illusion, misrepre-sentation, and the subconscious quickening of normal faculties. More and varied experiments are wanted, more and more accurate records of spontaneous phe-nomena; and at the present stage there should be no lack of either one or other. Most scientific inquiries demand of the investigator long years of special study and preparation, and an elaborate mechanical equip-ment. But experiments in thought-transference can be conducted by any one with sufficient leisure and patience to observe the requisite precautions; whilst telepathic visions need for their recording no other qualifications than accuracy and good faith. In fact Science, whose boast it was once

> " Aerias tentasse domos animoque rotundum
> Percurrisse polum,"

has now come down from those airy realms and turned its attention to the things of earth, and especially to the study of our human environment and the growth of human intelligence. And in this its latest phase Science has, of necessity, followed the tendency of the age and become democratic. Every parent can become a fellow-worker with Darwin in the laboratory of the infant mind; in investigating the faculties and idiosyncrasies of man, even the lines imprinted on his finger-tips and his shifts to remember the multiplication-table, there is not less need of the accumulated small contributions of the many than of the life-long labours of the expert. And in this newest field of scientific research there can be no doubt that results of permanent value await the worker who is content to walk upon the solid earth, and to turn his eyes from the mirage which has dazzled many of his predecessors.

INDEX.

———

THE WALTER SCOTT PRESS, NEWCASTLE-ON-TYNE.

CONTEMPORARY SCIENCE SERIES.

Crown 8vo, Cloth, Price 6s.   Illustrated.

MAN AND WOMAN:
A STUDY OF HUMAN SECONDARY SEXUAL CHARACTERS.
By HAVELOCK ELLIS,
Author of "The Criminal," "The Nationalisation of Health," etc.

Crown 8vo, Cloth, Price 3s. 6d.   With Illustrations.

THE EVOLUTION OF MODERN CAPITALISM:
A STUDY OF MACHINE PRODUCTION.
By JOHN A. HOBSON, M.A.

THIRD EDITION.   Twentieth Thousand.   Crown 8vo, Cloth, 6s.

ESTHER WATERS: A NOVEL.
By GEORGE MOORE.

"Strong, vivid, sober, yet undaunted in its realism, full to the brim of observation of life and character, *Esther Waters* is not only immeasurably superior to anything the author has ever written before, but it is one of the most remarkable works that has appeared in print this year, and one which does credit not only to the author, but the country in which it has been written."—*The World.*

Crown 8vo, Half Antique, Paper Boards, 2s. 6d.

THE THEATRICAL WORLD FOR 1893.
By WILLIAM ARCHER.

"That the literary drama dealing with social problems made great advance during 1893 is universally admitted, but if proof were wanted nothing could be more conclusive than Mr. Archer's series of thoughtful and pointed articles."—*Daily Chronicle.*

SECOND EDITION.   Crown 8vo, Cloth, Price 6s.

MODERN PAINTING.
By GEORGE MOORE.

"Of the very few books on art that painters and critics should on no account leave unread this is surely one."—*The Studio.*

London : WALTER SCOTT, LTD., 24 Warwick Lane, Paternoster Row.

DRAMATIC ESSAYS.

EDITED BY

WILLIAM ARCHER AND ROBERT W. LOWE.

Three Volumes, Crown 8vo, Cloth, Price 3/6 each.

Dramatic Criticism, as we now understand it—the systematic appraisement from day to day and week to week of contemporary plays and acting—began in England about the beginning of the present century. Until very near the end of the eighteenth century, "the critics" gave direct utterance to their judgments in the theatre itself, or in the coffee-houses, only occasionally straying into print in letters to the news-sheets, or in lampoons or panegyrics in prose or verse, published in pamphlet form.   Modern criticism began with modern journalism; but some of its earliest utterances were of far more than ephemeral value.   During the earlier half of the present century several of the leading essayists of the day—men of the first literary eminence—concerned themselves largely with the theatre.   Under the title of

"DRAMATIC ESSAYS"

will be issued, in three volumes, such of their theatrical criticisms as seem to be of abiding interest.

THE FIRST SERIES will contain selections from the criticisms of LEIGH HUNT, both those published in 1807 (long out of print), and the admirable articles contributed more than twenty years later to *The Tatler*, and never republished.

THE SECOND SERIES will contain selections from the criticisms of WILLIAM HAZLITT.   Hazlitt's Essays on Kean and his contemporaries have long been inaccessible, save to collectors.

THE THIRD SERIES will contain hitherto uncollected criticisms by JOHN FORSTER, GEORGE HENRY LEWES, and others, with selections from the writings of WILLIAM ROBSON (The Old Playgoer).

The Essays will be concisely but adequately annotated, and each volume will contain an Introduction by WILLIAM ARCHER, and an Engraved Portrait Frontispiece.

London : WALTER SCOTT, LIMITED, 24 Warwick Lane.

LIBRARY OF HUMOUR

Cloth Elegant, Large Crown 8vo, Price 3/6 per vol.

VOLUMES ALREADY ISSUED.

THE HUMOUR OF FRANCE. Translated, with an Introduction and Notes, by Elizabeth Lee. With numerous Illustrations by Paul Frénzeny.

THE HUMOUR OF GERMANY. Translated, with an Introduction and Notes, by Hans Müller-Casenov. With numerous Illustrations by C. E. Brock.

THE HUMOUR OF ITALY. Translated, with an Introduction and Notes, by A. Werner. With 50 Illustrations and a Frontispiece by Arturo Faldi.

THE HUMOUR OF AMERICA. Selected with a copious Biographical Index of American Humorists, by James Barr.

THE HUMOUR OF HOLLAND. Translated, with an Introduction and Notes, by A. Werner. With numerous Illustrations by Dudley Hardy.

VOLUMES IN PREPARATION.

THE HUMOUR OF IRELAND. Selected by D. J. O'Donoghue. With numerous Illustrations by Oliver Paque. [*Ready Sept.* 1894.

THE HUMOUR OF SPAIN. Translated, with an Introduction and Notes, by S. Taylor. With numerous Illustrations by H. R. Millar. [*Ready Oct.* 1894.

THE HUMOUR OF RUSSIA. Translated, with Notes, by E. L. Boole, and an Introduction by Stepniak. With 50 Illustrations by Paul Frénzeny.

THE HUMOUR OF JAPAN. Transiated, with an Introduction, by A. M. With Illustrations by George Bigot (from Drawings made in Japan).

London: WALTER SCOTT, LTD., 24 Warwick Lane.

Crown 8vo, about 350 pp. each, Cloth Cover, 2s. 6d. per vol.
Half-polished Morocco, gilt top, 5s.

COUNT TOLSTOÏ'S WORKS.

The following Volumes are already issued—

A RUSSIAN PROPRIETOR.

THE COSSACKS.

IVAN ILYITCH, AND OTHER STORIES.

MY RELIGION.

LIFE.

MY CONFESSION.

CHILDHOOD, BOYHOOD, YOUTH.

THE PHYSIOLOGY OF WAR.

ANNA KARÉNINA. 3s. 6d.

WHAT TO DO?

WAR AND PEACE. (4 Vols.)

THE LONG EXILE, AND OTHER STORIES FOR CHILDREN.

SEVASTOPOL.

THE KREUTZER SONATA, AND FAMILY HAPPINESS.

THE KINGDOM OF GOD IS WITHIN YOU. 2s. 6d.

Uniform with the above.

IMPRESSIONS OF RUSSIA.

BY DR. GEORG BRANDES.

London: WALTER SCOTT, LIMITED, 24 Warwick Lane.

THE SCOTT LIBRARY.

Cloth, Uncut Edges, Gilt Top.   Price 1s. 6d. per Volume.

VOLUMES ALREADY ISSUED—

1 MALORY'S ROMANCE OF KING ARTHUR AND THE Quest of the Holy Grail.   Edited by Ernest Rhys.

2 THOREAU'S WALDEN.   WITH INTRODUCTORY NOTE by Will H. Dircks.

3 THOREAU'S "WEEK."   WITH PREFATORY NOTE BY Will H. Dircks.

4 THOREAU'S ESSAYS.   EDITED, WITH AN INTRO-duction, by Will H. Dircks.

5 CONFESSIONS OF AN ENGLISH OPIUM-EATER, ETC. By Thomas De Quincey.   With Introductory Note by William Sharp.

6 LANDOR'S IMAGINARY CONVERSATIONS.   SELECTED, with Introduction, by Havelock Ellis.

7 PLUTARCH'S LIVES (LANGHORNE).   WITH INTRO-ductory Note by B. J. Snell, M.A.

8 BROWNE'S RELIGIO MEDICI, ETC.   WITH INTRO-duction by J. Addington Symonds.

9 SHELLEY'S ESSAYS AND LETTERS.   EDITED, WITH Introductory Note, by Ernest Rhys.

10 SWIFT'S PROSE WRITINGS. CHOSEN AND ARRANGED, with Introduction, by Walter Lewin.

11 MY STUDY WINDOWS.   BY JAMES RUSSELL LOWELL. With Introduction by R. Garnett, LL.D.

12 LOWELL'S ESSAYS ON THE ENGLISH POETS.   WITH a new Introduction by Mr. Lowell.

13 THE BIGLOW PAPERS.   BY JAMES RUSSELL LOWELL. With a Prefatory Note by Ernest Rhys.

London : WALTER SCOTT, LIMITED, 24 Warwick Lane

THE SCOTT LIBRARY—continued.

London: WALTER SCOTT, LIMITED, 24 Warwick Lane.

THE SCOTT LIBRARY—continued.

London: WALTER SCOTT, LIMITED, 24 Warwick Lane.

London: WALTER SCOTT, LIMITED, 24 Warwick Lane.

THE SCOTT LIBRARY—continued.

65 SHERIDAN'S PLAYS. EDITED, WITH AN INTRO-
duction, by Rudolf Dircks.

66 OUR VILLAGE. BY MISS MITFORD. EDITED, WITH
an Introduction, by Ernest Rhys.

67 MASTER HUMPHREY'S CLOCK, AND OTHER STORIES.
By Charles Dickens. With Introduction by Frank T. Marzials.

68 TALES FROM WONDERLAND. BY RUDOLPH
Baumbach. Translated by Helen B. Dole.

69 ESSAYS AND PAPERS BY DOUGLAS JERROLD. EDITED
by Walter Jerrold.

70 VINDICATION OF THE RIGHTS OF WOMAN. BY
Mary Wollstonecraft. Introduction by Mrs. E. Robins Pennell.

71 "THE ATHENIAN ORACLE." A SELECTION. EDITED
by John Underhill, with Prefatory Note by Walter Besant.

72 ESSAYS OF SAINT-BEUVE. TRANSLATED AND
Edited, with an Introduction, by Elizabeth Lee.

73 SELECTIONS FROM PLATO. FROM THE TRANS-
lation of Sydenham and Taylor. Edited by T. W. Rolleston.

74 HEINE'S ITALIAN TRAVEL SKETCHES, ETC. TRANS-
lated by Elizabeth A. Sharp. With an Introduction from the French of
Theophile Gautier.

75 SCHILLER'S MAID OF ORLEANS. TRANSLATED,
with an Introduction, by Major-General Patrick Maxwell.

76 SELECTIONS FROM SYDNEY SMITH. EDITED, WITH
an Introduction, by Ernest Rhys.

77 THE NEW SPIRIT. BY HAVELOCK ELLIS.

78 THE BOOK OF MARVELLOUS ADVENTURES. FROM
the "Morte d'Arthur." Edited by Ernest Rhys. [This, together with
No. 1, forms the complete "Morte d'Arthur."]

79 ESSAYS AND APHORISMS. BY SIR ARTHUR HELPS.
With an Introduction by E. A. Helps.

80 ESSAYS OF MONTAIGNE. SELECTED, WITH A
Prefatory Note, by Percival Chubb.

81 THE LUCK OF BARRY LYNDON. BY W. M.
Thackeray. Edited by F. T. Marzials.

London: WALTER SCOTT, LIMITED, 24 Warwick Lane.

London: WALTER SCOTT, LIMITED, 24 Warwick Lane.

GREAT WRITERS.

A NEW SERIES OF CRITICAL BIOGRAPHIES.

Edited by ERIC ROBERTSON and FRANK T. MARZIALS.

A Complete Bibliography to each Volume, by J. P. ANDERSON, British Museum, London.

Cloth, Uncut Edges, Gilt Top.   Price 1/6.

VOLUMES ALREADY ISSUED—

LIFE OF LONGFELLOW. By PROF. ERIC S. ROBERTSON.
  "A most readable little work."—*Liverpool Mercury.*

LIFE OF COLERIDGE. By HALL CAINE.
  "Brief and vigorous, written throughout with spirit and great literary skill."—*Scotsman.*

LIFE OF DICKENS. By FRANK T. MARZIALS.
  "Notwithstanding the mass of matter that has been printed relating to Dickens and his works . . . we should, until we came across this volume, have been at a loss to recommend any popular life of England's most popular novelist as being really satisfactory. The difficulty is removed by Mr. Marzials's little book."—*Athenæum.*

LIFE OF DANTE GABRIEL ROSSETTI. By J. KNIGHT.
  "Mr. Knight's picture of the great poet and painter is the fullest and best yet presented to the public."—*The Graphic.*

LIFE OF SAMUEL JOHNSON. By COLONEL F. GRANT.
  "Colonel Grant has performed his task with diligence, sound judgment, good taste, and accuracy."—*Illustrated London News.*

LIFE OF DARWIN. By G. T. BETTANY.
  "Mr. G. T. Bettany's *Life of Darwin* is a sound and conscientious work." —*Saturday Review.*

LIFE OF CHARLOTTE BRONTÉ. By A. BIRRELL.
  "Those who know much of Charlotte Brontë will learn more, and those who know nothing about her will find all that is best worth learning in Mr. Birrell's pleasant book."—*St. James' Gazette.*

LIFE OF THOMAS CARLYLE. By R. GARNETT, LL.D.
  "This is an admirable book. Nothing could be more felicitous and fairer than the way in which he takes us through Carlyle's life and works."—*Pall Mall Gazette.*

London: WALTER SCOTT, LIMITED, 24 Warwick Lane.

GREAT WRITERS—continued.

LIFE OF ADAM SMITH. By R. B. Haldane, M.P.

"Written with a perspicuity seldom exemplified when dealing with economic science."—*Scotsman.*

LIFE OF KEATS. By W. M. Rossetti.

"Valuable for the ample information which it contains."—*Cambridge Independent.*

LIFE OF SHELLEY. By William Sharp.

"The criticisms . . . entitle this capital monograph to be ranked with the best biographies of Shelley."—*Westminster Review.*

LIFE OF SMOLLETT. By David Hannay.

"A capable record of a writer who still remains one of the great masters of the English novel."—*Saturday Review.*

LIFE OF GOLDSMITH. By Austin Dobson.

"The story of his literary and social life in London, with all its humorous and pathetic vicissitudes, is here retold, as none could tell it better."—*Daily News.*

LIFE OF SCOTT. By Professor Yonge.

"This is a most enjoyable book."—*Aberdeen Free Press.*

LIFE OF BURNS. By Professor Blackie.

"The editor certainly made a hit when he persuaded Blackie to write about Burns."—*Pall Mall Gazette.*

LIFE OF VICTOR HUGO. By Frank T. Marzials.

"Mr. Marzials's volume presents to us, in a more handy form than any English or even French handbook gives, the summary of what is known about the life of the great poet."—*Saturday Review.*

LIFE OF EMERSON. By Richard Garnett, LL.D.

"No record of Emerson's life could be more desirable."—*Saturday Review.*

LIFE OF GOETHE. By James Sime.

"Mr. James Sime's competence as a biographer of Goethe is beyond question."—*Manchester Guardian.*

LIFE OF CONGREVE. By Edmund Gosse.

"Mr. Gosse has written an admirable biography."—*Academy.*

LIFE OF BUNYAN. By Canon Venables.

"A most intelligent, appreciative, and valuable memoir."—*Scotsman.*

LIFE OF CRABBE. By T. E. Kebbel.

"No English poet since Shakespeare has observed certain aspects of nature and of human life more closely."—*Athenæum.*

LIFE OF HEINE. By William Sharp.

"An admirable monograph . . . more fully written up to the level of recent knowledge and criticism than any other English work."—*Scotsman.*

London: Walter Scott, Limited, 24 Warwick Lane.

GREAT WRITERS—continued.

LIFE OF MILL. By W. L. COURTNEY.

"A most sympathetic and discriminating memoir."—*Glasgow Herald*.

LIFE OF SCHILLER. By HENRY W. NEVINSON.

"Presents the poet's life in a neatly rounded picture."—*Scotsman*.

LIFE OF CAPTAIN MARRYAT. By DAVID HANNAY.

"We have nothing but praise for the manner in which Mr. Hannay has done justice to him."—*Saturday Review*.

LIFE OF LESSING. By T. W. ROLLESTON.

"One of the best books of the series."—*Manchester Guardian*.

LIFE OF MILTON. By RICHARD GARNETT, LL.D.

"Has never been more charmingly or adequately told."—*Scottish Leader*.

LIFE OF BALZAC. By FREDERICK WEDMORE.

"Mr. Wedmore's monograph on the greatest of French writers of fiction, whose greatness is to be measured by comparison with his successors, is a piece of careful and critical composition, neat and nice in style."—*Daily News*.

LIFE OF GEORGE ELIOT. By OSCAR BROWNING.

"A book of the character of Mr. Browning's, to stand midway between the bulky work of Mr. Cross and the very slight sketch of Miss Blind, was much to be desired, and Mr. Browning has done his work with vivacity, and not without skill."—*Manchester Guardian*.

LIFE OF JANE AUSTEN. By GOLDWIN SMITH.

"Mr. Goldwin Smith has added another to the not inconsiderable roll of eminent men who have found their delight in Miss Austen. . . . His little book upon her, just published by Walter Scott, is certainly a fascinating book to those who already know her and love her well; and we have little doubt that it will prove also a fascinating book to those who have still to make her acquaintance."—*Spectator*.

LIFE OF BROWNING. By WILLIAM SHARP.

"This little volume is a model of excellent English, and in every respect it seems to us what a biography should be."—*Public Opinion*.

LIFE OF BYRON By HON. RODEN NOEL.

"The Hon. Roden Noel's volume on Byron is decidedly one of the most readable in the excellent 'Great Writers' series."—*Scottish Leader*.

LIFE OF HAWTHORNE. By MONCURE CONWAY.

"It is a delightful *causerie*—pleasant, genial talk about a most interesting man. Easy and conversational as the tone is throughout, no important fact is omitted, no valueless fact is recalled; and it is entirely exempt from platitude and conventionality."—*The Speaker*.

LIFE OF SCHOPENHAUER. By PROFESSOR WALLACE.

"We can speak very highly of this little book of Mr. Wallace's. It is, perhaps, excessively lenient in dealing with the man, and it cannot be said to be at all ferociously critical in dealing with the philosophy."—*Saturday Review*.

London: WALTER SCOTT, LIMITED, 24 Warwick Lane.

GREAT WRITERS—continued.

LIFE OF SHERIDAN. By LLOYD SANDERS.

"To say that Mr. Lloyd Sanders, in this little volume, has produced the best existing memoir of Sheridan, is really to award much fainter praise than the work deserves."—*Manchester Examiner.*

LIFE OF THACKERAY. By HERMAN MERIVALE and F. T. MARZIALS.

"The monograph just published is well worth reading, . . . and the book, with its excellent bibliography, is one which neither the student nor the general reader can well afford to miss."—*Pall Mall Gazette.*

LIFE OF CERVANTES. By H. E. WATTS.

"We can commend this book as a worthy addition to the useful series to which it belongs."—*London Daily Chronicle.*

LIFE OF VOLTAIRE. By FRANCIS ESPINASSE.

George Saintsbury, in *The Illustrated London News*, says:—"In this little volume the wayfaring man who has no time to devour libraries will find most things that it concerns him to know about Voltaire's actual life and work put very clearly, sufficiently, and accurately for the most part."

LIFE OF LEIGH HUNT. By COSMO MONKHOUSE.

"Mr. Monkhouse has brought together and skilfully set in order much widely scattered material . . . candid as well as sympathetic." — *The Athenæum.*

LIFE OF WHITTIER. By W. J. LINTON.

"Well written, and well worthy to stand with preceding volumes in the useful 'Great Writers' series."—*Black and White.*

LIBRARY EDITION OF "GREAT WRITERS," Demy 8vo, 2s. 6d.

London : WALTER SCOTT, LIMITED, 24 Warwick Lane.

SELECTED THREE-VOL. SETS

IN NEW BROCADE BINDING.

6s. per Set, in Shell Case to match. May also be had bound in
Roan, with Roan Case to match, 9s. per Set.

THE FOLLOWING SETS CAN BE OBTAINED—

POEMS OF

WORDSWORTH KEATS SHELLEY	COLERIDGE SOUTHEY COWPER	HORACE GREEK ANTHOLOGY LANDOR
LONGFELLOW WHITTIER EMERSON	BORDER BALLADS JACOBITE SONGS OSSIAN	GOLDSMITH MOORE IRISH MINSTRELSY
HOGG ALLAN RAMSAY SCOTTISH MINOR POETS	CAVALIER POETS LOVE LYRICS HERRICK	WOMEN POETS CHILDREN OF POETS SEA MUSIC
SHAKESPEARE BEN JONSON MARLOWE	CHRISTIAN YEAR IMITATION of CHRIST HERBERT	PRAED HUNT AND HOOD DOBELL

SONNETS OF THIS
   CENTURY
SONNETS OF EUROPE
AMERICAN SONNETS
	AMERICAN HUMOR-
	  OUS VERSE
	ENGLISH HUMOROUS
	  VERSE
	BALLADES AND
	  RONDEAUS
		MEREDITH
		MARSTON
		LOVE LETTERS
		
		BURNS'S SONGS
		BURNS'S POEMS
		LIFE OF BURNS,
		    BY BLACKIE

HEINE
GOETHE
HUGO
	EARLY ENGLISH
	  POETRY
	CHAUCER
	SPENSER
		SCOTT'S MARMION, &c.
		SCOTT'S LADY OF LAKE
		LIFE OF SCOTT, [&c.
		  BY PROF. YONGE

London : WALTER SCOTT, LTD., 24 Warwick Lane, Paternoster Row.

SELECTED THREE-VOL. SETS

IN NEW BROCADE BINDING.

6s. PER SET, IN SHELL CASE TO MATCH.

Also Bound in Roan, in Shell Case, Price 9s. per Set.

O. W. Holmes Set—
    Autocrat of the Breakfast-
      Table.
    Professor at the Breakfast-
      Table.
    Poet at the Breakfast-Table.

Landor Set—
    Landor's Imaginary Conver-
      sations.
    Pentameron.
    Pericles and Aspasia.

Three English Essayists—
    Essays of Elia.
    Essays of Leigh Hunt.
    Essays of William Hazlitt.

Three Classical Moralists—
    Meditations of Marcus
      Aurelius.
    Teaching of Epictetus.
    Morals of Seneca.

Walden Set—
    Thoreau's Walden.
    Thoreau's Week.
    Thoreau's Selections.

Famous Letters Set—
    Letters of Byron.
    Letters of Chesterfield.
    Letters of Burns.

Lowell Set—
    My Study Windows.
    The English Poets.
    The Biglow Papers.

Heine Set—
    Life of Heine.
    Heine's Prose.
    Heine's Travel-Sketches

Three Essayists—
    Essays of Mazzini.
    Essays of Sainte-Beuve.
    Essays of Montaigne.

Schiller Set—
    Life of Schiller.
    Maid of Orleans
    William Tell.

Carlyle Set—
    Life of Carlyle.
    Sartor Resartus.
    Carlyle's German Essays.

London : WALTER SCOTT, LTD., 24 Warwick Lane, Paternoster Row.

IBSEN'S PROSE DRAMAS.

EDITED BY WILLIAM ARCHER.

Complete in Five Vols. Crown 8vo, Cloth, Price 3/6 each.

Set of Five Vols., in Case, 17/6; in Half Morocco, in Case, 32/6.

"We seem at last to be shown men and women as they are; and at first it is more than we can endure. . . . All Ibsen's characters speak and act as if they were hypnotised, and under their creator's imperious demand to reveal themselves. There never was such a mirror held up to nature before: it is too terrible. . . . Yet we must return to Ibsen, with his remorseless surgery, his remorseless electric-light, until we, too, have grown strong and learned to face the naked—if necessary, the flayed and bleeding—reality."—SPEAKER (London).

VOL. I. "A DOLL'S HOUSE," "THE LEAGUE OF YOUTH," and "THE PILLARS OF SOCIETY." With Portrait of the Author, and Biographical Introduction by WILLIAM ARCHER.

VOL. II. "GHOSTS," "AN ENEMY OF THE PEOPLE," and "THE WILD DUCK." With an Introductory Note.

VOL. III. "LADY INGER OF ÖSTRÅT," "THE VIKINGS AT HELGELAND," "THE PRETENDERS." With an Introductory Note and Portrait of Ibsen.

VOL. IV. "EMPEROR AND GALILEAN." With an Introductory Note by WILLIAM ARCHER.

VOL. V. "ROSMERSHOLM," "THE LADY FROM THE SEA," "HEDDA GABLER." Translated by WILLIAM ARCHER. With an Introductory Note.

The sequence of the plays *in each volume* is chronological; the complete set of volumes comprising the dramas thus presents them in chronological order.

"The art of prose translation does not perhaps enjoy a very high literary status in England, but we have no hesitation in numbering the present version of Ibsen, so far as it has gone (Vols. I. and II.), among the very best achievements, in that kind, of our generation."—*Academy*.

"We have seldom, if ever, met with a translation so absolutely idiomatic."—*Glasgow Herald*.

LONDON: WALTER SCOTT, LIMITED, 24 WARWICK LANE.

THE CANTERBURY POETS.

EDITED BY WILLIAM SHARP. IN 1/- MONTHLY VOLUMES.

Cloth, Red Edges	1s.	Red Roan, Gilt Edges, 2s. 6d.
Cloth, Uncut Edges	1s.	Pad. Morocco, Gilt Edges, 5s.

London: WALTER SCOTT, LIMITED, 24 Warwick Lane

THE CANTERBURY POETS—continued.

NEW EDITION IN NEW BINDING.

In the new edition there are added about forty reproductions in fac-simile of autographs of distinguished singers and instrumentalists, including Sarasate, Joachim, Sir Charles Hallé, Paderewsky, Stavenhagen, Henschel, Trebelli, Miss Macintyre, Jean Gérardy, etc.

Quarto, cloth elegant, gilt edges, emblematic design on cover, 6s. May also be had in a variety of Fancy Bindings.

THE

MUSIC OF THE POETS:

A MUSICIANS' BIRTHDAY BOOK.

EDITED BY ELEONORE D'ESTERRE KEELING.

THIS is a unique Birthday Book. Against each date are given the names of musicians whose birthday it is, together with a verse-quotation appropriate to the character of their different compositions or performances. A special feature of the book consists in the reproduction in fac-simile of autographs, and autographic music, of living composers. Three sonnets by Mr. Theodore Watts, on the "Fausts" of Berlioz, Schumann, and Gounod, have been written specially for this volume. It is illustrated with designs of various musical instruments, etc.; autographs of Rubenstein, Dvorák, Greig, Mackenzie, Villiers Stanford, etc., etc.

London: WALTER SCOTT, LTD., 24 Warwick Lane

The Contemporary Science Series.

I. THE EVOLUTION OF SEX. By Professor PATRICK GEDDES and
  J. ARTHUR THOMSON. With 90 Illustrations. Second Edition.
  "The authors have brought to the task—as indeed their names guarantee
  —a wealth of knowledge, a lucid and attractive method of treatment, and a
  rich vein of picturesque language."—*Nature.*

II. ELECTRICITY IN MODERN LIFE. By G. W. DE TUNZELMANN.
  With 88 Illustrations.
  "A clearly-written and connected sketch of what is known about electricity
  and magnetism, the more prominent modern applications, and the principles
  on which they are based."—*Saturday Review.*

III. THE ORIGIN OF THE ARYANS. By Dr. ISAAC TAYLOR. Illustrated. Second Edition.
  "Canon Taylor is probably the most encyclopædic all-round scholar now
  living. His new volume on the Origin of the Aryans is a first-rate example of
  the excellent account to which he can turn his exceptionally wide and varied
  information. . . . Masterly and exhaustive."—*Pall Mall Gazette.*

IV. PHYSIOGNOMY AND EXPRESSION. By P. MANTEGAZZA.
  Illustrated.
  "Professor Mantegazza is a writer full of life and spirit, and the natural
  attractiveness of his subject is not destroyed by his scientific handling of it."
  —*Literary World* (Boston).

V. EVOLUTION AND DISEASE. By J. B. SUTTON, F R.C.S. With
  135 Illustrations.
  "The book is as interesting as a novel, without sacrifice of accuracy or
  system, and is calculated to give an appreciation of the fundamentals of
  pathology to the lay reader, while forming a useful collection of illustrations
  of disease for medical reference."—*Journal of Mental Science.*

VI. THE VILLAGE COMMUNITY. By G. L. GOMME. Illustrated.
  "The fruit of some years of investigation on a subject which has of late
  attracted much attention, and is of much importance, inasmuch as it lies at
  the basis of our society."—*Antiquary.*

VII. THE CRIMINAL. By HAVELOCK ELLIS. Illustrated.
  "An ably written, an instructive, and a most entertaining book."—*Law
  Quarterly Review.*

VIII. SANITY AND INSANITY. By Dr. CHARLES MERCIER. Illustrated.
  "Taken as a whole, it is the brightest book on the physical side of mental
  science published in our time."—*Pall Mall Gazette.*

IX. HYPNOTISM. By Dr. ALBERT MOLL. Second Edition.
  "Marks a step of some importance in the study of some difficult physiological and psychological problems which have not yet received much attention in the scientific world of England."—*Nature.*

X. MANUAL TRAINING. By Dr. C. M. WOODWARD, Director of the
  Manual Training School, St. Louis. Illustrated.
  "There is no greater authority on the subject than Professor Woodward."—
  Manchester Guardian.

XI. THE SCIENCE OF FAIRY TALES. By E. SIDNEY HARTLAND.
  "Mr. Hartland's book will win the sympathy of all earnest students, both
  by the knowledge it displays, and by a thorough love and appreciation of his
  subject, which is evident throughout."—*Spectator.*

XII. PRIMITIVE FOLK. By ELIE RECLUS.
  "For an introduction to the study of the questions of property, marriage,
  government, religion,—in a word, to the evolution of society,—this little
  volume will be found most convenient."—*Scottish Leader.*